Judgement OF Solomon

Anne Redmon has published four novels, *Emily Stone, Music and Silence, Second Sight* and *The Genius of the Sea*, the first novel in her *Byzantine Trilogy.* She has reviewed for the *Sunday Times*, has taught at the University of Michigan and at Wandsworth Prison, and she is a Fellow of the Royal Society of Literature. She was a recipient of an Authors Foundation Grant travel bursary awarded in 1992 by the Society of Authors. She is married, has three children, and lives in London.

By the same author

Emily Stone
Music and Silence
Second Sight
The Genius of the Sea

THE Judgement OF Solomon

Anne Redmon

SINCLAIR-STEVENSON

First published in Great Britain in 1995
by Sinclair-Stevenson
an imprint of Reed Consumer Books Ltd
Michelin House, 81 Fulham Road, London SW3 6RB
and Auckland, Melbourne, Singapore and Toronto

A CIP catalogue record for this book
is available from the British Library

ISBN 1 85619 522 8

Phototypeset by Intype, London
Printed and bound in Great Britain
by Clays Ltd, St Ives PLC

For Benedict, as always, and
for Peta,
who inspired the trilogy

Acknowledgements

THIS BOOK could not have been written without the help and cooperation of many people. Without an Authors Foundation Grant from the Society of Authors I could not have visited Istanbul, nor made an essential visit to the island of Chios where the main action of the novel takes place.

I am particularly grateful to members of the Calvocoressi family, who most generously contributed to my knowledge of Chios. Whatever sense I may have conveyed of the Kampos region of the island is entirely due to Miltiades Calvocoressi, who gave much time and energy to escort me and my husband around its unique country houses and to introduce us to many landowners from whom I was able to glean a composite picture. I am also grateful to his wife, Irina, who showed us around her own beautiful house. Chiote hospitality to strangers is a humbling experience to Western Europeans. I am also indebted to Peter Calvocoressi. He facilitated my trip to Chios and has answered many questions about Greece in general, and, in particular, about the island where his family has been established for many centuries.

I would also like to thank Elsie Donald, Jane Dorrell, Ann Shearer, Professor Nicholas Coldstream and Dr Nicola Coldstream and George Schöpflin, who have given time and thought to this project. In addition, I am happy to acknowledge the purely literary inspiration given to me by my niece Hilary Redmon, who listened to my story with a wisdom beyond her years and helped me enormously with the character of Xenia, who was roughly her age at the time of writing.

Other helpers have been Athina Mariou-Dimatopolou, Demetra Arlys, and David Moore.

Any errors in the novel are entirely my own.

I have consulted many books in an attempt to make the historical and geographical aspects of the novel lively and accurate. I owe much to the first two volumes of John Julius Norwich's *Byzantium* (Penguin, 1991); to *The Kampos of Chios in its heyday: Houses and surroundings* by Fanny Aneroussi and Leopold Mylonadis (Arritas Publications, 1992); *Nea Moni of Chios* by Andreas Axiotakis (The Holy Metropole of Chios, 1991);

Hagia Sophia by Rowland J. Mainstone (Thames and Hudson, 1988); and to guidebooks too numerous to mention; a novel by Nicholas Gage, *The Bourlotas Fortune*, was helpful in establishing some detail about the Greek shipowning community in Chios, although most of this I gleaned from my own research.

And finally, I would like to add a word of gratitude to my family in Kentucky, who entertained me with great kindness and hospitality when I last visited the United States, where I was born.

Cast of Characters

Charles Simon – *a publisher.*
Rosamund Simon – *his American wife.*
Francis, Dominic, Peter, Theresa and Mary Simon – *their children.*
Isabelle, Lady Simon – *Charles's mother.*
Catherine Phocas – *Charles's sister and wife of Theo Phocas.*
Beatrice, Sister Mary of the Assumption – *Charles's sister, a nun.*
Theresa Simon – *Charles's sister with whom Lady Simon lives.*
Caro – *Charles's lover.*

Theologos Phocas – *a Greek shipping magnate, husband of Catherine.*
Xenia Phocas – *their adopted daughter.*

Melissa Kavanagh (Missy, née Buchanan) – *Rosamund Simon's American first cousin.*
Tom Kavanagh – *Missy's third husband, elderly plutocrat and horse breeder from Kentucky.*
Romola Cardew – *Tom Kavanagh's stepdaughter from his first marriage, and half-aunt to Paolo.*
Paolo – *the six-year-old grandson of Tom Kavanagh, who is travelling through Europe with the Kavanagh entourage. His mother, Celia, is Romola's half-sister.*

Serge Mirkovsky – *a Russian nobleman, who played a large role in* The Genius of the Sea. *He lives in England.*
Helena Taggart – *his first cousin, who likewise played a large part. She has been an important literary critic and was the lover of Arthur Holt, a well-known poet, now dead, whose biography is being published by Charles Simon. She has retired to Patmos, a Greek island, where her family has owned a large house for many years. This is where Serge's mother died.*

(They refer to: Marina Holt, his widow; Dr Paul Mason, her second husband, and Serge's mother, the Princess Sonya Petrovna Mirkovskaya, all of whom were major characters in *The Genius of the Sea*.)

The main action of the novel takes place in 1992 on the Greek island of Chios, which is a very short distance across the water from the Turkish mainland.

Unlike many Greek islands, it is not dependent on the tourist trade. Many wealthy shipping families come from Chios. It is famous for its mastic gum trees. Although it is said that Homer was born on Chios, it is not a classical island, but Byzantine. The mosaics at Nea Moni are some of the finest examples of this period, and many churches throughout Chios are adorned with wonderful frescos and icons. Two wonderful medieval towns to visit are Pirghi and Mesta. The Chiotes themselves are independent and charming.

In 1822, the Turks perpetrated an appalling massacre upon Chios, which was commemorated by both Victor Hugo and Delacroix. It is talked about still, almost as if it had happened in living memory. A further catastrophe: the earthquake of 1881 devastated the island, and yet today the traveller is rewarded by a sense of peace and tranquillity. Although some of the great houses in the fertile Kampos region of Chios are still in ruins, many have been restored like the Phocas house in this book.

I

Isabelle Simon, bags packed, sat alone in the courtyard of the Phocas house waiting to be taken to Chios airport. It was only a few minutes away by car, and though Theo, her son-in-law, had undertaken to drive her there, there was no sign of him. She was anxious not to miss her flight, for she had had quite enough of the island, but only the keenest observer could have discerned her impatience. Although she was eighty years old, her posture was flawless and her expression never changed: she viewed her surroundings with patrician frigidity. Anyone else might have enjoyed the grace of her daughter's beautiful house, but she did not.

Theo and Catherine had a small staff of servants who helped to maintain their estate, and in a vain attempt to make the old lady's last hours in Chios palmy, they had enthroned her in a shady spot under a large and ancient vine. Greek coffee stood by her in an exquisite cup on an exquisite table, but she did not drink it. She appeared to concentrate on her tapestry, a cambric square clamped in an embroidery hoop. She threaded subtle wools through the rough material. She was making a kneeler for the Abbey at home. A rigid Lamb of God held a flag, the pole crooked in just above its hoof. Her heel, however, trembled irritably on the pavement beneath her feet. Theo Phocas was proud of this graceful mosaic: a pattern of fruits and flowers swirled in a spiral of black and white cobblestones across the whole courtyard. But Lady Simon disliked its association with him and thought it dangerous underfoot.

Theo and Catherine had established themselves in Chios many years ago. At that time, the house had been a shambles, but Catherine had made it her career, and with Theo's money, they had turned it into a little paradise. The architecture of the Kampos region of the island was unique, and Lady Simon's daughter had become obsessed with its history and morphology down to the very last detail.

Although reticent by nature, Catherine had a tiresome way of going on about the house, using Greek where English would do. A salient feature of the courtyard was an old wooden water-wheel positioned over a marble well. Catherine would call this a *manganos*, and would explain, to anyone who listened, the intricacies of water supply to the orange groves that lay beyond the house. In fact, she had got the ancient wheel to work, and it turned even now, making a gentle plashing in the background. Lady Simon had to grant that it was a pleasant noise, but the fruit trees were irrigated these days by modern methods, so it did seem rather a waste of precious water.

The whole estate was enclosed by mellow walls, which Catherine had restored brick by brick, almost with her own bare hands. Ancient arches and shady pergolas stretched out almost in an embrace to the beholder, but Lady Simon shunned the blandishments of the view. It did not appeal to her. She tried to think of the Abbey at home and how pleased the monks would be with the kneeler when she finished it, but her mind revolved upon her family . . . those she was leaving, and those awaiting her in England.

Where was Theo? With her taste for herbaceous borders, Lady Simon found the Greek garden somewhat dark and bare. The high walls guarding the property gave it an almost sepulchral shade in places. There were mastic trees and foreign pines, and the dark verdure of orange trees and trees that grew mandarins and limes strayed from the groves with their unripened fruit. The only colour in her line of vision came from a huge bougainvillaea with a startling magenta hue, which spilled itself down a sunny spot near the old stone stairway that mounted to the imposing front door of the house. Lady Simon considered Theo a drastic Greek. Somehow, the intense purple flowers of the vine, the shady courtyard, the fine, resurrected old mansion with its vaguely Turkish trappings, summed him up.

Theo was a shipowner, and Catherine had married him from school almost thirty years ago. He had inherited a small fleet and a large amount of money from an uncle, who had not seen his native Greece for half a century. Lady Simon's late husband had always had a weakness for Catherine, who had been wilful and difficult in her view, and he had allowed the match because she had claimed to be enduringly, passionately in love. It was true that Theo had been quite good-looking; he had reminded Lady Simon somewhat of Rudolph Valentino as the Sheikh of Araby, or whatever, and he had had the buccaneering charm, she supposed, to go with what in her day they used to call bedroom eyes. Even with the money, Lady Simon thought Catherine could have done better. One did not want to make too much of background, but to be absolutely frank, Theo was not quite the gentleman he claimed to be.

Of all things, his pretensions to this charismatic state, with all of its rites and inexplicable mysteries, irritated her the most. He claimed descent from the Byzantine nobility, and this was hard to challenge because none of his family had survived recent Greek history to tell the tale. She knew for certain that her ancestors had been Crusaders and could prove it from their cross-legged effigies that gloomily occupied the heavily vaulted Norman family chapel where she had been married, and indeed baptized. Lady Simon sometimes suspected that Theo had Turkish blood. After all, he was quite dark and his grandparents had come from İzmir, call it 'Smyrna' as much as he liked. His boast, without foundation, she suspected, had been a way of annexing the truly aristocratic Catherine, who had always shown a lamentable indifference to her lineage . . . to her cost.

Catherine had had more to endure in her 'enduring love' than she had bargained for. And if anything was at issue, the thickness of blood as opposed to water had created the ill feeling she always sensed now between her daughter and Theo. Well, maybe it was not ill feeling, exactly, but the marriage had shrunk rather than expanded. It had become a gnomic, dour relationship, difficult to penetrate, hard to prise open, even to her gimlet eye, and this was a disappointment.

Lady Simon eschewed the temptation to take her watch from her handbag and look at the time. Theo could easily have arranged for his driver Nikos to fetch her in the old Daimler that she was sure he kept for show. In this venerable car, Catherine was ferried about when she wished to make little purchases or visit friends; it took Xenia to and from her singing lessons in the Hora; and it met Theo himself from the boat or airport whenever he returned from his increasingly frequent trips to Athens. Of course, his shipping company did have offices in Piraeus, the world was in recession and he had no sons to carry on his business after him . . . only Xenia. Lady Simon had it in her head, however, that Theo kept a mistress in or near the *pied-à-terre* he maintained in Athens. It was a smart flat in a smart district, Kolonaki. To put it bluntly (and she was invariably blunt to herself if not to others) she always rather mistrusted money made from trade. She saw Theo as trading, always dealing, cards close to his chest, eyes veiled with guile. His urbanity unsettled her. He was not horsy, nor doggy, nor tweedy – simply rich. Lady Simon sometimes wondered if her late husband had been wooed by this unseemly shipping wealth into auctioning Catherine off. After all, the Simons hadn't a bean . . . well, not many beans.

This disloyalty to George's memory now caused her finger to slip on the needle. She pricked herself and quickly dropped the cambric so that she would not soil it with her blood. She allowed herself a sigh, but not the ladder-back of the chair. She had been a débutante and never slouched; in consequence, she had never developed the figure of a crone. Even so, she dressed architecturally in the habit of her class. She always wore a discreet string of actual pearls and spoke with stentorian distinctness. She had been a beauty in the twenties, all cream and roses, but it had not lasted. Catherine, let it be said, had never, by some miracle, aged. Of course, she had never had any children, and this might explain it, Lady Simon thought. Xenia was not Catherine's child.

Unable to bear it any longer, she fished her watch from her handbag – she did not like to have it on her wrist – and with considerable relief realized that she had wrongly guessed the time. Theo had at least another quarter of an hour to make good his desertion. She was not at all sure, but she thought she heard voices quarrelling deep within the house.

Although it might be supposed that Catherine Phocas could take her own mother to the airport, it was a sad truth that the two women could not abide each other. Lady Simon's annual visit always took place, however, on the premise that there was something vaguely intolerable about Catherine living abroad and that reparation had to be made for this. For two weeks each year they both executed their duty to this lie, and having wholly exhausted each other after ten days of suffocating intensity, they would be ready to drop with fatigue at the end of the stay. Had they been able to remain merely English about it, the visits might have tailed off, particularly as Catherine, Theo and Xenia went to England every spring after the Greek Easter and stayed for a month, but somehow, an Aegean sensibility seemed to have crept into Catherine's reckoning and, like an icon, her mother had become the object of ceremonious oblation. It was almost as if Catherine felt that ritual could achieve what she herself could not. In occasional dim flashes of insight, Lady Simon saw that she was quite cold to her daughter and always had been. In fact, if Catherine had married the Duke of Norfolk, Lady Simon would have found him wanting in the scales where her thumb tipped the balance.

Whatever the complicated reasons for this, a delicate adjustment seemed to be made at the end of every visit, and Theo would step in to do Greek honours for his mother-in-law, whom he supported financially as a matter of obligation. He would bottle her up in the Japanese car they used as a runabout like a tedious but necessary old spider, and they would make tense jaunts around the island. She had seen it many times, he had seen it many times – but they saw it again for good measure. There was

Mesta with its medieval walls constructed like tunnels against Turkish invasion; there was Pirghi with its houses marvellously etched with geometric patterns; there was the mastic region of the island where the trees had yielded up aromatic gum since biblical times; and there was the famous Nea Moni, a Byzantine monastery with outstanding mosaics. Theo always brought Xenia along and she sat in the back seat. The itinerary varied from year to year, but the conflict did not. Each time he made what he called 'The Grand Tour' with the old lady, he had a way of insinuating Xenia upon her. She was not Lady Simon's relation. 'Your granddaughter,' he would say in referring to Xenia. 'Our child,' he would call her as if she were Catherine's.

Theo spoke perfect English. In fact, he had both Greek and British nationality, for he had spent the larger part of his childhood and youth with his rich uncle, who had lived in Bayswater near the Orthodox Cathedral in Moscow Road. Theo still kept on the heavy Edwardian flat with its high ceilings. His uncle had sent him to Westminster and Oxford, but somehow he had never been 'quite right', although never really wrong either.

When he and Catherine had elected to settle in Chios a few years after their marriage, Lady Simon had thought the whole thing rather bogus. He had only a tenuous connection with the island through great-grandparents. It was not lost on her that the really old shipping families tended to congregate in Chios, and these passed muster with Lady Simon. The house, the grand address in Kampos, the Daimler and her daughter all had to do, she thought, with his monstrous vanity and ambition. And so, of course, did Xenia . . . above all. From her babyhood, Theo had softly insisted that every kind of familial recognition should be bestowed upon this adopted child. More softly still, but with greater penetration, Lady Simon had refused to grant it.

Where had Theo got to? Surely it was in his interest to get her to the aeroplane on time. She had to make a connection in Athens, and if she missed the flight, she had no intention of wandering around the dreadful city by herself while she waited for another aeroplane to London. If he did not come more or less at once, he would have to put up with her for another night! She looked up and around to escape stifling memories of this particularly awkward visit, her bright eye picking out details of house and garden. Beyond the water-wheel, continually turning underneath the shady trees, stood Xenia herself, apparently oblivious to Lady Simon's presence in the sheltered courtyard. She stood in the sunlight at the top of the groves, perhaps in readiness to say goodbye – a hopeful sign of imminent departure, Lady Simon thought.

Xenia was just eighteen years old, a slender, modest girl. She was blurred by the light, then suddenly vanished from it altogether, like a spirit, into the groves of fruit trees. Maybe wishful thinking had conjured up her image, Lady Simon thought, or maybe she had the sense that she was being watched, this apple of her father's eye. She was the heiress to a considerable fortune, but she comported herself with becoming meekness like a member of the Royal Family, groomed from the beginning. From the outset, however, Lady Simon had always thought her sly and, worse still, not at all the person she was supposed to be.

Surely, Catherine could see it! Lady Simon was never really sure whether she saw it or not. From the day they had acquired Xenia, newborn, she had been as spoiled as a little duchess in a heavenly white pram with pure white awnings in broderie anglaise. They had tricked her out in continental chic with dresses, cardigans, and even bibs purchased at great expense. Everything Xenia had worn had been of Italian design, all articles of furniture imported from London on Norland's authority. But even then Lady Simon had seen it, even when Xenia had been quite small. Theo had brought the little girl home one day, flanked by nurses, in an incubator. She had been a *fait accompli* for Catherine to accept, as if she had been the infant Heathcliff or a puppy. He had presented the baby to his barren wife just like that: no fuss, and apparently, no questions asked. It had been extraordinary!

And if her method of arrival on the scene had been outlandish, the tale of her origin was no less so. Xenia was supposed to have been the baby of an Albanian woman, who had died in childbirth while fleeing her native country, a stowaway on one of Theo's ships. The Christian child could hardly be posted back to Hoxha, or so the argument went, for the mother had received the last rites of the Orthodox Church, and her dying wish had been that the child should be brought up in a devout Greek family. The dead mother's body had been conveniently repatriated beyond Albanian borders and the reach of awkward questions. A document must have existed somewhere for Xenia to have later obtained a British passport, but Lady Simon privately thought the golden legend of piety left almost everything to be desired. She had not spent one moment in the child's company without being sure Xenia was Theo's natural daughter and Catherine had been trapped into bringing her up. The girl's resemblance to Theo was startling, embarrassing, and as she had matured, it had become more acutely so. Whatever Lady Simon's failings, she had never breathed a word of her suspicions to Catherine, for she considered silence on such matters to be a public decency, and public decencies she maintained. She could not help but feel hostile and queasy in the child's company, however, and as for Theo, she had come to suspect him on all counts as the Sultan of the high seas with a harem in every port that the Phocas Lines visited – and, of course, there was the putative mistress in Athens to be reckoned in with the rest. As for his friendship with Rosamund, her daughter-in-law in London, well, there was something too dark in this for her to contemplate, which she contemplated none the less. Lady Simon was not an impious woman for all her lack of charity. Indeed, she held dear the traditions of her English recusant Catholic family. And so she called upon the Virgin to defend her now from evil thoughts, and threw St Michael in for good measure.

At once, as if in answer to her prayer, the garden door flew open and her daughter emerged from the house. 'Xenia! Xen-i-a! Come and say goodbye to *Yia-yia*. She is going now.' It had been agreed that Xenia should call Lady Simon the Greek word for 'grandmother'. Catherine paused. 'Xen-i-a!' Catherine looked no older than thirty. She had an oval, unlined face and a rich head of light brown hair, which she generally wore loose. She espoused an utter simplicity in dress, and if this set off her beauty, it also gave her a slightly childlike air. Lady Simon supposed that this was why a confusion sometimes arose about Xenia and Catherine. They were often, quite genuinely, taken for sisters.

'Darling, you needn't bellow. I am quite sure she hears you,' Lady Simon said. 'I saw her only a moment ago at the top of the grove, or orchard, or whatever.'

Catherine gave her mother a look of controlled fury, ignored her, and marched over the cobbled terrace towards the water-wheel. A short flight of steps led up to the platform on which the hub rested, and it served as a vantage point. Catherine climbed up and stood feet apart, arms akimbo, and searched the garden with her eyes. She wore a thin muslin skirt of graceful length. As the wheel turned in front of her, Lady Simon could see the moving shadow of its spokes through the gauzy material. 'You should be wearing a petticoat,' she found herself saying without wanting to, but if Catherine heard this remark, she ignored it. Her voice sailed forth again, this time in a torrent of Greek. Catherine had become absolutely fluent in the language and spoke it like a native.

'Oh, do leave her be!' Lady Simon cried. 'I am quite sure she has better things to do than to say goodbye to me! In any case, I shall miss the aeroplane if Theo does not come directly.'

Catherine turned and looked at her; her eyes grew large and her nostrils pinched. With a wiry leap, she jumped off the steps. She wore beautiful sandals on her narrow feet. She had the waist of a teenager. 'Theo is not taking you. Theo is not well,' Catherine said, or rather growled. She sprang round a low wall, disappeared for a moment, then emerged with Xenia. The girl wore a shirt dress embroidered with leaves. She had a fine, long neck and translucent, olive skin. Her dark hair was caught up in a ribbon, and even Lady Simon had to acknowledge a kind of gawky beauty in her as she came up from the garden with her mother. Like primordial, unformed Eve, she was innocent because she was unaware. Yet, for all of her strict Greek upbringing, the veiled eyes, the muteness, the crossed ankles, there was, to Lady Simon, a voluptuousness about the girl which betrayed her origins. Xenia was being groomed for Oxford. She had completed one year of the sixth form at St Winifred's in Kent, Catherine's old school, and was set to do the Entrance Exam and A-levels during the coming academic year. She regularly spent week-ends and half-term holidays with Lady Simon's son Charles and his wife Rosamund. Lady Simon looked at her embroidery. She looked back at Xenia.

'I shall be seeing you in quite a short time, I expect, Xenia, so there is really not much point in your saying goodbye to me.' The girl looked down then up again from Lady Simon to Catherine, but she said nothing.

Catherine closed her eyes. 'We really must be going, Mummy. Theo thinks he is sickening for this dreadful summer cold that has been going around. He says it would be awful if he gave it to you.'

The corner of Xenia's lip twitched. 'Goodbye, *Yia-yia*, it was so lovely to see you. I shall be looking forward to seeing you quite soon.' She bent to give the old lady a social kiss. 'Give my love to Uncle Charles and Aunt Rosamund, won't you? Tell them I am longing to see them.'

Lady Simon thoroughly disapproved of the way Xenia had inveigled herself into the household of her son and his wife. She folded her crewel work and pursed her lips. Catherine with strong arms was swinging the luggage. Xenia helped the old woman to her feet, and taking her arm, accompanied her across the slippery mosaic of swirling fruits and flowers towards the gate. This was a portal of some magnitude and it would not have disgraced the seat of a Florentine duke. The Kampos region of Chios was famous for these triumphal arches to old houses. The whole area was a labyrinth of high walls and narrow lanes, which seemed to tunnel from gate to gate, landowner to landowner. Xenia delivered her grandmother to Catherine who simmered in the waiting Toyota she had driven from the garage, then she stood behind the massive grille of wrought-iron acanthus leaves and waved.

When the car was out of sight, Xenia turned and walked towards the house, smiling slightly to herself at the thought of her father's 'illness'. Lady Simon's general mistrust of Greek germs at least had the effect of limiting and controlling her visits. Although he was usually a stickler for truth, particularly when it meant Xenia telling it, he had certainly weakened this time. Nikos was setting his cases down at the foot of the courtyard stairs, making it evident that he intended to leave for Athens on the boat that left in an hour's time.

She could hardly blame him for the ruse. He had been especially long-suffering towards her 'grandmother' this time and thus might be excused the final hypocrisy of kissing the old lady goodbye. They all sneaked round her a bit. Xenia only wished that her mother was able to sneak more effectively in order to avoid Lady Simon's direct hits. Bombshell after bombshell would fall under the guise of innuendo, but there was never any mistaking the craters they left. She would have liked to have talked about this to her mother and express her sympathy, but somehow whenever she got to the point of this or any other emotional subject, the shutters went down and it seemed better to remain silent.

Xenia looked up and saw her father jogging lightly down the stairs. He was dressed for the city in a crisp linen suit and he seemed in the finest fettle imaginable. When he saw her, he stopped and hailed her.

'Xenia, I'll be off, then!' He came towards her, arms outstretched. He was large and heavy-set, but not fat. His embraces tended to engulf. 'I shan't be seeing you before you go back to school, but it is a very important term for you, as you yourself know.'

Her shoulders sagged. The lecture was about to begin. Listening to it with freshly eager ears each time was difficult, especially when she made real efforts to put the lessons it contained into practice. Xenia was always faintly shocked when her schoolfriends in England talked about rows with their parents. It almost seemed part of the Western ideal to rebel and even healthy to show disrespect for a mother or father. From time to time, she did get fed up with their nagging, and if she were to be really honest with herself, she and her mother did exchange words now and then, but she believed that both of them had her best interests at heart, and she wanted very much to please them.

She looked up at her father and into his eyes. The lecture usually contained a sermonette on the responsibilities that went with her fortunate position as his heir and the harrowing example of mindless hedonism given by other scions of other wealthy Greek families. Hard study and genuine attainment were the stoic antidotes he commonly recommended against the poison of the jet-set mentality. The virtues of religion, the consciousness of history, and the necessity of *noblesse oblige* were sometimes thrown in for good measure. One time, just before she had gone back to school, he had told her something else, something of great importance, but they had never referred to it again. She dropped her eyes at the memory of that conversation, always thinking the topic would return and mostly hoping it would not.

Evidently, he did not catch the drift of her mood, or else he only caught that part of it which pertained to cautionary tales, for he gently tugged a lock of her hair and laughed. 'Don't look so crestfallen,' he said. 'I promise not to go on about it any more. I think we have all had enough fault-finding recently to last us for a very long time to come!' And he rolled his eyes comically in the direction of the gate through which Lady Simon had departed.

Xenia smiled. She rather enjoyed the sly complicity they had sometimes, particularly over the old lady to whom they were both unfailingly polite. He kissed her forehead.

'I promise you, I will work hard,' she told him in order to reward his mercy at not telling her to. She was seized with a sudden affection for him and she gave him a little squeeze. He twinkled a bit, bent down and opened his handsome briefcase.

'Just a little thing for luck on the Entrance Exam,' he said, presenting her with a small parcel wrapped in gold paper. It was obviously a pen.

She was touched by the gesture. He rarely gave her presents. 'Oh, I see! A lovely book! Thank you.' They both laughed at her little joke.

'Not to open until the day, eh?' he said. 'Keep it in a safe place?'

'I will. I promise,' said Xenia.

'And give Rosamund and Charles my love when you see them, won't you?'

She nodded. She disliked seeing him go, really, but Nikos had brought the car round; she could see it through the gate of twined acanthus leaves. It depressed her, too, that he seemed to be on his way before her mother returned from the airport. She wished he would consider these little kindnesses a bit more, because she was quite sure it would help. Nevertheless, he was who he was and he did as he did. After all, he would return at the weekend after she herself had gone to London. He swooped up his bags in his big, heavy hands – she had called them 'bear's paws' when she had been small – and in a moment, he was in the snorting old Daimler. Again, Xenia waved from the gate, but this time with affection and enthusiasm. He really did look quite distinguished, she thought, as he sank into the red leather seat. He opened his briefcase again and took out what looked like an impressive dossier, full, no doubt, of crucial information. He raised his hand to her in farewell, then immediately bent his head, with its mane of iron grey hair, over the facts and figures on his lap. She supposed that she would have to do well on the exam now she had the pen. Maybe her singing really would boost her application. She did love music. She always had that.

II

IT WAS in mid-air that Lady Simon began to think of her daughter-in-law Rosamund. This was partly because she expected Rosamund to meet her at Heathrow, and partly because she had seen someone very like her daughter-in-law in Athens airport where she had had to change for her flight to London. Of course, it could not have been Rosamund – the woman's hair was nicely done, for one thing. For another, she had been tall and businesslike; but the face across the wide concourse had been so familiar that it had given Lady Simon a start. The woman was arriving, it seemed. She carried a neat case and swung smartly along. She vanished out of the pneumatic doors, fit for the broil of Athens, ready to tackle it. This was the sort of person Lady Simon had expected Charles to marry. Instead, he had been ensnared at an early age . . . but by an American.

The difficulties in her son's marriage had been the chief source of her dissatisfaction with her trip to Chios, and still she could not see why she should not have confided her misgivings to Catherine during the time of her stay. It seemed heartless of Catherine not to take an interest in what so nearly concerned the whole family, and not a little odd that she had fobbed off her mother's comments on what had, after all, become scandalous public knowledge – and recently, too.

Charles, Rosamund, Theo and Catherine had been close, not only as relatives, but as friends. Of her other children, one of Lady Simon's daughters was a nun, the other, Theresa, looked after her. It was impossible to discuss such matters with Beatrice, now Sister Mary of the Assumption, and dangerous to bring them too close to the surface with Theresa, who was inclined to be unpredictable whenever Lady Simon mentioned Charles. The sad truth was that Theresa had always been stupidly jealous of her brother. So it really had been beastly of Catherine to deny her a full audience, especially when the rumours of Charles's marital troubles had arrived in Chios while Lady Simon was actually staying there.

Lady Simon had always found Rosamund very difficult and had not felt comfortable with her from the outset, but it had been borne in upon her by her two single daughters that anyone who had married Charles would have had a hard task in pleasing her. She was reminded by Theresa that Theo had never gained her approval, and by Beatrice, now novice mistress in a Carmelite monastery, of Rosamund's virtues and merits. Rosamund, who had become a Catholic on her marriage to Charles, had taken to the Faith with commendable zeal. She had borne Charles five children, and had presided over his home with self-immolating, thorough-going responsibility. It was hard to fault her, but privately, and especially during the last year, Lady Simon had suspected that the marriage was beginning to buckle under stress. She had always sensed a hidden flaw in Rosamund, and these things always showed themselves in time.

Charles, of course, was a very successful man. Of his achievements, his mother was unreservedly proud. He had taken over a duff publishing house and had turned it into a respected and profitable concern. Naturally, he had had to make sacrifices in the personal sphere. Any woman should expect this. In fact, he rarely had time to visit her, but she offered this privation up for the Holy Souls. Rosamund sometimes openly complained that he worked such long hours, and often went about her daily duties in a martyred, self-regarding way that Lady Simon abhorred.

Socially, Rosamund was not entirely up to the demands of a man who needed his wife to entertain a great deal. Lady Simon supposed she was clever enough, but it was the sort of cleverness that made one tired. Was she a little boring? It was difficult to quantify that ephemeral quality, but Lady Simon knew what she meant by it. One could be too earnest and sincere. Even Beatrice, of whom Lady Simon stood in awe, had a lightness of touch. As for the emotions, well, she drew a veil over that sort of thing, but she suspected her son needed someone a good deal less complicated, someone who fit into the family ethos. Not to put too fine a point on it, Rosamund was gauche and intractable, a self-pitying neurotic, she was sure, under her supposedly exacting standards. She had a moral rigour that Lady Simon, despite all of her piety, disliked. And so, when the scandal came out, she was not at all surprised, nor could she find it in her heart to blame Charles. His weakness might be there for all the world to see, but who knew what a Cross he had had to bear in Rosamund?

Lady Simon looked out of the aeroplane window and down on Mount Olympus, but she did not recognize it. Though normally she enjoyed flying, the journey was spoiled by the thought that she would have to be driven back to London in that battered old Volvo by her daughter-in-law, who each year fetched her, put her up for the night in Holland Park, then dispatched her to Gloucestershire the next day.

According to the story in *Private Eye*, kindly sent to her by her closest friend Agnes, Charles had a mistress, one Caro Morris. ('Not "Caroline and Charles"! Oh, Mummy!' Theresa had cried over the telephone with a sort of witch's glee.) It was bad enough having a meal with Rosamund when Charles was about, but what on earth could she say in the light of his inevitable absence? She had assumed that Catherine would help her to prepare for this encounter with Rosamund, but Catherine had let her down as usual, actually refusing to speak of it when Lady Simon had been so dreadfully worried and had had so many questions to ask.

As she wanly regarded the clouds beneath her, she anticipated the icy breath of Rosamund's kiss at Heathrow. Their cheeks would graze. 'Did you enjoy your stay? How is Xenia?' (This always came annoyingly first.) 'How is Catherine? How is Theo?' she would say. Then there would be the litany of grandchildren's doings in the car. Lady Simon was convinced that Rosamund's children did not like their mother. Except for Mary, who was going to Edinburgh this autumn and who was taking a 'year out' in Zimbabwe, they all had jobs, lived in sin, and rarely saw their parents.

And yet, through all these years of mutual dislike, she and Rosamund had managed to keep up an exact and courteous pretence. Tonight, her daughter-in-law would serve up cold lamb and chutney she had made herself, salad and baked custard, for this was Lady Simon's favourite supper. Although they generally addressed each other through a barrier that seemed to be made of frozen cotton wool, there really might be no conversation at all. Lady Simon was not sure that she would be able to look Rosamund in the eyes, especially as, despite the Church's teaching on divorce, she thought this Caro person sounded more suitable for Charles. She prayed that he would actually be there for the sake of appearances; that he would reassure her; or that he would give her the chance subtly to reassure him. She knew whose fault it was.

Lady Simon, gloomily aware of the aeroplane's northerly direction, nibbled at the roasted peanuts that the flight attendant had brought with her gin. Lady Simon drank gin in solidarity with the Queen Mother, but she did not really like it so much as she liked the tonic. She had the obscure notion that quinine killed germs. Despite Catherine's excellent Chiote cook, Lady Simon was never entirely sure about Greek food, and she had often experienced phantom tummy upsets at the house in Kampos. Catherine brutally put these episodes down to nerves. It was no wonder that she had attacks of nerves after the sober meals in the dining-room which Catherine had been at such pains to restore.

There was a curious table, inlaid with Penthelic marble, that her daughter had, perhaps imaginatively, chosen. She had once heard Catherine pretentiously call it 'the spiritual centre of the house'. She would let no one clean it but herself, and got her mother to bring Antiquax Marble Cleaner in tins from England every year. It reminded Lady Simon of an altar or a tomb, particularly as meals proceeded in silence as a norm. Glasses clicked on the marble surface. An unspoken catalogue of forbidden subjects inhibited even Xenia, whose correctness as a young lady seemed to be more and more at issue every year.

Although Lady Simon appreciated manners in the young, Xenia gave the impression of a Lipizzaner horse, each meal, each greeting becoming a new event in dressage. If the child so much as peeled a fig, it had the aspect of ritual. She stood up for elders and opened doors with the mathematical perfection of a butler. Somehow, the whole exercise seemed a tribute to her father's grand design for her and to the money he had spent on it. Like a mask worn in some Far Eastern drama, the girl's features were perpetually schooled – not frozen, but ceremonial, excising her personality and sublimating it to the necessity of a greater end. She was the form and pattern of a maiden state, long since anachronistic in the West: she had an honour that could be defended, or, for that matter, lost.

It had been after one of these dreadful dinners that Lady Simon had attempted to discuss the *Private Eye* entry about Charles with Catherine. Theo, whose will, it seemed, was never directly contravened, had gone into the orange groves for a post-prandial cigar, and Xenia had been practising her singing. She was boosting her application to Oxford by trying for a choral scholarship, and it was true that she did have a good voice. She sang 'O, for the wings of a dove', Penelope's lament from *Il Ritorno d'Ulisse*, and arias from Mozart as Lady Simon and Catherine sat upon the terrace in the soft evening, the purity of the voice spilling around them. One might have expected a peacock to arise from this Xanadu and perch upon the wall, or the arrival of Kubla Khan. Sometimes, Xenia would sing a wailing Greek or Turkish folk song, Lady Simon was never sure which, and it was these Asiatic melodies that suited her voice best. For them she dropped the breathing and comportment appropriate to the concert platform. Husky and nasal, somehow ferocious with suppressed feeling, the song would drift a cappella like smoke on to the terrace and beyond, as if bound for Çeşme across the water, or into the general air where unrequited love still hurt people.

Each evening, Lady Simon and Catherine would sew by the light of the dying sun, and after dinner, by an oil lamp set upon the table just outside the music room. The terrace overlooked the water-wheel, the cobbled mosaic of the courtyard, and the trellised walk that led to the groves. Lady Simon worked at her kneeler, Catherine at a patchwork quilt of her own design. A love of fine handiwork was virtually the only thing they had in common, and they pooled this slender resource in a mild desperation to get on. Although Catherine gave evidence of listening to the young girl's singing, Lady Simon could always see the symptoms of strain in her daughter's face.

It was an unstated family commonplace that Catherine left something to be desired as a mother, although it was hard to know quite what that was. Xenia, who was clever, well educated and in good health, showed no signs of neglect. It was simply that Catherine treated the girl a little impersonally, as if they happened to be sharing the same first-class carriage, or as if they were the members of the same club and knew each other only slightly. Of course, Lady Simon had her theory about why this was. She also thought Rosamund had taken opportunistic advantage of the situation by stepping in to take up the slack that Catherine left. She could never tell if Catherine resented this, but rather thought she ought to. At any rate, whatever the matter really was with Catherine, Lady Simon knew one thing for certain. Her daughter's apparent attention to Xenia's singing, the garden nightingales and the splashing, turning wheel was only an evasion of conversation with herself!

That particular evening, Lady Simon had assessed the cliff face for a toe-hold. Her earlier attempts to discuss the exposé of Charles in *Private Eye* had been scuppered in the bland wash of Catherine's blue eyes.

'Are you sure that striped material goes with that blue?' she had asked. 'It looks rather like an awning, darling.'

'It's meant to be Greek,' Catherine said, clenching her teeth on a thread she had bound off.

Xenia was singing *Laudate Dominum.*

'Well, I suppose it's bold . . . striking.'

'Yes.' Catherine picked up a cloth lozenge of a chevron design, perhaps bolder, and knotted the thread at the end of her needle. She was hoping to have an exhibition of her Greek quilts in London the following year.

'I'm so sorry. I didn't mean to offend you.'

'You did not.' Catherine matched the lozenge to the bottom of a hexagon.

'It's just that I'm so awfully worried . . . you know . . . about poor

Charles and Rosamund.' Lady Simon lowered her voice at the end of the sentence, piercing the air with her stage whisper.

'Why do you worry? You never liked her anyway.'

'Well, darling, it *is* a marriage! And what will the children think, especially darling Mary?'

'Do children think?' Catherine paused, repentant, Lady Simon hoped, at this flippant remark. 'I think the whole thing will come out a great deal better if we mind our own business.'

Lady Simon completed the Lamb's knee and let her work rest in her lap. She looked out over the garden in a demonstration of the pain that Catherine really should be sharing with her in all of this. 'I do not see that I am interfering by asking you in private about the truth of these rumours. Surely you can see how unpleasant it is to have the family talked about in this way! It really would help me enormously to fend people off when I am back in England if I *knew*. Perhaps these ghastly gossip people have only invented the story. If they have not, one wants to be loyal in another way.'

'Meaning . . . ?'

Somehow, Lady Simon had flushed Catherine out. 'Well, one wants to stand by one's children.'

Catherine closed her eyes as if in mute appeal for patience, then opened them again, blistering the patchwork on her knee with a look of pure resentment. She had become more caustic with time. 'When have you stood by me?' she asked. In the lamplight, her face was studied and fearful, for she must know, Lady Simon realized, that this was the sort of thing one did not say.

'Darling, I think that is rather selfish. I have never had to protect you from nasty rumours!' She was pleased she had thought to say that to which there was no riposte.

Catherine evidently saw this. Perhaps she was sorry. She put her elbow on the little table and her head in a slightly trembling hand. She took off her half-moon spectacles and rubbed her eyes. 'You wish to stand by Charles's adultery, then? What would Father Henry say? Or Beatrice, for that matter . . . our own Sister Mary? They will be none too pleased. I think it highly unlikely that you mean to defend Rosamund!'

A picture of long ago came into Lady Simon's mind of Catherine and Rosamund sharing mugs of tea in the kitchen while Rosamund spooned baby food into the latest arrival. She could see them laughing and smoking – as they both did then – excluding her. Now, they spoke to each other with reserve, but excluded her still. 'And would you defend her? Knowing her as you do?' Lady Simon blurted this out in a sudden brainstorm, the sort she had with growing frequency and found unaccountable in herself. Her heart would pound, and, as the saying went, she would 'see red'. As she liked to think that she was very patient, such attacks frightened her.

Catherine held her in a bold, blue gaze and gathered her needlework to herself. 'Mummy, I think we are all very tired from this wretched heat, and it would be an awfully good idea if we went to bed!' She extracted pins from the patchwork, then stabbed them into a velvet pincushion, her grandmother's and a gift from Lady Simon. 'There will be no divorce. I am almost sure of it. And that is the last word I have to say on the subject. Rosamund is . . .' But she looked up and fell silent. Xenia had slipped out on to the terrace and was standing in the doorway. Catherine gave her mother a queer, humourless smile. 'You see?' she said softly. 'Don't you see how stupid . . . ?'

And Lady Simon had had to accept defeat.

III

Charles had tried to winkle his sister, Theresa, out of Gloucestershire to meet their mother's flight from Athens. He could hardly get 'Beata' (as Theresa privately called her) out of her convent, and he really did not want to mix the children up in all of this until they really had to know that Rosamund was gone.

He had quailed before the prospect of speaking with Theresa, on whose rough charity the family depended: Lady Simon lived with her. Theresa, a farmer, had been trucking off lambs to the abattoir, not a happy task for her, and with distinct unkindness had said 'You bloody get her! I'm bloody well not coming up to London, and it's time you faced things out just a bit. When she gets back from Chios, I shall have nothing from morning till night but your wretched love life . . .' and on it went until he had had to put down the telephone and get his secretary to cancel his luncheon engagement.

Charles had been gearing himself up to meet Marina Mason for some time now. Even though he had liked the sound of her when he had rung her, it was going to be difficult to talk with her about Edgar Jolly's biography of her late husband Arthur Holt. It was partly her own fault, for she had given his journals and unpublished poems to the children of his first marriage with a brief to dispose of as they would – and they had. Although Jolly himself was fair-minded about the poet's second marriage, to Marina, Holt's diaries were so scathing that it was difficult to see how he had gone on living with her. What was more, his children, the beneficiaries of her generosity, had vilified the poor woman, who simply refused to defend herself. Over calves' liver, or whatever, Charles had intended to go to some pains to make sure that she really did not want to offer her own side of the story to Jolly. Quite honestly, he did not want a libel case on his hands. But if he had been anticipating the lunch with mixed feelings, he regarded meeting his mother with pure dread.

Although Charles had wanted a more streamlined and high-tech existence, he drove the dowdy family Volvo, made shabby by dogs which had either died or been recycled into his children's lives, and on this day, he found it rather reassuring. It seemed somewhat less alarming to countenance his mother's veiled intensity in a familial car of such antiquity than it would have been in the Mazda to which he vaguely aspired. Charles disliked telling lies, and the worst aspect of his affair with Caro had been the deceit. He wished to negotiate the conversation in such a way that his mother might best understand the truth, and this would mean, he knew, going into contortions of small fibs and false trails. Whether or not he was going to reveal that his wife had bolted leaving no forwarding address, he did not yet know.

'Rozzy!' he said softly to himself. He paced the polished concourse of Terminal 2. Its expanse seemed relentless in the suggestion that all kinds of modern arrivals and departures had to take place against a backdrop of Tie Rack and The Body Shop. Caro had once worked for The Body Shop and still often smelt of mint or aloes. Roz would think Caro a person of the concourse, a young, modern person of goings and comings, herbs and green ideas. Although 'a girl of good family', she dressed with a touching modernity and thought with the thoughts of Anita Roddick and Channel 4. Even with her father's corporate grouse moor behind her, she did this, and it was brave of her . . . Charles knew.

He caught himself up. How had he allowed himself to think that Caro was 'a girl of good family'? Was this how he really did think when catastrophe bared the foundations? Rosamund, the American, would have said so. Had it been for the best that Rozzy had found out? Caro was emphatic that it was for the best. But for a week he had been steeling himself to discuss it with his wife, and when last night he had finally gone home to have things out with her, he had found her note, and had been seized with a panic more awful for its having been wholly unexpected. He looked away from The Body Shop in an effort to say to himself that he did not want not to want what he had thought he wanted and now had. He was, at least partly, relieved to be rid of Rosamund.

He looked up at the screen to find that the aeroplane from Athens had arrived and that the baggage was in the hall. He could see his mother in his mind's eye, propped upon her walking stick, pointing out her luggage to some passing young man, expectant of his help and gracious with her thanks. The youth would doubtless be saying to himself, 'What a sweet old lady! I wish my mother were like her, a world traveller.'

Charles grasped at the hope that his third sister, Cat, had manipulated things in his favour, for he was sure their mother's preternatural ears had picked up the gossip, and Cat loathed any form of unkind gloating. But then it was possible that she had not. Kit-Cat . . . Catherine, who had never had the family dogginess, except in the way of persevering loyalty. She was inscrutable, more contemplative than their sister, the nun, and less cheerful. A ludicrous image came to him of his sister treed in her orange groves, their mother making small rushes at the trunk. He should have written to Cat or rung her, but this would have involved admissions he was even now unprepared to make.

Charles in his grey suit watched the first trickle of passengers from his mother's flight as they meandered into the concourse wheeling luggage or shifting rucksacks on tired shoulders. In running shorts or shell suits the world's youth had evidently enjoyed Greece; men and maidens both, with bronzed legs and sweat bands looked as if they had run to London in a marathon. They carried souvenir bottles of ouzo or Metaxa in string bags, and despite the dismal English day, seemed on their way for a swim. Their teeth flashed in smiles at waiting relatives as if in an inadvertent ad for toothpaste or Pepsi. They returned with open lovers with whom they had shared Lilos naked on beaches for naturists. Oiled, they had browned all over in the Mykonos sun. Perhaps they were, in fact, students of archaeology or the Greek drama.

Despite the rigours of his wife, Charles and Rosamund had four adult children who all travelled this way now, more hedonistic, he thought, as a result of their mother's conscientious prudery. Mary, the fifth and youngest, was different, but there were reasons for that and not all of them positive. As for her elder siblings, there was nothing ardent about their love affairs. They somehow reminded him of a magazine called *Health and Efficiency*, which he and his friends had sneaked into school, with dreadful sniggering. Charles himself, in Jermyn Street shirts, had fallen in love with Caro. Greying, he had thrown himself at her young feet.

What a pickle! What a mess! If only he knew where Rozzy was, he could simply tell his mother she had been called away to it. This morning, he had intended to check out her favourite haunts until he had realized he no longer knew what they were. She had no family in England, and her friendships had always been loosely based around the children. In any case, Rosamund was too guarded to land on a chum, too proud to admit the failure of her marriage. Would it be possible to suggest to his mother that his wife had been summoned away to a deathbed in the States? All of her relatives were long-lost ones, but no theory about Rosamund was complete without the element of her origins coming into it. Far-fetched though this idea was, Charles suddenly wondered if she had, in fact, run off to Kentucky. He could somehow see her using this circumstance to get in touch with her much and darkly vaunted 'roots'. He shook his head. He was only evading his mother with these imaginings, and blunt though Theresa was, she was right. He must face his mother now . . . and with the truth.

His hand went up to the knot of his tie in preparation. And there she was.

As Charles had predicted, Lady Simon had commandeered a bearer. A youth with legs like tree trunks, his hirsute thighs bulging from denim cut-offs, swung her valise (for there was no other word for this heavy, pre-war suitcase) from his arm as if it were a handbag. He was wearing an Australian leather hat and looked as if he were about to burst into song from the sheer fitness he exuded. Although his mother generally held such people in odium, she smiled graciously up at the lad. She was dressed in a silk suit of black and white hound's-tooth check; her hair crowned her head in a perfect chignon; and she grasped her walking stick lightly like a wand, rather than a support, or a rod having to do in some way with the due process of law. With even dignity, she scanned the crowd; when she saw Charles, her whole face and body relaxed. He realized that she had been expecting, and perhaps dreading, a meeting with Rosamund.

'Thank you so much,' she said to the youth, 'but here is my son!' And with a forceful electric beam, she met Charles's shifting glance. Absently, she rummaged for her handbag, and for an awful moment, Charles thought she was going to give the young man a tip, but she extracted her handkerchief and dabbed at her nose as if perhaps earlier on she had been crying.

'Cheers!' the lad said, touching the brim of his hat. Hoisting his duffle bag, he fluxed away.

'Darling! So lovely to see you! So considerate of you to have come.' She tiptoed up and grazed both of his cheeks.

Inversely to her intention, perhaps, Charles thought of all the times he had not met her on her returns from Chios. She gave his hand an extra little squeeze, however, as if making a moot point. Her eyes gave him to understand that she knew he must have been through rather a lot.

For some reason, Charles wished he had not been wearing a yellow shirt. Caro had chosen it and he had put it on that morning for the sake of Marina Mason, a celebrated beauty. 'Did you have a lovely time?' he asked, knowing, of course, that she had not. 'How's Cat? How're Theo and Xenia? Well?' The yellow shirt seemed to advertise too bold a transition from Rosamund, disloyal to her somehow. Where was she?

'All well!' his mother said perkily, almost bravely in the effort of this assertion. 'There seemed an immense amount to do. I don't think darling Catherine realizes how old I have become. It was very tiring.'

Charles smiled to himself. Cat and Theo, in preparation for the annual visit, always devised schemes and itineraries to distract her. He took his mother's case and paraphernalia. 'My goodness! What have you packed in here, Mummy?' There was a dearth of family jokes, but everyone stuck to this one. Lady Simon was incapable of taking less than her entire wardrobe to Greece. 'What a weight!' They made towards the car park.

She made no effort to describe the exhausting round of social duties imposed upon her by Catherine: luncheons, dinners, teas and yachting expeditions with the Chios gentry. 'How is Rosamund?' she asked instead.

Why had he not simply hired a driver to meet her? In answer to his mother's question, he shrugged.

'Not unwell, I hope. She always comes to meet me.'

Could he say that one of the children was ill? That was only asking for trouble. Suddenly, the menopause struck him as an answer to prayer. 'Mummy,' he said, laying a hand on her shoulder as a prelude to a communication of some delicacy, 'Rozzy has really not been herself for the last six months. I am sure you understand . . . time of life and all that. Lately, things have been getting on top of her and we all thought it for the best if she took a little time to herself. Besides, you and I haven't really seen each other properly for such ages. Rosamund was worried about not meeting you' – and indeed the substance of his wife's note had been that her departure would make her unable to perform this duty – 'but I packed her off for a complete break . . . and here I am!' Charles could not help but bask in his mother. She obscurely melted his resistance to her ethos of finesse. In an oblique manner, she now understood that Rosamund had decamped, was being difficult, that the marriage was in trouble, but being weathered none the less. Rosamund would have gone at it head on – with a broadsword.

Lady Simon smiled. 'How lovely, darling!' she said. 'Such a good idea for Rosamund to have a little holiday.' They exchanged a look in which he admitted and she understood more, perhaps, than he had wished to say.

In the car park lift, an Asian family beamed approval on this filial pair. In tow, they had an old lady in a sari, who looked nettled in some way but, by and large, content. Charles wondered how much longer he could sustain this and how long it would take her to get round to the *Private Eye* piece. He thumbed frantically through his mind for a busy, noisy restaurant where he could take her without offence and where they would be unable to talk.

'Darling,' he said by inspiration, for he never called her this, although he felt she wanted him to, 'do you mind if I drop you off at Holland Park, settle you there and go back to work for a few hours? I have something rather pressing. Then I suggest we pop off to . . . Langan's. You must be so tired of Greek food. Then you can tell me all about your visit.'

They were driving along the motorway in the smelly old Volvo which had done so many school runs and supermarket trips. It was really Rosamund's car. Somehow it pained him to see her vivid in his mind now, staggering under loads taken from the car – shopping, tuck boxes, children's school trunks, bags of potting compost, tubs for the garden, lamps, beds, children's friends, dogs, aquaria, newts, and birthday parties lugged to the cinema to see the latest offering of death and horror. She was sturdy, draconian, unyielding, but unsparing of herself, tirelessly trying, unendingly offered for them, a holocaust and sacrifice. He could not believe she had really left him. When she was angry, she often said she had burnt up her life for him and the children . . . and of what savour was the smoke now she was gone? Was it sweet? It had been substantial. Some of her things were cleared, but mostly her room stood frigid and intact. He supposed he must get round to asking the children if she had told them where she was going, but that was so embarrassing it did not bear thinking about. They had not even met Caro, nor had they discussed the scandal with their father.

From the corner of his eye, he saw his mother's tireless back recline into the seat as if the whole thing were a merciful release. Her eyes closed, her mouth was in the faint curvature of a smile. Of course she did not mind being dropped at the house. She would love a little rest, she said.

Even Caro did not know about Rosamund's disappearance. And she must know. He must return to his office and ring her from there.

The Simons lived in a large family house backing on to a communal garden. Rosamund had seen to meals on the table, dishes in the dishwasher, prams, tricycles, bikes, telly, homework, Lego, boyfriends, girlfriends. She herself had not made friends so much as allies of the other mothers whose similar houses abutted the common ground. There had been bonfires and sausages on Guy Fawkes Night and on Bank Holidays, fun for all. The neighbourhood children had slipped into each other's houses for pyjama parties. They had jumped about breathless in the garden until nightfall, playing until the last minute when they had to be scrubbed and put to bed. In the end, a lot of the mothers with whom Rosamund had had tea had become unmoored from their marriages or had obtained liberation through work. Nannies and au pairs had taken their place, but never for Rosamund, who continued to bake fairy cakes, who had continued to be there when the children got home from school, who had done French verbs and algebra with them as the evening had drawn in . . . and Latin. They had a small garden which led to the large shared one, and she had taken an interest in that. She was a keen reader and sometimes would help Charles with awkward manuscripts. Once in a row, she had told him that she might have written something herself if it had not been for him. And yet, despite her resentment, motherhood had seemed the only vocation she recognized as worthy of her energies. She was an average housekeeper and had no feeling for neatness or design, but this did not disprove her function in any way, even when the children were gone. Somehow, she was always behind the glass doors coming up from the garden, or descending the staircase from the airing cupboard, or on her way out of the front door to the supermarket in his mind's eye. He never asked her what she did with her time.

As the years had gone by and the children had shifted, more and more space had become available in which they could avoid each other in the big house. It was not a question of their deliberately acknowledging a gulf between them. He, of course, worked all hours, and she, of course, needed her sleep. With no one around to chivvy, chide or help, narcolepsy had become her hobby, he often thought. She was often in bed by half past eight after a microwaved supper. She never even watched the news. She slept as if she were dead. And so, by degrees, they had come to operate from separate bedrooms, coming together infrequently, and in recent years hardly at all. He had found more and more to do, and although she had less, she never seemed to have the time to go to parties or launches with him. He had met Caro at one of these. She was a PR from another firm.

It was hard to remember that once he had known in close detail what Rosamund did with her day every day, even to the minutiae of her dealings with the greengrocer. The chasms of her innermost thoughts had been familiar to him. They had met at Cambridge where she had been a student on a special award from America, and he had found her strikingly different from English girls, who, next to Rosamund, seemed mannered and blasé. She had seemed a classless princess and had a quick wit which would flash through her American earnestness, giving her a piquant, elfin aspect. More soberly, she had written rather intense poetry then and even had a Gothic past, which she talked about endlessly to the tune of espresso machines in coffee bars. He now thought he had romanticized her because she romanticized herself.

At the time, her life history seemed to come from Faulkner, with even a fire thrown in for good measure. She had been at pains to establish that the house in which both her parents had perished had been something of a family seat. Rosamund had been at boarding-school in the East when the calamity had occurred, and after the event she had been taken in by an uncle in Boston who had organized her study abroad. Charles had been smitten, drawn in by her vulnerability. It helped that she was small and fragile, a figurine from Tennessee Williams's menagerie. And yet she was more austere than sad and slovenly. She was the august refugee from a New World disaster, and from time to time she would brood intimately on hints and forebodings she had had in childhood of a family history of which the fire had been the symbolic outcome. The inquest had found that an electrical fault had been the cause. Rosamund, however, suspected spontaneous combustion from a psychic source. And indeed, clinging to the edges of the story, there had always been, he felt, the faint curl of malice, as if someone or something had lain in wait for the Buchanans as they slept: not an arsonist, but some destructive ambiance reified by fire. Rosamund had unresolved feelings about her father, and 'Daddy' by Sylvia Plath had been her favourite poem. There had been times, in fact, when Charles had wondered if Rosamund had been abused by this shadowy man she rarely spoke about, for it would have addressed many questions, albeit in a simplistic manner. But as she was even now given to patches of vengeful ruminating and this had never emerged, he had decided that at least incest was not the lugubrious first cause with Rosamund.

Charles, with the tradition of Simons behind him, had felt the heady swell of gallantry. Rosamund, hemmed in by dragons, wanted rescue.

The worst of it was, a quarter of a century on, he seemed to have slain none of them. In a sense, he thought she kept them as pets and loved them more than she did the family she had so dutifully raised. After a breakdown in the seventies, her fragility had imperceptibly become brittleness. In their early days together, she had clung to him with rollercoaster fears, which in later years had reduced themselves to anxieties, some of them so petty as to be absurd. With the children she was brisk and able, but she landed on him with her binges of depression. Charles did not like listening to Caro's denunciations of Rosamund, but he could not help hearing them. He had grown and Rosamund had stayed in the same place, diminishing her store of tragedy into a locked-room mystery. Even with her good degree, she had become a wilful slave to house and garden. She had terminated the therapy he knew she needed. In fact, Charles really did know what she did with herself all day. She suffered.

He sighed. He suffered too. He suffered quite a lot from time to time, but not, of course, from such a distinguished cause as his wife, who would never let it be forgotten that the imaginary details of her parents' immolation possessed her. How could you get round such a catastrophe? Privately, he thought Rosamund lacked that European panacea, irony, which always stood by one at the walls of Troy. When he had first known her, he had thought how direct she was, facing out the conflagration, facing out the wilderness in hand-to-hand combat with her demons. One had been awed into submission by such bravery and had tiptoed round the pyre. Latterly, he had come to see self-pity in it. Kentucky might have been her Mycenae, but she was no Electra. And was it so ignoble of him to want a normal married life, a good career?

Whatever the rights and wrongs of the situation, Charles had girded himself to face her the previous evening. Since the publication of the *Eye* piece he had slept at his club, thinking it unmanly to cower behind Caro's skirts. He had rung the house to give advance warning of his coming, but had not been surprised to find the machine on, nor had he expected an answer to his message. Rosamund had to be there because she was the house's genie. He had left work early in full expectation of battle. She was squeamish about divorce, and so, in fact, was he. Nevertheless, the decision to get one might have to be the outcome. Somehow, it seemed the cleanest thing to do.

He let himself in at the front door, thinking it too strong a statement to ring the bell in what was, after all, his own home. She had neatly stacked his post on the hall table, but the answering machine still winked its one message. At 6 p.m. she would be in the kitchen or maybe in the garden with her roses in the late light of August. A shaft of sympathy went through him. She would be dreading this interview as much as he. Maybe they could crack a bottle of wine. This thought made him wince in nostalgia for old times. Caro did not understand, and so he could not tell her, that he loved Rosamund in a different way, almost like an old friend with whom he had fallen out. There was more to her than mere neuroticism. Although she had done nothing to foster it, he still admired her literary judgement. In fact, before the scandal had broken, he had left Edgar Jolly's rough draft of the Holt biography for Rosamund to mull over. Caro might know how to sell it, but Rosamund would be able to evaluate it. As it was bound to be controversial, he wanted her opinion. Maybe they could start that way. Maybe they could talk about the book.

'Roz?' he called out in the empty hall. There was no reply. He had the urge to fortify himself with whisky from the drinks tray in the drawing-room, but decided against it. Stupid, too, he thought, to imagine discussing Arthur Holt with Rosamund no matter how much she admired his poetry. He squared himself and descended to the kitchen.

'Roz?' She was not there. His eye trailed around the mathematical tiles she had oddly chosen. For some reason, she had decorated the kitchen clinically, against her unruly nature. The walls often reminded him of a sheet of graph paper; the utilities were plotted and planned. Usually, there was a mess erupting from this dour order, but the kitchen was vacant and tidy, the garden door bolted hard. Through the plate glass, he could see the neighbours' Dutch au pair waving children down from the monkey-puzzle tree from which Dominic had fallen years ago. Had he broken an arm or a leg? The communal garden was sear from the hot summer, and the sun was setting, a dense and turbid globe over Shepherd's Bush.

'Roz?' Maybe she was doing some late shopping. Maybe she had gone to an evening Mass at the Carmelite church. Once, she had been a daily communicant, but apparently some priest had offended her, and she now made perfunctory Sunday visits elsewhere. He thought she might well pray now. He decided to wait for her return.

Charles drank more than he ought, so Caro said, but not so much as to warrant real concern. He was thirsty and hot and dead nervous. Maybe there was some white wine in the fridge, or some tonic water so he could make himself a fortifying gin. He opened the door and there it was . . . her note. It was the only thing left on the chill and scoured shelves. It astonished him to realize just how shocked he was to see it:

Dear Charles,

This is to let you know that I have decided to go away. I was sure you would look in here. I am afraid I cannot fetch your mother from the airport tomorrow, and I must leave you to make other arrangements.

Re: the draft of Edgar Jolly's biography, I think he has done a good job, but you are right in wanting to persuade Marina to put her point of view, and surely it should be possible to get in touch with Helena Taggart no matter how barmy she has become. In every other way, it seems highly publishable, and I am sure it will cause much interest. I have left the ms. on the desk in your study with a few notes.

Rosamund

Charles, not stupefied, nor grief-stricken, nor forlorn, was all of these. A note in the fridge would have done a sub-acid female novelist proud, but not Rosamund. With her endemic moral earnestness, she would have meant it – and did mean it; would have seen it – and did see it – as an unmitigated symbol of an arctic, mechanical marriage shared on a subsistence level in which there was no nourishment. He felt as if she were dead. The note was typed and signed like a business letter which required no reply. He was irrationally angry that she had stood him up in this way. How did she know he would come to the house that evening, especially if she had not picked up the message on the machine? He was hardly a glutton, so why did she imagine he would look in the fridge? And hadn't she taken a bit of a risk with his mother? She could have left a message with his secretary after all!

Charles sat at the melamine table, the note before him, his head in his hands. He should have tackled Rosamund at once, but he had evaded the confrontation until the *Private Eye* piece had worked into her brain with its smug, smutty insinuations. The item had injured everyone. Suddenly, he too felt groped at and sickened. He got up slowly and blundered to the wine rack where he found a good bottle of claret, which he opened and drank, taking it in great gulps like medicine. He had formed the idea that he had sustained internal injuries which required minimal movement, and so he sat down and consumed one glass after another.

Perhaps it was like a death, after all. When Charles's father had died, they had all wanted him out of his misery, but when it had actually happened, he had been shocked. In the same way, he had often longed for some *coup de grâce* to his marriage and, even before Caro, had found it difficult to control fantasies of the very situation he faced now. He had mislaid his faith some years ago, and had not since bothered to look for it, but the habit of guilt, like anthrax, remained in the ground of his being unmitigated by compensating grace. It had been for the past few years at least his recurring daydream that Rosamund would go, leaving him the righteous mourner, in credit with his children and friends. Somehow he had never been able to imagine her with a lover, although it would have relieved him, he thought, if she had had one. Instead, he had visions of a clothing ceremony, with Rosamund entering a convent like his sister, her hair being ritually shorn, her body flattened crosswise in oblation, face down. He had fantasies of her taking the veil, having obtained special permission from Rome. She had gone through their wedding like that, pale, white and garlanded to the altar, and on their wedding night he had felt like a human knife.

Now that she was gone, he knew that the first thing he should do was to ring Caro, but so strong was the lingering sense of death in the house that it seemed a blasphemy. After a few glasses an unwelcome thought struck him. Suppose she was dead. It had seemed a bit mad to put the note in the fridge; perhaps it really was mad. Could she have committed suicide? Was this her way of telling him? Afraid of what he might find, Charles had apprehensively searched the house, going from attic to cellar and through the grown children's sealed rooms. There had been no sign of her and he had decided she had communicated metaphorically after all. It had been the corpse of the marriage he had found in the fridge – a bodiless entity, but with a tag of a note around its toe nevertheless.

Now they had arrived at the Cromwell Road, Charles looked at his mother, grateful for her silence during the journey up the motorway. It had not been tact, however. She had fallen asleep. At eighty, she was inclined to doze, and it always disturbed him to see her slack mouth, her crêpey eyelids. She woke when he made the turn to Kensington High Street and Holland Park beyond.

'Rosamund,' she said acidly, 'is certain to be back in time for Xenia, or so I should imagine!'

'God!' said Charles. He had entirely forgotten that his niece was to arrive at the end of the week in preparation for her return to school. The remark seemed to have surfaced from his mother's slumber like an oracular dream. There was no humanistic way to describe the fatality and hostility with which she habitually spoke Xenia's name. Invariably it was charged with bridled repugnance, and it usually heralded an unpleasant change of mood in Lady Simon.

'Do you really need to blaspheme, darling?' his mother asked.

He bucketed past the Sainsbury's faux-Egyptian Homebase Centre and shot the lights. 'I'm sorry, Mummy. I didn't think.'

'Well, Rosamund will not forget her little protégée. You can be sure of that.'

Charles wondered if his mother was spoiling for a fight and determined that he would not rise to the bait. For many years now, the sly inference had hung in the air that Rosamund had pushed her own children aside in favour of Xenia, especially Mary, who was only a year older, and very much Lady Simon's 'favourite' in consequence. As in most insinuations of this kind, the worst of this one was that an element of truth lay at the bottom of it. Whereas Mary was pale and dejected with Rosamund and was often subject to helpless bouts of rage, Xenia blossomed in the presence of her aunt. With the advent of Xenia even in the air, Rosamund's face would soften and thoughts of spontaneous treats would burst from her. It was not that she rubbed Mary's nose in this preference, and she was always scrupulously fair, but Charles could tell how relieved she had been when Mary had wanted to take her 'year out' in Zimbabwe, and even though he understood what lay behind Rosamund's feelings, it did bother him that they were there. Unlike his mother, however, Charles never blamed Xenia, nor even his wife, for that matter, for the fondness that had grown up between them. There was something touching about the way they gossiped and chatted. He always felt that Rosamund would have liked to be more relaxed with her own children, and that Xenia would have enjoyed a similar relationship with Catherine.

'I am thankful,' he said sharply, 'that my wife and my niece have found friendship in one another, and I am sure you are too!' He changed down and took Shepherd's Bush roundabout in a bold arc. It was only when they had reached the house in Pelican Crescent that he realized how significant it was that Rosamund had flown, even in the face of Xenia's imminent arrival.

He lumbered his mother's luggage into the hall, and heaved it down on the cold, tiled floor. The house was Edwardian and now fulfilled the pretension to which it had once only aspired. Even before this time, Charles and Rosamund had discussed selling the big place, but they had never got around to it. He supposed they would now. From Lady Simon's own treasury, donated when she had moved into Theresa's 'Granny flat' (a term she loathed and which Theresa consistently used) the house was furnished in the style to which it might have wanted to become accustomed. Below a large gilt mirror stood the Georgian hall table. Charles scanned it quickly for incriminating evidence. Perhaps Rosamund had returned in his absence and left another note. Maybe he had left some evidence of Caro there. In deference to antiquated custom, when people like the Simons had had one telephone in the hall to be answered by a butler, they kept the answering machine. A message winked, and Charles froze at the sight. Perhaps she had repented and rung him; perhaps Caro had heard the news from someone else (though from whom he could not imagine). Now the wall was down, maybe she had decided it was time to clamber across.

'May I get you some tea, Mummy, or would you rather rest?' he asked. His mother resembled a small, inquisitive animal, and even though he had chastened her she seemed to be sniffing the air for the quality of Rosamund's palpable absence. It was clear to him, however, that she did know she had gone too far about Xenia.

'Darling, thank you fetching me. Would it be all right if I had a tiny rest? Then I shall be fresh to go out later.' She was holding him to the restaurant. Before she could go on, he hefted her bag upwards, letting her strain up the stairs after him. The guest room was a tribute to Laura Ashley – Rosamund's idea – with curtains too winsome for Charles. But his mother seemed genuinely tired and sank with the gratitude of old bones into the bedroom chair. After pecking her cheek and ensuring she would be all right on her own, he sprang softly and swiftly down the stairs. He put his ear next to the speaker on the machine, turned the volume down, and played the message back.

'Hi!' said an American voice with a Southern accent . . . a woman's. 'Hi, Rozzy? This is Missy here. Are you OK? I hope so, because I haven't heard from you and I am really anxious to do so . . . er . . . it was just lovely seeing you the other day . . . and I . . . um . . . wondered if you had considered. Anyway, I really would love to hear from you soon. Bye, now!' The machine clicked, then clunked, then clicked.

Charles hunted for the button and played it back again.

'Hi! Rozzy? This is Missy . . .'

It took Charles a moment to recall that Missy was Rosamund's first cousin from Kentucky. He had met her – oh, perhaps twenty years ago – but the unpleasant memory lingered. He had disliked her on a primitive level to which he never normally descended, and he could not shake off the impression that the high little voice on the machine presaged some ill.

If Rosamund had vanished in this abrupt way, might it have something to do with Missy? It was foolish to think this, he knew. The woman had probably turned up in London with her begging bowl again, and Rosamund had simply fobbed her off. Still, it made him uneasy to think that

Missy was in the vicinity of a crisis. It was evident that she was anxious for something. Not only her words but her tone conveyed a sense of urgency. Charles replayed the message once more. Missy had not left her number and could be anywhere. Charles began to wonder. Without him there, Rosamund would be wide open to the woman's menace. That's what Missy was – a menace!

He tried to remember why he had thought this once so long ago, but could only recapture the sensation of disquiet.

Why was she anxious to hear from Rosamund? What did she want her to consider? Whatever it was, he hoped his wife had given it the most sceptical thought . . . or refused to have anything to do with it.

IV

LADY SIMON could be forgiven for not having recognized her daughter-in-law at Athens airport, for the transformation was complete. Rosamund had never been one for clothes that caught the eye. In her heart of hearts, dressing for effect had always struck her as being insincere. A face, she thought, should tell its own tale without benefit of make-up, and a figure should be draped in what was clean and decent. Whatever jewellery she wore was genuine. She was one of those small, wiry, intense women who are never really touched by age until quite suddenly they seem to implode and wizen. Although she had never been athletic, she looked as if she were about to set out on a pony trek. Her strong, regular features gave her the appearance of wholesomeness, an impression curiously undermined by an inward look that betrayed a tendency to morbid introspection. No frills, no fuss – that was Rosamund in everything but an essential isolation where complicated night blooms flourished beyond her conscious reach.

On that day, however, when she had arrived in Athens, she had thought it fitting to arm herself in the full regalia which typified the Simon clan. The day before her departure she had taken a taxi to Knightsbridge, marched into Harvey Nichols, and had given the American Express the drubbing she thought Charles deserved. As for Lady Simon herself, Rosamund did not notice her as she merged towards the boarding gate. Her English family was the last thing on her mind. She emerged from the airport into the hot pollution like a model stepping from a bandbox, and strode to the taxi rank in her new high heels, as if such shoes were second best. Her close-cropped hair had been tamed into a sleek cap and it shone with halo blondeness in the penetrating sunlight. Almost shocking herself, she had cut a swathe through the cosmetics department, and with the command of a former débutante, which she was not, she had chosen warpaint of the most subtle and discriminating kind. In her new beige linen suit and cream silk blouse, she looked like a woman of distinction on her way to a luncheon or private view. She did not wear gloves, but she carried them: stitched cotton gauntlets to be thrown down at Theo.

Rosamund had liked and admired Theo from her wedding day on. She had been young, lonely, and afraid of taking on marriage, a new religion, a new family and a new country at the altar of St James's Church, Spanish Place, which had been Lady Simon's spiritual watering-hole in London at the time. Her strained, Bostonian uncle, an uncomprehending Protestant, had thrown a reception he could not afford for people he could not understand at the Savoy: he and Rosamund had been looked at glassily from under hat brims. Only Theo had had the warmth to sense how frightened she was, and with a slight twinge of guilt, she had found herself eyeing him through the white tulle fluff she had only recently pushed back in church to allow Charles's blameless kiss.

Theo had always been a very good-looking man, dark, confident and physically imposing. He was somewhat older than the rest of them: Charles, Cat and Rosamund, who were all of an age. Very soon, she saw how he was always singled out for blame. Unlike herself, he had not transferred his allegiance to Rome, but had remained stoutly Orthodox – strike one, she always thought. Strike two was his breezy lack of inhibition at expressing feeling, a respect in which Rosamund had always felt herself lacking and even crippled. Many years later he was still on base, but without a comfortable margin for error. As time went by, it emerged that an unusual bond lay between Rosamund and Theo. If she had lost her parents in a fire, he had lost his in conflict. His extended family, prominent Greeks in Smyrna, had been massacred by Turks in 1921. He, too, had been an only child, and his father had been killed in Athens during the Greek Civil War in the late forties. His mother had fled with him to London, and had died of a broken heart, he often said, shortly afterwards. Like Rosamund, he had been brought up by an uncle, who had been a shipowner and an old bachelor renowned for parsimony. In the end he had adopted Theo, sent him to school and university in England, and had initiated him into the mysteries of the Baltic Exchange. He had left his small but successful fleet of cruise ships to Theo, who had taken the Chiote name 'Phocas' as his own. Theo was no Onassis, but he had expanded the business and become very wealthy.

For want of an external occupation, Rosamund had given the links between herself and her brother-in-law a lot of thought. She wondered if they had both married into the large, established Simon clan for similar reasons. Perhaps a passion for security was the common cause at the base of their bond, a marriage of true minds. They neither sought each other out nor corresponded, but their understanding seemed better for the impressionistic haze that blurred its edges. It often struck her that they alone in the family understood what it felt like when flames and anarchy got out of hand. They both knew what it was like to be an involuntary sole survivor of a lost Eden. Charles had once said of Theo that a Greek without a family was like a quadraplegic, and of her, that an American with one, was a freak occurrence. Rosamund had often remembered this with resentment, but at the present moment she remembered it again: this time as a terrible irony.

Theo! How could he?

She thought of him now (as she had, perhaps, always thought of him) in all his physical distinctness, and this time a faint abhorrence shuddered through her at the heavy shoulders, the large hands with which he cut the air for emphasis when he spoke. Curly black hair had once adorned the backs of these hands and his chest, but it was now grey. Sometimes it was possible to see the chest through the starched shirts he had made for him in London. He wore a gold medallion of the Virgin under these English vestments, and the masculinity he exuded was buttoned in the finest twill or duck from Savile Row so that he expressed power rather than carnal energy . . . or so she had always thought. With Rosamund, he seemed to curtail his strength as if an instinct to value her involved a certain sacrifice.

At family occasions, they were an odd sight with their heads together, the little starchy woman and her heavy-set familiar: they looked as disparate as two people could be. Charles had also offered the observation that Theo held her in high esteem because she had given birth to three sons. 'Very Greek,' he would say, 'and a bit unfair on my sister, don't you think?' And further, 'Somewhere inside you there is an unreconstructed capitalist to whom our venturesome Byzantine appeals.' He offered these as analytical theories rather than digs to her solar plexus, but long ago she had made up her mind that if Charles was jealous of Theo, he was on very shaky ground and she on terra firma. Besides, if he wanted to treat her as handsomely, he might see a wonderful change.

Rosamund was not thinking of this past allegiance, however, as the queue jolted forward in the wilting Athenian heat, nor of the perspiration that stained her new silk blouse, nor of Charles himself and the scandal for which she might be forgiven the taking of an unscheduled break. She was thinking, instead, of her Cousin Missy.

Wherever she looked, or had looked since Missy's completely unforeseen return into her life, her cousin's name and face were blazoned.

It winked at her like neon as she rocked on the unaccustomed stilettos.

After all this time and moot family speculation, the horrid innuendo was true: Theo was Xenia's natural father. But the domestic apocalypse that made light of all others, even this one, was almost too great to endure: Missy, it appeared, was Xenia's mother.

Rosamund edged her smart case forward with the toe of her smart new shoe. She stood shocked, stiff as a caryatid as the sun blazed down. She believed only what she could absorb. The larger part of her protested still that Missy had invented the whole story, and before she jumped to any conclusions, she had come to Athens to find out. The tale had the Munchausen unreality of a Greek myth. She might as well have believed that Xenia had been hatched; yet, like a myth, it also had an eerie, ulterior credibility.

Of course, it was true that Missy and Theo had met, and in her own house too, but before that time and after it, Missy might have lived in Mongolia for all she thought about her. It had never occurred to Rosamund, for example, to ask Missy to her wedding. It was as if she existed on another plane and in another time. Indeed, in her burnt-out family, Missy had been something of a joke, the wild card in a pack of sober, latter-day Calvinists. Rosamund had not found her funny in childhood, however. Missy had had a breezy cruelty and she had exercised it when, newly arrived from New York in her parents' project to become landed gentry, Rosamund had suffered terribly from shyness. Missy had made sure that Rosamund had felt a stupid, awkward Yankee, no equal to the matchless, columned house that nestled on a swelling hill of blue grass like a child contented at its mother's breast. The trouble was that Rosamund's father had bought back a family place, the estate of a distant relative. Whether or not it should have gone to Missy's father was hard to know, but he evidently thought so even though he had not done well in life and had become something of a poor relation. Most of this had gone over Rosamund's head, anyway. To her, the worst of Missy had been a taunting sexual precocity. Rosamund remembered a double date they had been forced into together. Missy and a beefy high school football star had whooped it up on the back seat of a convertible, while she and a dumb boy from Lexington had exchanged strained conversation, then none at all, on the front. This memory now flashed to illumine the present situation to Rosamund, but she as quickly doused it.

No, her cousin's allegation was the sort often lodged against rich men. Pop stars got it all the time. In the days of DNA, it was the wild action of a fool to make this kind of trouble. She would simply tell Theo that

Missy had turned up with an old and very much used lottery ticket, and he would scotch the story.

In the queue, Rosamund was wedged between two elderly German women much encumbered by paintboxes and easels. She tried to concentrate on them. It seemed that they were off to sketch in Patmos. Behind her were a couple of American fraternity boys whose loud ambition it was to get stoned and laid in Athens. Rosamund shrank. Missy had done the same, hadn't she? Or had she? One of the boys tripped on his rucksack and jostled her. 'Sorry about that, ma'am,' he said. She turned, intending to give him a courtly nod, but the sight of the two in idiotic Bermuda shorts infuriated her, and she glared instead. 'Jesus, lady, all I did was bump you!' said the boy, but Rosamund made no reply. She looked ahead again, oblivious to her own hostility. If what she suspected was true and blackmail was at work, the only conceivable approach was the direct one. Missy had not imagined that she would have the guts to lay the blueprint squarely in front of Theo, nor that she would act so swiftly. Not for the first time, she thought, had Missy underestimated her, nor was it the first time that she had saved her English family's bacon, though little enough thanks she got for it! She was sure Theo would be at his flat, for he normally spent the week in Athens. She would go straight to Kolonaki. He would laugh, oh, surely, he would laugh.

Suppose he did not laugh. Suppose the allegations were true. Rosamund stood very still to control the fit of trembling that this thought gave her. However implausible, the story was possible, and since meeting with Missy, her mind had become an incessant knitting machine, threading and knotting stitch after stitch of the pattern. The probabilities of where, when and in what manner this atrocious business might have happened wove themselves into a narrative so convincing that she found herself unpicking it again. A mass of ravelled thought entangled her. The unthinkable thought itself in her again. Her fondness for Xenia – had it been used?

Perhaps it was in her imagination that she and Theo had shared in the child, mute in their grasp of what things might have been, intelligible to each other in the pain of sacrifice. Had all those patient years been endured in the service of an illusion? It was too terrible to consider. It was as if she had spent a life learning an obscure language of little signs and subtle symbols only to find a Rosetta Stone that challenged every word. Well, if she had been such a fool, maybe she deserved it. Rosamund was given to these grim little measures of inner discipline, but they rarely had the effect of self-improvement she intended.

All at once, a flotilla of taxis arrived as if to clear up the mess of tourists and their impedimenta. Rosamund's driver smiled encouragingly at her fractured Greek, apparently relieved that she was distinct from the ravening horde and knew where she was going. Worry beads and icons swayed from his mirror as he sped towards the city, and Rosamund found herself avoiding the Byzantine gaze of a particularly authoritative Christ, whose eyes seemed to search hers from the dashboard. She looked instead from the window at the familiar scene of jerry-built showrooms, concrete blocks of shops and flats that lined the route. Her new shoes already hurt her, but she forbore to kick them off. Now she was really on her way, she began again to doubt the wisdom of this surprise attack. Maybe he would not even be at home. Billboards proclaiming the coming show of some celebrated Greek *chanteuse* punctuated the way. Plush and voluptuous, the crude picture of the torch singer yearned forward luring the beholder into the bold life of her exotic passions. Some triumph, after all, she seemed to say, emerged from love's treachery. It was a state to which loss was endemic and its cruelty was there for all to see. Rosamund looked back at the icon, hoping it would counterbalance this view and give some vindication to her mission, but its eyes remained thoughtful, the figure aloof.

Once he had remembered Missy, Charles could not get her out of his mind. Having fed, watered and settled his mother, he moved the telephone from his study to his dressing room and kept the bell turned on in case she should ring again. She had come before as bell-wether and banshee. Even though there was no concrete evidence that she had precipitated Rosamund's breakdown in 1974, Missy had arrived crucially right before it, in the way such figures do, a dark and even poetic figure on the doorstep. At her departure, Rosamund, who had recently been delivered of Mary, had cracked and had been hospitalized. His mother and Nanny had coped wonderfully well, but afterwards Rosamund had lived in a different relation to him and their children. She had become cut off and untouchable, and he had countered this finally with indifference. Romance had seemed more and more impossible with someone whose idea of rehabilitation was a grim contest with the scrubbing-brush and an implacable view of purity. In time, the edges of his wife's sharp and unspoken dilemma had become blurred, but the breakdown had brought some essential to the surface and it had never altogether gone away. He had forgotten how Missy had come to embody to him whatever this was, but now he remembered seeing her illuminated as the disrupting catalyst. It had not been a question of her having said or done anything to Rosamund. It was more as if her simple being had spoken to Rosamund's ulterior mode, a self she had hidden and had even tried to erase. Now, at yet another crucial time, she was once again in England and Rosamund had fled.

It had been Christmas Eve when first she had shown herself. Missy had arrived at an intimate time when he and Rosamund had been stuffing stockings in the drawing-room. Morning Mass and Christmas lunch had loomed in Rosamund's mind, he remembered. She had been fretting that she had not bought a present for the baby, even though it would have been virtually impossible for her to do so. Neither of them had wanted another baby, but this had remained unexpressed. Under the tree, Charles had been reassuring her.

When the doorbell had gone at nearly midnight, they had thought it too late for carol singers. 'Some drunk! I'll deal with him,' Charles had said and had gone to the door.

And there she was, standing in the porch light. 'Hi!' she said. 'Are you Charles? I'm Rozzy's cousin Missy from Kentucky. May I please come in?'

Back then, in 1973, she had been something. She was dark and slight with delicate features and slightly hooded eyes which reminded him of Rosamund. She was dressed altogether from head to toe in hippie chic, both outlandish and outmoded, a throwback to the sixties or a cast-off from them. She wore purple crushed velvet, a headband, and lots of fringe. Her hair was long and tangled, as if she had been sleeping rough. She huddled on the threshold out of the sleet, which drove in eastward needles outside the door. She was wearing suede boots, but she shivered. Her teeth chattered. At first, he did not believe that she was related to Rosamund. He called into the drawing-room and his wife came out, billowing still from her recent pregnancy in Laura Ashley corduroy. The two women eyed each other for a moment without a word. Roz, her hair bunched and flaccid, her face extremely pale, swallowed down what he knew was a deep resistance to this incursion.

'Why, Missy! So it is!' she said. 'You had better come in and warm yourself in front of the fire.'

This was the sort of Christian charity that Rosamund practised as a rule. She followed the Gospels like a recipe book and relentlessly added ingredients that it might have been more prudent to omit. Charles knew a scrounger when he saw one, and mentally cast about for alternatives to having her to stay. 'Perhaps you would like a glass of mulled wine and a mince pie,' he said briskly. 'We were doing the children's stockings and are about to go to bed.'

Missy looked at Rosamund with a tremulous air. She seemed Dickensian on Christmas Eve. Shivering in her glad rags, she was a living tableau of the crèche. Had she said at one point, 'No room at the inn?' She was not, it turned out, without irony.

Rosamund had been embarrassed and had flustered about. Before they knew it, Missy was at their fireside, perched on the padded fender and warming her toes. 'This is nice,' she said, checking out the house from cornice to parquet floor, from duffed-up leather library chair to the andirons. Rosamund jammed fingers of fudge into the children's stockings.

'Let me make you something,' she had said. 'I'm afraid the kitchen is in chaos because of tomorrow, but I'm sure I can rustle up some eggs.'

'This'll do fine,' said the wispy Missy, picking at the mince pie that Charles had offered her. She sipped the wine they had stored in a thermos for themselves while playing Father Christmas to Francis, Peter, Theresa and Dominic. Mary was in a carry-cot, stirring awake to be fed. 'Oh, have you had a baby? Isn't it sweet? What a cute baby,' Missy said in a perfunctory manner at the blob of Mary's head rooting at the flannelette sheet.

No one knew what to say. Missy licked her fingers. As she warmed, she sat straighter. In the lamplight, the firelight, the light of the Christmas tree, Charles was dumbfounded by a sudden, clear evidence of beauty. She looked like Pocahontas sitting there in her beads and feathers, a fine princess of the wilderness, who was not altogether daunted by London.

'It's a "she",' said Rosamund, gathering up the baby, 'and I'd better go feed her.'

Missy shrugged and took a tangerine out of the pile for the children's stockings. She peeled it, ate it, and cast the peel on the fire. 'Feed her here. I don't mind,' she said.

English though Charles was, he had been surprised at how little the two women had exchanged in conversation. Nevertheless, they seemed to communicate. It was almost as if they had anticipated each other. He noticed that Rosamund's anglicized voice had subtly changed.

But she stiffened at this. 'I'd rather not,' she said with an English *froideur* that would have done his mother proud. As she vanished up the stairs with the baby, however, he thought he heard her give a suppressed gasp.

Missy turned to him, evidently pleased at Rosamund's departure. Perhaps she felt more comfortable with a man. He had that sensation. It was disquieting. She turned and smiled at him. One of her front teeth was slightly crooked and it added piquancy to her perfect, oval face.

'I hope I do not intrude,' she said. 'I am sure I must, but I had no place to stay, and no money either, I'm afraid.'

He found himself offering her another mince pie. She almost snatched it. He knew she was hungry.

'Blood is thicker than water,' she added. 'Rozzy and I used to hack around as kids, and I had no other place to turn.'

He knew he should say she was welcome, but he could not because she was not.

'You see, I had to leave my husband – at short notice.' She smiled. 'Army. We've been policing Europe. We were going home for Christmas, but we were delayed at Mildenhall. It seemed a golden opportunity not to be missed.' She paused. 'Here!' she exclaimed, pulling up her sleeve. There was a large weal on her arm. In the shadow around the crook of her elbow, he thought he saw needle marks, but then again, he was not so sure. She seemed, in her bizarre way, to be the picture of sobriety. 'He's a redneck!' she added with contempt, 'and they behave like that. Everybody warned me, but I wouldn't listen – not me. Rozzy will tell you. There's more bruises where those come from, and I'm not taking any more. I got here with my last dime. You're in the phone book. Luckily, I remembered your name. I nearly didn't.'

Charles was stunned into silence.

'Don't worry. He won't come and get you. He doesn't know who you are. I never mention my fancy English cousins.' She said this, too, with contempt.

It had been agreed that no one had ever met anyone quite like Missy. It was hard to say that she ruined their Christmas, but she stayed for the duration. They could hardly turn her out. In fact, she was an almost perfectly convenient guest. She slunk like a shadow or a cat from warm spot to warm spot in the cold London house. She slept in what had once been the maid's room, the only available one, in the attic. She was into Indian religion and spent long periods in meditation. She seemed to have an array of silks which she often changed. They emerged from a carpet bag (quite literally – she had an old valise made from a Turkish rug) in proliferation as from a magician's hat. As exotic as she was, she bathed with irritating frequency and used hot water needed for poor Mary, who somehow got displaced as the Christmas infant. The older children were subdued and awed by her. Both Charles and Rosamund had been hot on manners from early on, and the little ones with their 'pleases' and 'thank-yous' and 'Cousin Missy would you likes' were flummoxed at her unexpected responses. She was not graceless, but crudely casual, and Charles knew that Rosamund was ashamed of her, especially in front of his mother who was scheduled to spend Christmas Day with them and who could not be put off. In addition to this visitor, Theo and Catherine happened to be in England that Christmas, and were coming to lunch . . . he remembered that. It had been the year before Xenia's arrival on the scene, and the Simons had been worried that the presence of the new baby might upset Catherine, and Theo even more. They pined for children.

He remembered that Christmas Day. At that time, for the sake of his young family, he had kept up a show of devotion, and even mildly felt it sometimes, though truth to tell, he was not a naturally religious man. They had all marched off to the Carmelite church for the Children's Mass with carols, Roz with Mary in her arms. He should have seen the signals. He had a clear memory of her pallor. In those days they had talked a lot, and he had tried to ask her about Missy, who had stayed at home saying she would do the Brussels sprouts. She seemed to experience some discomfort in a Catholic home. Charles suspected that this did not come from the Maharishi, whom she vaguely admired, but from a more fundamental layer. Rosamund had often talked about the rock-hard pioneer Calvinism in her father's family, and beneath Missy's headband Charles thought he caught a glimpse of bigotry.

'I don't like leaving her in the house on her own,' was all that Rosamund would say as they entered the church and crossed themselves. The four little ones were being very good, having been promised presents after Mass when their grandmother arrived. Their joy at the stockings had been frozen when, coming downstairs to show their parents what Father Christmas had brought them, they had encountered Missy, sleepy, sleazy with a cup of coffee, weary and frocked in saffron. After Communion, Rosamund had wept. 'I'm just tired,' she had said. She had looked completely defeated.

On their way back to the house, Charles had said, 'Why don't you talk to me about this? What is the matter?'

'It's "The Area", Charles,' she said. 'The Area' had to do with her Kentucky years. Sometimes she called it 'The Bermuda Triangle'. Whenever she spoke of it in this way, it signified a kind of fatalism she had. Any attempt to reach her in this mode was doomed to failure.

In the simple memory of that time, Charles was now seized with love and pity for his wife. Her arduous nature was shot through with many points of charm and graces. He remembered her holding her new baby to her tenderly, precariously, as they walked the cold way back to the house that day. There had been something poignant and forlorn about the little pair. How had he and Rosamund allowed themselves to lose each other by such venial and nearly imperceptible degrees? It was not as if the two of them had been vandals to the marriage, but the perpetrators of gradual neglect. He sat up in bed. He had disliked telling Caro that afternoon that Rosamund had gone. He had wanted to tell Rosamund that Rosamund was gone, and to share the coagulated sadness of time between them.

Charles heard a queer noise and started. His mother was snoring in the guest room and the sound came eerily to him as rustling leaves or papers. At that time, Rosamund had been heroically trying to impress her. She would knock herself out every time Lady Simon came to stay in an effort to prove herself worthy of 'the great family' into which she had married. Each Christmas dinner had been stuffed, laid and ornamented. He had tried to stop her, but she seemed to act out of a visceral compunction to be perfect, to achieve, perhaps, a *noblesse* which could only be conferred, and that by birth.

Perhaps it had been the arrival of Missy, perhaps the unwonted presence of Theo and Catherine that Christmas, perhaps it had been the grim determination to make a grand meal for everyone so soon after childbirth that had landed Rozzy in the clinic. He remembered her teetering in and out of the green baize door with course after course while the smoke from the candles rose, while the baby screamed in the corner, and while he and Catherine blundered about trying to help. Roz was manic, exhausted, intense. Francis, Peter, Dominic and Theresa huddled together.

Those four were as thick as thieves now; poor Mary the odd one out. She had done well, really, to get into Edinburgh. She was perhaps predictably fragile, a bit of a Daddy's girl, really. It was almost unbearable to think of her returning to London from her 'year off' to the mess her parents had made. Surely, Rosamund would come back to deal with this. She felt guilty about Mary. And now, of course, he did too.

He remembered having been intensely irritated by Missy, his mother, and also Theo, who he really rather liked. They had sat, a passive trio at the festive board as if they were the only adults present. In paper crowns, they had looked like the Three Kings while everyone had danced attendance. They seemed to hold each other's attention fully while Rozzy spiralled off into the outer darkness of the kitchen, then spiralled in again; while Charles carved and made silly jokes to lighten the atmosphere; while Cat became the maid . . . clearing.

Later on, he had tried to reassure the sobbing Rosamund that she need not have blushed for Missy. In the light from the Christmas candelabra, her gear, complete with tiny, flashing mirrors and sequinned scarves, had shone and glinted. For the ceremonial lunch she had changed into a silk caftan. He could not really say to his wife that Missy's hot beauty transcended all social categories. She had been simply thrilling, and he had sensed Theo's eyes standing out on stalks. Perhaps it had been her scintillating clothes, perhaps it had been his imaginative association with Theo, but Missy had reminded Charles of a mosaic empress of Byzantium. She shone, an Irene or Theodora, relieved to be released from the wall of a basilica. She was the sort of woman who picked up baubles wherever she went. On her hands she wore interesting rings. With the wine, perhaps, she became quite a conversationalist. She spoke with delicate gestures of ringed fingers about a projected trip to Kathmandu. At the time, full of zeal for his wife, Charles had eschewed all lustful glances at Missy, but he was not blind. In flashes, she might have been a priestess about to perform rites on a Himalaya. At other times, she looked perilously close to the sort of American who cracks gum and parks it under the table. He thought even his mother had been entranced. Poor Rozzy, and even poor Theo, had wasted so much energy in trying to measure up to his mother's standards. Missy didn't give a bugger.

As they sat around the table awaiting the pudding, Charles had found it hard to believe in the battering rednecked husband. Now, nearly twenty years on, it seemed more likely than not, and in part an explanation for Missy's almost preternatural dash and pluck. Then, however, he had been puzzled. He could see Missy dabbling in the slums, but never marrying into them, and he imagined that she had simply hitched a joy-ride with some besotted soldier-boy in order to get to Europe. And there was something about her that would have conned, forged, flattered and talked her way into or out of any situation. She would have done bull-dancing, tightrope walking or hang-gliding, but he could not see her settling down long enough to be beaten by anyone. She probably turned tricks for a bob or two now and then, he thought, and then was ashamed of thinking it. Her exotic Southern voice warmed the room like a hot, dry breeze, perhaps even bearing infestation. She was not a healthy person, but you could probably get her to do anything once. She would have been, he decided, a perfect courtesan. She was hanging on Theo's every word, quizzing him about the best and cheapest routes to the East, which she *so* wanted to discover. Charles wondered if she would end up winding some Sultan around her little finger. She had hard, sharp, darting eyes and he could see her walking away with diamonds big as eggs.

As she daintily begged his rich brother-in-law for the details of shipping routes, Charles had to exercise some self-control. The previous night, she had told him she was down to her last dime. Now she was considering cruises and the hiring of camel trains. Perhaps he had had too much to drink, perhaps he had been worried about Rosamund, who seemed to have disappeared into the kitchen for a very long time, but he had a sharp urge to expose Missy, to challenge her there and then. Mesmerizing as she was, he found he suddenly disliked her, like a dog which abruptly remembers that a familiar cat is yet a cat. His sister, an altogether more domestic feline, had slunk away from the contest. Instead, Charles had remained a host and said, 'Where's Mummy with that pudding?' to the children.

'I'll go see,' said Francis. He clambered down and trotted to the kitchen. He had been six that year. In a few moments, he returned. 'Mummy is crying,' he announced to the table at large. At twenty-five, Francis was becoming a newscaster with the BBC. Even then, he had known how to announce an event with proper solemnity. 'I think Aunt Cat is helping her.'

'I expect poor, darling Mummy is tired,' Lady Simon said to the child with more opprobrium than sympathy.

Before Charles could go to her aid, Rosamund had arrived with Cat in tow. Her martyrdom complete with a smile, she had looked like Joan of Arc as she had borne in the blazing pudding, a sprig of holly twisting in the flames.

Rosamund put her case down on the pavement and paid the driver over the odds. It was all very well imagining fiery confrontations, but now she was here, her empty stomach clenched with nerves, and she was awed by the task before her. In fact, she had impulsively asked the driver to let her down in Kolonaki Square, which was short of her destination. Why she felt at pains to conceal this from an Athenian cabbie, she did not know, but she gave him a very large tip, almost as if to silence him. It was in Rosamund's nature to be secretive, and although she had a horror of any direct lie, she sometimes gave way to an instinct to dissemble, often for no apparent reason. These little flights from her high principles disturbed her, and she tried to rationalize them. This time, she told herself that she had to gather her forces before she made the final onslaught. Even though the block of flats was a steep uphill climb away and her case was heavy, she liked the feeling of arriving on foot rather than having to be a plain spectacle emerging from a taxi at Theo's *pied-à-terre*. The whole force of her plan depended on the success of ambush. He would not have the foggiest idea that she was coming at all, much less why. Whatever her thinking, she picked up her tightly packed bag, swung it to her shoulder, and started to trudge upwards.

It was a hot afternoon and the square lay in torpor. Even the fleshy leaves of the sub-tropical plants in the central garden looked glazed and wilted. There were few people about and Rosamund noticed that she seemed the only foreigner. Kolonaki was a district where rich Greeks lived and plush shops flourished. Many of the older Athenian families disdained it now and lived instead out in Kifissia. Theo liked it and insisted on living there even though a flat in Piraeus would have been more convenient. Kolonaki might have become slick with telly stars and *nouveaux riches*, but it dominated Athens from the slopes of Mount Likavittós. Rosamund always thought it assuaged the death of his father for Theo to be able to command these heights. He was a man who wholly resisted the idea of becoming anyone's victim or murderee. He had the penthouse flat of a solid old building with an art nouveau front, and he especially enjoyed the view from the terrace with its yellow awnings and little potted plants. In the evenings, they would sit on spindly Italian furniture and watch the sun set. Shades of rose reflected on the distant Parthenon, golden shadows on the more distant sea. There was an edge to Theo, however, that always made Rosamund think that the balcony was a vantage point for him, an observation post, which any enemy would do well to acknowledge and shun. The tower girdled him, and sometimes when he gazed from it lost in thought, it was not too fanciful to imagine him dumping boiling oil or Greek fire on to the heads of potential invaders.

It was perhaps for this reason that Rosamund instinctively made a circuitous approach. Although in many ways Theo had a touching gentleness, he was not a man to be crossed, especially on a family matter. His chivalry to women, his gaiety with children, his kindness to subordinates, unfortunates, all had their origin in his unquestioning view of himself as a man of honour. He might have been a Southern gentleman, Rosamund often thought, but for a ruthless streak that evinced itself from time to time and in small ways. To confront him with Missy's story might invite a number of responses, none of them predictable. Although she had decided that her news could not be confided on the telephone nor confined to a letter, Rosamund began to wish that she had not taken quite so bold a step as to come 'on spec'.

As she neared the top of the square, a well-dressed Greek woman, accompanied by a groomed daughter, emerged from a café. It gave Rosamund a start to see them. With their Jaeger boxes and kid handbags, they might have been Catherine and Xenia, the Anglo-Greek lady and her pretty heiress child coming to consult the omens of fashion. Perhaps they themselves would be in Athens now, staying at the flat for some shopping before Xenia's school term began. Why had she not thought of this? What would she do if they were there? Well, she would have to flush Theo out and take him to one side. Whatever happened, it was far too dangerous to let Xenia return to England until her father knew the whole story. Reminded of this stated purpose of the journey, Rosamund took heart. Of course, she had had no alternative but to come! It was inconceivable that she should evade this responsibility.

Her case grew heavier and her shoes pinched as she ascended past the rows of cafés up towards Mount Likavittós. Athena was supposed to have alighted on its summit in classical times, but all goddesses were routed now. The slopes of the hill were overbuilt with 'desirable' real estate, and the district had a forlorn crassness about it. Rosamund found and climbed the stone steps that led to the upper reaches of Kolonaki. After her lunch with Missy, she had tormented herself with the thought that Catherine had known this all along, and perhaps Xenia too. She did not know what she would do if the whole family had concealed Xenia's true identity from her. In the shade of an acacia tree, she put down her heavy load to catch her breath. In her mind's eye, she saw the fair Catherine bent over her quilts and tapestries, a self-made princess in a bower, deliberately distant from everything but the little kingdom she had built in Chios. No, she would have been sealed against this reality, if reality it was. Rosamund, normally not intuitive, knew. And as for her beloved Xenia, it had seemed almost unbearable to think about her after

Missy's revelation. Suddenly, the young girl's buoyant openness came to her as if in a rush down the hillside. It stayed on the surface of her mind for a while, alighting there like the very breath of innocence, and then it was gone. No, neither Catherine nor Xenia could have colluded in such a deception! Nor, if the story were true, would she, Rosamund, connive in the lie. Of that, she was sure. Well, she was almost sure of it. If she had to sacrifice his friendship, then she would, wouldn't she?

She lifted the travel bag to her shoulder once more and resumed the steep flight with renewed vigour. At length, she arrived at a plateau a few levels short of the park where a piny wood began. From it, one could make a final, rugged ascent to the summit from which it was possible to view all Athens to the sea. A cable car went up there, too, but she had never taken it. She remembered walking in the pine wood with Theo, while the others were taking a siesta one hot afternoon. They had talked: about Xenia, of course, a legitimate concern. Was it because he was Greek, Theo had asked her, that he thought Catherine was cold to the child? He did not wish to be disloyal, but in whom else could he confide? A delicate silence of much aplomb had stretched between them, more expressive than anything that might have been said. She had given him to understand that she herself had more than enough affection to go round, especially where it touched Xenia, and, naturally, himself. She had given him the assurance that this would be made manifest if he were to make up his mind about the English boarding-school . . . and he had smiled. It had been blazing hot, a record summer. Theo was a keen conservationist, and had made donations to a committee which was re-wooding the mountain-side. He had offered her his arm over the slippery needles and had voiced his concern about forest fires up there in an extreme summer when people had been dying of the heat in the city below. She had looked up at the dry trees, in danger, he had said, of kindling up in spontaneous combustion. Rosamund was not, as it were, a man's woman. She had put it out of her head that she had had an exalted sense of their immolation together – the whole mountain in flames – but for a long time afterwards she had had disturbed dreams about the death of her parents.

Oh, surely in the depths of such intimacy as that, he would have told her on that day! Why hold back? On that afternoon she would have accepted anything, especially a truth of so private a nature. A shadow crossed Rosamund's mind and she tried to blink it away. When he had searched her eyes that day, had he seen Missy? Chalk and cheese though they were in character, the family resemblance had always been remarked on; as far as looks went, the genetic quirk that linked them had favoured Missy. No! It was intolerable even to consider this. Rosamund glanced down the slope. A large Orthodox church lay below her. Its silver domes shone with a dull glare; they nested beneath the hanging gardens of the smart apartment buildings that spread out before her. Theo was a pious man. No, these abominations were beneath him, she thought. Nevertheless, she steeled herself as she turned the corner on to the street where he lived. With its decks and terraces, the large, squat block of flats in which he lived looked like a cross between a ziggurat and an ocean liner. It had always seemed to her an absurd, expensive place to live. Again, her stomach churned. She adjusted her new beige jacket. Why had she not bought scent at the airport? She dreaded to think what she smelt like after the hot climb.

'Well, this is it!' she thought, and squaring herself yet again, she mounted the steps to the grandiose front door. A liveried porter rose from his desk to greet her, but as she swung forward in an effort to make a stylish entrance, the heel of her smart shoe snapped, and she tumbled forward with a wailing cry.

'Madame!' The porter lunged and caught her.

Suddenly, Rosamund burst into tears. She could not stop crying at the broken heel. The more she wept, the worse her humiliation was. 'My ankle!' she sobbed, lying.

The porter helped her to a chair. She found his green livery reassuring. He rushed back to retrieve the heel from the mat where it had snapped. Rosamund thought she recognized the man.

'I've come to see Mr Phocas,' she said. She kept trying to stop the tears, but they rushed down her cheeks blodging her careful make-up, clogging her nose. She did not know what to do. She rarely wept, but when she did, she had a binge.

'You are the sister of Mr Phocas, yes?'

She nodded, grateful at the convenience of this title.

'But he is not at home,' the porter said.

The shock sobered her. 'What!' Why had she not checked? She was becoming unhinged.

'He will be home . . . this evening.' He seemed uncertain of his English. He considered something. 'I have the key,' he said. 'He will be upset if I do not let you into his flat.'

Rosamund sagged, disproportionately relieved that she was going to see Theo. 'Thank you,' she whispered.

The porter looked at her foot with sympathy. The ankle was, indeed, beginning to puff up slightly, and it had started to throb. Without a word, he gathered up her case, her broken shoe, and collecting everything into the lift, he sailed her up to the top floor. He averted his eyes from her distressed state. With the pass key, he let her into Theo's flat and settled her on the sofa, propping cushions beneath her foot. After a moment, he was gone, bearing the broken shoe with him. He would get it mended before the return of Mr Phocas. Nothing, it seemed, was too much for Mr Phocas, nor his family by extension.

He had left Rosamund in the dark, for the shutters were closed, but she had no will to open them. In any case, the memory of bright times came to her in the shadowed outlines of the stark furniture. Had Missy visited this place? It gave her pain to think so, and so she lay very still, hoping the thought would go away. She had achieved her objective, and now all she could do was wait. In the dark, the ambush would be spectacular – beyond anything she had hoped for. Without really being aware of it, however, Rosamund was still crying. Her tears oozed slowly in a steady stream until, quite exhausted by them, she slept.

V

ONLY TWO days before her flight to Athens, Rosamund had been in the kitchen packing the freezer against Xenia's arrival in London. She normally indulged her niece in a modest riot of junk food in the annual week of preparation for school. Although Xenia was conscious of her figure – all girls that age were – Rosamund knew by instinct that she wanted and needed to be babied. Somehow, it gratified her to raid the shelves of Marks and Spencer in Kensington High Street for fudge cake and popcorn, little American treats that were still exotic to Xenia, and thus acceptable. In conscience, Rosamund always added guilt-free vegetables and salads to her basket. She might be a doting aunt, but she had standards.

That day, however, her limbs moved torpidly in resistance to the pleasant ritual of squirrelling away the hedonistic pizzas and gateaux that she would have hesitated to give to her own children. They, save Mary, of course, who was away, had come around to Sunday lunch the day before. Francis, Peter, Dominic and Theresa had all been decent enough to rally round in the wake of their mother's humiliation, and Rosamund had been touched. But the gossip column piece, which Francis had earlier shown her, had clearly shaken them all, and she had ended up dishing out the ceremonial chicken in an inhuman effort to act as if nothing really serious had happened. It had been rather a relief that she had not seen nor spoken to Charles, because she had been able to say that she could not confirm or deny the rumours that she knew to be true. They had left wanting to know if Rosamund would be all right on her own, but their eyes had slid away, and she had shut the front door with the bleak realization that except for Mary, who would be devastated, she was virtually on her own. None of them wanted to take her on, and why, she asked herself, should they want to? She was determined not to cannibalize their adult lives.

When, on the morning after this, the telephone had rung, she had had to compose herself before answering it. She and Charles had to talk it through some time, she supposed. She slowly closed the freezer door and took deep breaths. He had sent her a very civil note after the item about him had appeared in *Private Eye*. Could she give him a few days' grace before they discussed it? He would be staying at his club. Everyone needed time to think. How sorry he was if the regrettable piece had caused her pain. He so invariably took refuge in this kind of pomposity that Rosamund had laughed at the time. With bitter sorrow, however, she had expected to hear from him hourly.

'Hi!' said the voice on the telephone.

Rosamund laid her head on the wall next to the instrument that hung there. At Armageddon, she thought, one of her countrymen would be present with this greeting. Who could this one be, ringing at such a time? 'Hello,' she replied stiffly.

'Roz? It's me, Missy! Do you remember?'

Rosamund found she was shaking. She really had expected Charles. How much, she had not realized. Her cousin's voice seemed to come from an alternative reality, something conceived in the minds of mystics or philosophers. 'Missy?'

'Yep! I'm back in town. Do you remember, you all put me up one Christmas? I borrowed some money from you. I've come to pay you back.'

'That was twenty years ago, Missy,' Rosamund said faintly.

'Well, better late than never.' The optimistic Southern voice became slightly injured. 'Besides, it was only eighteen.'

'I didn't mean that. Oh, dear. I meant, keep the money.' She had lent Missy £200, partly in order to get her out of the house. They had received not so much as a postcard in thanks, not from Kathmandu, nor from anywhere else.

'It was for survival. I was very grateful. In fact, I owe you some hospitality, too.'

Outside on the lawn, the neighbour's dog was peeing on her shrivelled roses. She vainly rapped at the window. The garden lay in pre-autumnal stupefaction. Sweat poured down Rosamund. How could she get rid of Missy? 'Well, Missy, it's nice of you to get in touch, but I have rather a frantic week. Are you here for long?'

'As long as it takes,' she said.

'What do you mean?' Rosamund was near tears. She was in desperation to get off the phone. She wanted to scream at Missy.

'As long as it takes to see you.'

Rosamund said nothing. She pressed her lips together. Missy was the last straw.

'I have an important family matter to discuss,' her cousin said, after a pause. 'With you.'

What had it been in that voice that had compelled her to listen? Had it been her own vulnerability or Missy's character? Later, she realized that only a little frankness on her part might have saved them all. Somehow, she could not bring herself to say, 'I can't see you. My husband has left me' – not to Missy.

Her cousin's voice, now lowered to a dark purr, had continued. 'It won't take long. Just let me give you lunch. Today, if you like. No problem.'

'It's difficult.'

'Tomorrow?'

'OK, OK, today. Missy, I don't want to be rude. It's just an awkward time.'

To Rosamund's surprise, Missy had given her a smart address on the Embankment overlooking Battersea Park, '. . . right across from that Buddha,' she had said. Rosamund knew the spot. She and Charles had rich acquaintances who lived near there and who had complained when the borough across the river had put up what they called 'a garish Eastern temple'. Rosamund secretly liked it. Knowing she could not park and being pressed for time, she took a taxi. She had showered and had slapped on a skirt and blouse of medium grandeur. It seemed a hare-brained thing to do to roar out after Missy. On her way from Holland Park to Chelsea, she kept on seeing her children's faces in her mind's eye. Discussing the scandal with them had been confronting it. She was more unstrung than she thought. In the past, she would have relied on Charles to fob Missy off, or some avatar of Charles. 'Charles has a plan. Charles mentioned something to me. I will have to ask Charles.' Now she had to rely on herself, she had not known what to say. The taxi let her out in front of an imposing mansion block with mellow Edwardian brick and high, mullioned windows. Standing on the pavement, she suddenly felt underdressed. Surely, however, Missy would be more so. If Missy were staying here, she must be freebooting off of someone else. Perhaps she had actually become a Buddhist in Kathmandu; perhaps a colony of lamas was ensconced in the top flat. This would explain why Missy had mentioned the glinting landmark, which had its hand raised in perpetual blessing from Battersea Park. Of course! Missy had taken to Eastern religion as she said she would. Maybe it had improved her.

Rosamund could not believe her eyes when Missy opened the door. Her cousin stood on the threshold, dressed from head to foot in matchless elegance. 'Rozzy, hi!' she said a little languidly. 'How nice of you to come.'

She had not seen Missy in nearly twenty years, but there was no vestige left of what she remembered from her last visit, nor even a small remnant from childhood. Missy, now of slender mien, wore a dress of light grey linen. Her hair, with soft, grey wings, was caught up in a smart French twist. Around her youthful neck clung a choker of glowing pearls. Her little feet were embraced by patent leather shoes glinting with silver buckles, and from her wrist there hung a platinum bracelet studded with smoky semiprecious stones. She was a marvel.

'Why, you look all done in!' Missy cried. 'Do come in, Roz. Lovely to see you. I really do hope I haven't dragged you out.'

Rosamund caught a glimpse of herself in the hall mirror. She did not look bad enough to be called 'dragged out' or 'done in', but next to Missy, she felt dressed by Oxfam.

'Missy, you look so well!' She swallowed her pride. 'And here I've come empty-handed. Do forgive me. It's been one thing after another.' A bunch of freesias, at least, she thought, should have been offered to this goddess.

'Oh, for heaven's sake, you said you were busy. Come on. Come on.' Nevertheless, she passed a critical eye over Rosamund's giftless right hand as she swept towards the drawing-room door beyond them. Rosamund tagged after her.

The room was gracefully proportioned, high and sunny. A large bay window, mullioned and casting a milky light, gave a view to the river. A striking young black woman with pronounced cheekbones sat in the windowseat, and on her lap she encircled a child of about six. They made no move as Rosamund entered, but studied her as they continued to sit. The little boy had dark, creamy skin and a cloud of curly hair. He was very beautiful, and he inspected Rosamund with the confident air of a young African prince.

'This is Romola,' said Missy, indicating the woman, 'and this is my grandson, Paolo.'

'How do you do?' Rosamund said, but they made no reply.

Missy shrugged. 'Here, let me get you a glass of sherry.' She went to a drinks tray and poured a slug from a bottle into a wine glass. She offered none to Romola and took none for herself. She shoved the glass into Rosamund's hand. 'Drink up!' she said. 'I've got to check out the lunch.'

Rosamund was almost too stunned for speech. She looked around at each elegant appointment of the flat. The sofas were of faded chintz, and

Oriental carpets lay on the parquet floor. In the fireplace there stood an arrangement of peonies, and above it was an oil portrait of a lady, perhaps an ancestor of whoever owned the flat. It looked like Rosamund's own home, but she did not feel comfortable in it. The sherry was sweet. Rosamund sipped it for want of anything better to do. 'Well, you're my new cousin, then,' she finally said to the child. 'And it's very nice to meet you, too, a new member of the family,' she said to Romola, who must, by her evident affection for the boy, be his mother, she thought.

'We're not family,' said the young woman with subdued pride. 'Not yours. Paolo is Mr Kavanagh's grandson, and I'm just here for the ride. I am his aunt.'

'Oh,' said Rosamund. She folded her hands in her lap. 'I'm sorry, I do not know Mr Kavanagh. Who is he?'

Romola, from her expression, decided to take pity on Rosamund. 'Miss Melissa,' she said with heavy irony, 'married Mr Tom a few years back. She is very eager to be friends with us, isn't she, honey?' She addressed the child in fond conspiracy.

He wriggled on her lap. He was wearing a T-shirt with a tiger emblazoned on it.

'Don't worry. Tom isn't a black man,' Romola continued with the same simmering hostility she had shown from the outset.

Rosamund flushed. 'I have not had the time to form such an idea, much less to worry about it. My cousin might have married a black man if she pleased!'

'Hmpf!' said Romola.

All the time, it was impossible for Rosamund to take her eyes off the pair. In the mullioned window, they sat like some ancient configuration of mother and child, blessed by an aureole of light. It streamed over them, illuminating them.

'We're going to the zoo!' said the little boy suddenly. 'Do you want to see my tiger?'

He extricated himself from his aunt's grasp and trotted across the floor to Rosamund. 'See!' He pointed to his shirt.

'It's a super tiger,' she said, liking the child.

' "Super"?'

'In this country, that means "fantastic",' she explained.

'I know lots of new words,' Paolo said. 'We've been in France . . . and in Italy, where my Daddy is. I like spaghetti.'

'I like spaghetti too,' Rosamund said, stroking his cloudy hair. She looked up and caught from Romola a sudden, dazzling smile. She inclined her head and returned it.

The woman glanced out of the window. 'Oh, there's our taxi, honey. Come along, now, you hurry up.' She turned again to Rosamund. 'We are lunching at the zoo.' She gathered up the child's jacket and made towards the door. 'Don't let Missy lean on you,' she said with a dry smile. 'Imagine not telling you about Tom!' And with these impenetrable words, she swept from the room.

The moment they left, Rosamund heard Missy clicking up the hall. 'Come on, come on, lunch, lunch, quick, quick . . . sit!' she cried as she advanced on the room. Rosamund noticed a round table laid prettily in a corner. She rose, and her cousin entered bearing aloft a Worcester soufflé dish, attractively decorated with fruits and flowers. 'You'll *never* guess what this is! You aren't a veggie, are you? I should have asked.'

Rosamund was suddenly shy with Missy and wished Romola and Paolo had not left. 'No, no, I eat anything.'

'It's corn puddin'. Yes, indeed, I've been slaving away, you see. All over Europe, in fact. I have given collards to ambassadors, chittlins to opera singers. I have promulgated Southern cooking, believe me.'

She flumped down on a fragile chair. Linen napkins and bone china awaited them. Rosamund, endemically gauche, sat at an awkward angle. The risen top of the corn pudding sighed and fell in response to Missy's spoon. There was a good loaf, a green salad, and some white wine on the table. 'There!' She served Rosamund. 'Now, what do you think?'

'Mmm! Delicious!' There was nothing else to say. Indeed, the pudding was very good. 'Thank you, Missy.' Her cousin had gone to trouble even when she had been so ungracious on the telephone. It shamed her to think that if she had known of Missy's transformation, she might have been more forthcoming.

'Well, it's been a long time,' said Missy, as if she were making an obscure reference to this. Her eyes were all veiled triumph. She poured wine into the delicate glasses. 'Your health,' she said.

'Romola told me you had married a few years ago,' said Rosamund. There were slivers of Virginia ham in the pudding. 'We really have lost touch.'

'Didn't Sally Belle write you? I'm surprised. She couldn't be more pleased.' Sally Belle was Missy's elder sister, and was the only family chronicler they had.

'Sally and I haven't corresponded for years.'

'I would have sent you an invitation to the wedding, but then I've had so many weddings,' Missy said. She carved a bit of bread, then smiled raffishly. She had a slightly crooked tooth, and it gave her a piratical air. 'If it hadn't been for you that Christmas, I'd never have got out of the first marriage in one piece, that's for sure. He was a real goon.' She shuddered with mild distaste. 'Now, Tom is a gentleman – a racing person. Haven't you heard of him? Oh well, never mind. We live at Eagles – you know, on the Paris–Lexington Road. Mint juleps, a verandah, carriage dogs . . . Whoo!'

Rosamund did not know what to say in the face of this unabashed gloating. She remembered a venturesome spirit in Missy, but not vulgarity. 'I'm happy for you,' she said.

'It's very, very far from the Road to Mandalay, which I believe I was on when I last saw you,' her cousin replied. She wrinkled her nose and sipped the fragrant wine. Rosamund saw she was rubbing it in and looked down. 'We all grow up sooner or later,' Missy added. 'Tom is in Ireland now chasing some filly.' She gave a low chuckle to emphasize the saucy pun. 'Otherwise, I would have introduced you.'

'And your grandson?'

'Oh, he's not *mine*! I just said that to wind up Romola. He's Tom's. Oh, he dotes on that child. We travel in caravan. Tom wants Paolo to be a man of the world.

'And just in case you're trying to piece together the truly remarkable genealogy,' Missy added with a winking little snigger, 'Tom, who is as white as great Caesar's ghost, married Romola's Negro mother in the sixties, *much* to the consternation of his family. Let's say she wasn't just the maid. She was the ultimate radical chick, the pinnacle of achievement in his "Black is Beautiful" phase, and red-hot in more ways than one. Needless to say, it didn't work out. But on the way and by the by, *she* had a child by Tom called Celia, believe it or not, who is Romola's younger half-sister. Now it is my view that Tom spoiled those gals something rotten, but that's just my humble opinion. Celia wouldn't give a duchess the time of day, and she ran off with some ne'er-do-well Italian, who is Paolo's daddy. Clear as mud, ain't it? So Romola is only Paolo's half-aunt, see? Romola is dying to kill me. Did you notice? She is part Cherokee. I expect a hatchet any day.'

Rosamund found this line of conversation very distasteful. She blotted her mouth with the napkin and put it down on the table. She had forgotten the arcana of Southern bigotry, which she felt creeping from Missy's every word. 'I always thought *we* had Cherokee blood,' she said, narrowing her eyes.

Missy's mouth twitched, as if she had flushed out a liberal prig. She repressed a smile. 'Well, not on my side. So, your mom's people must have made quite a trek to pull that one off.'

Rosamund's mother had been a New Englander and had never been accepted in Kentucky. They called her 'the Yankee lady' even after the house had burnt down. Missy, quite a tease in her youth, had mimicked her mother's accent until Rosamund had cried. 'I can't talk about the fire!' she said sharply.

'Who mentioned the fire?' Missy shrugged as if she were talking to a crazy person.

'I didn't mean the fire. I meant my mother.' It was crazy. Why had she said 'the fire'? 'They hang together. I won't talk about my mother, the fire *or* Cherokees! It disagrees with me.'

'Oh, you're all right,' said Missy sulkily. 'You've done OK for yourself.'

Rosamund closed her eyes and swallowed hard. In her present state, she should never have come to see Missy. They had descended to childhood, and were squabbling like little girls. Odd, distorted memories came back to Rosamund like disconnected artefacts from a cryptic tumulus. She had pictures of her fine Bostonian mother, something of a bluestocking, and courtly, superior father, but she could not picture them. Now, she saw a vivid image of them sitting on the verandah of the newly acquired house drinking Bourbon with her uncle and aunt while she, Missy and Sally Belle were expected to get on because they were young and because they were cousins. They had sat in a row on a porch swing, saying nothing. As an only child, her ear was tuned to adult conversation and she remembered the discomfort and disquiet of the time. Rosamund's father had sold out a successful business in the North in order to reclaim and farm the land that had wandered in and out of the Buchanan family for generations. He and Missy's father might have been Cain and Abel, for all the love that was lost between them.

Her Uncle Liam was the elder of the two brothers and she remembered his curling lip, a sarcasm cloaked in 'good ole boy' humour, at the acceptable offering of her own father's success. That day, the house had seemed to represent too much. Missy's father, like Missy herself, perhaps, had been the family star in youth, good at sports, a popular handsome boy, indulged for general hell-raising. He had married young, but not well, to his high school cheerleader sweetheart, who perpetually felt snubs from the old and sporadically landed family she had blundered into. Thirty years on, Rosamund knew how her poor Aunt Rose had felt. Missy's father, however, was one of those broken, irresponsible people, who feel that life has cheated them. He had become a feed salesman, not likely to rise from his suburban house in Lexington to the spiral staircase and Adam mantelpiece of 'the old Buchanan place', as it was called. Missy had caused some trouble or other that day. Rosamund could not remember what it was. But heavy-jowled Uncle Liam had enjoyed it. Pioneer blood had run through the veins on the verandah. It had been an ugly moment.

'Look, I'm sorry,' Missy said. 'I suppose you don't get over that sort of thing in a hurry.'

Rosamund opened her eyes. 'You never get over it.'

'Coffee?' Missy asked. 'I forgot to make dessert. I can never see the sense in it.' Perhaps unconsciously, she smoothed her hand over her modelled hip. Unlike the wiry Rosamund, she had a treasured figure. She frowned. The emotion in Rosamund's voice seemed to trouble her. 'You know, you really should talk about it to someone.'

'I already have,' said Rosamund, but she had not nearly enough.

'What do you think really happened?' Missy's beautiful face seemed caught in the shadow of the event. Rosamund remembered that she had asked this question the last time she had been in London. It seemed to preoccupy her.

'I really do not know. Now, please, let's get off the subject.' She paused. 'Let me help you clear the table.' Missy was not transformed after all. She still had an odd, childlike streak that Rosamund now remembered. She talked about the fire in the same way that Paolo had pointed out the tiger on his T-shirt. It had impressed her.

'No, I insist.' Missy regained her poise as hostess and gave Rosamund a mannered and uneven smile. She loaded up the tray. 'There are some pictures of Eagles on the coffee table. Have a look at my album. I'll be back in a trice.'

She breezed from the room. Rosamund stood and went to the window in an attempt to shake off her mood. Boats were plying up and down the Thames under the impassive eye of the Buddha on the opposite shore. The tide was high, the river swollen. Everything seemed calm, heightened, illusory. The Buddha was an incongruously bright gold. What was Missy doing here? Why had she returned to London now when Rosamund's life in England seemed to be crumbling? She had dreaded questions about Charles and the children, but Missy had not alluded to them once. She seemed to have sailed back into London, freighted with old and ominous hints of the past, of a past in Kentucky which Rosamund preferred to forget. What family matter could she have in mind? Why this sudden ostentation from the former hippie?'

She went to the coffee table and sat down, obedient to Missy's wishes. A watermarked album lay on a pile of magazines: *Country Life* and *Harpers & Queen*. She felt at one remove from everything and flipped nervously through the book. There were photographs of thoroughbreds with long, chestnut noses, and an ante-bellum house surrounded by white fences. There was a picture of Missy lounging beside an indoor pool, and another one of her arm in arm with an older man. He was squinting at the camera as if in some obscure defiance of it. Missy gazed up at him with studied rapture. There was no question, the picture seemed to say, of who was boss. Rosamund felt antipathy towards these pictures. They seemed to falsify something. Perhaps in an attempt to convey an idea of Southern gentry, they had subtly missed its essence. She remembered old Kentucky relations, soft-spoken cousins, who would have shuddered at the glossy sheen on Missy and the whoops and hollers she had learned to give, perhaps at the knee of this small-time Paul Getty. All of a sudden, an ungovernable scent of the past overwhelmed her, the lonely grandeur of the columned house, her distant and equivocal parents. She shut the book with a snap, wild to get away.

Missy entered with a tray of fragile cups and plonked them on the table with the coffee. They rattled. 'Aren't these cute?' she asked, handing Rosamund a bone china cup. 'This place belongs to some English horse people we met in France. All very high-toned, isn't it?' A deliberate raunchiness gave piquancy to Missy's general air of elegance. She seemed above the rules of class and taste that concern others. Rosamund wondered how soon it would be polite to leave and decided she would not let this matter.

Missy sank into the sofa and lit a cigarette. 'Now the preliminaries are over, I think I had better get straight to the point . . . You don't mind, do you?' she added, indicating the cigarette. 'Sometimes I think I single-handedly support the tobacco industry.'

Rosamund disliked the smell of smoke, but said, 'I don't mind.' She looked up. Missy was regarding her evenly across the coffee table. 'What point?' Perhaps it was her cousin's look, perhaps an atavistic prescience that made her suddenly alert.

'I'll be blunt. What do you know about my daughter?'

'Your daughter?' She was relieved. Obviously, Missy had some wrong-headed idea about one of her children and could be set to rights. 'I didn't know you had a daughter.'

'Sure about that?' Her manner was heavy, almost hostile.

'I am quite sure. I didn't know you had any children.'

'Nevertheless, I think you do know her.' Missy pursued it with court-room rhetoric.

Rosamund began to feel uncomfortable, even a little offended. 'Look, Missy, I have my faults, but I am honest.'

Missy threw up her hands with a theatrical air. 'Honest. Yes, I believe you are. Good ole Roz! In fact, I have little doubt of it. So, you don't know, do you? He never told you. That makes him even more of a jerk than I thought.'

'Who? What are you talking about? Missy, please explain.'

'Oh, it's not your precious husband, if that's what you're worrying about.'

'Charles?' She put the fragile cup and saucer down on *Country Life*. There was the photograph of an Elizabethan manor house on the cover. 'Look, I do not know your daughter, and I do not know what "jerk" you are talking about.'

'Presumably, you know Theo Phocas, or have you lost touch completely? As I remember, he is your brother-in-law. Or was.'

'Of course Theo is my brother-in-law!' She paused. 'We are very close . . . to them,' she added.

'Ah, yes, he did say he was fond of you. So, he's still married to Catherine, is he? They still have a child, a girl?'

'Xenia!' Before bad things happen and it is too late to escape, the mind still makes futile efforts to do so.

'That's the one! I think it will interest you to know that she is my baby, my daughter.'

Rosamund paused in an airless moment. 'Are you saying that Xenia is the child of both you and Theo Phocas?'

Missy ground out her cigarette. 'You'd better believe it!'

Rosamund shrank at this sudden aggression, somehow terrified by it. 'No!' she cried. It could not be true.

'I did think you knew,' Missy added as if in apology for having gone too far in her cross-examination. She cushioned herself back into the feathered sofa, lit another cigarette, and rubbed her forehead with a pensive air. 'Could you tell me how my daughter is? Then, perhaps, I had better fill you in. You'll need to know the whole story.'

Rosamund was still thinking that this really could not be true, but she found herself saying, 'Xenia is very, very well.' She was on the verge of tears. She saw the young girl in her mind's eye – touching, coltish, pretty Xenia. Only an hour ago, she had been preparing for her visit . . . and now this. She denied it to herself. It was not possible.

Missy closed her eyes in satisfaction. 'I have not known for the last eighteen years whether she was alive or dead.' For some reason, it struck Rosamund as odd that Missy was not weeping.

After a pause, suitable to the gravity of her discovery, Missy opened her eyes. They were a clear, unusual green, deep-set and hooded. Apart from the colour, they were like Rosamund's eyes: they were like Xenia's. 'The story,' she said, 'is complicated in one way, but very, very simple in another. Of course, you will recall that you introduced me to Theo yourself, at your house that Christmas Day, and if I'd known what I know now, I'd have run screaming, but you know me, "I'm just the girl who cain't say no." Or I was until I met Tom.'

Missy embellished this last statement with the thin twist of a smile that could have meant anything. Rosamund sat with her hands in fists on her lap, and thought she must endure the pain, even of this flippancy, until some shred of evidence arose beyond the swamping sense she had of truth.

'You may remember that I had it in mind to get to Kathmandu. I couldn't face going back to America, especially after Dan – you know, the redneck. But, out of the frying pan and into the fire. That's me. Well, one thing led to another with Theo and me around your lovely dinner table, and at the end of the day he gave me his card, telling me that if I came to Athens, he thought he could arrange my passage on one of his cruise ships to Bombay. In fact, he offered me a job, or said he could find one. He was *very* cordial, and *very* handsome.'

A sharp and painful memory came to Rosamund of the occasion. She had been aware that Theo had observed her cousin's beauty from under his paper crown. A fit of weeping had overwhelmed her as she had tried to assemble the Christmas pudding. After that, there had been so much crying and for so long that she had quite forgotten the episode. 'And so you did . . . make your way to Athens?'

All at once, Rosamund started to wonder why she was taking this story lying down. Here they were talking about a living soul, Xenia,

Missy's own child, or so she said. What sort of mother would not thirst for the smallest detail? And all Missy wanted to do was to tell her about a backfired romance, just as if they had been two college girls. It was a question of tone.

'Oh yes, I made my way, all right – on the money you lent me. It was too good an opportunity to be missed.'

Rosamund found herself counting on her fingers. The story was rubbish! Xenia had been born in August. More confident, she sat back, waiting for the next real whopper. She wouldn't let Missy get away with this. 'And so you went straight to Theo? Theo asked you to stay, did he?'

'Not quite, not then. Things took time.' Missy sat back, obviously not wanting herself to rush through the narrative. 'In fact, at first, I thought he was quite embarrassed that I had taken him up on his offer. I remember I went to his offices in Piraeus, and they were about to sling me out when I demanded to see him personally. All that deep pile carpet, all those toy ships in cases, all that swank! But, to do him justice, he did come out to greet me, and hustled me into his inner sanctum – me in my wild gear past all those circumspect Greek secretaries? And he was as good as his word . . . well, sort of. Instead of putting me on one of his ships, he got me a job doing guided tours in one of those coaches.' Missy threw back her head and gave a harsh laugh. 'I thought it was because he was critical of my lifestyle! He even made me wear a uniform! Or that distant cousin of his who ran the tour company did. I believed he did not trust me on the high seas. But when he came to help me bone up on the Greek mythology and history I had to know for the job, I soon found out that he had quite a different motive for keeping me in Athens. So there I was, taking American tourists around the Parthenon and Delphi and Mycenae by day, and by night . . . well, let's put it this way, it was a scorching hot affair.' Missy closed her eyes. 'I was good at both jobs, you see. And Roz, I thought he was going to marry me.'

It was clear she had seen the offices in Piraeus. Rosamund began to falter. Maybe someone had told her about them, though. 'I thought you were already married, and so, of course, was he,' she said tightly, drily.

'My marriage was over. I thought his was as well. Old story, isn't it?' Missy angled her a look. 'You don't believe me, do you?'

A sudden blast of hatred for Missy shocked Rosamund. She tried to let it pass; she tried to ignore it like a bad cramp, suppressing the pain by saying, 'I do not disbelieve you.' For no apparent reason, she thought of Caro, the young woman she had never met, who had made forced entry into her own marriage, Caro, who wanted Charles. Who were these women who wiped their mouths and asked for more, who felt aggrieved that they weren't wives? 'What do you want, Missy?' she found herself asking in so subdued a tone that Missy had to get her to repeat it. 'What do you want from me?'

As distasteful as she found it, and probably because she was so angry, Rosamund had to acknowledge the genuine twinge of pain in her cousin's eyes. For a curious moment, it was vivid to her that Missy had really suffered. She jerked her head away from Rosamund and stared at the bowl of peonies in the fireplace, as if trying herself to gain control over too strong feeling. 'I suppose it doesn't do to review all the details,' she said after a moment. 'I got pregnant . . . by accident.' She shot Rosamund a look. 'But if you think he minded, you are mistaken. He gloried in it! He revelled in it! He moved me out to a ritzy love-nest in Kifissia, right under the noses of all those swells. He made me stop work and of course, there was no question of Kathmandu after that. God! He lavished me with jewellery! And I can tell you, I sold every last seed pearl afterwards. You have no idea what an antique situation it was. I reel when I think of how much of a fool I was to be taken in by something so perfectly Edwardian as that.' Missy's eyes were as hard and glittering as two emeralds, her mouth curved in an almost fatuous smile.

'And so Xenia was born in September of that year, then, was she?' Rosamund asked, unable not to play her only ace.

'As you know perfectly well, she was born in August. She was premature.' If Missy had hauled off and slapped Rosamund hard, the effect of these words and the force of their delivery could not have been more stunning. 'Listen, don't mess with me, honey. The bastard took my baby and in cold blood.'

Rosamund looked down at her hands, aghast, and suddenly frightened of Missy. She could say nothing, for her diaphragm had solidified and she could hardly breathe.

'You see, all that time, he was waiting for me to drop, and only when she was born safe, alive and well did his tune change. Do you love your children? Well, I'm sure you do. And you know as I do what childbirth does to a woman. I was far too weak to fight him, far too weak. And in the end, he drove a very hard bargain. Do you want to know the deal?'

Rosamund wanted to stop her ears, but she simply blinked at Missy.

Missy lit another cigarette, her hands shaking from powerful emotion. 'He's a better businessman than you know.' She blew the smoke in a hard stream from pursed lips. 'First of all, he spooked the baby out of the nursing home. They told me she was sick and needed an operation! And then, you can more or less use your imagination about the rest. Either I relinquished Xenia to him for a good lump sum and my fare back to the States, or – '

'Or what?' Rosamund really could not believe this. This was too grotesque.

'Or, he released certain information to the police. An elaborate fiction, I may say, but one so well concocted that I really had no choice. I have not seen my baby girl since her birthday.'

With that, Missy crushed out the cigarette and sat back, her case apparently ended.

For a few attenuated moments, Rosamund sat unmoving while her mind made feeble inner protest, not only at the allegations that her cousin had made against Theo, but at the idea that she and Missy were even in the same room together. She did not know whether to challenge the story or simply to ignore the fact that it had been told at all. After a long pause, she spoke with that semi-automatic, blurred practicality that comes with sudden death. 'Missy, why didn't you go to the American ambassador? You are talking about abduction and blackmail and these are crimes.'

'Hah! You think he would have believed me over Theo?'

'Well, then, why is it you have waited so long to tell me about this? Or confront me? Surely, if you thought I knew that you were Xenia's mother, you could have written to me and at least found out if she was all right.'

'Don't you think I have every day of my life since then wanted to do just that?' Rosamund cringed into the chintz sofa at this explosion. 'I'm sorry, I'm sorry,' she found herself automatically saying, and then wondered why she was apologizing.

'Look,' said Missy, 'I know I shouldn't shout at you, because obviously he's even a better liar than I thought and it really isn't your fault, but there is a lot at stake here. Xenia was, in fact, legally adopted, although how legal our private deal was is anybody's guess. If I'd had any money, I would have contested it in court, but I was broke . . . no power, you see. As for you, I've torn up a hundred letters to you because how could I know what you would do with it all? Now I am married to Tom, things have a different complexion. Plus,' she said, shrugging, 'Xenia is now eighteen.'

'So your husband knows?'

'Knows? Why he's fixing to set aside a little room for Xenia at Eagles . . . if, of course, she ever wants to come and stay.'

It was all very slow. The movement, the sense of speaking, the dawning of what Missy required of her. 'So, you want me to be the go-between. You want me to tell my niece?'

'Honey, she is not your *niece*! She is your *cousin*!'

Before Rosamund could answer, the door to the room opened and Romola stood on the threshold. At the sound of her entry, Missy jumped and turned. 'What are you doing here!' she asked sharply.

'Back from the zoo. Started to rain,' said Romola, giving Missy a look exquisite for its depth and knowledge. 'Now, just what have you all been up to?' she added with an exaggerated Southern drawl. 'Looks like you've been doing a lot of catching up.' Romola strolled in, not only at ease with the situation, but somehow in command of it. The child peered out from behind the door jamb and, seeing Rosamund, trotted in.

'We saw the tigers! They were great!' he said. 'See?' He took out a paper bag of postcards and fished one out. 'It's a Bengalian tiger,' he said, showing Rosamund the ferocious, crouching animal.

'Bengal,' said Romola, looking out of the window. It was, indeed, raining.

In one swift glance at Missy's face, Rosamund was sure that she had told at least one lie. Whoever this Tom Kavanagh was, she was fairly certain that he knew nothing of what Missy had just told her. Missy was not, after all, angry at Romola's intervention, she was frightened by it.

'Why you look all done in after your nice lunch,' Romola said to Rosamund. 'You must come back some day and meet Tom, mustn't she, Missy?'

Missy said nothing. She sat, holding one knee in a basket of hands, her back slightly hunched.

'I like your tiger a lot,' Rosamund said to the child. Sensing something, he put a soft hand on her knee. The atmosphere was very awkward. Rosamund did not know whether the interruption was a good or bad thing, but suddenly, she was glad of Romola. Did Romola know anything about this, or had she only guessed that Missy, who probably called up disturbances wherever she went, had called up one now in Rosamund?

All at once, she found the urge to escape irresistible. It was as if her cousin had pinioned her to the sofa and had been raining blows down on her. She felt like the victim of a mugging. Out of desperation, it hit her what to say. 'I think,' she said to Missy, 'that all of this requires careful thought. Don't you?' She edged towards her handbag. 'Why don't we talk some more later in the week. Jot down your number for me and I'll give you a ring.'

A blank, impenetrable stare passed between Missy and Romola.

'Perhaps Paolo would enjoy the adventure playground in Holland Park,' Rosamund continued, then it struck her with force that Xenia herself was scheduled to arrive on Friday. She had not forgotten this, but its awful relevance had eluded her. She improvised. She had to get away. 'On the other hand, my house is an awful shambles at the moment. We could see the dinosaurs at the Natural History Museum and have lunch out,' she said. She was relieved that her mind had grasped at this protection. How had she remembered dinosaurs?

'I've seen the dinosaurs,' Paolo said.

'Never mind, we'll find a castle.'

'That's really nice of you,' said Romola. 'Paolo,' she added, turning to the child, 'if someone offers to show you something, you don't say "I've seen it", you say "thank you very much".'

If Missy was confounded by Rosamund's haste in departing, she gave no evidence of it. Perhaps she herself was relieved at the intervention of Romola and the child, but her face was too opaque to read. It was clear, however, that some wrinkle in their domestic situation made it impossible for her to ask Romola to leave them alone for a few moments more, for in normal circumstances such a request could not have caused offence. But Missy simply rose, went to a desk by the wall, and wrote energetically on a piece of paper. She returned it to Rosamund.

Above the number, it said, 'I don't want you to tell Xenia about me. I just want to see her with my own eyes, only that. I'll deal with Theo myself. Believe it!' And pinned under the note with a paper-clip was a cheque for £2,000.

VI

A BRIGHT LIGHT woke Rosamund, and for a moment she was confused into thinking that she had had an accident and had been taken to hospital. A general overbearing whiteness, combined with a sense of being drugged, made her blink and thrash, but no sooner had she called out in alarm than she realized where she was. Sitting across from her in a tubular steel chair was Theo.

'Rosamund,' he said. He leaned forward, his hands hanging loosely between his knees. He watched her. Instinctively, she made to cover herself, but of course she was already dressed. 'How on earth did you get here?' he asked. Somehow, she had expected a different sort of welcome.

She shook her head and sat up. Her suit was creased, her blouse awry. She tried to rearrange herself, then gave up with a helpless gesture. 'Oh, Theo!' she said.

'Are you all right?' he asked. He did not move. He had large, prominent eyes, and they were vigilant.

'Didn't the porter tell you? I broke my shoe and twisted my ankle.'

'When did you arrive?' he asked. 'The night porter is on duty now.' He touched his fingers together. 'It is quite late.'

He most certainly was not challenging her right to be there; nevertheless, she felt uneasy and defensive. 'Well, I hope it was all right to wait for you. The day porter said it would be. I suppose I have been here since about three.'

He leaned back. 'It's lovely to see you.' He was dressed quite formally. 'I've just come back from a reception at the Argentine Embassy,' he said by way of explanation. 'If I had known you were coming, I would, of course, have cancelled the engagement.'

'I'm sorry if I gave you a shock,' she said. He looked squat and substantial sitting in the Milanese chair. An immaculate dinner jacket encased his muscular frame, and his starched shirt creaked as he moved. Like many rich and internationally connected people, Theo often seemed incidentally Greek, and somewhat sentimentally patriotic. Suddenly, she felt as if she had stumbled on some foreign cavern in him where he was truly at home and she was not. She felt humbled and disoriented. 'Do you mind if I have a wash?' she asked.

'Please do! Have you eaten anything?'

She shook her head. Deep in her imagination of this scene had been the anticipation of his warmth. In times gone by, how lively had his enthusiasm been for the visits of Rosamund and her brood! He had taken uninhibited pleasure in showing them Athens. Each cold marble bore a tale of gods and goddesses, which he would relate like fresh gossip. The children had all adored him. With a shock, Rosamund realized that he was perhaps the only other adult with whom she had ever shared simple pleasure. 'I've eaten nothing all day.'

He showed mock horror, an encouraging shadow of his former self. 'Well, we shall have to do something about that. The fact is, I need a hungry guest. My maid thinks I starve and makes me vast quantities of food. I never know what to do with it and she gets her feelings hurt if I do not eat it. Actually, I barely touched a morsel myself at the party because of these mountains of moussaka. So!' He slapped his knees and rose.

Missy could not have been telling the truth, she thought. Theo had aged into a picture of distinction, a man of substance courted by ambassadors. He was a friend . . . now charming.

'I am sure that Catherine, and especially Xenia, will be happy to see you,' he added, moving towards the kitchen. I think she is very nervous about this term.' He raised a quizzical eyebrow.

So that was what had worried him! Xenia was due to arrive in London on Friday, and here was her mentor, dishevelled in Athens on Wednesday. What could she say? Rosamund dived into the bathroom and shut the door. She looked into the mirror above the sumptuous bank of basins with their slick chrome taps. Her tears had made dark runnels through her make-up, her hair was frowsy and there were creases on her face where she had been sleeping. How was she going to put it? Now she had seen him, it seemed an impossible task. She had an impulse to throw off all her clothes, stuff them in the linen basket, and wash all over in the continental shower with its snaking hose. She rolled up her sleeves, however, and scrubbed to the elbows, as if for an awkward operation. She doused her face, over and over, and at last, thinking herself not too bad in the mirror, she padded out into the sitting-room in her stocking feet.

Theo was whistling in the kitchen. The flat was in direct contrast to the house on Chios. It was scrupulously modern and had always reminded

Rosamund of a ship. In his youth, he had spent some years at sea in order to gain firsthand knowledge of his business, and she had always thought him a captain *manqué*. He had a passion for order and an instinct for the elements. How could she tell him about Missy? He had opened up the shutters leading to the balcony and she hobbled out on to it. Her ankle throbbed, but was clearly not sprained or broken. Dressing for this occasion had been a nonsense. It was only Theo, and he had opened a bottle of wine for them, which stood on a glass-topped table. The terrace garden was in bloom with lilies, geraniums, and a potted fig tree, and a veil of scented jasmine cloyed the night. The vine curtained a view of Athens, where beyond the distant, rumbling traffic she could see the Parthenon, lit up for the *son et lumière*, a feature for tourists. There, once, Theo had described the deeds of Athena to her and her children. All of a sudden, the sheer absurdity of Missy struck her. The vulgarity of her story belonged to the gutter, not to these heights.

Theo emerged on to the balcony with a laden tray. He was proud that he had once worked in a ship's galley, and he liked to do for himself. In assembling the meal, he seemed to have brightened considerably. 'Microwaves are brilliant,' he said. 'You see what a lot she has made? She must think I have orgies here when her back is turned.'

Rosamund tried to smile at this. She helped him to unload the tray, then she sat across from him. It was a vague aubergine dish, hot from the eerie rays of the oven. She was terribly hungry, but she was sick with nerves.

'I do not know how to put this delicately,' he said after they had eaten for a moment in silence, 'but we have heard there has been a very unpleasant rumour . . . none of it true, I am sure. Our mother-in-law was full of it. Are you . . . ?' He paused, a forkful in the air.

'Taking refuge from Charles?' It had occurred to Rosamund to say this to Catherine or Xenia, if they had been there, but this reason was so far from the actual purpose of her visit that it gave her quite a start when Theo broached the subject. 'I have not spoken to Charles in weeks.'

Theo became silent. It took her by surprise that he seemed slightly shocked. 'He does not know you are here?' He considered her across the table. He had always seemed capable of great shifts of distance in short spaces of time, and she could not read him now.

'No,' she said. Giddy for a moment, she decided to plunge. She had to before she lost all will to confront him. 'I thought it would be best if no one knew I was coming,' she said.

He frowned slightly, perhaps in concentration, and the muscles in his jaw tensed. Had her fear triggered some response in him? He was a highly intuitive man.

'I have come about Xenia, Theo,' she said, laying her fork and knife together. She could eat no longer.

'What about Xenia?' His eyes were opaque, but he communicated alarm with a small jerk of his heavy hand on the table.

She looked at the humble meal, the shared wine. She could not say it.

'What about Xenia?' he repeated. He was slightly crouched, his voice aggressive with subdued anxiety.

She scraped back the chair. 'Now that I am here, I don't want to say. Theo, you don't want to know this.' In a flash, she took stock. Of course, he did. Obviously, he thought Xenia had got herself into some kind of trouble in England. He blinked with feral power from the shadows. 'Actually, I am sure the whole thing is quite silly,' she continued. 'It can't be the day before yesterday, but it was. I have a cousin from Kentucky – Missy Buchanan – you met her a long time ago. She turned up . . .' but the words dried. His face was livid.

For a long moment, they were held in complete silence. 'Missy,' he said, at last.

She heard a speedy rushing in her ears. 'You remember her,' she found herself saying stupidly. She did not want to have to believe, not just yet.

He said nothing. He was the spectacle of a man to whom bad news has come.

She had to drag onwards. Why let the scotched snake writhe? 'What she told me could not be told to anyone but you, and certainly not in any other way but face to face. Theo?'

They held a glance between them; a last fragment of shared sensibility, she was later to think. 'So you know,' he said.

She could not really believe it even now. 'I had to tell you!' she said, though. 'It is true, isn't it?' Suddenly, his eyes became peculiarly cold, and for a moment, he studied her. She retracted slightly, alarmed by him.

'She has broken her contract,' he said at length, as if this statement contained the sum and degree of his feelings.

'Is that all you have to say?' She blurted this out, then covered her mouth with her hands. It was too large an admission of pain. She sat stiffly with her eyes closed in an effort to regain self-control.

'You were never meant to know this. That was part of the deal,' he said with businesslike distinctness.

'Theo, how can you? This is something terrible!'

'What!' he shouted. He gripped the table and the cutlery rattled on the glass tabletop. Rosamund shrank, eyes wide open now. 'What? That that creature is Xenia's mother? Yes, I will admit that is terrible!' A startling look of revulsion appeared on his face like a bruise rising.

Everything seemed to be getting out of hand. 'I didn't know!' she cried. 'You never . . .' But it seemed the wrong order of priorities to mention her own feelings in the matter, and so she left the sentence unfinished.

'I never told you that bitch was the mother of my child? You resent this? I would not mention her name to any decent woman, much less to you!'

It was hard to believe that anyone nowadays could speak in this way and carry conviction, but he delivered the words with a thundering force and she was curiously relieved at the distinction he made between Missy and herself. 'Theo . . .' She had not meant to sound quite so abject.

After a long pause in which he sat very still, he spoke. 'I apologize,' he said. 'My indiscretion has cost me more than you can imagine.'

'Look,' she said a little wildly, 'I hold no brief for Missy . . .'

He interrupted her. 'Rosamund, why did she come to see you? It is crucially important to know what she intends!' His voice cut the humid air. Rosamund might have been his secretary.

'She came in order to find things out. I don't know.' She was wounded.

'What things?'

'How Xenia was . . .'

He made an expression of disgust, like spitting.

'Theo, I never liked Missy! I think she wanted me to arrange for her to see Xenia . . . incognito. Apart from everything else, she gave me a cheque for £2,000. Needless to say, I tore it up.' She carried on through his gasp of disbelief. 'Luckily, I was able to escape her before I committed myself to anything. That is why I came directly here. What more could I do?'

'Under no circumstances will she see Xenia. Is that clear?'

Rosamund looked down and bit her lip at this insult to her selfless efficiency. The atmosphere was heavy between them. 'I think you would do well to remember that Xenia is eighteen,' she said in an injured tone. 'This is not lost on Missy.'

'I see at last!' he cried. 'She thinks she can fool you into thinking that that makes a difference to our bargain, does she?'

'I don't know what the bargain was, Theo!' Rosamund burst out. 'Why don't you tell me? I'm involved too, now, you see.'

'It was a pact with the devil,' he muttered. 'She is an evil woman!'

'Theo, it's absurd to say things like that. It's medieval. Can't you at least tell me what happened and leave me to judge? I am quite sure I would believe you almost any day over Missy. Can't you trust me?'

He said nothing, and she could not bear to search out his eyes in the shadow. She looked instead into the distance where the lights trained on the Parthenon jerked mechanically around it, revealing its salient features. She suddenly had the mad impression that he was tangled up in the thick vines that grew behind him. He threw up his hands; his expression was intense and inward, as if he had been enmeshed with some internal complication of this matter for a very long time.

'Theo, something has to be done, and if I don't know, it will only make matters worse.'

'Are you sure?'

This struck her cold, but she nodded, avid, all at once.

He turned his head to one side and for a while let his gaze drift out over the balcony towards dark Likavittós beyond. 'I was mad about her,' he said. Rosamund concealed a sharp intake of breath, but he glanced at her all the same. 'Can you imagine how desperate I was at that time? I met her at Christmas at your house. I don't expect you to understand. She is the sort of woman who can drive a man demented. But,' and he leaned earnestly towards her, 'I did not think I had any plans to get involved with her. I simply found her attractive, and when I gave her my address here, it never occurred to me that she would take it up. She seemed to have a genuine passion for travel, and I suppose I had mentioned something about finding her a job on one of my cruise ships so that she could get to Bombay and overland from there to Nepal.'

Rosamund's throat was very dry. She drank some wine. She became conscious of her foolish, rumpled suit and nervously smoothed her lap.

'I suppose one must never underestimate the enterprise of your countrymen,' he continued wryly, 'but I was astonished when she turned up a week later in my offices in Piraeus, and I was not a little chagrined to come face to face with her there. My staff had never seen anyone like her, dressed as she was in those extraordinary clothes just like an alien being. She had come about my job offer, she said, but had changed her mind about going to Kathmandu. Maybe she could do something a little less ambitious . . . guide trips to Turkey, for instance. She had conceived a passion for Sufism and wanted to see the dervishes! I ask you!

'Whatever her purpose, and whatever her feelings, two things stood out in my mind. The first was that she happened to be your cousin and this put me under an obligation. The second was, that on seeing her for a second time and on my home ground, I could tell she was quite unsuited to working in any capacity on one of my ships. So, as I had a corollary travel business here in Athens run by a distant cousin of my own, I told her she could gain experience – if guiding tours was what she wanted to do – in taking rich Americans around the Peloponnese. I know now that I deluded myself, but I thought then that I should keep an eye on her. I had considered what she had said about travelling in Turkey, and it had occurred to me that she might have had a more compelling reason to visit that country, with which, of course, we were virtually at war then. Mind you, I did not have her cast as a Mata Hari, but I could see her doing deep research into the hashish market, or worse. I'll never forget trying to explain the Cyprus situation to Missy. I was amazed that she did not know that Greece and Turkey had ever been at war!

'Now, I am not so sure that she was as naïve as she pretended to be, but perhaps it was just that naïvety that appealed to me. For all her . . . gameness . . . she had a pristine innocence. Her idea of suffering was to be deprived of a telephone or not to have a hot shower. She really had no idea that anyone ever starved to death or that one's next-door neighbours could betray or murder one's family. She was a complete hedonist, but not in the European way. She was an epicurean without the attendant despair. It was a positive thing with her. She believed that anything that intensified her pleasure was a good thing. What I did not see until it was too late was that she would do anything at all for gain. It simply did not occur to her that anything or anybody should get in the way of what she wanted.

'At any rate, to make a long story short, I did get her a job, and I staked her a loan on a little flat . . .' He stopped here, looked down and was silent for a while. Clearly struggling with himself, he continued. 'I'll be honest with you, Rosamund. I paid for it. You do not know how deeply ashamed I am of this.' He looked at her searchingly. 'Catherine is very cold. That came about when she knew she could not have a baby. It was gradual, but by the time I met Missy, well . . . In my weakness, there have been some women over the years, I'll admit, but nothing like that! There she was in her pert little uniform showing stockbrokers around the tomb of Agamemnon by day . . . I was starved to see her by night.'

Rosamund sat stiffened with as many gaping wounds as the founder of the House of Atreus. In her wildest moments, she had never imagined a confession so awful as this one. He paused, and she wondered how aware he was of her shattering. She had erected great palisades of fantasy against this final assault, and now she was left exposed. Was he looking at her to see just how much she was now at his mercy? The only light on the balcony was an insect-repellant candle. Theo detested moths. She could not tell why he was skewering her on this spit. In full flood, he sat back, his face shaded.

'And then two things happened,' he continued. 'One afternoon, my cousin rang me with a bit of a "problem". It seemed there had been a complaint about Missy. Oh, I'll have you know she was a very good guide,' he said in a grim aside, 'and she was quite a linguist in her way. She picked up Greek. It also seemed that she had been picking up other things. In broad daylight, in Delphi, of all places, she had been observed exchanging a small packet for large money, and as brazen as you please, had taken it back to Athens on the tour bus in her handbag! My cousin wanted to know if he should tell the police. He knew I was involved with her, but even myself I did not know how much. Stupidly, I told him to fob off the law – we have rather a different way of looking at things like that here – but I guaranteed him that I would deal with her myself. And I did.

'It is difficult for me to explain to you the very complex feelings I had for Missy. On the one hand, I was furious at her, but in another way I was sorry for her, and frightened for her too. At that time, there was something almost wistful about her. Her great pleasure principle seemed to stem from a belief that if we always remain children, we are saved. I knew she had experimented with drugs in the past, but I felt a sadness for her that she was still messing around in the sandpit in this way. I suppose I thought that our affair had grown her up, somehow. But it enraged me that she was dealing. Apart from anything else, it seemed to put our love at terrible risk. What was more, it filled me with dread on every level to think of Missy in a Greek prison. Can you imagine? It is sentimental, I know, to say that it was like thinking of a wild bird trapped, but that is how I constantly saw it. This *rara avis*, fit for a king, would not find hot showers or telephones in one of our jails!

'Well, as you can imagine, there was a dreadful row! I had decided to send her back to the United States. I simply could not risk her future or my reputation if this thing got out of hand. Besides, she had betrayed the trust of my cousin, and we are inclined to take things like that quite seriously here.'

Theo leaned forward out of the shadow and rested his arms upon the table. The small, shaded candle lit his face to dramatic effect. In the last few years he had aged and, on the whole, he had gained distinction in the process. Now, however, he looked as defeated with regret as an elderly man stranded on a park bench. Rosamund averted her eyes, not wanting him to be pitiful somehow.

'I have never been able to discover,' he continued, 'what, if anything, Missy did take seriously, but the outcome of the row was what you might expect. Even as I threatened to send her home, I suppose I was begging for a reason not to, and, of course, the greatest reason of them all emerged. She told me she was pregnant.

'I tell you, Rosamund, my joy knew no bounds.' He shot her a pleading glance across the table as if his whole case rested on the one circumstance of his happiness at that moment. 'All at once, Missy seemed a saint to me. By her condition alone, she was utterly redeemed in my eyes. She glowed. And if I had ever thought her wretched or trivial, she completely transcended herself as she pleaded her case. Yes, she had transferred the drugs, but she had done so only for the money. As much as she loved me (or so she said), she had planned to leave me anyway, to have the child by herself and to look after it without telling me. She told me she could think of nothing lower than to use a rich man and said it would have been beneath her dignity to have told me about the baby, a baby I worshipped from the first moment I heard of it! Rosamund, I really, truly took her seriously!

'I am not sure how well you know Missy,' he continued bitterly, 'but I have had a real education in her. She had taken me totally by surprise and I would have given her literally anything. Now, I think she was desperate for cash to get an abortion, for she knew I would never have sanctioned such a thing, but then, I believed everything she told me . . . that she had planned to go back to the States and have the baby without complicating my life. And she did have that defiant independence of spirit. There was a pride in her that might have made her do this. You see, from the very outset I had told her that I would never leave Catherine, who could never remarry because she remains a Catholic. And, despite everything, I have always had a loyalty to . . . my wife. I took her away from her home when she was so young, you see, and she has tried so hard. The baby, of course, made everything ten times worse. I do not think you can have an idea, Rosamund, of how terribly Catherine suffered when she had to recognize that she was barren. Her womb is malformed, you see, and really nothing could be done. It was I who had not wanted to adopt a child, and we had quarrelled dreadfully about this. If I had then left her for another woman made pregnant by me, I think this would have killed her. Then again, I was so intensely in love with Missy that I could not imagine a life without her. What should I do? I felt I could not abandon either of them, but I was really torn. I did not want the only child I was ever likely to have to be born illegitimate, but I could not think of marrying Missy.' Theo threw his hands out expressively towards the candlelight. The misery on his face in chiaroscuro was vivid. 'Don't worry, Rosamund. I knew I deserved my suffering. Not all Mediterranean men swagger around with macho smugness at such situations. I was quite aware that something that had begun so lightly had so quickly turned destructive. But it is not in my nature to bemoan what cannot be helped, and I tried to find the least terrible solution.

'I thought that Missy and I were facing out the dilemma together. I can promise you that I would have sent her home in luxury to have the baby there, if that had been what she wanted, but she declared that she wanted me as much as I wanted her, especially now that I was so happy that she was pregnant. We chose a little flat out in Kifissia near the nursing home where she was to give birth, and I supplied her with every amusement and convenience. Oh, she was to be a very rich woman, I left her in no doubt of that! I visited her every day, and went home to Chios each weekend, riddled with guilt. Do you think not? Catherine had poured all of her energy into rebuilding the house. She did it, you know, practically with her bare hands. There she was, so cheerful, so occupied, so determined not to sulk because she was barren! And there was Missy, bulging like a fertility goddess – myself, an idolater towards her belly! My wife is an honest woman, Rosamund, and deceiving her was peculiarly hateful to me. A million men in my position might have felt otherwise, and I confess, I have winked at my own peccadilloes at other times. But this was not a peccadillo. It was the grace of love and the sin of betrayal all rolled into one. I could barely look at Catherine without remembering what I had loved in her from the beginning, and knowing that Missy was of far less worth.

'Nevertheless, as the pregnancy progressed, I became more and more convinced that I had no choice but to put my wife aside for the sake of the child, and I was on the verge of telling Catherine when the blow struck – the blow that is responsible for everything that has followed in the last eighteen years.' Theo lowered his voice and leaned closer. 'I do not like to tell you this because it brings shame on your family, but you must remember that it brings shame on Xenia too. Terrible shame!

'It was in August of that year when my Cousin Dmitris – the one who had employed Missy – came to me on a night like this, at a time like this . . . a dreadful hour! One for witches, don't you think? Although he understood that Missy was a delicate matter, he did not know the whole truth. He wanted to advise me to get Missy out of Greece as soon as possible. He had substantial evidence, which I keep to this day in my bank vault, that Missy was no amateur when it came to trafficking in drugs. She was no hippie doling out hash. She had been dealing heroin. What was more, she had a large connection with professional racketeers. She had used his company as a front, and he was justifiably worried that he might be implicated. He was not a wealthy man, but I am, and that concerned him more. I was, of course, very shaken by this news, but nothing prepared me for what was to come. I am afraid to tell you, Rosamund, that I was not your cousin's only client. Missy had found herself rich pickings in Greece . . . the tourist trade, you might almost say. Dmitris had incontrovertible proof that Missy was a whore.'

For a long time, neither of them spoke. Rosamund could not be sure, but she thought she heard the sound of Theo weeping and she glanced aside. A cold, deathly calm had descended on her. She had sat immobilized throughout his story. She did not know how late it was. The lights had long since gone out over the Parthenon, and the distant rumble of traffic from the city seemed muted now. At the very worst, she had expected to be told that Xenia was the result of a drunken fling with Missy. That he had loved her with such intensity struck Rosamund as having to do with the ends of things: it brought her to a place where time stopped. The disoriented stars seemed to wheel about this fact as around a still, turning point of irreducible pain. She felt sluggish with the shock. What a quaint irony it was that he assumed her concern was for her family honour! The seamy details of Missy's life were nothing to her next to the central evil of his loving her. After a while, he reached for his glass, swallowed some wine, cleared his throat and went on.

'You must get it straight in your mind, Rosamund, that I had proof of this, and you must also know the lies that she had told me. It broke my heart. Even now, when I am sure that Xenia is my child, I feel soiled by Missy. It is not only women who can feel this way. It disgusts me! She was Judas Iscariot to me. At first, I wanted to kill her, and then I became afraid that I actually would kill her, throttle her!' Theo paused, his whole body clenched like a fist. In the low flame of the candle his face looked unfamiliar, almost gross in the distorting shadow. 'It was Dmitris who finally persuaded me to let him go to Missy and send her packing. I think he truly thought I would murder her . . . or go mad, I don't know which. But I am not sure you will ever believe what happened next. Even I, who lived through it, find it almost impossible. It was like something out of Euripides . . . no, I dignify it! It was more the sort of story that you might read in some sleazy rag!' He gave a grating laugh, and his eyes never left Rosamund's face. 'But that's Missy! A real cat among the pigeons, you understand. She rang me. I expect you imagine she was hysterical . . . in despair? She was none of these, not she! She told me very coolly that unless I stuck by her, she would tell Catherine – and she named a sum. When I refused to be blackmailed, there was a little pause. I shall never forget this as long as I live. "Then the baby is dead," she said. And the receiver went "click". Just like that.

'Of course, at first I did not believe her. How could anyone believe a thing like that? Nevertheless, I had some instinct about her. She was flamboyant enough, but not one given to melodrama. Missy was never an emotional woman, you understand. She would not have tried to get my attention in that sort of way, but even if this was her motive, I found I simply could not take the risk. I went out to Kifissia and let myself in with my key. Missy was sitting in the bath, a knitting needle in her hand. She had broken the waters and her pains were on her. I tell you, she was like something made of stone. She did not even flinch.

'It is only by the grace of God that Xenia is alive today. I called an ambulance and rushed Missy to the private clinic where we had arranged for a very different experience. At that point, I did not care whose baby it was. It was attempted murder!' He put his head in his hands. 'Now do you see?'

Rosamund said nothing. She simply watched him for a long time, unable to think of anything but Missy, impassive, crouched and swollen in the bath. 'I wish you had told me this before,' she said. It seemed irrelevant but there was nothing else she could think of saying.

'What was there to tell?' He threw up an expressive hand. 'As far as I am concerned, Missy does not exist. Have some brandy!' he said suddenly, rasping back the iron chair on the stone terrace. He got up, paced to the edge of the balcony, then paced back. He disappeared through the French doors, and emerged with two glasses and a bottle of Metaxa. He poured it out and she accepted it, at once feeling the need for it. It was too painful to look at him, and so she closed her eyes. She had eaten of the apple, and now this ugly, sensational story would tell itself any time it chose. In her rose garden, in the supermarket, in the back of taxis, in sleep, in church . . . wherever she was at her most unguarded, this night would remember itself. 'And now I have been quite open with you, Rosamund,' he said, 'perhaps you will tell me a little bit more about your interview with Missy. You see I have never believed for these eighteen years that we were entirely done with her.'

Rosamund opened her eyes. He was looking at her with fearsome intensity. 'I hardly know what to say in the light of what you have just told me.' She swallowed the fiery brandy. 'Needless to say, Missy left out some salient details of your story. It is her contention that you abducted Xenia and bullied her into relinquishing the child. I did not know what to make of it then. I do not know what to make of it now.' In some dim recess of herself, Rosamund could see how Missy might be driven to violate her own womb and to want to keep the baby at the same time. What worse revenge could one take on a man? And what greater triumph could there be than to walk away with the thing he wanted most, living in your arms?

He exploded, but somehow she did not shrink. 'If Missy wants a thing to be true, then to Missy it *is* true! It was a perfectly straightforward deal. She got safe passage, a ticket home, and the money she needed to buy and furnish a house. I got the baby she tried to kill, and a clear, legal undertaking from her that no other claims would be made. She most certainly did not want Xenia, but her scope for further blackmail was considerably widened once I had the child. She could have blurted the story out to you. You might have told Charles, and Charles might have told Cat . . .'

Suddenly, Rosamund could bear it no longer. 'Theo, I came all the way to Athens to tell you! I have not told Charles nor any other human soul!' She heard her voice choking. 'And do you know how I feel? I feel that all these years you have not trusted me! You used me because you knew . . . you knew . . .'

'Knew what?'

'Nothing!' She felt ungainly and exposed. She tried to get a grip. 'You must have known always that I would never have betrayed you to Charles,' she murmured.

Theo had marvellous clarity. 'I knew that you could not take it,' he finally said, and the observation was too direct, too true to be offensive.

'Well, I took Xenia,' she replied. 'I took in everything to do with her, except, of course, that I did not know that she was my cousin.'

'And that does have to be addressed! Of course, it does. You did take her in. You do. She loves you. And every time I look at you together, it cancels out the fear that I have that one day she will become like her mother, like Missy. You and Xenia have the same blood. Your grandparents are her great-grandparents. Your children are her cousins, her real cousins, not just adopted through Catherine and Charles. And you are a woman who is day to Missy's night. You are virtue, she is vice! I am grateful to you in a way that you cannot know. In my mind, it is you who are Xenia's mother, and whenever I see Missy in her face and in the very little things that show they are of the same blood, I am also reminded of your face, and that you are a good woman whom I respect and honour.' He sat back and folded his arms.

'I thought it was something else, Theo.' It was all she could do to muster the strength to say this. She felt as if she had jumped from the balcony, but she had needed to say it. Her face was suffused with shame, and tears pricked at the back of her eyes.

There was a long, tense pause, but if she had confounded him in any way, he gave no sign of it. 'Thank you so much for everything, Rosamund,' he said at length. 'Thank you for coming to tell me this, for what we must do now is to stop her. Under no circumstances is she ever to reveal her identity to Xenia.' He reached out and patted Rosamund's hand. They exchanged a look, and her confession was consigned to an oubliette. 'Tomorrow, I will get on to my lawyers. Xenia is safe from Missy in English law, but if there is even the smallest chance of harassment, then my daughter will not go back to England. Presumably you did not tell Missy that Xenia was studying there?'

Rosamund shook her head miserably. 'I told her nothing.'

'Good! As far as Greece is concerned, Xenia is well defended from her mother, who is not a welcome visitor in this country. Still, I think a little reminder might be in order and it ought to be quite sufficient to deter Missy.'

Rosamund's hands were shaking and she clasped them together hard. Like a snubbed adolescent at a dance, she cringed, abased as he whirled around with these considerations. 'Missy is rich now,' she found herself saying. If her tone was spiteful, she did not hear it.

He raised an eyebrow, cautious. 'In all of this, I did not ask what had become of Missy. She has married?'

'A racehorse owner, a breeder called Tom Kavanagh. I did not meet him.'

Theo snorted. 'And does he know about Xenia?'

'She says he does, but I think he does not. You are not considering a bit of blackmail yourself, are you, Theo?' She bit her lip, regretting this last.

He put his two fists on the table, lightly clenched. 'I do not think it needs to go that far. Missy knows she has no legal right to approach Xenia, and though it would seem that she could approach you if she wanted, extra provisions were made against this. If she makes any other kind of trouble, well, we may find ourselves fighting fire with fire. We shall see. It is she who is the blackmailer, not I.'

'Suppose Xenia wants to know who she is. She once told me that she often dreamed of her natural mother.'

Theo leaned forward, his head held heavy like a bull. 'As you know full well, Rosamund, Xenia's mother is dead.' His eyes lit with a peculiar loathing. 'And I only wish she were. You cannot possibly know how I revile that woman. I told you the story of what happened, but nothing could tell you how. That is the key to everything, isn't it? The quality of the deed. There is only one other person who knows as much as you do, and that is an old monk on Patmos where I made a pilgrimage when all was finished, said and done. Even though I had never been religious before, I made my confession to him. He told me that my sin, this child, had converted me, and it is true. But, try as I might, I cannot forgive Missy, nor can I expect she wants to be forgiven. If she has come to see you and if she has tried to get you to connive in her seeing Xenia, then I promise you there is only one thing she wants, and that is revenge. All of these years, she will have been preparing. Believe me. And it is not because she ever loved me, but because I thwarted her.

'I see it in your eyes that you do not understand, Rosamund, but you must try. However much you are tempted, I must beg of you that you tell no one, no matter how close, what has passed between us, and that to your dying day, you will never reveal to Catherine or to Xenia that Missy is her mother. I want your oath on something holy . . . your solemn word.'

Rosamund looked at Theo for a long time with bitter regard. 'My word has never been otherwise,' she said.

VII

FROM DEEP within the house, Catherine heard the bell – or thought she did. She was wrestling Xenia's trunk from the box room thinking that there was no time like the present to get the fundamental packing started. St Winifred's was hot on order, Xenia was not. Every year they had a struggle over the list of things Xenia was to take, but she invariably left something behind that then had to be posted. Catherine had supposed that now she was a sixth-former Xenia would take charge of these arrangements, but one nag had followed another unheeded, and it was time to start. It never seemed to occur to Xenia that if she did not do a thing, her mother would have to, but Catherine supposed it was pointless to carry on about it. All the same, if she did not pull her socks up, she really would not get a place at Oxford. Catherine gave a little sigh. She doubted the wisdom of Xenia applying at all, but as in everything, she was contradicted by Theo, and overruled in London by Charles and Rosamund. They knew best.

The bell sounded again. She groaned. Yiorgia had gone to town with Xenia to do some shopping and Spiro was in the groves beyond recall. Visitors rarely came to the gate, but then she remembered that her friend Anna had wanted to show her some curtain material and this would take some time. Anna was almost comically indecisive, but she had a touching confidence in Catherine's 'English' taste. Although she wiped her hands on her skirt with an irritable sigh, Catherine was glad of the distraction. Anna's chatter soothed her. The estates of Kampos, connected by tunnelled, shaded lanes, brought landowners together in an understated camaraderie. If neighbours popped in, they were welcome.

Catherine made her way into the courtyard and looked at her watch. Xenia would be back from her voice lesson in half an hour. Maybe she would get Yiorgia to lay an extra place at lunch and ask Anna to stay. Catherine always found herself unaccountably nervy and waspish the week before Xenia had to go back to school. Even though she wanted to be serene and kind, she found herself grudging, snappy and fault-finding. Xenia was always thrilled at the prospect of staying in London and this obscurely irritated Catherine, who had developed a morbid dislike of the city. Anna had two married daughters, and over the years had gained profound insight into teenage girls. Catherine never confided in her friend exactly, but she listened for such auguries as fell from her lips. Yes, she would ask Anna to lunch. In this way, she would gain the added benefit of fobbing off the prodding, anxious questions that Xenia had been asking about Charles and Rosamund ever since she had overheard that unfortunate conversation on the terrace. Catherine really was fed up with her mother. Imagine exposing Xenia to that sort of gossip!

With a smile, therefore, she opened the door in the heavy gate, only to come face to face with a stranger. Catherine gave a start. A well-groomed, smartly dressed woman stood before her. She had striking features, and in particular, large, bold eyes of an unusual green with which she stared at Catherine. She wore a suit made of ivory linen, but the jacket was slung casually over her shoulders as if she were not bothered about what she wore or how she wore it. For some reason she seemed familiar to Catherine, but she could not quite place her.

'Madame Phocas?' the woman asked.

'Yes . . .' Catherine retreated slightly behind the door.

'My name is Melissa Kavanagh.' She put her head to one side in an interrogative way. 'I think you are a relative of my cousin Rosamund Simon.' She paused. 'In fact, I know you are,' she continued, laughing. 'You mean she did not write to you?'

Catherine noticed that the woman had parked a jazzy little red car on the gravel shoulder by the house. So that was why she looked familiar. She looked like Rosamund. 'No, I'm sorry, she – '

'That is so like her!' the woman interrupted, rolling her eyes. 'Well, I'm very sorry. She vowed to me she would.' Missy turned as if to make for the car.

In inverse proportion to any sinking of heart were Catherine's good manners. The dazzling woman appalled her somehow. 'Oh, please do come in,' she said faintly.

Before she knew it, Missy was through the gate and standing in the courtyard. 'My! Isn't this beautiful!' she said. 'This is so nice of you.' She looked around in a dreamy manner. 'It's just lovely.' She inclined her head and looked at Catherine. She seemed almost sleepy, and the corners of her mouth were turned up in an inscrutable smile. 'I hope I'm not putting you to any inconvenience,' she said, 'but I am in Chios literally for the day before I set off for Turkey to join my husband. I'm just dropping by, and you're not to do anything for me at all.'

Catherine had no plans to do anything about her and was wondering, now she was in, how to get her out again. After an inner struggle, though, she offered the woman coffee.

'Certainly not! I'll say not! I wouldn't put you to the trouble.'

'It's no trouble,' Catherine lied.

'That's so kind, but I've just had some in town. To tell you the truth, I'm just shamelessly interested in your house and Rozzy told me she didn't think you'd mind showing me around. I've been doing a course at the University of Kentucky on worldwide domestic architecture . . . it's really just "Old Houses for Old Ladies",' she said in a fudgy, confidential tone, 'but I thought I'd wow them if I did a little project on something like this.' She looked around herself again, wide-eyed. The inflections of her voice went up, ending every sentence with a little sigh. 'Rozzy told me how you all had done up this fantastic old place, and I thought to myself "Just the very thing for my little circle in Lexington! That'll shake 'em out of the magnolias," I thought. "Something different." '

Catherine, who mistrusted Americans, decided that this was a peculiarly American thing to do – to barge into someone's house unannounced and study it. In a moment, she would probably take snapshots.

And, indeed, with a flourish, Missy produced an expensive camera from the depths of a kid shoulder-bag. 'Would you *mind* if I took a few pictures and then just scurried off?' Notwithstanding this culturally immature gesture, the woman's movements and expression were of a svelte refinement. She had a fluid eloquence that belied her curiously childish voice, and her eyes darted around the enclosure, alert and observant.

'No, please let me show you around,' said Catherine. She was slightly mollified by the vague idea that the house's fame might spread abroad. It was her glory and her joy. Besides, as much as she sometimes resisted being swallowed whole by the country of her adoption, she had absorbed that Greek article of faith which made hospitality to strangers a necessity, and the acknowledgement of relatives, no matter how distant, a mandate.

'Well, it's just so sweet of you,' said Missy, wrinkling her nose. 'Tell me,' she said, putting her head to one side, 'is your husband at home?'

Catherine was a little taken aback at this apparent *non sequitur.* It seemed a bit intrusive to mention him at all. 'He is in Athens,' she said shortly.

'No . . . I was just wondering if I could give you all lunch. Roz made him sound such a fascinating man.'

Catherine felt a low growl rising at the back of her throat in response to this dimity archness, and she determined not to be forced into asking Mrs Kavanagh to a meal. She was beginning to get the idea that she had met this woman before, but she could not think how or where. 'That is very kind of you,' she said, 'but my daughter and I are preparing for her return to school.'

'You have a daughter?' An eyebrow shot up. 'So do I. How old is she?'

'She's just eighteen.'

'Me too. Same here,' said Missy. 'About to go to college, is she?'

'We're hoping for Oxford, actually,' Catherine replied, grateful for once to say this of Xenia. She wanted profoundly to move the conversation from the personal. 'Now, where shall we start? The courtyard where we are standing is, if I may say, of some interest.'

The woman seemed entangled in some foreign thought, perhaps of her daughter, but she snapped her eyes to attention and looked mildly enough around. 'My husband and I have tried to be as faithful as possible to the original,' Catherine continued.

'Well, I know. We have a *very* pretty ante-bellum house near Lexington, and we have slaved . . . not so much for restoration as for revival. It is terribly important to be tactful with these old places. You have to treat them like bad-tempered old ladies.'

Despite herself, Catherine smiled at this remark. 'If your house dates from before the American Civil War,' she said with a generosity born of effort, 'it is probably older than ours in most parts . . . except, of course, for where we are standing. The foundations of this courtyard date back to the seventeenth century when rich merchants from Genoa settled here. The arrangement of the water-wheel and cistern, the mosaic pavement, date from that time, but there was a fearful massacre in 1822. It's a foul story. The Turks slaughtered practically the whole population of Chios, and many of those who survived were sold into slavery. They still talk about this on the island as if it had happened in living memory. I looked up all the old records when we bought the house. The family who lived here escaped the massacre and abandoned the house, which, in any case, partly collapsed in the notorious earthquake of 1881.' Catherine felt she was waxing on a bit. The woman's eyes flitted about the scene in a haphazard way, not settling on her or what she was describing.

She said, however, 'I was struck by that water-wheel the moment I came in. It *is* the most beautiful thing! I hope it isn't tactless for me to ask, but those plaques that line the cistern . . . they look Turkish to me.'

Catherine was impressed. The woman seemed to have some acumen after all. 'Indeed, they are Ottoman in influence.'

'It was the carnation motif that struck me,' Missy said blandly.

Catherine was gingered up . . . inspired. Imagine knowing about the carnation motif! She expected the woman did have rather a nice house of her own in Kentucky, perhaps with horses. Had she not met one of Rosamund's relatives once? She had a vague memory of someone of a completely different order from this woman.

'May I?' Missy asked, raising the camera. She stepped prettily back on the slippery cobbles and snapped the striking arrangement of water-wheel and cistern. She moved closer in, athletically crouching, and photographed the marble plaques with their ancient designs of flowers and cypresses. Catherine, who had a weakness for shoes, admired Missy's simple pumps.

She eyed the whole costume. 'Valentino,' she murmured.

'This old thing? It is, as a matter of fact.' Missy brushed down the jacket, thumbing the fine stuff like a rag. 'I got it *ages* ago,' she said. 'I always cling on to my little investments, don't you?'

This attitude corresponded to Catherine's own predilection for thrift. As rich as Theo was – in fact, because he was so rich – she detested ostentation. She owned a Balmain evening dress, a Chanel suit, and a few understated effects from other great couturiers. She admired the workmanship in them and wore them only on state occasions. The rest of the time she made do with simple clothes bought off the peg, and she always looked for a bargain. 'Now, the house, you may be interested to know, was virtually a ruin when we bought it twenty years ago.'

Missy inclined her head, absorbed. 'I know.' She paused for the second Catherine took to find this odd. 'Roz told me.'

'To tell you the truth, I virtually did it over myself. Husbands, I find, are hopeless at this kind of thing, or at least mine is. Theo's work takes him to Athens a great deal, and abroad, so I oversaw architects and builders. It was like a bomb site, and I lived in the back wing for years. These estates in the old days were really serious business concerns, and they often had workshops attached to them where the local people would come to spin silk and weave fine cotton cloth for export. I put up a camp-bed in the old mill and watched the house grow from there. Now, I have turned it back to its original use. It is my studio. I work in textiles. I'm a weaver, and I also make quilts and things.'

'Oh, I'd *love* to see it! D'you have a loom?'

For some reason, curious in that the instinct was abrupt, Catherine balked at showing Mrs Kavanagh this room. In fact, she did not know why she had mentioned it. The workroom was her sanctuary and she kept it locked. 'As I told you,' she said, changing the subject, 'the foundations are seventeenth-century, but after the 1881 earthquake a Greek family took over the property. By Greek, I mean not Genoese in origin. In fact, they claimed descent from the Byzantine aristocracy. This is a Byzantine island, and actually my husband's family has its roots here from that time on his mother's side. The great medieval lord, Bardas Phocas, was exiled here in the tenth century by the Emperor John Tzimisces and he left many descendants.'

Mrs Kavanagh seemed very interested in all of this. 'Intriguing,' she said.

'Anyway,' Catherine continued, 'the family which took this house over built it up to great magnificence at the turn of the century, but they lost their money in the Great Depression, and when the last male heir died, the house was once more abandoned. Luckily, the structure was sound, but the so-called caretakers of the place had chickens in the drawing-room, goats in the kitchen! And look at that vaulting and those *arcatures*, won't you? They were all plastered over!' She stood looking at the house, wanting to interpret it for her visitor.

To Catherine, the house had a deep intelligence, which uttered of itself only in solitude. Especially in the shades of evening, it became an evanescent presence to her like the scent of fruit trees and the balm of groves. The moment she had discovered it, she had loved it. She had come upon it suddenly a few years after she and Theo had decided to live in Greece on a more or less permanent basis. Threading through the winding lanes in a little hired car, she had entered deeper and deeper into Kampos. Behind old walls and high gates, profoundly shut against the world and spiked with wrought-iron filigree, under old and twisted trees, had stood the shadowed mansions. The arched loggias and magnificent staircases all seemed to have grown by themselves to charmed proportions of height and sprawl, Italianate and graceful. Sequestered here and veiled from sight, the houses seemed like the jewels of a seraglio, so precious that they must be guarded from unseemly glances. Not fanciful, when she had found it, she could have sworn their house had summoned her.

When they had bought it, the task of renovation had consumed her. It had been she who had spotted the original features, she who had dug out broken pillars and pilasters, often with her own hands. The whole exercise had been like doing an enormous jigsaw, fitting it all together without disturbing a subtle intactness the place had, its ruin notwithstanding. At her command, slender columns had risen to be boughed with trellised vines; and the shattered, magnificent outdoor staircase once more swept up to the first-floor entrance for which she had found carved lintels. The old place had surrendered to her; theatrically, it had unfolded. She remembered the moment that she had been able to descend the balustraded staircase down to the refurbished courtyard. She had stood on the top step in a pitch of pure happiness, the restored, cobbled mosaic unfurling beneath her. From its own inner eye it had seemed to swirl out, black and white, and to churn, almost as if it had been in motion.

'It's lucky you have someone to leave it to!' said Mrs Kavanagh. Was her tone sharp, or was this statement at odds with what Catherine imagined she was thinking? Missy had been staring at the house, apparently bewitched by masonry. Perhaps it came from living in an Eastern country, perhaps it was her own English reticence, but Catherine found this and other small allusions to her family (to whom Mrs Kavanagh had not been introduced) somewhat unseemly. Perhaps sensing this, the woman continued in a different vein. 'The stone is a particularly attractive colour, so mellow, especially where the light strikes it. Is it local?' She waved her hand at the upper loggia with the handsome cross vaults Catherine had restored so lovingly.

'Yes, it comes from a local quarry which has been used from classical times. You do know that Homer was supposed to have been born in Chios?' Mrs Kavanagh seemed uninterested in the sublime, blind poet. 'I had all of the new stones made to measure from that very place.'

'You know, you really ought to write a book. You could get Charles to publish it!' Missy clasped her hand to her chest in a gesture of one thrilled at an inspiration. 'Why don't you?'

This idea had more than once occurred to Catherine, but the thought was always swallowed up in that diffidence that was endemic to her nature.

'Why, this place is unique!' Mrs Kavanagh continued with renewed, breathy, Southern gasps. 'It makes Eagles look like a li'l ole shack!' Parenthetically, she added, 'Eagles is my place.'

Catherine was beginning to wonder if her visitor were not some kind of social climber after all. Despite her noticing the Ottoman bas-relief, she seemed to be interested in something else besides the house. Her eyes darted everywhere, over the doorways and the gate, down the trellised walkway to the orange groves. 'There are some books already,' Catherine said, her stateliness recalled. 'And in any case, the last person I could impose upon is my brother.'

Missy slipped the noose of this veiled snub with an uninhibited chuckle. Brandishing her camera once more, she nipped across the cobblestones looking for angles and shots. 'Well, I guess not,' she said, 'but I'll send you all any of these snaps that come out. I fancy myself as a bit of a photographer. I just worship this place!' And, indeed, with a kind of cold, professional eye, she set about capturing salient features: a marble tub planted with geraniums, the stone balustrade of the stairway, the vaulted limestone arch that led to cool offices and storerooms below. The process made Catherine feel nervous, as if the BBC had moved in with cameras and displaced her.

So it was with some relief that she heard the car draw up and the doors slam with the debouching of Xenia and Yiorgia. They were back, and help was at hand. 'Oh, that must be my daughter and our cook,' she said.

Missy crouched by the boll of a plane tree and snapped an urn. She rose from her haunches and stood. 'How nice,' she said.

And Xenia entered. She was wearing a shapeless garment she had bought in Kensington Market and which Catherine disliked, not a little because Xenia would call it 'an antique' from the sixties. It was modest enough, however, and could be allowed on Chios. Her long hair was fetched up in a dark knot at the nape of her neck, and she was carrying a bag of loaves for Yiorgia, who followed her, burdened with shopping. They were conversing rapidly not in the Athenian Greek which her parents encouraged, but in Yiorgia's raw dialect. Yiorgia had served as a nanny to Xenia, and they were very fond of each other. On seeing the visitor in the courtyard, Xenia drew to a halt. She and Mrs Kavanagh looked at each other, almost staring, Catherine thought.

'Melissa Kavanagh,' Missy said, extending a hand. '*Ti kanis?*' she added in Greek.

'*Hiero poli! Kala, ephcaristo, ke esis?*' Xenia replied, greeting the other.

'This is my daughter, Xenia Phocas.' Catherine felt the urge to break in and return the exchange to English. 'Xenia, this is Mrs Kavanagh, a cousin of Rosamund, who has come to see the house.'

'*Kala*,' Missy said in Greek to Xenia. She almost breathed the word. It meant 'well', 'I am well'.

'So, you have been to Greece before?' Catherine asked stoutly.

'I've been around the block a few times. I'm a real globe-trotter. I lived in Athens for a while.' All along, her eyes never left Xenia. 'Pretty dress,' she said to the girl.

Xenia looked down at the rusty old gunny sack from Biba. 'Oh, thank you! How is Rosamund? She is my aunt, but I call her "Rosamund", you know. We're tremendous friends.'

'Oh really, I didn't know that,' Missy said with a thin smile. It struck Catherine that Melissa Kavanagh did not like her cousin, and this was not entirely to her discredit. Rosamund always seemed to know best in Xenia's eyes, and in Theo's. Catherine supposed she had good motives.

'Yes, I'm going to stay with her next week. I always do when I go back to St Winifred's.'

'So you're going to England next week? You go to school there? Odd that Roz didn't mention it, but then I suppose she had so much else on her mind.'

Catherine thought this a sharp tone for a small omission, but the thing to do now was to get Mrs Kavanagh to leave. 'Speaking of England, I've started your packing, darling. And we really must press on.' At this she expected her visitor to declare that she could no longer detain them.

'I hear you're going to Oxford. You must be pretty smart.' Mrs Kavanagh produced an oddly mirthless laugh.

'I won't get in,' Xenia said, 'not unless they take me for my singing.'

Catherine felt herself to be an irrelevance to some ulterior dynamic. She often sensed this when Rosamund and Xenia were together, and she disliked it. Maybe Americans were good with young people because they were juvenile themselves. From time to time, waves of resentment at her sister-in-law welled up in Catherine, but she turned a blind eye to them. When all was said and done, it was she herself who had done the donkey-work for Xenia. She had never really abandoned Xenia to Yiorgia. Her own mother had plonked her down with shifting nannies and she had been sent away at the age of seven. She had wanted Xenia to go to St Winifred's only because she had never been happier anywhere else herself. And if there had not been close family in England, Theo would never have agreed to give the girl this supreme advantage. So Catherine tolerated Rosamund and considered it mean to think ill of her.

'How was your singing lesson, darling?' she asked. The admiring eyes of Mrs Kavanagh stimulated a little eddy of pride in Catherine. Xenia really did have a very nice voice.

'Well, she was a bit despairing of the Mozart, but the Monteverdi impressed her. It really did.' Xenia blushed at the boast. 'Oh, Mummy, that reminds me! I'm afraid we forgot her cheque. And she does so hate to say.'

'Xenia's teacher was at La Scala in Milan,' Catherine said. 'We're terribly lucky. She settled here with her Greek husband and started to give lessons when he died.'

Throughout this conversation, Mrs Kavanagh stood unnaturally still and withdrawn. 'Madame Phocas,' she said in a husky rush of words, 'I am so sorry to trouble you, but do you think I could have a glass of water? I suddenly feel faint. I dashed around in the heat this morning and I had no appetite for breakfast. I really should have accepted your offer of coffee.'

'Oh, you poor thing!' Xenia cried. She reached out and grasped Mrs Kavanagh's arm and led her to the well that fed the water-wheel. She took out her handkerchief, dipped it in the water, and tenderly bathed the face of the stranger.

'Oh dear,' Catherine said, 'I'm sorry.' And she was. Especially in front of the merciful Xenia, and particularly at a quarter to one, it had now become impossible not to offer the woman a meal. Catherine reached for the bands of self-control and tightened them. 'Perhaps you would like to lie down for a moment,' she said to her guest, 'and of course, you must stay for lunch.'

With a flourish, Xenia broke off some of a loaf she was carrying in the plastic bag. 'Eat this!' she said, 'You will feel better.

And Missy looked up at her with a thinly veiled intensity.

VIII

CHARLES TOLD Caro that he had better stay at home in case Rosamund had done something silly.

Caro wondered what he meant by 'silly'.

Charles asked her how she would feel if something had happened to Rosamund . . . something awful . . .

'Like suicide, you mean?'

'I can't exclude that possibility. Suppose I were with you when the news came. Suppose she's done some other drastic thing. No, Caro, I think we had better wait until we have found out what has happened to her.'

There was a long, repressed silence at the other end of the telephone. 'Very well, Charles, if that's how you see it.' She paused. 'I think I shall be going up to Scotland after all, in that case. My parents have been through hell over this. Perhaps I owe it to *them* to spend a little time . . .'

He had visions of Caro, the vegetarian, drilling grouse; Caro in a padded jacket with dogs sniffing the clean air. In the early throes of it all, he had promised to accompany her to Scotland to meet her father, no laird at all, but a businessman, who yet took a dour view of the romance. 'Look,' he said, 'the children are in a bad way about this.' He had the feeling this was taken for a flimsy excuse, but he could not prove it. 'I spoke with Francis this morning. He thinks his mother may be . . . well, self-destructive.' This was not the only thing Francis had said, nor the reason he had given for it.

'Wasn't she always? Isn't this what she would do to keep you? I'm sorry, Charles, but if you are willing to buy that melodrama, then . . .'

'Then, what?'

'I'm sorry, darling, but I do "smell the smell of burning martyr".'

He remembered the quotation from a *Fawlty Towers* episode. Couldn't she at least be original?

'From everything you have told me, this is just the sort of thing she would do. She's like my mother! If you give in now, your life will be nothing but crisis management from now on out!'

Francis had said something of the kind, only the nature of the criticism had been different. He had said that Charles had substituted Rosamund for his own mother. Francis had asked his father when he intended to grow up.

The conversation, having veered towards these treacherous depths, steered itself once more into the shallows, where neither Charles nor Caro felt prepared to admit that they had made a mistake. It seemed very cowardly for him to dump her under this pressure, not that he was sure he wanted to. Caro had a brave little flat on the wilder shores of Notting Hill with only stairs to climb to the umpteenth floor. It was a garret, but not a slum, and she owned it. He bent a little, saying that he might be over that evening, but doubted that he would spend the night. He would take her to dinner, maybe. She had been so patient. Could she not be patient for just a little longer? Of course, she could. Caro had a thing about her biological clock which alarmed Charles not a little. But she did see it. Of course, she saw it. If Rosamund were into some grand manipulation, then surely it really would be the worst thing to bolt. They would only pay for it later. There was every kind of sense in that.

Charles put down the telephone, suddenly exhausted. He had stayed home from work in order to take his mother to Paddington and to talk to his son, who had blazed up the garden path that morning with murder in his heart. It had been a terrible interview. The small democracy of the Simon children had voted Francis their delegate, for his family role had always been that of arbiter. Charles had squared himself for his son's logic but he had been astonished to find angry, personal wounds. Francis had put it to him that Rosamund had been the only parent they had; a charge, Charles felt, that was grossly unfair. It was clear, however, that the children were closer to their mother than he had thought, and it now seemed extraordinary that she had not told at least one of them where to find her. There ensued a miserable ringing round to Dominic, Peter and Theresa, who knew nothing of this latest development. Theresa said she had always thought Rosamund had a secret life, adding that her mother had needed one.

Following these conversations and his son's departure, Charles was shaken by the revelation that he, the more tolerant parent, was seen as less loving than his wife. He had thought they were frightened of her. In reality, they were frightened of losing her and the background her solid justice had always provided.

He began to wonder if his shame at the affair had less to do with the opinion of him held by Francis, Dominic, Peter and Theresa, and more with his own true feelings. If he really loved Caro, wouldn't this have been its own defence? Surely, he should be angry at Francis if he loved her? And why, too, was he so anxious about Rosamund? Without sparing him, Francis had reported how worried they had been about her at Sunday lunch. She had had no plans to go away then. She had been holding her ground, waiting for Charles, trying not to upset them. Everybody knew she had suffered in the past from severe bouts of depression. It would be beneath his mother's dignity, her son had said, to write a suicide note, for she would never plan such an act. It wasn't beyond her, however, to run away and then, on the spur of the moment, do herself in.

Charles surveyed the street gloomily from the window of his study. In self-defence, he remembered that he had given the best room in the house to Rosamund, even though she appeared to do little more in it than brood. He mused upon the tired, late summer trees in the road, their leaves too dusty to be an augury of change to winter. He supposed he would have to get on to his sister Catherine and tell her that Xenia might not find Rosamund at home when she came. He wondered if he should ring Marina Mason too. Apparently, she had come all the way up from Oxford where she lived with her new husband, a doctor, and she had missed him the day before. He wondered if she had felt like this when she had run off with Arthur Holt. Holt's diaries showed him to be a man of no conscience, who had felt he was entitled to do what pleased him, and he seemed contemptuous that Marina had agonized about breaking up his first marriage. Charles would have liked to confide in Marina. He thought he would confide in almost anybody, given the chance, for he had never felt more wretched.

He looked down and saw that he had been doodling on his memo pad. He had been drawing arrows going in all directions; whether they were vectors of confusion or a general expression of hostility, he did not know. With a sigh, he put his pencil down and looked again out of the window. To his surprise, he saw a primly dressed black woman coming up the garden path with a little boy in tow. He ducked, thinking this might be some new onslaught from the Jehovah's Witnesses, who had recently been targeting the area, but she had caught his eye. Charles was sour on religious enthusiasm and he shook his head. She beckoned again, however, with enough urgency to make him go for the door. She'd have a job to save his soul. He would send her off with an impenetrable Catholic defence and then he would ring Cat. Rosamund would have had the woman in to tea.

Whatever her mission, she stood on the threshold, crisp and authoritative. 'Yes?' Charles asked curtly.

The woman eyed him from head to toe. With one hand, she clutched her charge close to her skirts; in the other she held a furled umbrella. Altogether, she had a stately appearance and Charles's hand went to his rumpled hair. 'Is Mrs Simon at home?' she asked, rather as one would address a butler. She was an American.

'I am afraid she is not,' Charles replied.

She advanced a foot. Charles fingered the latch. 'When do you expect her?'

'I'm not sure,' he said frowning.

'My name,' said the woman, 'is Romola Cardew, and this is my nephew Paolo. I met Mrs Simon at her cousin's on Monday.' She paused for a moment. 'It is of some importance.'

'Oh, God!' he cried. He had forgotten about Missy in all of his analytic ravellings. 'You mean Missy?'

The woman nodded. 'Are you Rosamund's husband?' she asked.

'Yes. Is Missy with her?'

'I think I had better come in.' Her swingeing look disgraced Charles. 'That is, if you don't mind.'

'I'm sorry,' he said.

Romola and Paolo stepped into the hall; the child wiped his feet on the mat, even though it had not been raining.

'Say "How do you do?" to Mr Simon,' his aunt instructed.

The little boy did as he was told and beamed an engaging smile at Charles.

'Has something happened to Rosamund?'

'Not that I know of,' said Romola. 'It is Missy who concerns me more at the moment.'

He was at once relieved and confused. He found the crisply buttoned woman and her charge incongruous with the hippie Missy. 'Will you have some tea?' He opened the drawing-room door. 'Come and sit down.'

'I won't put you to the trouble of getting us tea,' Romola said disdainfully, 'but perhaps we could talk for a moment.'

'May I take your umbrella?'

She spied the Chinese umbrella stand in the hall, and stabbed the instrument into the tall vase. 'Thank you,' she said, as if he were improving. She swept into the drawing-room and he motioned helplessly for her to sit. She perched with the child, angular on the sofa's edge.

'I'm sorry,' he repeated, not knowing quite what for.

'It's all right. We're used to it,' she replied with asperity.

He realized that he had been rude to her at the door. 'Sherry, perhaps? Would you like a drink?' He flushed. He had made a large assumption about her from the colour of her skin. He could not imagine anyone less like a Jehovah's Witness.

'That would be nice. You see, Missy has dematerialized.'

Charles's eyebrows shot straight up. 'Oh, I see,' he said. He experienced a great sinking of heart. He went to the drinks tray and fumbled with a bottle of Manzanilla. No, he could not see Rosamund going off to live in a commune. He remembered Missy's beads and feathers, her ashram outlook. But the ominous expression in Romola's eyes unnerved him. 'I . . . uh . . .'

'What does "dematerialized" mean?' the child asked. He leaned into his aunt and looked up at her.

'I say! Would you like a lemonade?' Charles asked Paolo heartily.

The boy nodded shyly. ' "Yes, please",' said Romola, nudging him. She looked relieved that he had acknowledged the constraint imposed upon them both by the child.

'Look,' he said, suddenly remembering it, 'we have a playroom full of toys downstairs. Come with me and I'll get you a drink and we'll open it up.' It seemed emblematic to him, suddenly, that they had never cleared this room, but had left it as it always was. Charles gleaned from Romola that this had been a good idea. She seemed in the habit of sending heavy messages with her eyes.

Paolo trotted after him into the hall and they descended. 'It's a little scary,' Charles said.

'It's not scary,' said the child. 'I'm not scared of anything.'

In mid-afternoon, the shadows were sharpened and the high, deserted kitchen felt forlorn and abandoned. Charles switched on all the lights and opened the old playroom door where there was a rocking-horse and a box of Lego on a small table surrounded with diminutive chairs.

'I'm afraid of lots of things,' Charles said to Paolo. Rosamund could not have run away with Missy, could she? The foreboding that seized him was all the more potent because it was irrational.

'Wow!' said Paolo at the rocking-horse. 'May I ride him?'

Charles got lemonade from the larder and a glass from the cupboard. He dusted down the horse and tested it with a heavy palm to make sure it was not broken. He did everything in a slow, deliberate manner, as if to break a spell. 'We'll be upstairs if you want us,' he said, but Paolo, in transports over the rocking-horse, was urging it on with a jockey's expertise.

'Now,' said Charles, as he entered the drawing-room once more. 'What, indeed, do you mean by "dematerialized"? As it happens, my wife has vanished too.'

'What!' Romola put the small glass carefully down on the table. 'With Missy?'

'That is rather what I wanted you to tell me.'

'I have no idea! It simply crossed my mind that she might have come here, and that is why I came. Has she *been* here? That's the question now.'

Charles shook his head. 'I don't know. I don't think so. She did, however, leave a message on the answering machine. It must have been Tuesday or Wednesday, but she left no number.' He looked down. 'I am afraid my wife and I have been estranged recently. I thought she had left me.'

Romola sized him up as if she knew whose fault this was. 'What did Missy say?' she asked abruptly. 'Now, I'm sorry,' she added. 'You see, I'm very worried.' Their eyes engaged.

'So am I. Missy wanted to know if Rosamund had considered something. Maybe they planned a trip. She said she was anxious to hear from her. You see, I met Missy only once . . .'

'But once was enough, eh?'

He forbore to answer.

She gave a sharp laugh. 'Don't worry. I understand. I do it all for Tom, you know. Or for his own good!'

'Tom?'

'People are inclined to think,' said Romola, 'because I am black and Tom is white that I am Paolo's nurse. In fact, I am more in the way of being Missy's. Tom is her husband, my ex-stepfather, and a very wealthy man. He is Paolo's grandfather. The situation is extremely complicated, partly because my sister, her child and a very large sum of money are involved. Another complication has to do with Missy herself, and yet another has to do with my own feelings. See?'

Was this woman Missy's minder? Charles was suddenly alert to the dangers of her needing one. 'Not really,' he answered.

Romola looked at him shrewdly for a moment. Perhaps she took pity on his confusion, but she seemed to thaw a little. 'I suppose all of this is a little deep-end and up-front especially if you are English, which of course you can't help. And I guess my association with Missy has made me blunt. She has a coarsening effect. But believe it or not, I liked her when first she married Tom and I felt sorry for her. She seemed original, to say the least. I got the impression that she was a glamorous woman of the world taking early retirement, and I sort of assumed she'd been pushed around a lot by men. It's difficult to explain about Tom. I have very mixed feelings about him, but taking in waifs and strays is his hobby and there's no stopping him. His other hobby is horses and he met Missy in France at the races. It thrilled him she was a Kentuckian. Her pioneer blood exercised him a lot.' Romola gave an ironic smile. 'He has a romantic notion about the wilderness, and I believe Missy exemplifies this to him. He thinks she's a "wild thing", and he always says if he kept her indoors she'd tear him to pieces, which I would say is a fairly accurate reading of the situation.' Romola gave a fastidious shudder. 'To make a long story short, it soon began to transpire that Missy had little "turns", and so he lets her wander. Up to a point. That point has now been reached.'

Perhaps it was the surreal quality of the story, perhaps it was the forceful way in which Romola told it that made the unease in Charles spread and deepen. The tack she had taken made all sorts of assumptions about what he knew. ' "Turns",' he said, bewildered.

'You must understand that it is important for Missy to keep her agreements,' Romola continued. 'These little contracts make our lives much more agreeable. The way it goes is this: she can go where she likes when the mood strikes her as long as she informs Tom or me of her geographical location . . . you know, in a rough sort of way. It would not be good enough, for instance, to say "Scandinavia", or in fact "Norway", but "Oslo" would do. She was in Wyoming last year and had a great time raising hell, but nothing got broken – not crockery, not laws, not heads – and she came back just fine. Sometimes she'll call up from a place – New York City, Acapulco – and that's all right too. This time, however, she has been missing for two days with no word and no call . . . and whatever was said on Monday between your wife and Missy sure set her off. She was brooding and thrashing and giving me all sorts of lip.'

'Are you trying to tell me that Missy is insane? Are you a psychiatric nurse?' A little shiver ran through Charles.

' "Not quite" is the answer to both of those questions,' Romola said. 'But I am not the servant that Missy takes me for! My qualification is, in fact, in psychology, but as it happens, I am a sculptor. Tom lends me a barn. I lend him a hand. I've had an exhibition in SoHo, you know,' she added as if he were bound to disbelieve her. She looked down at her hands, which were strong and supple. 'I am sorry to be so defensive. I can't tell you what an invidious position this puts me in.'

Charles could see that it did. 'Can't you . . . ?'

'Leave? Even if I were not frightened for Paolo, I could hardly take to my heels and let her plant the flag in my sister's birthright. Frankly, it has become a contest: her or me. Pioneer blood, indeed she may have, but we go deeper.'

He suddenly saw her splendidly unfurled, a banner on her own. They sipped at their sherry. 'I'm not sure it ever did Rozzy much good,' he said. 'Maybe so. Who knows?'

'Your wife's all right,' Romola said after a moment's thought. 'I liked her.'

'Look, Ms Cardew, don't you think we could get to the bottom of this in some way if we put our heads together? I can't tell you how it upsets me to think that she has run off with Missy.'

'It would bother me,' said Romola.

'My wife did leave a note, and she did not mention Missy, but neither did she say where she was going. Can you remember what was said on Monday . . . anything that might prove a clue?'

Romola yielded her back to the sofa and looked at Charles for a while in an opaque way which was not unsympathetic. 'I only wish I did know what they were talking about. I took Paolo to the zoo while they were having lunch. Missy was showing off like hell, and I didn't think I could stand that. She's kind of trashy, you know? When I came back, I heard her saying something about a niece, then something about a cousin. I must say, I thought she was up to something, because she clammed right up when I walked into the room, but I have literally no idea what they were talking about. Your wife looked quite upset. In fact, she used my return to beat a hasty retreat, I thought . . . Oh, I remember Missy giving her something. It looked like a cheque – but it was not a happy atmosphere at all.'

'Niece?' Charles said. 'We have only one niece, Xenia, and she is Greek. Mind you, she stays with us often because she is at school in England. In fact, she is coming here at the end of the week. I suppose Rosamund could have been using this as an excuse not to see Missy again, if she was as uncomfortable as you say.'

'No, she told Missy . . . that's right – like the answering-machine message – that she would consider something, and she asked us to lunch, Paolo and me as well.'

Charles realized what this must mean: if Rosamund hadn't had the intention of going away on Sunday, it appeared that on Monday, when Romola had seen her, she had not changed her mind. He looked up, surprised to see open pity on Romola's face. He must look in a bad way. He was in a bad way. 'You say Rosamund was upset? I don't want to demonize Missy or lay too much at her door, but I have to tell you that the last time she was here, my wife went into a very serious decline. In fact, she had a nervous breakdown. To be fair, there is no evidence that Missy caused it, but you yourself must know that they are a rather unstable family . . .'

'Well, you know what they say back home. They say that one of those Buchanans fired that house. Was that your wife's?'

Charles was staggered. 'No! I mean, yes, it was her house, and her parents' too! Was it Missy?'

'Oh, she must have been only a teenager! Her father was a bit of sleaze, though, and there was always some degeneracy on the fringes of that family. When you think how Missy gives herself such airs! . . . Look, I'm sorry I spoke. It's just nasty gossip. It makes me realize how much I've come to hate Missy. Truly, I did not know that it had anything directly to do with Rosamund.'

Charles was on the verge of calling Interpol. Had Missy told Rosamund something about the fire? Their fathers had been brothers, so one had been the uncle of the other, which gave both of them the status of 'niece'. And Missy and Rosamund, of course, were cousins. 'Could she have *said* something about the fire, though?'

'Listen, Missy would say anything to gain her own ends, and sometimes they are obscure! Because, you see, as for causing trouble, she has come near to destroying us all with her craft and her downright lies! I would put absolutely nothing past her, and the word "fair" is in a category she does not recognize. She has come between Tom and his daughter, and one day, she'll get between Tom and Paolo! You wait and see. She's either too old or too vain to have any children of her own, but bless me if she would not adopt a baby to push us all out of Tom's affections and Paolo, in particular, from his will!' Romola looked at her fingernails. 'Do you think that sounds crass? In a manner of speaking, my family were landowners in the area long before any of them.'

'I'm afraid I'm still with the fire. You see, I always thought . . . my wife always . . . Oh, she used to be very mysterious about it. It's come between us in an odd way.' He looked up at the direct, unusual young woman with her Mary Poppins collar and her eagle eye. 'Actually, it was my impression that it was Missy who had a profound respect for money. I was remembering it only last night. She used to be a hippie, did you know that? But . . .'

'You counted the spoons when she was gone? She liked this place, I guess.' Romola looked expressively around the drawing-room. 'Love Tom as I do, his taste is all in his mouth, whereas, low-down as Missy is, she has an exact knowledge. Funny to think she was a hippie, but I suppose it was a caterpillar stage. I have a theory she was also a jailbird, though I can't prove it.'

'In for what?' Charles asked with sudden attention.

'I said, I don't know. I only imagine the most unpleasant things about her. All I do know is that there is something in her past. She never rests, she is always alert. And either she has told Tom an edited version of her story or she has told him nothing at all. She does not think she needs to, he is so besotted!'

'Do you think this "past" might involve Rozzy at some level?' This seemed ridiculous, but Charles was combing the sand for clues.

Romola sighed. 'She wheedled her way on to this trip, and as in my experience she does nothing without an ulterior motive, it may well have to do with your wife. Then again, who knows? It could be anybody over here, because she makes a big deal about having "lived abroad". But the worst of it for me is that she's given me the slip and that is probably because she knows that Tom will do anything at all to get her back . . . even if that means getting rid of me.' Romola said this in a perfectly even tone. She finished her sherry and put the glass on the table. And then, in a moment, as in the reeling crash of a sudden storm, she began to weep. She threw her head into her hands and sobbed.

'Oh, dear!' said Charles, 'Oh, dear!' He began not to like the sound of this 'Tom' at all. She seemed to be emotionally shackled to the man, some crypto-racist Lear, who might throw his stepdaughter out on a whim. It was obvious that she loved Kavanagh but it suddenly seemed odious to Charles that she lived in a fealty of dread to his caprices. 'Look, we'll find her! We'll find Missy. I'll help you if you like and in any way you like. And if she's got Rosamund, maybe you can help me.' He wrung his hands. He hated to see women cry.

Romola extracted a handkerchief from her sleeve and miserably blew her nose. 'You're not to think ill of Tom,' she said. 'It's her.'

Charles considered this, but said nothing. 'Look,' he said at last, 'have another drink. I tell you, I need one.'

Sadly, Romola shook her head. 'I must check on Paolo. I must get back,' she said, but she sat still and kneaded her handkerchief.

When the telephone rang, they both started with nerves. She looked up at him wildly. 'Do you think . . . ?'

'Maybe,' he said and he strode to the hall to answer it, motioning her to follow.

From downstairs in the playroom, they could hear the child rocking on the horse. He crooned something to himself in a monotone.

On edge, Charles picked up the receiver. His shoulders sagged at the voice of his sister Catherine.

'Charles?' she asked, 'I'm surprised you're there. May I speak with Rosamund?'

Charles glanced at Romola and shook his head. 'Rosamund is not here. Listen, Cat, something has come up. I was going to ring you myself later on.'

'I know,' she answered drily.

It suddenly occurred to Charles that Rosamund might have gone to Greece. He had not even thought to check if her passport was missing. 'She's not with you?'

'With me? Why should she be with me?'

'Cat, I haven't seen Roz for days. I'm beginning to worry. I thought with Xenia about to arrive here, you really ought to know. You said you did "know" and that confused me.'

'Huh!' said Catherine, 'I know all about your scandal. That's what I meant.'

'Oh, thanks for the sympathy! It's been a nightmare.' Charles had been close to his sister in childhood, but slowly she seemed to have drifted away from everyone in the family. 'Well, why did you ring?' he snapped. 'Maybe I can help *you*?'

'It's really no matter, I suppose,' Catherine said, bridling. 'I simply wanted to check on something. A woman who called herself Rosamund's cousin turned up here yesterday – one Melissa Kavanagh – and I simply wanted to know – '

'What!' Charles wildly signalled to Romola, who was leaning in a defeated manner against the door jamb. 'What did you say? Missy

Kavanagh is in Chios?' He and Romola galvanized into one unified expression of amazement. 'It's my sister . . . in *Greece*!' he hissed, cupping his hand over the receiver.

'Oh, my God!' Romola cried. 'Greece?'

Catherine said, 'Charles, what do you know about this?'

'Catherine, I have a woman here who has just come to tell me that Missy has disappeared from London. She is very concerned to know her whereabouts.' Romola was grappling for the receiver, but Charles went on. 'Tell me, did she mention that she had been with Rosamund or anything like that?'

He made pleading gestures at Romola, who started to pace the hall.

'Charles, is there anything wrong?' Catherine's voice sounded strained with fear.

'Tell me, Cat!'

'Well, I would hardly have asked to speak with her if I had thought she was with the woman. I just wanted to check something. You know how paranoid Theo can get, and I suppose it's contagious. The thing is that Xenia went off to Çeşme this morning on a shopping trip with this Mrs Kavanagh. I had objected to her going alone but it did seem unreasonable to make a fuss about her going with Rosamund's cousin. It's stupid of me to worry. After all, I can't do anything about it now, but I started to wonder if she really was Rosamund's cousin, you know. She told me that Rosamund had sent her to me because of the house. Charles, you're making me very afraid.'

'My niece is in Turkey with Missy,' Charles whispered to Romola, guarding the mouthpiece with his hand. 'The niece! You overheard them talking about our niece!'

Romola stood still. 'Find out more,' she said.

'Look, Cat, I'm sure there is nothing to worry about. Missy is actually Rosamund's cousin. You forget, you met her once. She was here . . . that hippie who came to Christmas dinner.'

'This is no hippie, Charles!'

'But it's the same woman. I've established that. It turns out she's married an American millionaire . . .'

Romola made a face and shook her head. 'She sure did that!'

'Is his name Tom?'

'That's the one.'

'Then why are they looking for the woman in London when she told me she was meeting her husband in Constantinople?' Catherine's voice was charged with fear. 'And why did she not remind me that we had met before?'

Charles made a decision not to put Romola on the telephone. He did not want his highly strung sister to hear the character sketch of Missy that Romola was likely to give. On the pad by the phone, he scribbled a message: 'Is Tom going to Turkey?' Romola shook her head. 'Cat, Cat, I'm certain this is Missy Kavanagh. I have just heard that Rosamund had lunch with her on Monday, and she might well have suggested that her cousin call on you if she were travelling through the area. As far as I can make out, this Missy has an eccentric habit of taking off on her own from time to time. In fact, her family is quite used to it. Fits in with the former lifestyle, doesn't it? But what on earth it has to do with Xenia, I cannot imagine. You go to Çeşme yourself from time to time, and Xenia knows it well. It's only five miles away from Chios, and she'll be back on the evening boat, you'll see. Let's talk again when she arrives. She may have news of Rosamund. Shall I ring you at nine your time? By then, Xenia will be tucked up safe and sound and you will feel better.' Charles had never improvised a soothing tone more fully. What had possessed Cat?

'Charles,' Catherine said in a subdued tone, 'I'm sorry I was beastly . . . about your marital problems, I mean.' She paused. 'It isn't easy for any of us. If I've made a mistake in letting Xenia go off with this woman, then Theo will – '

'You can't keep her wrapped in cotton wool. She is of age, you know, and I'm sure everything will be all right.'

His sister exhausted him; deceit exhausted him. In his family anything unpleasant always had to be denied. To do otherwise was to commit a solecism of the highest order. It was quite true that Theo had a morbid fear of kidnappers. Catherine had always objected to this, saying they would suffocate the child if she were not allowed to lead a normal life. This had been a running quarrel between them, and though fundamentally Charles was on his sister's side, he did think it might have been more politic in this instance to fortify Theo's position. She could even have appealed to it with Xenia. By unwritten Simon law, however, he was quite unable to say, or even hint at any of this, and so he put down the telephone feeling drained. He shook his head, trying to dislodge his apprehension about Missy. The woman was simply barmy – a misfit who had found a soft billet with an American plutocrat. She would hardly threaten her position by leading his niece into trouble. 'Did you catch all of that?' he asked Romola.

She moved from her post back into the drawing-room. She had a wonderful carriage; she glided, lost in thought.

'I'm sorry, I didn't dare give you the telephone. My sister was very overwrought,' he continued.

'No,' she said, waving it away, 'I could see that. I'm simply feeling my way through it. You say that Missy claims she is on her way to meet Tom in Turkey?'

'That's what my sister said.'

'Well, it won't be the first lie she's told. I gathered that she had been with your sister's family in a place called Chios?' She paused. 'You see, that rings a bell with me. It was something she once said . . . some influence she had there, perhaps . . . only I cannot remember what it was.'

IX

Missy and Xenia had caught the bus to Istanbul by a whisker, having made the journey from Çeşme to İzmir in a harrowing twenty-minute ride. Although Missy had styled herself as a world traveller, Xenia had not associated her with speed and efficiency. On the boat from Chios early that morning, however, her air of mandarin vagabondage had given way to hustle. Missy had flourished maps and schedules with the competence of a seasoned campaigner. She had worked out a route, she said, just in case Xenia decided to come. And of course, as everybody knew, the Varan bus was the only real way to see Turkey. As she did not want to spend the night in İzmir, the only option was to catch the damn thing before it left at 9.30. So, the moment the boat had docked, Missy had muscled her way with Xenia through the queue of straggling Greeks, Turks and tourists, fixed the customs officer with a charming smile, and had marched straight through to the taxi rank where she surveyed the cars on offer as if she were royalty in a paddock.

'That one!' she said to Xenia, pointing out a white Mercedes. 'Come on, move it!' And she had propelled the panting girl forward. In a Babel of Graeco-Turkish-English, she offered the astonished driver a wad of hard currency, demanding that they be delivered at the Varan depot in time for the Istanbul bus. Xenia noticed that she was wearing a large sapphire ring. Whether this, the money or her tone of command had impressed the driver, Xenia could not tell. 'Drive like hell!' Missy had said. 'Step on it!' She turned to Xenia with a grin. 'I've always wanted to say that to someone,' she said. They settled in the vinyl-coated back seat. 'We'll make it. You'll see. If not, we'll get the driver to take us all the way to Istanbul.' Having said this, she closed her eyes with an almost exultant air of unconcern as the taxi shot forward.

Xenia had never met anyone like her. She was bewildered by the speed at which everything was happening. Before she knew it, the white Mercedes had left the familiar Turkish port with its mellow old fortress and had plunged north into the interior, a desolate scrubland which she had never seen before. She reminded herself once again that this had been her own decision. Missy had been very firm on that score – that she,

Xenia, should make an adult choice. But somehow, with the car going so fast, she felt the situation leave her hands like an insecurely held balloon. Of course, she had to hear Missy's side of the story, and of course she was planning to go for only a week, if that. Still, now she was actually on her way, she felt awed by the enormity of what she was doing, and not a little frightened by the woman beside her. It was one thing to consider such a truancy from the perspective of good old Çeşme, but quite a different matter to hurtle into the bleak and threatening cosmos of Islam, the territory of the ancient enemy. Even the mustachioed driver looked like a bandit as he gripped the wheel. Suppose he and Missy were going to use chloroform and ask her father for ransom? Xenia dismissed this as a childish response to chauvinistic horror stories. What was more, she had ample proof that Missy was her mother, proof that condemned her father as a liar. And if Missy were bent on kidnap, why would she have gone to such lengths to ensure that Xenia brought her British passport and her credit card? She could buy a ticket out of this any time she liked! If things really went badly, she could always fly directly to London and take sanctuary with Rosamund, who would explain everything to everyone . . . or so she hoped. Nevertheless, she found herself surreptitiously rummaging for the passport in her smart rucksack, just to make sure she really had it. She loved this pouchy accessory, which was usually a tangle of books and make-up and forgotten earrings. It made her feel like a proper student, not a sixth-former, and she had bought it in a French shop in South Ken. The bag comforted her. There it was, a badge of independence, unchanging in the midst of chaos. Of course, the passport was there and a letter too, from her best friend Sarah. Xenia touched it for luck. Sarah would be all ears for this story, she thought, and then it struck her that it was not exactly the sort of story one told . . . not lightly, anyway. Perhaps not at all. She tried to shake off the implications of what it might mean to bear so weighty a secret. She was tired enough from bearing one already. No, she could handle this. It was time the truth was out and very soon it would be.

Xenia stole another look at Missy, testing her again for reality. She had an urge to ask her to produce the American birth certificate again, the one she said she had obtained on application to the Embassy in Athens just before the adoption had taken place. It had looked official enough, typed, signed and sealed on a green rectangle of paper. However, she thought better of it. More absolute in its way was the defining resemblance between them, oddly more convincing for its subtlety. The realization had struck Xenia like an optical illusion where one saw either a white chalice or two black faces, depending. Once the faces had been pointed out, there was no going back to the chalice. Once Missy Kavanagh had revealed herself, there was no getting away from it. Everything made a different kind of sense now in Xenia's new perception of her own image. Her eyes, her brow, her jaw . . . even her hair verified the double helix that she and Missy shared: one body, one blood.

All the same, Xenia was not sure she had taken it all in. Only a simple action on her part had resulted in all of this. Not twenty-four hours ago, she had been having lunch in the dining-room at home with her mother (mother?) and this stranger. The conversation had been strained, and would have died altogether if Mrs Kavanagh had not kept up her end with diverting anecdotes of travel, fond memories of Greece from her distant past. The irony was that if her mother had not been very nearly rude, and if Xenia had not been mortified by this, she would not be in the taxi now.

Although there did seem a curious inevitability in it all, Xenia did not know how this would have come about if she had not offered to show Mrs Kavanagh around the orange groves before she left, in response to her mother's coldness to a stranger. What was said of strangers? In the stranger one saw Christ, or taken at its weakest possible interpretation, an angel. In fact, the oldest and most valuable icon in the house, admired by Mrs Kavanagh and presiding over the very dining-room table of which Xenia's mother was so proud, depicted Abraham entertaining the Holy Trinity in disguise. Xenia hated her mother's snobbishness, her clannishness. She had felt instinctively that her mother shuddered at Mrs Kavanagh's high, wide and handsome manner. It infuriated her that her family thought itself so special! What was more, the poor woman was a close relative of Rosamund's, and for that reason alone should have been treated with respect, even if she had been a complete outcast! This was Xenia's ideal, in any case. Shamed by her mother's silence, her iciness, Xenia had hotly volunteered a guided tour. And now, nothing would ever be the same.

Xenia inwardly upbraided herself for the cliché. Her English teacher went at such banalities with an exterminator's ruthlessness. The truth of the matter was that at one moment she had been sauntering along the pergola with Mrs Kavanagh in the assumption of one reality, and in the next moment she had been rendered incapable of ever making an assumption about reality again.

There was a belvedere halfway down the vine-covered walk. It had benches in it, and from it there was an attractive view of the house. Mrs Kavanagh had wanted to take more photographs, and it had been in this wish that Xenia's mother had refused to oblige her guest. 'Why don't you take some pictures here?' Xenia had asked with a compensating graciousness.

'Actually, honey, I really didn't come here to take any old pictures, though I admit it is a very pretty sight. I might as well take the bull by the horns and come straight to the point. I came here to see you.'

'What do you mean?' Had Xenia's scalp prickled or was this the evidence of afterthought?

The visitor had motioned towards an old stone bench, too mossy for her fine skirt. 'Come sit by me,' she had said nevertheless. 'I have something to tell you.'

There actually had been a warning, had there not? There must have been some perceptible foretoken, because her stomach had gone cold and her limbs had felt heavy.

'Do you know who I am?' Mrs Kavanagh had asked in a light but confiding tone. 'Do you have the teeniest, weeniest idea of who I might be?'

There had been no way of keeping her eyes away from that face with its especially clear green eyes. The arch voice had heightened Mrs Kavanagh's singularity, for it seemed quite at odds with an intensity that kept Xenia from moving or speaking.

'You don't know, do you?' the woman had continued. 'How to tell? What to say?' She shrugged. 'Well, I haven't got time to beat around the bush. I am in and out of this place before you can say "Jack Robinson", and that is for a reason that will unfold. You are my daughter.'

'What?' Mrs Kavanagh's voice had connected with the half-heard insinuations of dreams. 'What did you say?'

'Sorry to be so blunt, but I am your mother. It's true. I've got about five minutes to convince you, and you can take it or leave it. Only remember, I have come a very long way and have taken a very long shot.'

Xenia was sickened, immobile. 'No!'

'Look, this is a big risk for me!' the woman added in a faintly aggrieved tone. 'You have no idea how big. You want me to prove it? I can prove it. If you want to run into the house and tell Mrs Theo Phocas, then run in and tell her, and I'll be right on out of here. But I have been watching you every second since you first came in that gate, and I sort of have the feeling I can count on you. All I can tell you is that this is your only chance to hear me out, and I think you should take it.' Mrs Kavanagh pulled out a packet of Marlboro cigarettes and a Zippo lighter. 'You smoke?'

Xenia did . . . illicitly.

The woman lit up for both of them, then gave Xenia a cigarette. 'Stressful, isn't it?' she said, taking a drag.

'You are my mother?' Xenia asked in a tone of disbelief. 'I don't think you can be. You see, my mother is dead.' At this, Xenia started to tremble. As a child, she had had long colloquies with her dead mother, imaginative in the lonely nights, and then by imperceptible degrees, she had come to doubt the story.

'Is that what he told you?' Mrs Kavanagh gave an incredulous hoot. 'I guess he wished I was.'

Xenia sucked at the cigarette. Her hand shook so much that the ash fell in her lap. 'I don't think I believe you,' she said, but she looked up at the strange woman whose gaze bored into her with unflinching directness.

'That's as may be,' Missy shrugged, 'but it doesn't alter facts. Look at you! You're the spitting image. I'm no more dead than you are.'

Xenia struggled for words, her chest heavy with tears and confusion. 'My father . . .' she gasped.

Mrs Kavanagh tossed her head. 'You know that much, don't you? It would not be in his nature to suppress that particular bit of information for long!'

Xenia nodded slowly. On her thirteenth birthday, two weeks before she first went off to St Winifred's, her father had told her that she was his natural child. For some reason, he had seemed to think that this knowledge would comfort her, and although in one way it had, it had shocked her deeply too. He had sworn her to secrecy, and her way of keeping the pledge was, for the most part, to weaken the bond with denial. Now she was not so sure that this had been a good idea. She should have quizzed him about her other parent, the cardboard Albanian, even though he had reasserted at the time that the woman was no longer living. She had died a penitent, he said, a saint.

'Your father and I met at Rosamund's,' Mrs Kavanagh continued. 'Strange that Mrs Theo Phocas does not remember the incident – or me. The following week, I was in Athens, and seven months later you were born in Kifissia, a little premature, but healthy enough, I dare say. You have a moon-shaped birthmark and an "outy" navel.'

'Rosamund told you that!' It was not so much a cry of protest as of defeat. The woman's conviction was in itself hypnotic, horrifying in that it almost certainly conveyed the truth.

'Why should she?' Missy asked simply.

Xenia had a sudden, violent urge to push Mrs Kavanagh off the bench. 'I don't know. She could have.'

With her cigarette dangling from her lips like some tough girl in an old movie, Missy fished around in her handbag. 'She knew nothing about this until the day before yesterday, but you can call her and check. Your father neatly suppressed every evidence but this.' She handed Xenia an envelope. 'I went to great trouble to get this. He never knew I had it.'

And there it was at last, the proof of her identity, official under the seal of the United States of America. Xenia gazed trancelike at the document, then back at Mrs Kavanagh. 'Oh,' she said weakly. There was no doubt about it. Her mind had no more room for manoeuvre.

'Do you believe me now?' The woman's eyes were animal proof of motherhood. For a split second, Xenia was terrified by the consummate wolfishness in them.

'I don't know what to say. I suppose I do believe you.'

'You'd better! You'd better believe it! And if you're ever inclined to doubt, you may as well know that I have never given up. Not for eighteen years . . . never, never, never. You see? I wanted you, you know, but he got you! If you knew what I had gone through just to get here, just to see you . . . if you knew what he would do to me if ever he found out, then you wouldn't need any ole birth certificate to tell you I'm your mother. You'd know and for sure.'

'What shall I call you?' Xenia found herself asking. It seemed a wholly irrelevant question. Her head felt numb and buzzing. The fumes from the Marlboro rose, suddenly acrid in her nostrils. She ground the cigarette out underfoot.

The woman put her head to one side and thought for a moment. ' "Missy", I guess. You can call me "Missy". Everybody else does – and "Mom" would be a bit too much. Yes, definitely too much for now. Anyway, you probably think of *her* as your mother.' She indicated the house with a jerk of her head.

A sudden, covert tenderness for Catherine crept into Xenia's heart. 'What does she know about this?' she asked sharply.

'Nothing! At least, not as far as I know. There were certain lengths *he* went to to prevent her from knowing. Now, I'm not saying she would have kicked you out of the house or refused to bring you up if she'd found out. All I'm saying is that he wouldn't take the risk. You follow me?'

Before she knew the ache had started, it had spread – a dull, cold feeling which was an acknowledgement of what had always lain between herself and 'Mrs Theo Phocas', as Missy had called her mother. Ever since her father had declared his paternity to her, Xenia had been a prey to fears that Catherine suspected the truth. Before that time, she had taken for granted that mothers in general maintained a strict control on their children's behaviour; afterwards, however, uneasy thoughts had cropped up in Xenia. The edge of a cross word was sharpened, the silence behind a closed door was more profound. But it had never reached so blunt a point as this. If Catherine had known the truth, would she have rejected Xenia? Would she have refused to have anything to do with her infant, illegitimate self? If given the choice, would she have returned her to Mrs Kavanagh? Perhaps she would have done that. Perhaps she would have attached a haughty note to Xenia's swaddling-clothes. For a fleeting moment, Xenia saw the face of Lady Simon in her mind's eye, Lady Simon, who watched them all with reptilian coldness. *You're bringing up his bastard*, the look seemed to say when trained on Catherine. Mummy. Is that why she got so cross at the old lady? Not because she guessed it was true, but because she hated the truth she guessed? Xenia was that truth.

'Well, that's water under the dam,' Missy said, breaking into Xenia's awful reverie. 'The point is what we do now. And there isn't any time for heavy breathing!'

Xenia looked around, startled. She thought she had taken it all rather well, and certainly without histrionics.

'Not to mince words, I'm going to Turkey tomorrow, and I want you to come with me.'

'Turkey? What? You want me to come to Turkey?'

'Don't look so bug-eyed, miss! Why not?'

Suddenly, the full force of the blast hit Xenia and she seemed to be floating with imponderances in a surreal calm. The house in front of her and the garden beyond her seemed to reel around the central point of the belvedere, as if she were flying with an improbable genie, who was so used to overturning the laws of the natural world that she took the resulting chaos as a matter of course. 'I can't just go with you to Turkey. They wouldn't let me!'

'Do they have to let you?' Missy asked with an air of indifference. 'You're eighteen and hardly a pauper, and I bet you have your own passport. If you want to come, why shouldn't you come? You don't have to tell them anything.'

'But . . .'

'Look, I'm not in the white slave trade, if that's what you're worried about. And I don't want anything out of it financially speaking either. I'm as rich as God, or at least as rich now as Theo Phocas! Come for a day, come for a week, come for two weeks, two months, ten years, if you like. As long as it is by your own free will, there is absolutely no way it won't work out just the way you want it to.'

'But they'll worry!' Xenia cried.

'So that's the cardinal sin . . . making them worry! That's it, is it? I'll bet it's nothing compared to what I've been through these eighteen years of hell. Let them worry! A day or two of worry won't kill them. You can call them from Istanbul. In fact, I'd like you to,' said Missy, pausing for a moment as if in some relish of the thought. 'But I cannot stress to you enough, Xenia, that this is my final offer and that is because it has to be. Your father arranged things in such a way that it is unsafe for me to stay in Greece . . . plus, my own domestic situation would make any further attempts to see you very difficult. It's now or never, pet. See?'

Xenia had no idea what to say. She had never crossed the road before without her parents fussing and fuming. Her one small act of disobedience had been to sneak out one night in Athens with her friends Anna and Eleni, and only then at 9 p.m. to giggle at the boys in Plataea Kolonaki. Her English St Winifred's friends had been amazed when she told them that she had been sent away to boarding-school for this reason. Even by Greek standards, she realized it was a bit draconian of her normally kind father. Almost paralysed, she looked at Missy. 'I can't! I can't! I . . . haven't the nerve.' It was a sudden, fearful admission that she knew she should not have made.

'Oh, yes you can!' said her mother, fixing her with the emphasis of each word. 'You are not a child any more, and you have the right to know me if you want to. In fact, you might even have legally applied to find out who I was if you hadn't been told I was dead! You can come with me if you want to. You can, Xenia. You can do whatever you like!'

Xenia looked away. 'I'm not sure.'

A moment passed in silence and Missy tapped her fingers on the bench. 'Right,' she said. 'I'll go. Don't bother to show me out. I think I can find my own way. It's a shame, but it is your decision. All I ask is that you tell no one until I have taken the boat to Çeşme tomorrow morning, then tell anyone you like. Can you do that?'

Xenia nodded, feeling wretched.

'I guess I have dreamed of this moment for so many years that I have let fantasy step in and take over.' She stood and brushed her lap. 'I could see us in Pandeli's in the Spice Bazaar eating cakes and peeking into the hubble-bubble shops. In my imagination, I have toured Beyazit with you and the tombs of the Sultans, and have looked at the emeralds in Topkapı Palace. Well, never mind. They say it's a good thing to face reality, and maybe it is. Maybe later, sugar plum, you'll remember this day and come to the reality of me. But, sure as hell, your Daddy'll never utter one kind word on my behalf. And how will you know? You never will.' She extended a hand, then impulsively clutched Xenia's hung head to her waist. 'Bye, honey. I'm glad you look well.' She released her.

Xenia looked up. 'Do you have any other children?' she found herself asking. It seemed important. Her voice was hoarse. It had moved her terribly that Mrs Kavanagh had wanted to give her cakes at Pandeli's.

'Ah, sadly no,' Mrs Kavanagh had said. 'You are the only chick and child. Remember before you ever go in for it, the lot of a mistress is not a happy one.'

'I can't stand this,' said Xenia. 'This is awful.'

'Well, sweetpea, it's up to you. I'll be in the Hotel Kyma, you know, the one on the front, and I will be on the boat at 8 a.m. If you change your mind, call me, or just be there. But if you do decide to come, bring your own money and you can be free to do as you like. Do you have a British or a Greek passport?'

'Both,' Xenia mumbled.

'Then bring the British one. And one more thing. I am trusting you not to tell a human soul. No one. Do you promise?'

'I promise,' Xenia had said, and she had watched transfixed by the sight of her mother as she had drifted up the pergola and vanished out of sight. As she had heard the jazzy red car starting outside the gate, a memory from childhood came to her, thick like nausea. She had asked her father if they could get special permission to visit Albania and put flowers on her mother's grave. Now things had opened up, she had been making clandestine plans to go on her own to Tirana, where her mother was supposed to be buried. She had even learned a few words of Albanian secretly. Greeks loathed Albanians, and any prejudice against them had always distressed Xenia immeasurably. What had Missy said? 'If you had known that I was alive, you might even have tried to find me.' Of course, she would have done! She would not have rested until she had found her!

From a part of Xenia that she barely understood came a cold trickle of rage, like a deathly current in the sea . . . and she knew that she would go with Mrs Kavanagh.

X

THE DAIMLER burrowed down the darkening lanes of Kampos like a heavy, old animal. Many of the roads were too narrow for the car, so it lumbered slowly along the accustomed, tortuous route to the Phocas house, its breadth sighing and scraping against the hedgerows. Nikos, the chauffeur, spoke no English. He had met Rosamund at the airport, his eyes eloquent with crisis. Now, she sat in isolating grandeur in the back, gnawed by anxiety. Her clamminess met with the smell of old leather, and produced a harsh, acrid scent.

Rosamund felt the pain of her position very strongly. She did not know what to expect from Catherine. She did not even know if Catherine wanted to see her. In fact, all she had to go on was the command of Theo himself, Theo who was not Theo any longer, but a fixed mask of rage.

Ironically enough, he had spent all yesterday with his lawyers, and had returned triumphant to the flat with the news that a letter was making its way to London, a letter that Missy could not possibly ignore. Rosamund had spent the day listlessly gazing at icons in the Byzantine Museum, giving them cursory appraisal as if they had emptied themselves of meaning and become mere abstractions. There seemed no virtue, no beauty in which she could cloak the starkness of her inner situation. She drifted past walls of lambent Nativities, Pantocrators and Crucifixions unable to find an intelligible clue to what she was experiencing. He was in love with Missy still. She was certain of it. Rosamund stared at an Elijah contemplating a raven from his cave. Unlike the prophet, who had been fed by carrion birds, Theo was fed upon, still victim of a passion he had renounced. Or was Rosamund his victim? It was unclear, she thought, who was dining on whom. Suddenly she wondered whether Missy was subject to the same appetites as everyone else. Did she even have feelings? For some reason, Rosamund suddenly remembered Missy at her parents' funeral, dressed to the nines in black. Had Missy really hummed a little tune on the way back from the cemetery? Rosamund wondered how low could she sink. Her memory must be playing tricks on her. She kept finding excuses for Theo now she knew the worst.

On her return to the flat, she had felt stifled and exhausted. In view of the way she was now compromised, she thought of booking her ticket back to London. Rather than spend another evening with Theo, she should simply go home, her duty having been done. She reached for the telephone, then found she hadn't the energy to pick up the receiver. Maybe she would take a little holiday, visit an island she had never seen. Maybe she would make her way to Delos and see some classical remains, or make the voyage to Patmos. Later, she would ring the children and explain that she had had to get away.

When Theo finally returned to the flat, gloating at the way he was going to pay Missy out, her misery reached its nadir. She opened her mouth to speak, but she had not known what to say to him. He was so flushed with success, so expansive. Could he take her out to dinner now that it was all dealt with? Rosamund wanted to be finished with him, but she could not look at him and tell herself she was. She found herself agreeing and even wondered what she would wear.

When the news had come, Rosamund had been in the shower, and even through the powerful jet she had heard his sharp cry of fury. She had dried herself and dressed quickly. She had stood in the hall, not knowing what to do as the force of his rage crashed down the telephone. He had been yelling at someone in Greek. She had gone to the door of his study and had stood there. He briefly acknowledged her. 'Missy has taken Xenia. Catherine let her into the house,' he said, picking up the phone again and dialling. She was shocked, appalled. She was there. What were friends for? Could he give her the details? What had happened? Apart from telling her that Xenia had not returned from her trip to Çeşme, he had told her little else. She had sat on the sofa all evening long, virtually invisible to him as he gripped the telephone to his chest, shouting down the receiver, barking orders to nameless subordinates.

Rosamund gathered her skirts around her in the grand old car and smoothed them. If ever she had doubted the weight and substance of Theo's power, she felt now the force of its reality. He had spent the night waking up ministers, calling in favours as he instigated a search for Xenia at the highest level. He was not only willing, but able, it seemed, to unleash thunderbolts. What was more, his words of the night before had not been rhetorical. He might be wretchedly bound to Missy, but he intended lightning to strike her with lethal precision. Rosamund could barely come to terms with her hurt and bewilderment. Did he think this was all her fault? He had been so coldly, so exactly indifferent to her that anyone might have thought she had planned the whole thing. She had even gone to bed without her supper, as if she had been a child.

The following day, she had been relieved that he had decided to dispatch her to Chios. He had curtly informed her that if she wanted to be of use, she would be better employed in supporting Catherine than in getting underfoot in Athens. Not that he had put it quite this way, but his tone had conveyed it. Rosamund still could not believe that this was really Theo speaking to her. His outrage seemed to scythe away anything in its path, and she herself was too wretched to consider an alternative plan. But now, as the car rounded the corner and pulled to a stately halt before the stately home with its ducal gates, she realized that she should have run in the opposite direction. Although Catherine had been informed of her arrival, Rosamund was not at all sure of a welcome. And what was worse, Theo had gone to great pains to remind her of her oath. Under no circumstances at all was she to reveal the true nature of Missy's relationship with Xenia. Rosamund was aghast.

Nikos handed her out of the car and collected her luggage. The house faced east, and its façade was sunk now in the umbrous gloom of evening. Behind it, the setting sun made points of the roof glow so that something like a nimbus shone, lending the whole scene a charmed light. Theo had threatened to disinherit Xenia if Rosamund betrayed the secret of her origins to Catherine, and if he discovered that Xenia had gone willingly with Missy, he might disinherit her anyway. There had been no way of getting through to Theo. He had roared like a blinded animal at the meekest suggestion that the truth was bound to come out. Rosamund felt for the place where she had loved Theo. It was numb. Was it empty? All she knew now was the slow, creeping vastness of her involvement.

She shrugged this thought off. In the airport that afternoon, while she had waited for her delayed flight to Chios, she had remembered Xenia's only other act of insubordination to the unspoken rule of her father's will. To Western eyes, it had been a trivial thing, meriting only a scolding. When she had been twelve years old, Xenia had sneaked out of the flat in Athens with two of her friends, and had joined the evening promenade in the Plataea Kolonaki. They had been three little maids from school, full of naughtiness. In the make-up, gear and clompy shoes they had bought clandestinely, they had thought themselves enormously stylish. Their faces top-heavy with lipstick and mascara, they had stood in a nervous, giggly huddle and watched the boys. Around 9 p.m. each evening the cafés were thronged with young people whose vicious tendency it was to drink iced coffee – the ubiquitous *frappé*. Sometimes Fanta came into it, and now and then a small can of lager. At any rate, the girls were discovered by a passing neighbour, and Theo had been beside himself. Rosamund shuddered slightly at the disturbing sense his reaction now made. Missy, when young, would have made talented contribution to the Greek evening *volta*. Theo would have seen in Xenia her mother . . . strutting her stuff.

Rosamund could not decide whether she was flying apart or he was. He was ringing Interpol and Ankara. Would he next implore the Patriarch in Constantinople to call down curses on Missy? Surely a man of Theo's sophistication could see the ugly stamp of Freud on his motives! Even if Missy had prostituted herself at one time, this did not give him licence to suppose that her very being contaminated his child! Perhaps there was some cultural bias against promiscuous women, but it certainly did not account for his violent reaction. No, he was simply beside himself with worry. He would never deny Xenia her inheritance, for he loved her too much. Soon he would calm down. He would have to.

Rosamund shrank before the house, feeling like an intruder. If she were not to speak the truth to Catherine, what could she say? It seemed that no one had really thought this out. Nikos, however, led her up the fine stone staircase to the front door as if she were a welcome necessity. They passed under the chaste, formal lintel into the tiled, formal hall. He took her cases and motioned to her that she should wait in the drawing-room while he fetched Catherine. A look of warmth and sympathy filled his eyes. Rosamund was family and was where she ought to be – rallying round.

Well, what on earth could she say? How could she edit the story without lying or breaking her word? She would have to account for Missy somehow, but how? She slipped into the darkened drawing-room, familiar from old visits, happy times when they had all been friends and had enjoyed each other's company. In the early days, they would get a little tiddly and silly and would play at backgammon at which Theo was a devil, and Scrabble at which Charles was. She had never known whether Theo anglicized himself for their benefit or whether he had hellenized himself for Chios and found the company of English people a relief. Whatever, he had always been at pains to offer a good single malt, at pains to spend evenings at home, making a family occasion, making a fuss over Rosamund's children. As Xenia had grown, everything had changed, though slowly and almost imperceptibly. The customs of the household had shifted and had become almost entirely Greek.

Rosamund did not want to sit. The room seemed poised in its beautiful tact to resist what she had brought into it. Catherine had bought Turkish carpets of great beauty and value: spindly eighteenth-century furniture stood perched upon them. A lovely Italian chest stood against a wall. Catherine had gone all the way to Genoa to find it. In one corner, there stood an antique hookah, the property, once, of a local pasha. Everything was to scale; everything reflected the history of the island. In the old days, the drawing-room had been less grand, a place to curl up in. Rosamund looked around herself. It was about as comfortable as the V&A now. How could Missy have invaded this place? How had she managed to do it? All at once, Rosamund saw what had happened and she gave a little gasp. Here she was, thinking that Missy had blundered in seeking her out. Here she stood having acted out a strategy based upon that blunder. And all along, it had not been a blunder at all. There was only one thing Missy had needed: she had needed to know who knew. If Theo had been honest with Catherine and Xenia from the outset, her scheme would have collapsed. It had been Rosamund herself who had unwittingly given Missy the key, and now, like the Trojan Horse, she had broached the gates, a spoiler and a scourge.

Rosamund sensed eyes on the back of her neck and turned around. Catherine stood in the doorway, her face in shadow, her body a willed rictus of composure. 'Hallo, Rosamund,' she said.

Normally, they greeted each other with a familial kiss, but they did not do so now. 'Cat!'

Catherine entered the room. 'Good of you to come,' she mumbled at last. Her face looked scrubbed and her hair was severely tied up. With a shock, Rosamund saw she had been crying and had tried to wash off the results. Charles's family had Roman virtues, and it always unsettled Rosamund if there was any breach in their stoicism.

'Is it good of me to come? I wish it were.' She blurted this out, not quite knowing why, but Catherine frowned in concentration as if the words had special meaning. 'Have you had any news?'

Catherine shook her head. She looked waxen. 'You don't suppose she's gone to England or anything like that? Her passport is missing . . . her British passport.' They looked at each other, sharing out the dart of fear between them. 'You see, she was so looking forward to getting back to school . . . seeing her friends . . . you know.'

Rosamund was sure that Theo did not know about the passport. 'Have you rung the airlines? Have you rung Charles?' Maybe Xenia had gone to London, Rosamund thought. Especially if Missy had told her the secret, Xenia might be very frightened. She might be using London as a bolt-hole. 'Theo is thinking of checking passenger lists in Turkey,' she added. In fact, he was doing this already, but she did not want to alarm Catherine. 'Though why she should go anywhere in Turkey I don't know. She's probably just missed the boat, Cat. You know how daft girls that age are. They think you are psychic and don't bother to phone.'

Catherine looked positively hieratic in her anguish. She seemed almost unable to speak except through a very small space between her frozen lips. Rosamund did not understand why she had never seen this aspect of Catherine before. It was generally assumed that she was indifferent to Xenia. 'I have spoken to Charles,' she said. 'He knows you are here now. He was very worried.'

Rosamund shot a glance at her.

'Presumably, you came as far as Athens with your cousin Mrs Kavanagh – '

'No!' She was quite wild to deny this.

The question of why she was in Greece lingered on the air between them. 'You sent her here,' Catherine said, her voice more dead than accusing.

'I promise not! I promise you, Catherine!' Slowly, Rosamund began to become aware of her real predicament. In the panic that had followed the news of Xenia's disappearance, it had not occurred to her that a whole intricacy of lies would have to be spun from the central one. 'I did see her in London . . . for lunch. She asked after you. She remembered having met you.'

'Well, she did not remind me of that. She told me that you were sending a letter of introduction.'

'You must believe me that I did no such thing, nor did I promise to, nor did I intend to.' She suddenly saw where this self-justification was tending. She chose her next words with a desperate casuistry. 'I suppose I might have told her what a lovely house you had in Chios.' She swallowed drily. 'She was keen to show me pictures of her own.'

But Catherine was not to be deflected. 'She did not come for the house, although that is what she said. I knew she had come for something else, but it never struck me it was Xenia.' She was standing very still and she swayed slightly like a stricken animal. 'She came for Xenia. I know it.

Why?' Catherine seemed to have developed preternatural gifts. 'Why did she come for Xenia? Why does she want her? Where has she taken her? Rosamund, I want to know!'

Rosamund seized on this last. 'I don't know where she could have taken her . . . if she has taken her. She is unlikely to have kidnapped her, isn't she? She is a very rich woman.' The more she prevaricated, the more Rosamund longed to tell the truth. She felt swept down and almost overcome by a desire to speak the simple, painful words.

She peered at Catherine, searching her face. Their eyes met and engaged in a curious instant in which Rosamund nearly spoke and Catherine suddenly looked away. 'She said she was meeting her husband in Constantinople.'

'Then maybe she is there! Let's ring the Hilton! There's bound to be a Hilton, and it's just the sort of place where Missy would stay.'

'She spoke Greek to Xenia, but she called Constantinople "Istanbul",' Catherine said dreamily. 'Do you think she would harm Xenia?'

'Goodness me, no!' Rosamund exclaimed in her old, brisk manner. They looked at each other again, however, and held the gaze in the twilit room. 'If she does, though, I will kill her,' she found herself saying as a matter of fact. 'I will tear her limb from limb, and I will enjoy it.'

Catherine responded with a glittering eye. 'I know who she is, but I can't prove it,' she said.

There was a moment's pause. 'We will just have to wait,' said Rosamund. 'We will have to wait and see.'

'You know, don't you?'

'I know that you are in a state of shock. I think the doctor should come.'

'I don't need the doctor,' Catherine said. 'I need to be treated as an adult.'

Rosamund could barely endure this enforced silence. 'You are an adult, but you are an adult in shock,' she said, thankful for the one true thing she could say.

'Did you sleep with my husband?' Catherine asked.

She was in shock. They both were. 'No,' Rosamund said; then she added, 'He doesn't fancy me.'

Catherine put her head to one side and looked at Rosamund for quite a while, then she gave the ghost of a smile. 'Nor me,' she said. 'But that's a relief. I thought it was all so involved and special because he did. He made my daughter into your project.'

Rosamund was so ashamed. 'I have been very much deluded, Cat,' she said. She stepped forward and took her sister-in-law by the shoulders.

Catherine ducked her head and turned aside. 'I think I am glad you have come.' She hesitated. 'You must be tired. You must want a wash after your journey.'

XI

'My God! It *is* Serge Mirkovsky, isn't it?'

Serge was trying to cross the road from Taksim Square with a rug he had ill-advisedly bought in the Old Bazaar a weary hour before. It was intended as a peace-offering for his wife, whose misgivings about his trip to Constantinople were being borne out, he now felt, by the sudden apparition of the woman whose name he could not remember, but whose face rang an ominous bell. It was getting dark and his feet hurt. What was more, owing to Serge's complete lack of Turkish, the taxi driver, who had ferried him expensively across the Galata Bridge, had let him down in the wrong place. Now, he was cornered. With the unwieldly carpet and the traffic, there was no escape. Before he could pretend he had not noticed her, the woman was upon him, she and a timid girl of about sixteen.

'Well, I never! It *is* you, Serge! They do say it's a small world.' She was somewhere in her mid-forties, he thought, immaculately turned out, her hair done up in sleek wings. Where had he met her before? The lacunae of his drinking days were a sore point for Serge. There were patches of his life he could not remember. 'You don't recognize me, do you?' The woman was an American, all varnished and pearled. She had quick, hard eyes and a slightly wolfish look. Whatever the memory was, he was almost sure it was not pleasant. 'Missy!' she cried, as if this ought to make his day. 'Missy Buchanan that was, Missy Kavanagh that is. And I'd like you to meet my daughter Xenia, who is staying with me in Istanbul. Xenia,' she said, turning to the girl, 'this is Prince Serge Mirkovsky.'

It always sounded a warning in Serge when people used his title and in that tone. He tried for the memory, hoping he could get it before the woman got him. Had he met her in Canada? A few years ago, he had spent (or rather misspent) several months there on a fruitless and humiliating mission, and it was never far from his mind that this lost time of benders and disillusion might rise up and hit him with a bill for obliterated misbehaviour. The memory of his folly was always with him, but not with any precision. The woman looked at him coyly and he wondered if he had actually spent the night with her at some point. He shrank. When he had returned from his wild fling, he had finally had to acknowledge what his long-suffering wife Fiona had always tried to make him see. He was an alcoholic. He had gone in for extensive therapy, and now, dry for over a year, he had thought he had been able to guarantee that he would not drink if let loose in Istanbul. After all, he had argued to his wife, Turkey was a Muslim country and Muslims did not drink. What was more, his journey had the kind purpose of helping his cousin Helena. Serge still felt threatened, though, by his repented past. This sort of thing was what the shrinks called 'a trigger', and he looked at the Missy person as if she were a loaded gun.

'How do you do?' said the young girl, formally extending a hand. She stepped forward. 'Xenia Phocas.' She added the surname to her mother's introduction with a faint but determined emphasis. Serge had once met a shipowning Phocas at his London club. Maybe that was the connection. The girl had an English accent, he noticed, and what his mother would have called 'deportment'. No, he had probably met this Missy at some garden party or racing event. For all of Serge's sins, and he did berate himself for them, he was not a social snob. He was unhappily aware, however, that others were. She had the look of the sort of harpy who wanted to push a nubile daughter into a certain set. 'I'm terribly sorry,' he said, turning to the woman, 'I am sure we have met, but it quite escapes me where.'

'It'll come back to you!' She gave an arch but guarded look at her daughter, whose downcast eyes did not register her brazen glance at him.

Serge groaned inwardly. The general idea of his new regime was, however, to confront things when they arose so that they would not get out of hand later. 'It wasn't Ontario, was it?' he asked nervously, hoping that this covered a lot of territory.

She shook her head and smiled knowingly. 'I can't *imagine* Canada,' she said as if the thought were too dreadful for words.

'I know a Phocas,' he ventured. 'Maybe that is – '

'I don't think so!' the woman said abruptly. The young girl looked up suddenly and started to speak, but apparently thought better of it. Her mother's eyes narrowed to pinpoints, but then widened again. Swiftly restoring the air of a guessing game, she cried, 'OK! You give up . . . I give up! Paris . . . the Arc de Triomphe . . .'87!'

So it was the races after all. Serge felt relieved. On the whole, he had kept his nose pretty clean in Paris. His mother had spent winters there with his thoroughly respectable sister Varya, who was now married, of all things, to a mousy French librarian.

'Perhaps you block on it because of Philippe Renais,' Missy added, her voice rising on a delicate, interrogative note. 'Remember now?'

He did and with total, aghast recall. Renais had seemed just another hedonist with a private income, a modest string of horses, and a taste for the tables – a taste shared by Serge. Towards the end of her life, when he had found visits to his mother particularly intolerable, he had fallen in with Renais . . . and, of course, Missy Buchanan. She had been very chic, a glossy hooker with a raucous voice, who drank men under the table. In the end, there had been a stinker of a scandal. Renais had been uncovered as a mobster, and was still in prison, for all Serge knew. But the Sûreté had come to his mother's flat, had questioned him – and even Varya.

Serge looked at the tender girl Missy had in tow with pity. He did indeed remember. He had always thought Missy had been supporting a habit. Now he wondered if she had been doing the sad thing of whores, educating her child in some expensive convent deep in the country and fortified by nuns. 'Oh yes, of course . . . Missy,' he said. There had been something he had liked about her after all. She had been quite devoid of hypocrisy.

'Well, we've changed a lot since then!' she declared.

'Indeed, yes,' he replied firmly. 'You look very well, Missy.'

'In the end, I married well,' she said demurely. 'How's your Mom? You used to talk about her a lot.'

'She died a few years ago . . . in Greece.'

'Before the "Evil Empire" crumbled? That's a shame,' Missy said.

Had he discussed his mother's obsessive views on Russia with this woman? He could not imagine having shared such intimacy with Missy. Of all things, he hated the knowledge of lost time, the disconnecting erasures of blackouts. Here he was, standing on a Turkish traffic island being addressed by a total stranger as an old comrade-in-arms. It was his life story. He fell into people as if they were swimming baths and then drowned in the consequences of his rashness. To recall Renais and Missy was to bring back the weighted string of ill-conceived friendships, trusts made in bars and broken later in sobriety. 'Hard to talk about it, Missy,' he said.

All at once, a gap opened in the traffic. 'Right!' said Missy. 'Charge!' and hoiking up an end of the rolled-up rug, she led the plunge across the road, where at last they stood panting at the top of İstiklâl Caddesi, a broad boulevard lined with European shops. Only charming Edwardian trams clanged up and down this pedestrian sanctuary, where the crowd was thinning out for the evening. 'That's better!' Missy cried. 'We made it!'

'Grand,' he said. 'Well done! I expect I would have been standing there all night if you had not come along.'

'Well, send for the cavalry,' Missy said. 'It's the only way.'

Serge did not remember her thus. She seemed to be lighter, somehow, with her whoops and jokes. It was coming back to him that she had borne life some kind of grudge. She had been a kind of ironist. Under whatever new dispensation, she appeared to be more good-humoured now. Perhaps it was the presence of her child. Serge had children of his own, all grown up now, but he had always had a benign affection for young people. He glanced at Missy's daughter and took her more fully in. With her dark hair and voluminous clothing, she seemed faintly Asiatic. For all her perfectly enunciated English, she had the veiled and modest look of a Turkish girl, perhaps from an old Ottoman family. She hung back from the conversation with noncommittal eyes, as if it might even be impolite to take too strong a notice of what was going on. For all that, she looked tense . . . even frightened. Her pretty brow was contracted in a frown that is habitual in highly nervous people who doubt themselves. She seemed young for this expression, and again he felt sorry for her. 'Have you been sightseeing today?' he asked her gently. 'I expect you would love the Old Bazaar. I did . . . rather too much, I am afraid.'

She made to speak, but Missy interrupted. 'Making a killing on the kilims, eh? God, I wish! Maybe I will.'

'It's for my wife,' he said, thankful, suddenly, to be advertising her existence to Missy. 'I think I may have been talked into it.'

'I'll have a look. I know something about it. If they've gypped you, you can take it back,' said Missy. 'Where are you staying?'

Serge was interested that the young girl looked appalled at this pushiness, but again she veiled her eyes. 'Ah,' he said in desperation, 'that's very kind of you, but I am waiting for my cousin Helena, who may be arriving at any moment.'

'Well, we are at the Büyük Londra,' she said, making it sound Turkish.

So was Serge. 'In that case, I suppose we shall be meeting at breakfast,' he said firmly distant, 'for we are staying there too. Mind you, I am a very early riser.' Why, oh, why had he not insisted on the Pera Palas hotel?

'I like to get up early myself!' Xenia said suddenly, charging into the gap in the conversation rather in the way that her mother had crossed the road. 'I want to see Agia Sophia tomorrow. I have always wanted to see it.'

He noted with surprise that the girl looked at him with a penetrating wistfulness, as if, inexplicably, he could give her the answer to some imponderable question.

'We'll go. Crack of dawn if you like,' Missy told her somewhat sharply. 'I spent some time here between husbands and know Istanbul well. D'you?' Missy asked Serge as they descended the boulevard. A party of Germans bulging with knapsacks overtook them. With loud, horsy laughs they plodded down the street commenting and pointing at everything they saw. 'They will be making for the beer in Çiçek Pasaji,' Missy said with a genuine shudder of distaste. 'Best to avoid that, sugarplum,' she said to her daughter. Despite her raw presumption, her glad eye, this brought a memory back to Serge of Missy's elegance.

During her incarnation as Renais's mistress she had decked herself out in *haute couture*, which she had worn with an air of absolute indifference to its cost. She had been, he thought, something of a work of art: expensive, relating to herself alone, and having no point but being. Nevertheless, it distressed him to see the timid young thing trail behind this ageing geisha. In fact, he suddenly noticed what a bizarre picture they made together among the veiled Muslim women who followed their husbands up and down the boulevard and who eyed them with covert opprobrium. Serge wondered if the girl were afraid of Missy or if she had been too strictly brought up. As they threaded their way through the trickle of late shoppers, he noticed the flash of an Orthodox cross glint from her dark dress as the streetlight hit it. She was Greek – of course, she was – and Missy certainly wasn't. Her name was Phocas, and she had pronounced 'Agia Sophia' perfectly. Serge had spent forty-odd summer holidays in Patmos where his family owned a house. He knew where he was with her now. But where was she with Missy?

Now he fully remembered the circumstances in which he had first known Missy, it seemed more than a little odd that she should be at such pains to renew the acquaintance. As they made their way down the street towards the hotel, the young girl's innocent air seemed more and more to be her striking feature. Missy had obviously gone to some pains to shelter Xenia from the common old garden soil of the real world. Why, then, expose her to the indelible stain of the *demi-monde?* Serge would not have introduced one of his own daughters to his reprobate self, and would have kept them absolutely from anyone who had kept company with Renais. Well, the world was odder than one thought. This Serge knew. He supposed it was possible that Missy had adopted a sane policy of candour with her daughter. Maybe she, too, had learned that avoiding the truth stored up more trouble than dealing with it.

Since his recovery, Serge had become the advocate of therapeutic honesty. He supposed this approach had been an American invention all along. With some amusement, though, Serge observed Missy's sheer incongruity with Constantinople. With her bold looks and confident stride she seemed to challenge the ancient city with New World assertions. It might have the prestige of wars and heavy centuries, but Missy was having none of that. Somewhere at the back of his mind, it occurred to him that Missy was in Constantinople to have a good time and that, *ingénue* daughter or not, she was going to achieve this aim.

They turned into the little side-street that led to the Büyük Londra, 'The Grand London Hotel'. How on earth was he going to negotiate the way between Missy and Helena? Serge was easygoing, too easygoing for that matter, but the whole reason for his trip to Constantinople had quite genuinely been his poor cousin. Since the great débâcle in Patmos four years ago she had not set foot in England, preferring to stay on in the house where his mother had died. On his last visit he had been shocked to see how much she had aged. The awful business about Arthur Holt and Marina had shattered her nerve, and there had seemed no way to reach her. He often thought that it would have been better if Helena had broken down completely, but a strength of will that had made her intolerable in the past had also given her stoicism in the face of pain. Having been brittle with the thick veneer of a studied English manner, Helena had become morosely Russian. She suffered and wore black, but he had to hand it to her that she did have dignity. Now, he had some bad news to break to her, and he did not want to have Missy in the vicinity when he got round to it.

It had been a few weeks ago that Marina had telephoned him to tell him that Charles Simon had commissioned a biography of Arthur Holt and that a rough draft was already in hand. It had been Helena's dream to get a first crack at this project, and although she had ruthlessly manipulated Marina for her dead husband's papers, Serge could not help but feel sorry that things had turned out this way. In the first place, Helena was a far better writer than Edgar Jolly, and in the second place, she knew her subject, for Arthur had been her lover in the distant past and she had understood him only too well. What was more, it appeared that Jolly had not yet approached Helena to discuss her point of view. Surely he would, and a letter out of the blue would be devastating to her. All of this was mixed up, too, with her feelings about Marina . . . as Marina herself acknowledged. It was a messy situation and not one to be accompanied by the tinsel sensibility of Missy. Serge shook his head at the irony. He had hit upon Constantinople partly because it seemed to fit with Helena in every way. She was, and always had been, an exquisite mass of contradictions and layered thought. She had exhausted herself with obscure inner conflicts, and yet a patina of encrusted brilliance had built up around her, and perhaps even held her in place. Serge had been brought up with Helena and regarded her as his sister. Whether he liked the manner of her survival or not was a moot point. She was, in his eyes, phenomenal.

If Helena's suffering had ennobled her, Serge would have been surprised, and indeed it had not done precisely that. It had, however, necessitated a kind of simplification in her. She had quit her job in London, renounced her ambitions, and now lived in the big house on Patmos in a way that might have been described as ascetic if she had had any religion. He had been struck on his last visit by how little she consumed. It was not as if she had found, like the mystics, an alternative source of fuel for her existence. She mortified ordinary needs without belief, and Serge found that chilling. All the same, the process was somewhat akin. Something non-material kept her going. It was certainly not love of life itself, for Helena was far too negative a woman to rejoice in mere being. It was almost as if one unceremonious coal had improbably continued in a dead fire, glowing hotter for its singleness. Her face was lined and she walked with a stoop now. Perhaps she had become transmogrified intelligence in the absence of desire, blinded but for a single eye.

At first, she had refused to come with him to Constantinople, especially at his expense. Serge had needed to persuade her, for he did not think she could sustain the final blow to everything having to do with Arthur and Marina if she stayed on Patmos and he merely came and went. He felt horribly like he had when he had taken his last dog to be put down – trusting, it had wagged its tail. Well, maybe she wouldn't mind so much after all. In any case, to be absolutely frank, he really did need a bit of a breather from Fiona, who, good soul that she was, had taken Russia on her shoulders and was staggering around with it like an ant with a vast bit of bun. When they had been invited to attend the reconsecration of the Cathedral in Moscow, Serge had found scores of forgotten relatives. Fiona had found more . . . hordes, in fact, of impecunious Mirkovskys, good causes all. She had started by doing out cupboards for them, and had ended by marshalling racks of denim, shelves of tins, and whole pharmacies of medical supplies, which she stuffed into their Land Rover each year now, and ferried overland. The base had broadened, and recently, they had applied for charitable status – or Fiona had. Third cousins in Chiswick, elderly ladies from the church, had been sending gifts too, and now the winter was at hand once more. Serge had slipped away from Fiona's good works in Moscow and had crossed to Turkey from Odessa. She had it in mind that he should bring Helena back with him, thinking it would buck her up to do some good for someone else. Serge smiled but not openly. His wife and cousin were contradictory beings. Fiona was trying to outdo the Good Samaritan, crossing not only the road but the continent in order to effect mass rescue. As for Helena, the rest of the human race was a matter of complete indifference to her. This, Serge knew, was because she herself lay bleeding. So here he was, unfit for heroism but unable to turn away from Helena, if the truth was to be told. He could not let her find out about Arthur's biography from a stranger, and so he had come, he thought wryly, 'to the holy city of Byzantium' now that he and Helena were in their sixties and needed one another.

The Büyük Londra stands in wholehearted defiance of the modern world near the more sumptuous Pera Palas where Serge would have stayed had Helena not insisted that she must pay her own way. While the *fin-de-siècle* elegance of the grander establishment is polished to the degree one would expect in an international hotel where Agatha Christie had a regular room, the Büyük Londra seems to paint a softer picture of the past. It would not be fair to say that it is crumbling or unhygienic; the bald patches in the carpet are darned, and although the maroon velvet curtains are in need of some refurbishment, they are handsome and they are clean. The lobby is really like the comfortable drawing-room of an elderly aunt who has seen better times but won't give in. Brass pots of dried ferns stand on an Ottoman sideboard that looks a bit like Nelson's catafalque. Over the bar, somewhat improbably, hangs a large sepia engraving of St Thérèse of Lisieux. In her nun's habit, the Little Flower benignly oversees the drinking habits of a tasteful clientele: she sets the tone, somehow, for moderation. The hotel itself is happily placed so that south-facing rooms overlook the Golden Horn, and it is possible to watch the sun setting in the west over the Mosque of Suleiman the Magnificent. Altogether, it seems to rise above the aggression of bazaars, the ceaseless pushing of rugs and shoe-shines offered by desperate or impoverished Turks: the staff are positively deferential, and they shoo beggars from the door discreetly.

Xenia observed the Russian prince from under a fringe of lashes. She was surprised that her mother knew this man . . . and she was deeply relieved. Throughout the ten-hour bus journey from İzmir to Istanbul, her fear had mounted and her misgivings had grown. When her mother had booked them into the hotel, Xenia had become more and more anxious. It was nice enough, but it had begun to dawn on her that Missy neither wanted nor needed to save money either in travelling by coach or by staying at the Büyük Londra. The itinerary had been chosen, she began to realize, so that her father could not find her. Of course, it was not that Xenia wanted him to. She was not sure that she ever wanted to see him again, but then there was very little she was sure of now. If Missy was truly her mother, then what sort of man had her father been all along? Had he loved Missy? Had they loved each other? Why was Missy supposed to be dead?

Xenia had expected at least one or two answers to the almost infinite number of questions that buzzed like spoiling flies around her head. When they had boarded the Varan bus, she had assumed that one of many explanations might be forthcoming. It was an air-conditioned double decker with stewardesses in lip gloss who brought coffee with napkins and biscuits. Once they were settled in comfort, it seemed obvious that she and Missy would fly, as it were, into each other's arms . . . mother and daughter. A gauzy image of this reunion was not at the forefront of her conscious thoughts, but it had lurked more potently on the border between her thinking and her feeling mind. If her artificial mother was a mass of 'noes' and distances, complexities and anxieties, then her real mother would be one vast 'yes'. Her entire last night in Chios had been taken up with breathless anticipation. Frankness, boldness, a lack of reserve typified her actual parent. They would tie the knot and make the bond. Xenia would return confident and strong – if she returned at all. What was more, in the watches of the night, everything that surrounded her and all that she had loved grew horribly synthetic in her new vision of things. Even her beloved bedroom with its pretty chintz had seemed plastic and unreal, a little shrine to her father's hypocrisy, and she its votary. Although she had been brought up to be truthful, lying to Catherine that morning had been ease itself. Her whole life had been false after all; the path of integrity lay in Missy.

Ten hours in the Turkish countryside, however, had not realized this fantasy. From the outset, Missy had been peculiarly silent, and when they were truly under way and Xenia had turned timidly to her new-found mother, she had been amazed to see that she had fallen asleep. Xenia had not quite known what to do or how to react. She had argued with herself that it was part of her mother's honest approach not to push things at first, but it made her deeply uneasy all the same. She had thought they would have a little talk. What was more, now she was launched into the trip, she began to notice little things about Missy that made her uncomfortable. She seemed fearful of something, watchful. Xenia had seen films in which guns had emerged from handbags, in which hostages were taken. Was it too fanciful to suppose that her real mother actually was dead and that this woman had invented the whole story with false papers? No, she could not credit that. All the same, when the bus had stopped for lunch, Xenia had been frightened. Any moment she expected terrorists in balaclavas to spring from behind the counters of the cafeteria and seize her. Her mother had eaten . . . impersonally like a courier or Universal Aunt delivering the children of strangers from Point A to Point B. Added to this, there was a curious coarseness about Missy that Xenia tried to deny but could not altogether. She seemed irritated by Xenia's nervousness, or there was something else that bothered her. She explained herself simply by saying that she was tired and that they would talk once they got to Istanbul, but it seemed to Xenia that she was oddly preoccupied for someone who had found a long-lost daughter. Once or twice, left alone with her thoughts, Xenia had found herself making desperate calculations. If her father had wanted this woman, what were his hidden urges? She dropped such thoughts as if they were scalding hot. They were indeed both tired, she and Missy, and she was bound to have a distorted view of everything for a while.

Nevertheless, the mere sight of Prince Mirkovsky had struck Xenia as an augury of deliverance. Just when her spirits were at their lowest, Missy had hailed him in Taksim Square and there he was, conjured out of nowhere, as kindly and respectable an old gentleman as she could imagine. He had even recognized the name 'Phocas'. Here, at last, Xenia was on familiar territory, and undisputed too. He wore a linen jacket and a Paisley tie. He had the faint, refined Slavic appearance she loosely associated with Athenian gentlefolk, the sort Catherine had taken her to call upon from childhood, who lived behind walled gardens in pockets of the Plaka, in Glyfada or in parts of Kifissia and who always gave her sweet things to eat. He treated Xenia with their grave concern, their courtly touch of grace, and, what was more, he had known her mother . . . and in Paris, too. As they entered the hotel lobby, Xenia realized what she had not quite dared to admit. She had been terrified. Now with the imprimatur of the old Prince, Missy had a slightly different stamp. Xenia reminded herself that she had come on this mad journey principally to learn. She must and would maintain an open mind.

They had not got as far as the reception desk when they were suddenly confronted with a frail, elderly woman dressed in mourning. She wore a well-cut black suit and an onyx ring. Xenia immediately took her for a Greek. She was above average height for a woman, very thin and she had startling aquiline features. With her close-cropped white hair, she might almost have been a man, for her face was strong, her jaw set firmly. She sized up the little party as it entered the hotel and a thin smile came to her pale lips. She reminded Xenia of a certain kind of schoolmistress, the rigorous martinet whom pupils loathe then later respect. Again, it was most reassuring when the Prince greeted her. 'Helena!' he cried with an unnaturally hearty boom. 'Have you been waiting long?'

The woman, for all of her wizened appearance, glided to meet him. They kissed in the style to which Xenia was accustomed, grazing the air with both cheeks. 'Not for very long,' she said.

'Darling, how are you? Did you have a ghastly journey?'

'Not more than usual,' Helena said, and turning to Missy and Xenia, she gave a gracious nod which offset a shrewd inspection of them both. She made a gesture at the Prince, a request to facilitate an introduction.

'Oh, I'm terribly sorry . . . by an extraordinary coincidence, I happened to run into an old acquaintance of mine, Missy . . . ?' He made a comic grimace of remorse at forgetting her name, and Xenia was a little wounded at the distance this implied.

'Kavanagh!' Missy said abruptly. 'And this is my daughter Xenia.'

'My cousin, Helena Taggart.'

Xenia was not at all surprised when the woman greeted her in Greek, but she realized that Missy was. Madame Taggart spoke with a very faint English accent as Catherine did, and she had the same handsome manners. They conversed about nothing. 'Charming girl,' the woman said to Serge in English when they had completed the brief exchange. Xenia felt she had been interviewed, and flushed; nevertheless, she was glad she had passed muster.

She turned to Missy. 'And so you are here for a holiday?' Helena continued. Xenia thought the Prince looked nervous.

'There is so much to see,' Missy said, her head on one side. Xenia was surprised. Her mother and the singular old woman looked at each other in a moment of exchanged fascination. In a subtle way, Xenia could see the faintest modification of her mother's behaviour in the presence of Madame Taggart.

'Ah yes, churches, palaces, mosques, carpets, bazaars . . . I am looking forward to it.' Helena turned to Serge. 'I sailed from Samos. Exciting to arrive by ship,' she said. For some reason, he beamed at this remark.

'I thought the sea air would do you good,' he said, 'but you must be very tired.' He turned to Missy and Xenia. 'Forgive me, but my cousin must find her room and unpack.'

'We will undoubtedly meet later,' Helena said with a slow smile. 'Indeed, I should hope so.' And they made towards the lift.

'Well, you cleared that fence, cookie,' Missy said to Xenia with a short laugh, 'and without a hoof touching. What's this place you go to, a finishing-school?'

'Sorry,' said Xenia, looking down, although she did not know why.

'Sorry? Sorry for what? You did OK. Didn't I just tell you so? You were great . . . an asset.' But Missy frowned, and Xenia realized that in some oblique way she had caused offence.

XII

'I'M STARVING!' said Missy.

Xenia was too, but she had been brought up not to say so. By this time, she was also exhausted. Unlike her mother, she had been unable to sleep on the bus and she had been travelling since six that morning. Flagging as she was, however, she could not take her eyes from Missy, who sat across from her on the verandah of the Haçi Baba restaurant. Not only did the wooden porch creak with every move and shake with every footstep, it also overlooked the grounds of the Greek Orthodox church near Taksim Square, thus giving Xenia doubt in spheres temporal and spiritual. Missy had done herself up to go out and had ordered them a vast meal of stuffed mussels, koftë, imam bayeldi and pilaff. She was dying for a drink, she said, and she had already made inroads on a bottle of wine which stood between them on the table. She splashed some into Xenia's glass. 'Go on, be a devil,' she said, even though Xenia had a Coca-Cola to hand. She extracted a packet of Marlboros from her handbag and jiggled one in Xenia's direction. 'Want one of these?'

Xenia shook her head. By now, she was almost incapable of speech. She had already sensed the waiter's disapproval of the alcohol, a bottle being a large quantity even in Greece, and especially for a woman. If Xenia smoked as well, what would they think? Missy might have noticed too, but she did not seem to mind. She shaded her hand over the lighter flame against the faint breeze that wafted from the church garden, and emitted a stream of smoke from her mouth. 'That's better,' she said.

Xenia glanced at the dark, shut church, which stood back in the shadows, and quivered suddenly at the memory of history. Most of the time, she preferred to think of even recent martyrdoms as legendary, noble in themselves, but exemplary. There were stories of current Turkish atrocities, even modern-day crucifixions. Xenia never knew what to believe. It was all such a puzzle. All the same, she touched the cross under her blouse, ensuring that it was still there and that it was hidden. She did not want to bring her religion into disrepute nor to give the Turks any fuel for thought. She could not forget where she was even if Missy could. Constantinople made her edgy. That very evening, they had heard the

Muslim call to prayer permeating the city, one mosque taking up the chant where the other left off, blending almost fugal in a pure cacophony of single-minded devotion. Her mother had said, 'Oh good, I'm back in Istanbul,' but it had sent a grating shiver through Xenia.

It was not as if she wanted to adopt the prejudiced views of her elders; far from it. Since she had been at St Winifred's she had been given time to think much more in abstract about matters pertaining to the ancient struggle. She had even gone so far as to wonder if the Greek attitude towards the Serbian concentration camps in Bosnia was just. Was the press coverage merely Western propaganda? Xenia did not know. She did know, however, that it was not in the spirit of Orthodox Christianity to hate. Not all Turks were monsters. They had nervous systems, they had bloodstreams. Some of them were quite civilized, really. Breaking down barriers was crucial, love and understanding should be the key to everything. And yet, as she sat upon the Turkish balcony, a vision of whizzing scimitars flitted across her mind. Piles of severed Greek heads had been stacked like melons in a market in the port of Chios during the 1822 massacre, and Greeks had thrown themselves off the walls of Anavatos rather than submit to the ignominy of slavery. Chiote children had literally been sold off to Turkish families. What was more, her own great-grandparents had been massacred in Smyrna . . . and that, within living memory. A stiff portrait of them hung in her father's study. They had startled, prognosticating eyes, and were solemn, as if the camera had caught them in an oracular mood. Surrounding them had been their clutch of children of whom the only survivor had been Xenia's grandfather. The family had been burnt alive in the church where they had taken sanctuary. No one forgot these things in Greece, and right now Xenia was not sure how they could. And then there were the Kurds . . . now, today. Her father did business with the Turks, but he loathed them. Why was she thinking of him? He was the last person she wanted to think about. Xenia hated politics. All her life, she had wanted to believe in people instead.

Her mother, perhaps more to the point, raised her glass. 'A toast,' she said, 'to new beginnings.' Because of the flit, Xenia had not had the luxury of clothes to change into, but Missy had. Even though the restaurant was little more than a taverna, she wore a stunning purple frock made of silk jersey. But for the subdued tone and severity of its design, it would have looked out of place, yet the opposite was true. It made the other diners look wan and dowdy. The clinging material revealed a beautiful figure, but only an ayatollah could have objected to the dress with its long, tight sleeves and buttons to the throat. Xenia could not stop looking at her mother, nor could she fail to recognize the covert glances of the men on the verandah. Almost against her will, she found herself raising her glass in response to the toast. The wine tasted surprisingly good, and she had some more, a little sip and then another. 'Cheer up, honey!' Missy said, 'You look as if you've lost your last friend.'

Xenia wondered if she noticed a tone of command in the voice. 'I am sorry. I am very tired, and I suppose I am hungry too.'

'Well, here it comes!' The waiter appeared with the feast and unloaded it with telling lack of ceremony on to the table. Xenia was obscurely hurt at this implied criticism of her mother. Perhaps she was inventing the vague snubs she had sensed all day. She was grateful, however, for the food and for the distraction of it, so she fell to. It tasted delicious.

'So, now we are really, truly here, you can tell me about yourself,' Missy said when they had eaten enough to sustain them. 'It's not as if we have been able to talk with all this cloak and dagger stuff going on. I mean, do you like French, spinach, hockey, *The Sting*? You are my only child and I don't even know if you are frightened of spiders or won't eat greens.'

The creaking balcony seemed to sway slightly and Xenia had the sensation of rocking about on a potential of extreme emotion. The tenor of these questions made this heave a bit. She did not know what she was feeling, but tears pricked at her eyes. Maybe she was tired, but the tragedy of the situation hit her. Missy was looking at her too, and with great curiosity. Her fringed green eyes were wide and she blinked as if at a rare animal or a miracle. 'I suppose I don't really have any preferences,' she said. 'They have been rather discouraged.' This was true.

'Ha!' Missy cried, causing heads to turn slightly. 'Meant to be docile, aren't you?' She looked Xenia critically up and down. 'You must like something . . . I don't know . . . noodles, Vivaldi, tennis, knitting. You're a person. You matter.'

Despite herself, Xenia had to laugh. The expression on Missy's face was so comical that it seemed almost to guy her elegance. It was as if a pixie had taken the form of a goddess and peeped out from behind the mask. 'All right, I like . . . cream buns, though I know I shouldn't . . . um . . . I hate tennis and all sport, though I know I shouldn't. And I would rather be reading music at university than law – and that I really mustn't!' She spoke lightly, but felt treacherous.

'Law? How you're going to do law and be so submissive at the same time beats me! You have to be willing to have a bit of a scrap if you do law.'

'Maritime law,' said Xenia, who was tempted to sigh but did not. 'It's my father's idea. It's why I can't always do what I like. He means to leave me his business.'

'*Really!*' Missy seemed truly interested. 'To a *girl*? That does surprise me.'

'What do you mean?' The moment she had mentioned her father, Xenia's heart began to pound, and now she felt her pulses jump, her stomach contract. She did not know why.

'Oh, it's nothing.' Missy prodded at an unfinished meatball on her plate, then ate it. 'I suppose I got it into my head that you'd have one of those predestined marriages, all mapped out with goods and chattels to grandsons.'

'My father's not like that!' Xenia said a little hotly. 'He is very modern in his outlook.'

'Well, sweetness, you must have changed him,' Missy replied. 'He was hardly what I'd call a feminist when I knew him.'

There was something in Missy's eyes that made Xenia look away. 'My father loves and respects women,' she said.

'And here all along I was fixin' to send in the Marines!' Missy said wryly, her Southern accent broad once more. 'As I say, you have converted him. He was so desperate for a boy.'

Before she could stop identifying the deep and empty sadness she had never put a name to, Xenia had recognized it. She was proud that her father loved her, *qua* human being, that was, but she had always sensed the ache of his wider lack. He wanted a son. 'Well, I'm not a boy,' she said with spirit she did not really feel.

'That's the stuff!' said Missy. 'You sho' don't look like one.'

Xenia was self-conscious about her body and this was why she often draped it in baggy clothes. From time to time she went on faddish diets, eating only lettuce leaves or beans or whatever. In the last few years she had taken to keeping the Orthodox Lent strictly. It could be severe, so she got forty days of fasting without being nagged about it . . . not that it seemed right to use a holy time for vain purposes. She was not vain, she hoped, simply not piggy, she always said. Catherine fussed and fretted about this, and Rosamund always bought her fudge cakes, which she would eat then panic about. As for Missy, she did not seem to have a single ascetic principle. She had just polished off an enormous dinner, and when the bus had stopped for lunch, she had heaped her plate in the cafeteria too, declaring how much she loved Turkish food, even at the humblest level. At the same time, she had a better figure than Xenia herself. Xenia wondered if Missy had been commenting on this. She suddenly felt ashamed and looked down at her half-full plate.

'Do you have a boyfriend?' Missy asked, changing the subject. 'Or do they keep you chained up in that ole school?'

Earlier, it had surprised her that her mother seemed to disapprove of her being educated by nuns. She had made some remark or other. 'There's a boy who likes me,' she replied blushing. 'I think he does. We met at the Ampleforth dance and he did write to me.' She swallowed in the pain of truthfulness she felt bound to. 'Not this summer, though.' Some of the girls in her form were sexually experienced, and although at times she borrowed their sophisticated manner as she did their skirts and shoes, they really did shock her. Some of the more pious Catholic girls were still virgins like herself, but she felt stupid and Greek . . . a sore thumb. Everyone knew her father was really rich. Everyone thought she was really spoiled and so she bent over backwards not to be, even though she wasn't, even though the reverse was true and her parents were harder on her because of her expectations. One of the beastlier girls had once called her 'Christina Onassis' and it had stuck for a while, making her life a misery. At home, that unfortunate heiress was her parents' bugbear and bad example. Xenia longed to be like everybody else, so she had taken to doing menial tasks for people when she could find them. This, coupled with her innocence, had only gained her a reputation for being a 'saint', which was somewhat the kiss of death. She was sure this was why Cosmo had not written back to her. It was Sarah's opinion also. Well, her father would not have approved anyway. There she was, back at her father again.

'Oh, you'll learn soon enough. Don't worry. There's plenty of time,' Missy said wearily. 'Now as for me, I'd had one too many boyfriends when I was your age, and two or three more in my life than I should. But you know? There's one thing I've never regretted, and that was having you.' She wrinkled her nose in a kittenish smile and patted Xenia's hand across the table. 'But no way are you to follow my example!' she added. 'No way! Not, that is, if you can't hang on to your baby.'

A dark swell of feeling threatened Xenia again. Her throat ached and she had the impulse to escape. 'What do *you* like?' she asked in a desperate bid to change the subject. 'I don't know you either.'

Missy withdrew her hand, drank another gulp of wine and leaned back, displaying her breasts to advantage. For a woman of her age, they were surprisingly firm and voluptuous. Xenia looked away. 'Let's see,' said Missy, '. . . men, booze, smokes, clothes . . . what else? Horses, dogs, grand opera, travel, hunting, old houses . . . chocolate fudge sundaes. The only thing I truly cannot stand is a prig.'

For some reason, a blackness overwhelmed Xenia. The whole tension of the day swamped her. Although she could not fathom why she found it so, she felt a kind of insolence in Missy's nonchalance. 'I forgot to tell you. Another thing I want is lots and lots of children. And Charon himself could not ferry them away from me, no matter how hard he tried!'

Once this was out of her mouth, she was horrified. Her mother, however, gave a curious little smile. 'That's right, honey! You put your cards right on the table and then we can all see 'em. I tell you from the bottom of my soul that that man took you from me by force, and the Angel of Death ain't in it!'

'I'm sorry,' Xenia muttered. She was mortified. How could she have said such a thing?

Missy, however, did not appear to be angry. She flashed a platinum card at the waiter instead. 'It really is OK, sweetness. You can't read unless you've been to school, can you? And I have attended the University of Life. What you need is a few ABCs about your Daddy, or alpha, beta, gamma, if you prefer. But enough's enough for now, eh? And tomorrow we'll have some fun.'

'Thank you for the meal,' Xenia said, ducking her head, but a wild feeling of dereliction caught in her throat and it was only with great effort that she did not cry.

XIII

ROSAMUND CAME down the next morning to find a policeman standing in the hall, but before she was able to fear the worst, another one arrived, bumping equipment in at the door. She looked down the stairs. Wires trailed. A monitor like a seismograph was being lumbered in.

'*Siga, siga!*' the overseer ordered. 'Slowly, slowly!' On seeing Rosamund, he halted her with an upraised hand. '*Kalimerah, kiria*,' he added, politely wishing her a good morning. The operation was completed, and he motioned her to pass like a traffic cop.

What news had there been in the night? Rosamund panicked. Where was Catherine? She turned this way and that, wondering where to look when Theo emerged into the hall, giving rapid instructions to the vanishing policeman. He wore an open-necked shirt with sleeves rolled up, as if he were prepared for hard labour. She had thought he was still in Athens. She glanced aside at the sheer awkwardness of seeing him, but he looked straight at her, as if nothing had changed between them. Perhaps it had not.

'This is a crime,' Theo said. 'Kidnap.' He gestured towards the study behind him. 'We are setting up operations.'

'Has Missy . . . ?'

'Made demands? No, but she will. You can be sure.'

'Theo, when . . . ?'

'The trucks arrived from Athens by the dawn boat. I flew.'

'Catherine!' She was floundering, unable to complete any one thought.

'She is being interviewed now by an officer from the special unit. I was going to fetch you. You must speak to him too.' He paused. 'You did not tell our secret? Good! It is irrelevant.'

'What? You mean the police do not know who Missy really is? I would say it is highly relevant . . .'

'I am counting on you,' he said. 'I trust you.' He raised his index finger and looked at her over its tip like someone adjusting the sights of a gun.

She was too confused to protest. 'What shall I say, then?'

'Missy's Turkish connections are important. They want a description. Xenia may be a hostage.'

'Turkish? Hostage? What?' She paused. 'Theo, Xenia has taken her passport. You do know that?'

'Catherine told me,' he said stonily. 'It makes no difference. Xenia was . . . beguiled.' He had to search for the last word. Normally, his English had no trace of a Greek accent, but now it thickened his speech. 'She has taken Xenia to Turkey when she knows . . . *she knows*!'

'What?' Did Theo really believe that there was a political motive behind this? The whole idea was absurd.

'That my grandparents were assassinated . . . burnt alive! I told you only the other day of Missy's interest in Turkey.'

'Theo, Missy is not a Muslim! What possible reason could she have . . . ?'

He leaned into it with passionate emphasis. 'Missy is anybody's! She is anything as long as they pay her enough.'

'Then I suppose you don't want me to tell the police that she is married to a rich man and that she has never, as far as I know, had a political thought in her empty head! Theo, the truth is going to come out . . . and soon. Catherine already suspects it. It was everything I could do last night to keep my word to you. I only just managed not to tell a direct lie!' She said this last *sotto voce*, gesticulating her helplessness in the air.

Theo's eyes were inky black, the pupils distorted. 'My government is taking a serious interest in this matter. A girl from a prominent Greek family vanishes into Turkey with a woman who has a criminal record. This is the priority. For the moment, Catherine's feelings are not.'

'Theo, what criminal record has Missy?'

He glared in silence.

'Theo, Catherine is desperate.'

'Then let that be the punishment for her having let Xenia go to Çeşme with a complete stranger.'

'But she did not think Missy was a stranger. And she was not a stranger, Theo, not at all. Catherine is terrified. If only she knew – '

'Rosamund!' His tone was like a slap. He lowered his voice. 'Catherine's desperation is nothing, really nothing, next to what it would be if she knew the truth, no matter how much she suspects it. I am afraid you really must believe me.'

Rosamund did not dare venture any more. The door of the study, which lay beyond the archway where they stood, twitched slightly open as if someone's hand were on the knob. 'They're coming out,' she hissed. 'Theo, you never told me Missy had a criminal record.' It bemused her. She was not sure what to believe.

'You'd be surprised,' was all he said. The door opened fully and Catherine came out.

Rosamund winced. Catherine looked pulped and haggard, suddenly middle-aged. She was wearing dark clothes, almost as if she were in mourning, and her hair was scraped back in a bun. 'Oh, Cat!' Rosamund said softly.

Catherine looked from Theo to Rosamund. She said nothing, but her eyes rested on her husband in a way that made Rosamund doubt that their marriage could survive this. 'He doesn't speak English,' she said at last, jerking her head towards her interrogator, who sat at a distance behind the door arranging papers on Theo's desk. 'So, you will have to interpret for Rosamund,' she added to her husband, 'as I am sure you will.' The mixture of outrage and irony in her voice was exact.

Rosamund darted a glance at Theo. He really had left nothing to chance. She spoke no Greek, and she imagined Missy was not fluent. It did seem odd that a bilingual agent could not be found. If Missy rang, it would be Theo who would manipulate the call. She was certain he would ensure that.

With a sudden lack of reserve, Catherine clawed at Rosamund's arm. 'You have nothing to fear, Roz,' she said oddly. 'Thank you.'

'Nor have you!' Rosamund grasped her hand and squeezed it. 'I believe you have not.'

The Greek agent was a dry, spare man, who smoked constantly. He wore a black polo-neck sweater and had a hectoring voice. Rosamund noticed that the telephone on Theo's heavy Ottoman desk was connected to a tape recorder and amplifier. Other telephones had been set up too. She stepped over a maze of trailing wires. The agent's name was Tsamakis, and meaning business was what he was all about. If he had human frailties, he kept them in reserve for family occasions. He seemed unimpressed by the opulent surroundings. It was one of Theo's ambitions to set up a collection in his name, and the study was like a small museum. The bookcases gleamed with first editions that Theo actually read. There was a priceless carpet slung (but not casually) over a divan. He owned an archaic kylix said to date from the time of Homer, and it had been unearthed from Chios soil. Had it belonged to Homer? The family collectively dreamed that it might have and liked to imagine him taking the cup and drinking from it. Theo took an interest in classical antiquity and in Byzantine art. There was an ivory panel from a reliquary depicting the Four Evangelists, and a framed silk chasuble embroidered with the Lamb of God kneeling: it was deeply enriched by pearls.

Despite her incoherent mixture of feelings about Theo, Rosamund suddenly feared for him in the presence of this Draco, who would not take kindly, she imagined, to his time being wasted on a sordid domestic matter. Theo seemed unaware of this. He looked at Tsamakis like a brother. Almost overnight, he had become obsessed, a Cyclops with a single eye to damaging Missy. It was as if he would hurl wife, family, cattle into the air or over a cliff in order to get at her. Tsamakis's questions rattled out like dried peas. Theo interpreted them with heavy emotion like a singer reading music from a sheet.

'What is your relationship to Mrs Kavanagh?'

Rosamund explained.

'When did you last see her?'

Rosamund told him.

'Did she give you any indication of why she might visit Chios?'

Theo chose the words carefully. His finger was on the button. What could she do? 'She did not indicate to me that she planned to visit Chios.' Theo was pleased with this. The policeman grunted when he translated the remark. Theo added something.

'I explained that you had come to visit us . . . by coincidence.'

It struck Rosamund forcefully that the agent actually believed the spy story and that some suspicion hovered around her. She had forgotten where she was and what the political stakes were. The implacable militaristic tone of Tsamakis was not Ruritanian but authentic. They were five miles from the Turkish coast. Despite the stories of atrocities perpetrated on Muslims in Bosnia, stories that had horrified the English that summer, the Greeks appeared to have some sympathy with the Serbs. She shot a glance at Theo. Would he sacrifice her to Tsamakis? All of a sudden, she realised that something had been orchestrated in advance of this interview. The vector changed and Tsamakis pursued another line of questioning. What did Missy look like? What were her habits? Where did she come from? To whom was she married . . . and so on. A man of few words himself, he was satisfied with very little. He took notes. He wrote down Missy's London address and the name of Eagles in Kentucky. He wanted a profile of Missy. Rosamund described her as a rolling stone, unstable in the eyes of the family, a black sheep. Tsamakis took Rosamund in with a gauging eye, and she looked down at her hands. Her done-up hair was now a flat cap of silvered mouse, and her clothes had the eminent humility of years' wear. Even Mata Hari might have dowdy relations, his eye seemed to say. Her respectability met his scrutiny and passed the test. With a sudden stab of humour, Rosamund gave him the name of Missy's sister Sally Belle. A call from the Greek Secret Service would enliven her bridge game for years to come. With the proviso that she might be needed again for questioning, Tsamakis dismissed Rosamund. He waved her away.

She stood and looked at Theo for a moment, wanting recognition for her loyalty, but he only glanced up from the leather wing chair where he sat controlling Tsamakis. That was what he was doing, controlling the policeman. He was the very model of outraged father and patriot. He and Tsamakis spoke in the harsh, clicking language, a forbidding tongue. Rosamund had lied – this mattered to her – or rather she had suppressed the truth. The men spoke with tremendous speed like two oncoming trains. They were wholly absorbed in the rhythm of each other's gestures. Rosamund crept from the room, bone-weary, although she had not even had breakfast.

She shut the door behind her, then heavily made her way to the dining-room, hoping not to find Catherine, for again she would be bound to prevaricate. Suppose Theo did know something about his wife that made a lie the lesser of two evils. Maybe he did, but Rosamund could not imagine what that could be. She hated the thought of looking Cat in the eyes. To her relief, the room was empty except for an array of food, which looked oddly ridiculous on the grand, shining, inlaid marble table. Rosamund took fresh bread and yoghurt, but could not eat them. She had forsworn herself to the Greek authorities. Could she be prosecuted for this? Theo had expected this sacrifice as a matter of course. Suppose Missy had a genuine case in law against Theo. Suppose he really had taken her child against her will. Was Missy the kidnapper or was he? Suppose she could establish her claim. Could she ruin Theo? Rosamund had never talked to the police before. She recoiled, feeling that she had touched pitch.

She poured herself some juice made from tangerines grown in the Phocas groves and frozen for use throughout the year; it had the nectared taste of honey and was always thought to be a bit of a treat. She sipped the juice and traced her finger round and round the dull, green rhomboid shapes of the inlay as if she were trying to make sense of the larger pattern of the table. She looked at the pretty, polished marble avidly and tried to think rather than capitulate to tears. Suppose Missy really had been a prostitute and a hardened criminal to boot. Did this make any difference to the justice of her cause? All the images she had of Missy were insufficient to make a coherent picture. Granted, she was not chaste or respectable, but she was the child's mother. Did she want to be? Wasn't this the deciding factor? Rosamund shook her head. Missy was a casualty of the sixties, probably terminally infantile herself. If she had accepted money in return for favours, she most likely looked upon this as a fair exactment from an unfair world that expected its citizens to be grown-ups. That was it! That was the key. It had always been unfair . . . unfair, for example, that Rosamund had lived in the big house, unfair that her father had the money to buy it, unfair that the divine right of social importance should have passed down to the wrong brother. But was it actually unfair that the rich and powerful Theo, no matter what his advantages, had taken Xenia and lied? Suppose Missy had, in desperation, tried to rid herself of the baby at seven months. Theo's story had been so fluent, so extreme. Maybe she really had loved him. Maybe he had broken her heart. Maybe, fired by guilt, she had wanted the baby even more after the actual birth. Was she Medea or was she simply a sad, confused pot-head who would have pulled herself together for her daughter and grown up in the process? In any case, Rosamund began to wonder if she could believe Theo at all.

She decided she must count the lies, enumerate them. Xenia thought her mother was dead. Her mother was not. Catherine thought Xenia had been abducted, and was probably at this very moment awaiting the post in anticipation of a severed finger taped to a cassette full of pitiful pleading. None of this was likely. What was more, Theo had induced Catherine to believe that she was entirely to blame. This was not true. The case against him built. It was terrible. Rosamund felt as if she had opened a door to inspect a vague, crackling noise only to discover a sheet of flame – the explosion of his wrath, the pyrotechnic blaze of his denials. Now, to top it all off, he was wiring the place for Hezbollah, persuading even the gimlet eye of Tsamakis that it saw what was not there. If he could do all of this, he most certainly could take her for a ride. Why would he scruple?

Rosamund longed for the clarity this insight should give her. Indeed, she expected it, but it would not come. She should hate him. She tried again. She meant nothing to him. He had used her. He admitted it. It seemed to cause him no shame at all that he had schemed at entailing her heart so that she would serve his ends with Xenia. She had tried to make herself angry at his arrogance, stabbing herself with thoughts of it, but they made shallow wounds to the body of her sympathy for him. The day after she had learned the truth, she had spent herself pacing up and down the Kolonaki flat, trying to come to terms with it. In a corner of the living-room there was a little Japanese piano which Xenia used for practice when she came up to Athens. Her picture was on top of it, a lovely photograph in a silver frame, and the glint of it caught Rosamund's eye. She had looked away, but not before she had seen a resemblance to Missy, one that could now never be erased. It had almost been past bearing, and she did not know why: the subtle confluence of bones and brow were knit irrevocably into features that would never fail to strike her as having to do with her own.

Rosamund got up, troubled by this thought, and poured herself a cup of coffee from a hot plate where the brew had been left. She had done everything possible to erase Kentucky from her mind, and yet, in the person of Xenia, it had crept into the midst of her deepest and most hidden feelings. She had treasured Theo's daughter, hoarding Xenia to herself as a sacred trust. It had been a way to love him honourably to make much of his child. The little similarities between herself and Xenia had seemed secret signs of a spiritual affinity with Theo. But it wasn't that at all and it never had been! The connection between Xenia and herself was purely animal. It had always been a question of blood.

Rosamund put the coffee down because her hands were shaking. Her own flesh and blood! How she loathed it! All her life, she had longed to be somebody else. Indeed, every route she had taken had been a departure from her own genetic map. She sat down cautiously like someone suddenly aware of a hidden injury, and out it came as if the anger were a boundless entity that she had buried for years under the decency of mourning her parents, under the guilt at surviving them. The fact that she existed at all was only accidental, she was sure. In all probability, she was the result of one of her parents' many marital crises, for they had not repeated the experiment. No wonder she found it difficult to remember them. They had consistently forgotten her, her needs and wishes. Their cold, loveless marriage had no room for a lonely little girl. She had wanted so much to please them, yet no matter how hard she had tried, she had seemed charmless and ugly next to the distant glamour of their selfish lives. They had wrapped themselves up in the columned house as if this showed that their unhappiness at least had style, but in the light of their awful fate, it had achieved the status of a tragic grandeur that in actuality it had lacked. Rosamund had been so isolated, and no one had cared. Even Charles and five children had never made up for the family she had never had. It had never occurred to her until now how unfair it had been to expect them to make up for it.

Why had she not thought about this before? Here she was at the end of a long and hard-worked marriage because she had not had this out with herself from the very beginning. Instead of a family, she came from 'stock' like a horse. Her father had wanted to find his 'roots' as if he had been a plant. It had been borne upon her from her earliest childhood that she was the 'seed' of pioneers, an impersonal construct deriving from ancestors who had gone out into the wilderness, not with native bearers, but with tooth and claw. Blood was the issue, and they had had an atavistic attitude to the sticky stuff, whether it was spilled or whether it flowed in the veins. There had been no mosquito netting between them and their experience, only the gauze of flattering histories.

And yet what honest historian could forgive what they had done? They were no better than Lady Simon's much-vaunted Crusader ancestors, and maybe even a little worse. For some reason, Rosamund saw them in her mind's eye, barbarously self-righteous as they marched straight through the primeval forests, hacking them down. They had done without the blessing of any Pope; instead, they had achieved it all with an Old Testament rectitude, making up rules as they went along, cleansing themselves of Europe in the blood of slaughtered Cherokees. But in their innocent ruthlessness they had not imagined how large a place they had taken on, nor how wild it really was, nor how dense were the thickets against their poor spiritual resources. Her ancestors had been brave, but had they really tamed the vast opponent of the land? In attempting it, perhaps they had bitten off more than they could chew, and from the great pool of genes they took such pride in they had spat out her, and they had spat out Missy!

Rosamund found herself quivering with fury. She had no idea that she really felt like this, and at once accused herself of being treacherous, and more than a little unjust. Maybe it was because of the fire, an unusual trauma for anyone to absorb. Surely, it was unfair to reject her entire genealogy because of an overheated electric plug! She remembered the old house and the exquisite patience of its long-standing oaks, its cornices, her father's library where she had spent shaded August afternoons delving in old leather volumes. There had been the lavender-smelling great-aunts with their fine courtesies and chivalrous male cousins who seemed to step back in time and bow from a graceful world which wanted to remain dreaming that it was civilized. And just because of Missy and Liam Buchanan, she could not deny that there had been both rigour and honour in her family. In fact, in some ways, there had been rather too much of it.

All of a sudden it struck Rosamund that perhaps it was she who partook more of the grimness of her early forebears than Missy. Her unswerving back had consistently stood in the way of her own happiness and had cast a shadow over her entire married life. Between her starch and Missy's disdain for what got in the way, they made a distinct pair, both throwbacks to a time when such qualities were necessary to the killing of bears. Perhaps they were both the logical outcome of the conquest, a vengeance exacted by some spirit of the pure forests. No wonder the Buchanans had a tragic fixation with the land! They'd stolen and razed enough of it.

She pushed the coffee cup from her so hard that it clanked and sloshed over the hard marble surface. She had never thought about being the consequence of history. In European terms, she had none, and so she had got used to seeing herself as a *tabula rasa*. She had always been clever – that she knew – but early on she had realized that she had a boring mind, not gifted with creativity or imagination. If only she had looked imaginatively into her own past, she might have evaded getting caught up so utterly with Theo and this house. She would have branched out and done something instead of standing still, in awe of the magical enclosure on Chios. Here lived the king, the queen and the princess, beyond time's ruin, beyond her own dull life of shopping trips and necessary evils. Because she had refused to think beyond her parents' frightful death she had bound herself mystically to them, living their dream through Theo instead. It was as if their desperate experiment to create Tara in Kentucky had really worked after all . . . only a continent away, in Chios.

Often, on the cusp of sleep, Rosamund would see the dreamy light cast meltingly over the Greek courtyard. She would catch the scent of spiced breezes bearing up from the groves the perfume of ripened mandarins, just as if she were the heroine of some bad romance caught up in the exciting clutches of a bold Eastern potentate. She had served this fairy tale all these years, an ardent royalist basking in the reward of the king's vague smiles. Every gratification she derived from him bore on it the subtle message that her childhood had not ended in a smouldering wreck; that her parents had not been sad, failed and only too human. The approval she had sought was granted to her, and the handsome king, just slightly and so safely out of her reach, was always about to bestow the waking kiss. That he couldn't give it had kept the dream afloat. And now he never would. Missy had scuppered it. What had she called Theo? 'A jerk'. Somehow, the stupid, slangy expression had reduced him to inglorious proportions, and perhaps true ones.

Rosamund was fretful with the crawling energy these thoughts gave her. The coffee tasted like poison. Not knowing what to do with herself, she wandered back into the hall. Theo was evidently still closeted with Tsamakis behind the closed study door. The proofs of his indifference stung her very hard indeed. The inhibitors of shock were wearing off and her nerves were reconnecting. Why didn't she just blaze on in there and let him have it, insist on telling Tsamakis what she knew? Surely, he had some idea by now that Missy was no spy or terrorist. This absurd allegation of Theo's could only slow down the search for Xenia. She wondered if he had taken leave of his senses. On hearing the rumble of voices behind the door, however, she took fright. Whatever was in Theo's mind, it had the momentum of something too dangerous to stop with mere evidence.

Rosamund tiptoed up the stairs and found her way to the vaulted loggia which overlooked the grounds. The hot morning sun was pearled by the faintest haze of early autumn, but it parched the fruit trees nevertheless. She stood and leaned on the stone balustrade and fiddled a flowery weed out of a crack with her fingernail. Suddenly, it struck her what the distracting charade about Turks was all in aid of. If they actually tracked down Missy, what mightn't they do if she lay under this suspicion? Rosamund stamped on this horrifying thought as soon as it entered her head. Theo was not the Mafia, after all . . . was he? No, it probably had more to do with giving Missy a hard time, separating her from Xenia if they were found together, putting doubts in Xenia's mind, slowing things down, strewing red herrings about. At the very least, Missy's assertions of maternal love might seem a little weak in the light of these considerations and any attempt at blackmail could be thoroughly quenched.

She looked over the shady pergola twined with leaves. Where was Xenia? If she was with Missy, did she know? Maybe she was not with Missy at all. Maybe Missy had gone on to Istanbul by herself as she had said. Perhaps she had kept the secret as she had promised Rosamund she would do if only she could see her child again. Maybe she had left Xenia in Çeşme. Maybe someone really had abducted the girl. Her father was not fantastically, but very very rich. This would be locally known. Was Xenia dead? Rosamund could almost hear the sound of time in the silence. She withdrew from the penetrating sunlight into the vaulted shadows of the porch. Its cool, Italianate construction put her in mind of a cloister, and distractedly, she tried to pray. The tension of the moment should have stimulated this remedy in her, but she felt frighteningly cut off, unable to raise her eyes to Heaven, as the parable of the tax collector had it.

A faint, but intelligible sense came to her that a large, outstanding debt to Catherine lay upon her. It irked her to think of it, but to feel the weight of it was worse. Rosamund shifted under it. Had she directly wronged Catherine? What had she intended? Surely she had not consciously wished to divide her from Theo and Xenia? Well, of course not. She had only meant to help. In fact, she had never uttered a word against Catherine to Xenia and had always made light of their little skirmishes. Hadn't she? If she bucked Xenia up and dazzled her a bit, well, what was the harm in that? Rosamund knew all too well what the harm had been. She rested her head against the golden wall and looked up at the slender iron bars that held the arches of the loggia in place. Until the other night, she had not realized how much Catherine loved the child and how painful that feeling was. Or had she not bothered to look for the signs, see the likelihood of love rather than coldness, notice that the shy, defended woman could not express what she felt for Xenia?

Suddenly it occurred to Rosamund why Catherine had let Xenia go. After all those years when she must have wondered, after aeons of enclosure, penance, prison, lies, the chance of truth might have presented itself in Missy, seen yet not seen, known but not acknowledged. Yet what a risk it was if Xenia were never to return! Rosamund shuddered. She could see Catherine in her mind's eye, walking, haunting, her shade appearing after they were all long dead, being sighted in the garden, along the wall, in the cool half-shadows of the evening, looking for the gateway back to the moment in irredeemable time when she might have recognized Missy for who she really was and stopped her. Could she have stopped her? Could Rosamund have stopped her, and would she too ghost the day when she could have prevented this all with one simple telephone call to Athens, a call she had nearly made which would have changed the course of these events absolutely? Instead, she had gone shopping and bought finery for Theo. That had been the who and why of all her actions. 'Did you sleep with my husband?' She remembered Catherine had asked that, and the question had plucked at her all last night in dreams. No, she would not indulge in this speculation. The right thing to do now was to go inside and seek Catherine out, see how she was, sit with her. Maybe she was in her workroom with her knitting and her quilts, eking out the stretched and terrible seconds with stitch after stitch, plying her needle to her grand design, waiting it out. What else could they do? How she wished the telephone would ring . . . with Xenia on the other end, perfectly well, blithely unaware, and feeling idiotic for some silly, quite explicable mistake.

She stood, trying to shake off the thoughts that grasped at her . . . the guilt. Every effort of her adult life had been to make it as predictable as possible, ruling the surfaces of things so that nothing would escape or explode. But, she told herself, not even Theo had imagined that Missy would go to these lengths. As she turned to go back into the house, she heard the sound of voices in the courtyard below. Rosamund froze. Perhaps there was news. Maybe Xenia herself had simply returned. It was too much to hope. She crept back to the balustrade and peered over. To her astonishment, Charles was standing on the swirling mosaic of fruits and flowers. Before she could stop herself, she gave a little gasp, and he looked up.

'Rosamund?' He shaded his eyes. He looked embarrassed.

She was disconcerted, thrown off balance by this. She supposed he was coming about a divorce. What a time to choose! She turned away. The shock of it was that she was instinctively relieved to see him. That would change soon, she thought.

She peered over the balcony again and saw that he had been joined by two others. Standing beside him in the courtyard was Romola, the woman she had met at Missy's lunch, and leaning on her arm was an extraordinary gnome of a man dressed in a baggy suit. He wore a white, embroidered shirt done up at the neck with a string tie, and he carried a straw fedora. It was Tom Kavanagh: she recognized him from the photographs Missy had shown her. Charles looked sheepish.

'Hi!' said Romola. She waved a timid hand at Rosamund and Kavanagh looked up at her. Even from this vantage point, Rosamund could see that he had very blue eyes, so faded with age that they seemed to stare past her in a blank, sightless gaze that gave him the appearance of a Roman bust. Stringy, white hair curled at his forehead and stuck damply to it in the heat. He might have been Nero or Trajan.

'Rozzy, where is everybody?' Charles asked finally. 'Didn't Cat tell you we were coming?'

'No one knows whether they are coming or going here!' she snapped, then flushed for having spoken to him in this way in front of strangers. 'I'm sorry,' she added. 'I did not know you were coming. It's been terrible.'

Charles shook his head slowly from side to side. 'It is I who am sorry,' he said, and she could tell that he meant it. Charles would think it discourteous to spring himself on her at this juncture without having given her due warning. 'I spoke to Cat on the phone last night. She told me you were with her but you had gone to bed. I assumed . . .'

'She's in a dreadful state!'

'I gathered that,' he said. He frowned at the mosaic beneath his feet. 'Rosamund, can't you come down? This is Missy's husband, and of course you have met Romola. They are very upset too.'

'Glad to meet you,' Tom Kavanagh said. He had a quavering, high-pitched voice and spoke like someone out of a Western. He looked as if he had more to do with Texas or Arkansas than he did with Kentucky. She was surprised to see how old he was. It seemed absurd to carry on the conversation in this way. She could hardly go on shouting from the balcony at Missy's aged husband – nor, for that matter, at her own.

She entered the house once more. Her eyes were dazzled by the sunlight, and she made her way down in a green darkness. Did Theo know that Charles was coming? And with Missy's husband? She doubted it. The ramifications struck her. What on earth would he do, especially with Tsamakis there? 'Theo?' she called. There was no answer. The study door was still closed. She knocked, then entered. More equipment was up: computers, a bank of telephones. Theo was on one of them, rasping into the receiver in a delirium of Greek. Tsamakis was on another, making laconic replies. It was almost as if they were speaking to each other through separate instruments. A third phone, with tapes and winking lights, stood at the ready. She signalled helpless gestures at Theo, but he raised his heavy hand in a swatting motion. He had a pencil and was making notes.

'What shall I do?' she thought. There was nothing for it but to go into the courtyard. Perhaps she could get them to go away. Perhaps she would even go with them. She could not think what had possessed Charles to bring Kavanagh and Romola, nor could she imagine how he had even met them.

As she made her way towards them she determined not to embrace Charles, yet the moment she was face to face with him the temptation to fall upon his neck was almost more than she could bear. She had not seen him for weeks. Did he look thinner? He looked uncomfortably at her, as if he did not know whether he was pleased to see her or not. He gripped her hand and then let it go, a little gesture of helplessness.

'I'm glad to see you in one piece, Rozzy,' he said.

'Romola!' she cried, avoiding him. His quick touch had brought tears to the back of her eyes. She did not want to look at him. He made her so angry. 'Romola!' She extended a hand, but Romola seized her and hugged her.

'If you're wondering what we are doing here, it is a long story,' Romola said. 'I guess yours is too.'

Rosamund nodded. She sagged into the tall young woman's bony embrace with a real warmth of gratitude. She remembered how much she had liked her. How could Catherine have failed to warn her of this? It seemed extraordinary not to tell her. Rosamund wondered if they had brought the little boy as well. What a gathering! 'Where is Paolo?' she asked a little nervously.

'He saw a butterfly,' Charles said. 'I didn't think anyone would mind if he chased it. He's been cooped up in an aeroplane for hours.'

Beyond the water-wheel in the garden, she saw the boy's head bobbing in the sunlight like an advertisement for some wholesome product. What would Tsamakis make of all of this?

'He won't kill it,' Romola said anxiously.

'My grandson takes an interest in all forms of natural life.' Tom Kavanagh spoke, his voice a gaspy wheeze. Everyone turned to look at him. He had given ponderous weight to this simple declarative statement, as if it had large and important implications, perhaps for the future of the planet. He must have been about eighty years old, Rosamund thought, and in itself, this would explain Romola's dim view of Missy. So that was it. She was an old man's darling; a schemer. Rosamund had formed the impression that Kavanagh was somewhere in his sixties.

'How do you do?' She greeted him with some formality. The ropes of his neck stood out over the buttoned collar of his Mexican shirt, and his tongue flicked spittle from the corners of his mouth like a reptile. 'I am Rosamund Simon, your wife's first cousin.'

His hand was dry and bony, but for all his frailty, he had a strong grip. 'Well, just fine, thank you, Cousin Roz, how're you?' His faded eyes seemed impersonal, almost otherworldly. 'Nice place you got here.'

'It isn't Rosamund's, Pop. I told you, it belongs to Charles's sister and her husband,' Romola said, prompting him. She clutched at his thin elbow, fussing over him.

'Tom brought us in his private jet,' Charles said loudly. Rosamund could tell that whatever the situation was, it had become socially difficult.

'Aw, it's only a rented one,' said Kavanagh. 'It seemed the least I could do in the circumstances.'

'Did you fly here all by yourself?' Rosamund asked. She did not know why it seemed necessary to flatter the old boy, but the general mood seemed to require it.

'Well, I have my licence, but I'm none too confident in Europe.' He pronounced it 'Yurp'. 'We hired a pilot.'

'Tom feels an obligation to Cat and Theo,' Charles said. He shot Rosamund a glance freighted with barely communicable meaning, and yet it spoke to her. She turned aside, again oddly near tears. By the look she understood that he had been trapped into this journey in some way. It seemed almost unbearable that not too long ago it would have meant that he could not wait to tell her the whole story.

'Just you wait till I catch that Missy!' Tom Kavanagh exclaimed. 'She's a scallywag!'

'She's a tramp,' Romola muttered, just out of his hearing. 'Just what is she up to?' she asked in a louder voice. 'Is there any news since last night?'

'Nothing from Xenia. The police are here.' How was she going to explain this? 'They are taking it very seriously. It's getting a little out of hand.' She looked wildly at Charles. 'Did Theo know you were coming?' She slid a glance towards Kavanagh. 'I think it might come as quite a shock. He is beside himself.'

'Can't say I blame him,' said Kavanagh. 'Whatever you say or do with Missy, she just doesn't think.' A distant, fond look came into his watery eyes. He might have been talking about a wayward child caught with its hand in the cookie jar.

'On the contrary, Pop, she thinks a good deal!' Romola said with asperity.

'Oh, she's bright enough. I'm not contesting her intelligence. It's more truth and consequences. She can't link 'em.'

Romola threw up her hands at the old man's speech. 'Pop, I think Rosamund is trying to tell us that these people here are *really* cut up about their daughter. I am sure everyone is going to know soon enough that you intend to help find her – and Missy. But for the moment, it might be tactful if we went and found our hotel. This is a different country from ours. It might be hard for Mr Phocas to accept your offer straight away. That is what you mean, isn't it, Rosamund?' She put her head to one side in a gesture of special pleading for Kavanagh's years.

Rosamund was awash with relief at her good sense. Why couldn't Charles have thought of this? He fidgeted, bursting, she was sure now, for an opportunity to explain everything. Maybe he did not want a divorce. Maybe she did, though. She concentrated on Romola. 'You have put it exactly. Xenia has been brought up very carefully, Cousin Tom, which is the Greek custom. Missy may be unconnected with her disappearance, but Xenia is the apple of her father's eye, and meeting you just now might upset him a great deal. Do you see?' She explained this in perhaps too distinct a tone.

'Oh, I see! I do see,' said the old man. His cloudless eyes suddenly focused to a pinpoint, and though his expression was entirely without rancour, his voice was tremulous and a little defensive. 'I do see,' he repeated. 'We don't want to treat this place like Vietnam!' He waved a hand at the restrained opulence of the house and gave a dry chuckle. 'Send in the Marines, eh? Nuke 'em. Not my style at all.'

This had gone on long enough. 'Where are you staying?' she asked briskly.

'The Villa Argenti . . . where else?' Kavanagh said. 'We phoned ahead and booked.' He paused. 'Racing is a brotherhood, you know. We connect all over the world.'

The fame of the Villa Argenti was more potent for its not being widespread. Its prestige depended on word of mouth, and one did not precisely 'book' a suite within its walled sanctum. It was more a question of being a discreetly paying guest of the proprietor, whose family had owned the estate in Kampos for centuries. 'Theo will like that well enough,' Charles said sourly. He had always thought his brother-in-law a bit of a snob. 'I am staying here, however,' he added, looking self-consciously at Rosamund. 'Catherine begged me to.'

Romola cleared her throat. 'I think we'd best be going,' she said. 'I'll round up Paolo.'

'You'll need a taxi,' Rosamund said nervously.

'Oh, they won't,' Charles said with a short laugh. 'I'm surprised the whole world does not know we are here with what is parked outside. They hired a Rolls.'

'Well, "if you've got it, flaunt it!" ' Romola said with a mean smile, and she vanished down the garden walk in search of the child.

Charles, Rosamund and Kavanagh stood in silence for a moment. The water-wheel had not been activated that day and there was only the sound of cicadas in the trees. The old man looked at them, uniting them in one glance as if they were still a couple. 'Missy!' he said, shaking his head. 'Missy!' There was a heartbroken sound in his cracked voice. 'You are married people. You will understand. I cannot talk to Romola about it. She resists Missy so!'

Charles raised his eyebrows at Rosamund. 'She does this sort of thing all the time it seems, Roz,' he told her.

'She does?'

All at once, she remembered. How could she have forgotten it? Missy had told her that Kavanagh knew everything about Xenia and was preparing a room for her in his house.

'Footloose! That's what she is,' Kavanagh said, shaking his head sadly. 'And it's pointless to think that she will ever settle down.'

Rosamund was not listening. Did he know? Would he tell? 'Cousin Tom?'

He started from his vacant reverie.

'Cousin Tom, you don't happen to know of any reason why Missy should want to tempt Xenia away? This is a question I know you will be asked.' The words came out clumsily. The tone was wrong.

She was taken aback by the sudden force of his gaze. Her carefully masked question had jolted him into a marked shrewdness, and at once she could see the horse-dealer in him. 'What do I take that to mean?' he said sharply.

'Nothing.' She shrugged. 'It's the burning issue, that is all.' Why was he looking her over with such speculating acumen? She felt she had a hand of twos and threes.

'Not for immoral purposes, I am sure,' Kavanagh said, which seemed a very odd defence.

'I didn't mean that!'

'Then what did you mean?' He asked her mildly enough. Charles looked at her too. Was she exuding uncertainty?

'Catherine thinks Missy is a kidnapper,' she said at last, imparting this half-truth with conviction.

In a sudden display of ostentation, Kavanagh gave a loud laugh. 'That's rich!' he said. 'Could be the other way around, you know.' In a more serious tone, he added. 'I do understand the fear of kidnappers, though. It's with me day and night over Paolo, and when Missy takes her little "vacations", she doesn't *realize* – '

'No!' Rosamund said with a vehemence that surprised her. 'She does not realize!'

Their attention was diverted by Paolo and Romola coming up the pergola from the orange groves. The little boy trotted ecstatically in front of his aunt. 'Grandaddy, I saw a monster lizard! Ugh!' He gave a delicious shudder as he arrived. 'It was disgusting.' He stopped, and on seeing Rosamund, he greeted her. 'It's you!' he said with pleasure. 'How did you get here?'

'We'd all like to know that, Paolo,' Charles muttered.

'This is like my Daddy's house,' the boy said, 'in Verona.'

When the child mentioned his father, the old man's face clouded, occluding the radiance with which he had greeted Paolo's emergence from the groves.

'Look at your hands!' Romola cried with distracting verve. 'What have you been up to?'

'If you see a lizard, you try to catch him, don't you?'

'Dumb question, huh,' Romola ruffled his hair.

Everyone looked at the child with strained fondness.

Rosamund became aware that Catherine had joined them. She had come up so quietly that no one had seen her. She stood very still with her feet together on the cobbles, her hands folded precisely. 'Oh!' Rosamund cried. It was too late to spirit the visitors out now. How could she have failed in this?

Catherine stepped forward, but everyone else was rooted to the spot by the solemnity of her appearance. With her sober clothes and scraped-back hair, she looked Greek. A vertical frown had etched itself down her pale forehead. She inclined her head. 'How do you do?' she said to Kavanagh and Romola. 'I am Catherine Phocas. You must be Mrs Kavanagh's family. How kind of you to come! Charles, darling, thank you.' She was positively alabaster. She pressed her cheek to her brother's, then gravely shook hands with everybody. Paolo looked awestruck.

'Cat . . .' Charles hugged her, patted her shoulder, then hugged her again, almost giving a little sob as he did so. Her eyelids were swollen with crying and slanted with meaning. She seemed locked into a terrible sureness of what she was doing.

So she had not only expected the visitors, she had invited them! Rosamund was puzzled, but Catherine was magisterial.

'I am sorry. I did not realize that you had arrived. I was resting and I expect Yiorgia did not want to disturb me. But I see that Rosamund has already greeted you. Please, you are to come and have coffee,' she said, 'because I want you to meet my husband – unless, of course, you wish to rest after your long journey. Was it very tiresome?'

XIV

XENIA WAS footsore. Missy was not. She was, it seemed, an indefatigable tourist, and was determined to leave no sight unseen. By 2 p.m. they had visited umpteen mosques and combed the Old Bazaar, and now they were 'doing' the tombs of the Sultans, which lined the route to Agia Sophia. Xenia had lost track of which Sultan was which, but Missy appeared to know each one personally. As they went along, she held discourse on the delicate tracery of marble, the fretwork and the cupolas, as if Xenia happened to be an advanced student of architecture and she a cicerone with a specialized knowledge of Muslim funerary art.

They had spent the morning shopping. If Missy had meant them to remain undiscovered (as Xenia had suspected the night before) then she was certainly going about it in the wrong way. 'We have to improve your wardrobe, honey,' she had said upon rising, with a bold stare at the floppy dress Xenia had bought for herself at Gap in London. They had sallied forth in the best tradition of shopping women, and before she knew it, Xenia had been suited up in a swishing cord skirt and a jackety cardigan she really did like. 'There!' her mother had said, making her feel somehow that all wardrobe choices before had been part of a mistaken general ethos. A seemly frock for dining out had then been provided along with slips and knickers and bras, and then they had hit the shoe shops. Missy had bought a few pairs for herself too. All of these purchases were lavishly dumped on the American Express, and Xenia realized that the flimsies were bound to turn up on someone's desk when it was time to pay. It was obvious that Missy's husband must know where they were or would not care when he found out. She talked enough about him.

When Xenia's hands were fully stuffed with bags, Missy had wrinkled her nose. 'I do not think I can resist the temptation any longer,' she had said. 'I've just got to drop in on Artizan and see if they can squeeze me in.' They had hiked a frightful distance to the Turkish couturière and Missy had fitted in just fine. She was the sort of person who never needed an appointment for anything. Xenia had never met anyone so self-assured. Her mother had come out with a caftan in rose taffeta worth $1,000. The sleeves were inset with antique panels from an Ottoman court dress.

'What d'you think?' she had asked her daughter as she tried it on. There had been no 'thinking' about it. It dazzled. In another time, her mother might have been the darling of a seraglio.

Xenia had a painful vision of her father. The legendary Albanian mother was supposed to have had every desirable characteristic but a wedding ring. Everything that Missy had done since they had arrived hinted at a very different sort of woman, a concubine of rare gifts. Xenia knew that no lady would have flashed rings and platinum plastic in the way that Missy did. There was a knot of shame in Xenia's chest at the snobbery implied in this thought . . . and the embarrassment of watching Missy buying. She wanted to say, 'Please don't. It's vulgar.' No one else in the city seemed to think so, however. The shopkeepers doubled themselves in two.

It was when they had returned to the hotel with all their plunder that Xenia had struck the wrong note. 'I think it is time that I rang . . . home,' she had said. She was unable to use the words 'father' and 'mother' comfortably now. She realized now that she often spoke about her parents to her friends. They absorbed her in a crucial way.

Missy had stiffened. With a thin mouth, she had laid Xenia's new clothes on the bed like so many bribes. There was tissue paper everywhere. They had come back to change and they were planning to have lunch in the Old City. A full programme for the afternoon included Agia Sophia, the Blue Mosque, and whatever else they could squeeze in; Topkapı Palace, perhaps. 'Let's not spoil things,' she said evenly. 'You said you'd hear me out first. Call them tonight. Why not?' Her tone was soft and pressing. Although it would have been ease itself to lift the receiver and ask for a line, it seemed impossible to Xenia. The chill barrier of Missy's will stood absolute between herself and the telephone.

Xenia wished that she was not frightened of Missy. Perhaps she was simply shy of her, given the circumstances. It was difficult to imagine anyone more open and direct than her mother, and this had a breathtaking effect on one accustomed to the polite obliquities of her 'parents.' But as her eyes adjusted to the unshaded glare of Missy's approach, Xenia became uncomfortably aware of a faint menace in her. It was hard to define.

They shared the same room in the Büyük Londra hotel, 'the penthouse suite.' It was a little seedy, but the view across the Golden Horn was a picture postcard, the Mosque of Suleiman the Magnificent across the luminous water a promotion for the mysterious East. Even though their beds were far apart, Xenia had lain awake the night before with a sense of their radical connection across the enormous room. As tired as she had been, she had not dared to sleep until she had heard Missy's faint snores, which had come late, very late . . . so late, in fact, that Xenia had been sure of her mother's conscious attention. And while Xenia was grateful that she was not expected to put on displays of affection for this virtual stranger, there was something fundamentally disturbing about the lack of maternal warmth in Missy. She might have wanted Xenia, but now she had her, it seemed that she was not sure what to do with her. As they made their way down towards Agia Sophia, it became clear that any flagging or complaint of blisters would invite her scorn rather than her solicitude.

Xenia trailed numbly in her wake. Why had she not been able to pick up the telephone and ring her father? It was probably cowardice and nothing to do with Missy, who was treating her almost too much as another adult. At dawn, she had jolted awake, her father's image summoned from a dream. It was as clear as speech that his anathema lay on this whole exercise. In the beginning, she had not thought this would matter. In fact, she had some anathemas of her own to hurl. Once she had slept off the initial fever of her flight, however, she had sobered into an awareness that it might come to matter a lot. She had felt raw and squeamish all morning, and by the time she had decided to telephone, she had worked herself into a pitch of anxiety. If ever he had exacted one promise from her, it had been that she should avoid all contact with strangers of either sex. His wealth imposed restrictions on her. He had enemies. Xenia had often tried to imagine who these were. Although he was conservative, he had a grudge against the Colonels from the seventies. His own father had been killed by Communists and he had a low opinion of these. He had business dealings all over the world, and in such matters Xenia knew him to be an unsentimental man. And then there were the Turks. It was in his character not to elaborate on the specific dangers he foresaw. There were many things about his past that he never discussed. On the whole, however, Xenia had never expected explanations from her father in questions of obedience. Everything between them came down to trust. He had trusted her that she would trust him. They were that close. Now, however, it was all too easy to see what he had feared. The enemy had been within all along . . . her mother, this stranger, this Missy was the seed of her own self. Like Eve, Xenia had been proffered the dangerous fruit of knowledge, and she had eaten it whole. No, it was not Missy who had prevented her from lifting the receiver; it had been, rather, the fear of the death-blow in his voice . . . his wounded and outraged love.

All the same, she wished that her mother had not looked so slighted when she had suggested making the call. Xenia was certain that she was still angry. She had not said so, but instead of the leisurely lunch they had planned, they had picked up a kebab in a coffee shop, a place far from atmospheric. It was more like Burger King and Missy had sulked into her pitta sandwich.

Xenia wished that she had not worn the new shoes, but she had done so to indicate her gratitude. She decided to try a conversational tack in order to appease the giver of the gift, her long-lost parent, who might, in fact, want to get lost again. It made Xenia very anxious to think that she was not hitting it off with Missy. She cast about for what to say, and decided that a flattering reference to her mother as a world traveller might stimulate a happier atmosphere.

'It is wonderful how very well you know this city . . . Missy.' She still found the name difficult. 'Did you live here?'

'I spent some time,' Missy replied enigmatically.

'You seem to know a lot.'

'I'm a quick study . . . I hated school, though.'

Xenia was nervously glad to see signs of a thaw.

'Tell me, do you really want to go to Oxford?' Missy asked.

'I expect so.' Xenia was not certain that she did.

'Well, I suppose it is your Daddy's Alma Mater. He never let me forget that he had taken the British on at their own game and won. And naturally, he would be thrilled if you followed in those giant footsteps.'

Xenia wondered if she was being ironic. She pictured the vast imprints of her father and saw herself tracking after them, short of breath, exhausted from trying to keep up with him and his expectations of her. But she said nothing. She wanted to get off the subject of him.

'If you sing, why don't you study to be an opera singer instead? There's a big-deal opera here, you know. Last time I was in Istanbul, I dated one of the stars. Maybe he's still here. Maybe you could meet him. He could have gone off to Ankara, though.'

'I could be a choral scholar, but not a star,' Xenia said truthfully. 'I haven't a big enough voice.'

'Why do you always run yourself down?' Missy cried. 'You wear baggy clothes and you say you can't sing. You ought to be more positive about yourself. At your age, I was having loads of fun and here you are at eighteen bowed down with responsibilities. This is the time to experiment. You'll never get it back again.'

With a little jolt, Xenia realized that travelling with Missy was her experiment. It bucked her up to think this. Why not try it? Although she had a subtle sense that Missy herself was a woman who had never let the burden of any responsibility get too heavy, it was also true that her mother's words had struck a chord. When she thought about it, her parents strictly vetted her visiting list and the only fun she ever really had was eating pizzas with Rosamund and giggling with her school chums. And was this really so marvellous when she was terrified of getting fat? At school dances, she was as hangdog as a fourteen-year-old. She had suffered torments when Cosmo had not replied to her last (emotional) letter. In fact, she sometimes wondered if she had more in common with the nuns than with her own classmates . . . as far as life experience went, that was. To the vast party she imagined life to be, she had not been invited.

'I do have fun,' she said, though.

'At boarding-school?' Missy was incredulous. 'But then, I suppose the only person I ever knew who went to boarding-school was good ole Cousin Roz, and of course, you know all about *her.*'

'No, what?'

'Miss Hoity-Toity!' Missy said with startling vehemence. 'She with her airs and graces. She always was a bit of a hypocrite, which is why, I guess, she is *so* keen on your Daddy. I wouldn't be at all surprised . . . well, never mind.'

Xenia tried to puzzle out the meaning of this utterance, and then with shame she realized what it implied. A soft, remote look did come into Rosamund's eyes when she spoke of her father, but she had never imagined anything degrading about it. Missy's tone hinted at a smudge. Now she had seen the stain, it remained with Xenia that the motive of disinterested love was less powerful and less likely than that of sex. A shock of cynicism ran through her, sudden, unaccustomed, and quite cold. She wondered if her father and Rosamund had slept together. She wondered like Missy did.

Before she could consider this any further, however, they had reached their destination . . . the broad plateau of major tourist sights. Resplendent Byzantium spread out before them, and with it a gaggle of touts pressing rugs and tours and postcards. They had been beset all day by wheedling individuals whom they had studiously ignored, but now they were hemmed in. Missy looked at them with insolent amusement, almost pleased, it seemed, to let them crowd her. Then, in a few obviously well-chosen words of Turkish, she addressed them with extraordinary hostility. They backed away, lurked angrily, then dispersed. 'Taste of their own medicine,' Missy said. 'I hate the bazaar mentality. Give me a shopping mall any day.'

Xenia felt uncomfortable that she had treated the men like so many curs. Although she had felt menaced by their proximity, she knew that they were poor. Some people existed rather than lived, she wanted to say to Missy. Her father had always made her conscious of the needy and aware that her wealth should be self-taxed when she attained to it. Perhaps he would not have extended this largesse to Turks, but there was a sense in which he understood them better than Europeans . . . and she did too. She did not dare to contradict her mother, though. There had been a real, relished malice in her tone. A wave of fear came over Xenia, but she was not sure why.

Missy took her arm in a confidential manner. Perhaps she had seen Xenia retract. 'Well, here you are, sugarplum, Agia Sophia, Sancta Sophia . . . whatever you like. You said you wanted to see it, and your wish is my command. Feast your eyes on that!'

Before them sprawled the massive, pink bulk of the basilica. Beyond and to the right, the delicate minarets of the Blue Mosque shimmered in antiphonal response to the vast complex of domes. 'Oh!' Xenia cried with the sudden pleasure of seeing an old friend. All her life, the Church of the Holy Wisdom, dedicated in the reign of Justinian, had invisibly dominated her mental map at the epicentre of some unknowable sphere – as the contiguity, perhaps, of two spheres, the temporal and the spiritual. And there it was, as old and grand as her idea of God, sublime in its majesty, rooted in the depths of Greek History.

'Isn't it a dreadful pink?' Missy said.

Xenia felt she had to summon the courage to rally round it, the anchor of Christendom. In a veiled glance, she defended its position as splendid.

'Oh, are you Orthodox? You probably are. Odd to think of my child in that way,' said Missy. They walked along towards the stunning edifice. Xenia thought she did have the grace to look abashed.

'I expect I am a bit of both,' said Xenia. 'I have been brought up Orthodox, but I go to a Catholic school.' She wanted to add that her mother remained a Catholic and that this had somehow impressed her, but then Catherine was not her mother, was she? She was faced with three mothers now. The ersatz Albanian mother was said to have given her up on the condition that she should be brought up in the Orthodox tradition, and Catherine had thus conceded her rights in the matter. Now, she discovered that this fictional character had done nothing of the kind. She wondered what the real mother believed in. 'Before the schism, this church was both too. Like me,' she added, somehow comforted by the thought.

'OK, then it's a great pink.' Missy shrugged.

'Do you believe?' Xenia wondered if this were a proper test of character. The question seemed to puzzle Missy. 'Do you have faith?' This seemed more precisely what she wanted to know.

'Not in the same things you do, honey,' Missy replied. She frowned slightly in thought. 'I used to be a bit of a Buddhist, but that wore off. I'm not good enough for a religion,' she said, and for the first time since Xenia had met her, she gave an unguarded smile. 'I'm no good at rules.'

Xenia had a suspicion that rules were not the essence of it, but she said nothing. Her mother's answer satisfied her in some way. They bought tickets. More shocking than the colour of the great building was the realization that it was now a museum. They strolled through a shaded courtyard full of fallen marbles, antique capitals of columns that once supported great vaulted arches. Xenia shuddered slightly at the tragic ruin. A coach tour of some oddly non-specific Europeans crowded in at the west door.

Xenia looked up at the façade of Agia Sophia. She had expected a revelation of Byzantine glory, but she found it strangely depressing. Perhaps it was a sense that Islam had won the day, wiping it clean of all Christian imagination. After all, the Muslims had added minarets to the basilica and they prodded admonishing fingers at the sky. In an awful wave of sadness, Xenia realized that she had always thought of Constantinople as her father's idea. He loved to tell stories of its remote centuries as if the schemes, schisms and plots had happened only very recently. In her mind's eye, she had always seen the great church as a backdrop to lordly processions led by jewelled emperors in purple robes, empresses with crowns of radiant gold, saints and prelates, wily eunuchs, doomed princelings. Her father was even superstitious about Tuesdays, and did not like to make decisions on the day of the Fall of Constantinople, even though he often had to. In fact, he had made the tale of this sad event so vigorous with spurting blood and whizzing swords that she had been quite old before she realized that it had all taken place in the Middle Ages. It seemed wrong, somehow, to respond to Agia Sophia in his absence. She remembered he had once promised to take her there, and she would have seen its holiness and its greatness reflected in his eyes.

There was no alternative to going in once they were there, though, and so they entered the dark narthex. She gazed up at a rich gold mosaic above the old Imperial door where an emperor cringed in penitence before Christ, Who was seated in majesty. Was this the one who had married once too often for the Church's liking? She could not remember. And then, without suspecting it would happen, Xenia found herself cringing, but in awe. Looking through the lofty portal, she saw the reachless grandeur of Agia Sophia.

Missy gave a low whistle. Somehow, it was not out of place. 'Isn't it breathtaking?' she said softly. 'It grabs you every time.'

For a moment, they were united. They seemed to flow together into the basilica. Xenia was dumb with it. Her eye travelled up and up to the consummating dome which seemed to float unaided above the massive complex of piers and columns, arches and apses, upon which it rested. It was as if the outer edge of the universe hung above them, balanced from the finger of God. Streams of light, refracting through high windows, radiated down vast reaches to the floor like so many Jacob's ladders. It amazed her. She drifted in, forgetting Missy altogether. She gazed into the misty upper ether of the dome at the vast and heavy chain which hung from its navel, and she followed it down until it ended in an enormous chandelier. A numerous party of Japanese stood huddled under its wrought-iron branches as if sheltering from the hugeness of the place. Now and then, some of them snapped flashbulbs, but the hectic squalor of tourism was completely swallowed up in the lofty, numinous space, and for a moment, Xenia was lost to its mystery.

'There is your curious little pair,' said Helena. She leaned over the marble parapet of the South Gallery and gestured towards the eastern part of the nave far below them.

'Where?' Serge asked. He peered through the veil of mote-filled sunlight that flooded the dome and semi-domes that vaulted above them. 'I am assuming you mean Missy and her daughter.'

She nodded. 'Just beyond that party of Japanese tourists . . . by that vast column there. They are looking up at the mosaic of the Virgin. See?'

But Serge was looking instead at his cousin, who was incongruously framed by golden seraphim, hazy in distant pendentives. These faceless, winged messengers of God seemed almost alive, as if the mosaics themselves were avatars of pure being. Helena stood by a porphyry column. There was no doubt about it. She was an old woman now; her skin was as grey and fragile as the Byzantine capitals of fern and acanthus leaves. Her face was as intricately lined. How was he going to tell her about Arthur Holt's biography?'

That morning, he had thought it apt to break the news in the great basilica, for it seemed large enough to absorb any shock, but once they had arrived, Serge had had to admit defeat. He felt a dreadful sadness about Helena. Her beady eyes darted here and there, picking out the heft of a marble pier, the sweep of a colonnade, but in some elemental way he could not define, she seemed to reduce the transcendent loftiness of the monument to bricks and mortar. The mosaic portraits of emperors and empresses, stiff and hieratic, had brought a thin smile to her face, as if she were giving credit to the sheer artifice of power, but by and large, they might have been in a Russian Metro for all it inspired her. In fact, she had even cast a withering eye over the famous portrait of Christ which remained on the wall of the gallery where they stood. In latter years, Serge had discovered belief: Helena believed in nothing. Still, it annoyed him that she was unmoved by Agia Sophia. As they looked out over the parapet, they seemed to hang like spirits in a contemplative immensity of the Divine Wisdom. Even if she did not feel its spiritual power, surely she must understand how the Emperor Justinian had cried, 'Solomon, I have outdone thee!' at the great temple's completion.

'Don't you see them?' Helena repeated a little impatiently. Her voice had cracked since they had last met. Especially if she was crossed in any way, she would speak now in a reedy quaver. It irritated Serge, and it irritated him even more that she had taken such interest in Missy and Xenia. In an attempt to be unselfish, however, he tried to concentrate on the tiny figures below. After all, he had invited her to come on the trip, and if they amused her, he supposed he ought to indulge her . . . up to a point.

'Ah yes, you are right. There they are. Do you suppose we can scoot out before they see us?'

As he spoke, however, Xenia stretched out her arm and pointed up at the Mother of God enthroned above them all in the dizzying apse above the nave, and he was seized by the poignancy of the gesture. It was as if she were appealing to the figure which, for all its gold and majesty, had been wrought to convey a curious, touching humility. All the might of empires, it seemed to say, rested in this simple, gentle woman whose hand rested protectively on the infant Christ. The figures both stared out in mild amazement at all the pomp and glory of the vast building, bewildered that they had redeemed the universe; they would not have been out of place on a park bench. Serge looked down at Missy. She shaded her eyes, glanced up at the mosaic, then restively looked away.

'I have no wish to avoid them,' Helena said. 'They are just the sort of *rarae aves* one might expect to find in Istanbul.' She peered keenly at them through the voluminous air of the temple – like a hawk, Serge thought, at rabbits. Xenia and Missy moved across the marble pavement towards the centre of the basilica. With a sudden movement, the girl broke free and went to stand directly under the branching iron chandelier which descended like a plumb-line from the dome. 'Wasn't that spot supposed to be the centre of the universe?' Helena asked. 'Typical of an adolescent to seek that out!' She gave a dry husk of a laugh. 'I am surprised you do not see the potential in Missy and her daughter, Serge.'

'Potential for what?' Why was she taking such a perverse interest in the two? He had always defended Helena in all her whims and obstinacies, but he drew the line at Missy.

Helena shot him a killing look. It almost cheered him that she had not lost the taste for battle. They had enjoyed many rows in the past. 'I don't know . . . for being interesting. They seem like something out of Henry James, you know, like Madame Merle and Pansy. A Greek Pansy at that! Only she seems to have a little more to say for herself.'

'Henry James is not my cup of tea,' Serge said. 'And I really don't think you want to get to know Missy in any depth. I am sure you are sympathetic to a woman with a "past", but not one quite so mercantile as Missy's.'

Helena's eyes kindled with amusement. 'Bless me! She's a whore, is she? Serge, you are getting pompous in your old age!'

'Poor kid, though, don't you think?'

Helena mused on this and craned her neck over the barrier to get more of a look. Missy had joined Xenia at the *omphalos*, the navel of the world, and they were both lost to sight under the branches of the chandelier. 'Do you know her profession because you used her services?' she asked.

'Certainly not!' he said righteously. 'Do you remember that French crook that Mama and Varya got so upset about? Missy was a call girl, and she became his moll!'

He had forgotten that Helena was capable of spontaneity. She burst out into a fresh laugh that pealed all over Agia Sophia. 'Darling, I have never been able to understand why you have got mixed up with such people, but I think it must be because you are exceptionally innocent. In any case, the emphasis she put on being "Mrs Kavanagh" makes me think she has retired. By the magnificence of her ring, I should think she has found a sugar daddy and is grateful for the permanent prostitution that is marriage.'

Serge shot her an old-fashioned look. In her long life, Helena had espoused every liberal cause, but often there was an absurd disjunction between her opinions and her true feelings. She simply liked to be contrary, he thought.

'But, yes, I do feel sorry for the girl. She is clearly *bien élevée*, and she seems very lost.'

'Well, Missy is certainly not, how do you put it? – *bien élevée* – and thus could not have had a hand in bringing up the well-brought-up child.'

'Don't be so starchy! Missy has "class", as they say. It's just not yours. She is remarkable. I think she means to be a challenge to the world. Arthur would have had her in his pantheon.'

Serge winced. Holt's most famous poem had been about the goddess Aphrodite. There would be reams about Helena in his journals. It really did seem awful that she had not been allowed to read them directly, but Marian had insisted that his ghastly children should make the decision, and he supposed that was right. He would take her to the Bazaar. He would tell her over tea.

'Look!' Helena said, 'They are coming up to the gallery now.' She was staring down at the little pair. Patterns of tourists formed like shoals of fish on the marble floor of the nave. Missy and Xenia were heading towards the narthex.

Serge pulled a face. It occurred to him that Helena and Missy might have something in common. They were both radical and a little cold. He did not want to spend his entire holiday proving that theory, though.

'Oh Serge, don't be boring. I only want to satisfy my curiosity about them.'

They left their vantage point and began to stroll in the general direction of the western gallery. Helena was proving to be quite an effort, Serge thought, although he was not sure why. Ever since his best friend Paul Mason had married Marina, Helena had drifted more and more into a meaningless life. He could not understand why this had been a point of crisis for her, but it had. He supposed it was another way of losing Arthur to lose the friendship of his widow, for Paul and Helena loathed each other, but Serge believed that there was more to it than that. Often, he had wanted to discuss his friends with her. They had had a painful time of it, principally because they had not been able to conceive the baby they had so desperately wanted, even though they were getting to the age when most of their friends had grown-up children. There was something humiliating about the tests they had subjected themselves to; they were fragile and expectant of a fruit they would not bear each other, as if it were the only one to have, and he felt it would be nice if they could simply enjoy the love they did have and leave it at that. But somehow Serge hadn't the heart to give Helena pleasure in the trouble they were having. And it would have given her pleasure. He sighed to himself. Helena was not a nice person, and she never had been, but at least she had been sharp and articulate.

Since her arrival in Constantinople, however, their conversations had petered out into silence, and for a horrid moment he had wondered if she were descending into early senility. With a little shock, he remembered how self-willed she had been, how self-determining. It was this which was missing now. Like a rag-picker, she was gathering what came to her along the way. Her eyes had been darting around the city, alighting on strange objects of interest. She had been fascinated by a sweetshop, for instance, that sold nothing but Turkish delight, and in the Blue Mosque she had spent elongated moments gazing at a remote figure who had been hoovering the acres of carpets. But when she had abruptly asked after Paul and Marina, she had hardly listened to his careful reply.

They wandered down the exquisite colonnade under arches and cross-vaults which sprang from capitals in lacy filigree. Golden patriarchs stood sentinel across the basilica to the north, St John Chrysostom, St Ignatius Theophorus, their hands inclined towards instructing bibles. Maybe it was a good thing to encourage Helena in an interest in Missy and her daughter. Even as a diversion, it might help to reconnect her to the human race. That morning, they had watched a gypsy prodding at a dancing bear on the street. The poor creature had lumbered, a ring through its nose, and Helena had studied it without pity. Now, she looked down the long gallery in the same discomfiting way. At the very least, he supposed, Missy and Xenia were rare enough specimens for her collection. Her eyes hunted. 'Maybe they have seen the gallery already. Maybe they have gone,' she said.

As she spoke, however, Missy and Xenia rounded the corner of a large pier. For some reason, they startled Serge. He did not know why they made him feel uneasy. They gave at once the impression that something was wrong. Serge was thoroughly broken into rows between women. His wife and daughters had fought. Varya, Helena and his mother had fought, but there was something really unnatural about the girl's hunched form. Although they walked together, there was a disjunctive space between them and a sense of hostility exuded from Missy. It was probably only some stifling undercurrent battle about clothes or freedom going on between them in which angled statements had been made in perfectly sadistic innocence, but when Xenia raised her eyes from the floor and spotted him, the transformation was from misery to relief. He wondered what Missy was up to.

As for Helena, he felt a massive shift in her attention. In a swift glance at her, he recognized that her mind was cocked and on full alert, as if a current had been switched on. Her electric intellect, fallow for so long, lit the scene.

'Hallo!' she cried in the very social voice of an English gentlewoman. Helena had been raised in London, and somewhere in that neolithic time had been forced to become a débutante. 'I suppose it is not a coincidence that we meet in this place,' she said languidly gesturing at the light-filled dome as if it were something cooked up by the Turkish Tourist Board.

Missy stopped and cocked her head. 'Well, hi!' she said. Her voice carried over the distance but softly and with an intimate tone. She wore a silk shirt of duck-egg blue that picked out the dulled colours of old Islamic frescos painted in the arches. Serge observed Helena observing Missy's clothes. Why did she always seem to wear black now? She had been very smart in the past. 'How're y'all gettin' on?' Missy drawled. He was sure the accent was exaggerated. He remembered Missy guying herself in Paris.

'Quite exhausted!' Helena said, rolling her eyes. 'Why is it such a tiring city?' They stood together by a marble pillar that supported an elaborate lamp.

'Istanbul?' Missy considered. 'It can't make up its mind what it is about. The conflict just wears you out!'

Helena laughed at this apposite remark. 'Is it the beginning of Europe and the end of Asia – or the other way around?'

'Whatever it is, it hates itself,' Missy said. Serge noticed her glance in an oddly contemptuous way at the girl.

'Of course, that is why it is so disconcerting,' Helena countered. She was beadily inspecting Missy.

Xenia edged closer to Serge and looked up at him with a tentative, meek smile. 'I think Agia Sophia is wonderful,' she said. 'Do you?'

'Wonderful!' he replied, glad indeed to share that wonder with someone. 'I saw you way down there, as tiny as a little mouse.' He was annoyed at himself for talking to a young woman in such a babyish way, so he was taken aback by her expression of huge gratitude. In some way, too much was being asked of Xenia, he decided.

Xenia peered over the parapet. 'Gosh!' she said at the view below. Whether she was going to lunge over the balcony or straight at him, he did not know, but for a second, she reeled as if some desperate course of action had occurred to her. 'It makes me giddy,' she said, looking anxiously at her mother. Serge wondered if iciness was Missy's routine form of discipline.

'And so you know Istanbul well?' Helena asked Missy, filling in an awkward gap.

'I worked here,' she said. She gestured airily and a diamond ring flashed in a beam of sunlight. 'I spent six months conducting guided tours for an American company, if you can believe it.'

Serge could not believe that she could have been doing anything so respectable. A combination of her know-all ostentation and the girl's cowering vulnerability goaded him. 'A little low-key for you, wasn't that, Missy?' he asked drily, raising any eyebrow. 'When was that?'

It had been the wrong thing to say and he regretted it at once, but he was startled to see her abrupt change of mood. 'None of your goddam business!' she snapped.

Xenia was staring at her mother in nervous perplexity in the appalled silence that followed.

'In that case, you will be able to tell us if the Topkapı Palace is of real interest,' Helena said smoothly. 'Is it worth our struggling on to see it?'

Missy was frosty, but once more in command of her temper. 'Well, the seraglio is heaven,' she said. 'It must have been with no men but one boring old Sultan to please once in a blue moon. And, of course, I happen to have the *most* vulgar interest in emeralds. Diamonds, rubies, sapphires . . . they're good too.' She gave a nasty little smile.

'We must see the "rocks", then, mustn't we, Serge?' Helena clasped her hands as if enchanted with the idea of Eastern opulence.

' "A girl's best friend",' Missy retorted.

It was hard to know exactly what had gone on. Xenia looked pale, and her mother was regarding her with a curious fixity. 'We must get on, sugarplum,' she said, 'and get a load of those mosaics.'

Xenia smiled apprehensively at Serge.

'Incidentally,' Missy added, as if they had just completed the friendliest conversation imaginable, 'Russians generally like to eat at Réjans. It's right near the hotel. Catch y'all later!' And with a cute little wave of her ringed fingers, she was gone down the South Gallery with Xenia in her wake.

'Well!' said Helena. 'You certainly put your foot in it!'

'I know,' Serge said miserably.

'There is no one more virtuous than a reformed tart, and you were implying – '

'I know, I know. I can't imagine what got into me!'

'Do you get the impression that those two have only just met?' Helena asked, looking after them. 'I can see Missy fostering that girl out and coming to claim her like a checked hat.'

Serge laughed. 'Good old Helena! Back on your feed!'

'Why do you detest her? I could almost feel your tail switching.'

'I'm not being moralistic. It's the saccharin that makes me ill, and the sense of menace underneath it. She's brutal.'

Helena shrugged. 'She wants to impress the girl.' They strolled towards the stairwell, now finished with the monument to Byzantium, its lapidary beauty. 'I expect she ran off and left an ill-advised marriage with some Greek and the father got custody, don't you?'

'Ah,' he said, 'I think you have it.' No wonder Missy and Xenia seemed awkward together.

'Did you notice that the child is entirely kitted out in new clothes? It is one of those sad treats given by the defeated parent. They haven't a clue what to say to each other, and I should think the lass is giving *maman* a hard time for having sought fulfilment elsewhere.'

The logic of this scenario was so perfect that Serge could not understand why something in it did not sort with his instincts.

'*Maman* has a chip on both shoulders.'

'I can't think why they interest you so,' he said impatiently.

'You knocked one of them off.' Helena was thinking aloud.

'Do we *have* to go on taking an interest in them?'

'Oh, yes, we must!' she said, clapping her hands. 'I have to get to the bottom of them somehow.'

Serge offered Helena his arm as they descended the stairs, and wondered how diverting she would find the strange pair once she knew about Arthur Holt's biography.

XV

THE ILL-ASSORTED group in Catherine's drawing-room sat suspended in silence as Yiorgia trundled amongst them offering coffee and the tall glasses of water which are an invariable accompaniment to this murky brew. Her seamed face gave away nothing, her feelings were as enclosed and defended as the island itself and all its ages. There was a plate of small pastries on the tray as well, but everyone refused these except Paolo, who crumbled flakes of pastry on the Turkey carpet as he ate. Even Romola ignored this lapse. She sat very straight, frowning with intense concentration at her hands tightly clasped upon her lap. Catherine had gone to the study to fetch Theo, and they were waiting for him to appear.

Rosamund's ears sang with nerves. She and Charles sat braced apart upon a spindly sofa, slippery with its tight, striped upholstery. The silence her oath to Theo imposed on her was becoming a lie. Although she did not even glance at Charles, the temptation to share this burden with him, and at once, was almost unbearable. It seemed intolerable to her that he did not know. Had he come all this way to see her? It made her throat ache inexplicably with tears to think so. But rather than test this hypothesis by checking her husband's face, she looked across at Tom Kavanagh, who had accepted the hospitable coffee and water, but who did not touch the cup or glass on the brass table next to him. His hands hung loosely from the arms of his chair, and he gazed vaguely at the oil painting above the mantelpiece.

It was an attractive picture of Chios from the nineteenth century. A man and a woman in traditional dress stood dwarfed by the ruins of Anavatos, a village on an escarpment which had been decimated by the Turkish invasion of 1822. The painter had been an English visitor to the island, Catherine had once explained, and this perhaps accounted for the bloodless rural romance of the scene and its subdued colours. Nevertheless, it was a rather good painting, and it gave the room a detached, historical tone that seemed to say time healed all wounds.

It was like a sad time before the reading of a will, Rosamund decided, with each mourner awaiting a different verdict from the deceased. Yiorgia eyed them all with the dead irony of one whose grief had gone entirely unrecognized. A cold trickle of fear went through Rosamund. Xenia loved her nurse and would not wittingly have caused her anxiety. Perhaps she had not gone with Missy of her own free will after all. No, if Missy had told her the truth, it might have blown all other considerations from her mind. More still, Rosamund thought with a deeper shiver, there was something about Missy herself that would have mesmerized Xenia into submission. She was like one of those Celtic spirits which took children up in a terrible rapture to a magic place where all duties and allegiances were forgotten eternally. Rosamund found the silence intolerable. They waited and waited, sipping the dark, sweet coffee, their cups and spoons clacking on the saucers. The little boy looked wide-eyed around the room. Rosamund thought if he said something cute or precocious she would scream.

All at once, they heard some urgent, staccato whispering outside the door, and Theo entered the room followed by Catherine. He had put on a jacket and tie, and he arrived, indeed with the dreadful formality of a lawyer . . . but at a trial. Instinctively, everyone rose to greet him, but he motioned them to sit, like an official. Tom Kavanagh, however, got up and wavered to the centre of the room where he stood and extended a hand to Theo.

'Mr Phocas,' he said. 'How do you do, sir?'

Theo could have snapped the old man in half with his big hands, and for a moment he looked as if he wanted to, but he did not refuse Kavanagh's greeting and he made a courtly nod. 'Good of you to come,' he said. He had the stuffed manner of royalty showing its mettle under fire. He shot, however, a savage look at Charles, who made a gleeping little face at Rosamund.

'Well, I hope you think so, sir,' Kavanagh replied, 'and I thank you for your hospitality.' He indicated the untouched coffee.

Theo looked slightly mollified by these sentiments. Rosamund watched alert as Catherine flowed behind him, circumnavigating the men until she reached a straight-backed chair which dominated the semicircle. She sat. Kavanagh noticed this and was thus obliged to sit. Theo sat. He greeted Romola and Paolo with a nod. The child gazed at Theo, hypnotized.

'As Mrs Phocas knows,' Kavanagh continued a little less effectively from his chair, 'I have come to apologize to you, sir, for any disruption my wife might have caused you and your family, and to do what I can to help you find your daughter.'

Paolo turned his head very slowly and looked at his grandfather. His eyes seemed completely round.

'Before I continue, Mr Phocas, I wonder if you might prevail upon your servant here to mind my grandson while we talk, as he might inhibit our frank discussion of this matter. You see, I would prefer my stepdaughter, Romola, to remain with me.'

A look rich with depth and complexity passed between the old man and Romola. It was hard to know what it signified. Theo summoned Yiorgia from the door where she stood, and in a moment the child was gone without protest, persuaded, perhaps, by the warmth of her sudden and unexpected smile.

'Mr Kavanagh,' said Theo, very much in an old-world manner, 'it is extraordinarily generous of you to offer your compassion and your help. I am sure you have nothing with which to reproach yourself, but I fear the matter is no longer in our hands. The disappearance of my daughter is being dealt with at the highest level. Xenia may have been kidnapped. She may have been taken hostage.'

The old man's frail back curved into the chair, making his chest concave. He looked as if he had been picked up by a puff of wind and blown there. His Roman consul's head bobbed on his thin neck. He reached up a gnarled hand and adjusted his string tie under his hard Adam's apple, engorged by age. His blue eyes, however, were astute and they registered the surprise of a dealer and breeder of horseflesh faced with dubious bloodlines. Did he know about Xenia? Rosamund wondered. 'Well, now, Mr Phocas, I wouldn't distress myself with that if I were you, not if Missy had anything to do with it. If she is at the bottom of this, then there is no need at all to get the police involved, I can assure you.' He looked bird-eyed around him. 'Now, as this is a matter of some delicacy, I wonder if the ladies – '

'Ladies stay!' Catherine said abruptly. Everyone turned to look at her. She had been completely ignored, but now she entered the scene with bodily conviction. Her eyes travelled from Theo to Kavanagh like pointed guns. 'I think you should tell us all what you know.'

'Pop!' Romola exclaimed. 'For God's sake! These poor people! Out with it!'

Rosamund felt acutely sorry for him. He looked wanly around the room with his watery old eyes as if hoping for some reprieve from sadness. 'My wife . . .' he began, but faltered. Theo sat very still, but Rosamund noticed an involuntary flex of his jaw at these two words. His whole affect radiated molten intensity.

'My wife,' Kavanagh continued, 'is a very special lady, a lovely and gracious hostess, and a fine companion to me. She has beautified my home.' At this, he gave a rare smile, as if a very distant beam of light had struck him and come to his aid. 'But she has a little problem . . .'

Theo's eyes glittered with irony. He was unaware, Rosamund noticed, that Catherine was watching him, not Kavanagh, from the other side of the room. She was as camouflaged by her breeding as a panther would have been on a dark branch.

'. . . and it's a problem we *understand*, don't we, Romola?'

Romola raised her eyebrows and closed her eyes.

'It's just that Missy never grew up somewhere in herself, you see? It's not that she means any harm, it's just that she doesn't think, does she, honey?'

'She thinks,' Romola said.

'Now, it's my suspicion that Missy simply took a fancy to young Xenia, just like a magpie with a pretty diamond ring. You see, she goes off and flies away with anything bright and shiny.' He said this with a sudden and inexpressible pain. He took out his pocket handkerchief and wiped his eyes. 'She wanders, and often we do not know where she is or where she's gone, do we, Rommy? And this is where it is so embarrassing, but I owe it to you, sir, to tell the truth. It's with men. She wants to go with men from time to time and raise a little hell. But I can promise you that she would no more think of hurting your daughter than she would fly to the moon. And she wouldn't even influence her to the bad, because in her own way she's kind of puritanical, though I can't expect you to believe that. If she did take Xenia, it would have been from no motive at all. Maybe she wanted somebody to play with . . . someone of her own emotional age. Don't you understand? I've had to face it, though it hurts me so because I love her, that I am the father to her she never had. Saving your presence, Cousin Rosamund, your Uncle Liam was not a good man. And maybe that is why, no matter what she does to me, I can never abandon her. I'll always be true.' Tears ran down his cheeks. 'Don't, I beg you, get her involved with the police! She doesn't need to kidnap anybody, for my fortune is at her disposal. And what on earth would she take a hostage *for*? Missy doesn't have *reasons* like other people. And if your daughter went with her, then all I can say is that my wife has a charm I cannot describe. It is the charm – '

'. . . of the devil!' Romola said emphatically.

There was complete silence. No one had expected the old man to give tongue in such a way. He had spoken with the simplicity of utter sacrifice, and the beauty of it filled the room. The strain of exposing his agony to the Phocases was cruelly evident. His top-heavy head with its white curls nodded convulsively from palsied effort and his blue eyes were clouded with pain.

Theo made a noise in his throat. His hands were clenched into hams upon his knees; his head swayed from side to side like a punch-drunk fighter. For a moment, Rosamund thought he was angry at Kavanagh, but when his eyes, which had been blinded by emotion, cleared, he looked upon the old man with a terrible pity, as if he now were an added cause for wreaking dreadful vengeance upon Missy.

No one had expected Catherine to speak. She began quietly enough, clearing her throat, and they all looked around as if at an interruption. 'There is a reason,' she said, 'and it has nothing to do with kidnappers, or hostages, or Mrs Kavanagh's charm. There is a reason why Xenia went with Missy.'

It struck. Theo and Rosamund started with alarm. A swift moment was too late. Catherine had done all the sums. Her face was the answer.

'Theo,' she said, 'you know this woman.'

He was caught, cornered into bluster. 'We both know her. We met . . .'

'Theo, you know her a good deal better than that.'

All of a sudden, his hulking shoulders gave way and his whole body withdrew from her tremulous lucidity. He tried not to look away. His face was a mute appeal for a stay of execution.

Catherine glanced at Kavanagh as if to do him justice or to ask for it. The old man's head kept on wavering and undulating. Romola put her hand on his knee and he clasped it blindly.

'I have reason to believe,' Catherine said, 'that Missy is the natural mother of my child . . . by my husband. Missy inveigled her way into this house, and I believe she told Xenia the secret. That is the reason why Xenia ran away.'

Rosamund gasped without meaning to.

'*You* know!' Catherine turned her head slowly. 'It's true, isn't it?' She asked the company in general, appealing to each one of them. 'Perhaps you did not know that Xenia was adopted,' she added by way of explanation to the stunned Kavanagh.

'Cat!' Charles exclaimed. 'Cat, really!' But he stared at Theo and everyone followed his gaze.

'I wouldn't try to deny it, Theo,' Catherine said, as calm as a hangman. 'Long years of speculation have gone into this and you have had the mercy of my blind eye until now. I have never deceived myself that you were not Xenia's father, although I have tried to. But who the mother was . . . well, I never quite knew what to think. I imagined you had bought her off somehow, and as time went by, I was lulled into a false sense of security – in which I was never secure, I may add. Never once. Not for a minute. But the last person I imagined it to be was Missy until you yourself gave the game away. Ever since Xenia disappeared, every inflection of your voice has proclaimed a personal, and even intimate *understanding*. When I rang you in Athens to say she was gone, you *knew* Missy with a special repugnance. It was as if you had been waiting longer years even than I have for this moment. Confess, Theo. It will make you feel better, and the truth will get Xenia back here sooner than ever Tsamakis will with all of the false trails you have given him.'

Theo sat for a moment. His jaw pumped as if he were quite literally pulling on resources nearly dry. 'Catherine,' he said.

'It's true.'

He thought, then finally nodded in assent. 'I'm so sorry.'

Catherine closed her eyes and leaned back in the chair in the awful peace of her vindication. 'At last!' she said. After a few moments, she opened her eyes again. 'You knew,' she repeated to Rosamund. A sombre outrage seemed to possess her. 'How could you . . . ?'

Charles gave an astonished cry. 'All these years?'

Rosamund had no idea she was weeping until the tears fell on her hands. How could she justify herself? Her whole life had been taken up in being seen to be in the right. Suddenly, she did not care if she was. 'Not all these years. Just the other day, when Missy came to see me, and even then I did not believe it.' She looked up at Catherine. 'The awful thing is that I might have concealed it from you had I known, for I did conceal it after Theo confirmed it. I gave my word, you see.' There was a little emotional ping and then a crack. From his eyes, she knew she had lost Theo.

'I wish,' Tom Kavanagh said very quietly, 'that someone had told me. Did you know anything about this, Rommy? Did Missy ever tell you anything about a baby?' He looked around the room at all of them with a strange expression in his vague, wide eyes. It was as if he had found himself translated to the Gobi Desert and did not understand how to extricate himself from some barbarous custom involving human sacrifice.

'Oh, Pop!' Romola said with some distress. 'I always suspected something in Missy's background, but who could ever have guessed at this?'

'Cousin Tom, Missy told me that you knew all about this,' Rosamund said, suddenly enraged by her cousin's lies. 'She said you had prepared a room for Xenia to stay in.'

'My word!' he said. 'That would be Missy all over. She likes to fantasize. You'd think to hear her talk about me I was Buffalo Bill.'

'Frankly,' Romola said, taking them all in with a summary glare, 'there is one little thing I do know about Missy and that is . . . she is crazy.'

Suddenly, Kavanagh shook himself all over like an elderly white bantam rising from a fall to fight another round. He extricated himself from the depths of the chair in which he had been crouched with the misery of it all and he craned himself forward. 'Now, I'm going to say something once and for all!' he declared, glancing with pointed even-handedness around the room. 'Missy is my wife. I took her for richer for poorer, and the poorer she is, the richer I love her. Maybe she is a little crazy. Maybe I took that on board. And maybe, just maybe – though I'm not making any accusations – she's crazier than need be because she lost her baby. Now, I'm not saying that Missy isn't perfectly capable of mislaying a baby . . . she never reckons what a thing will lead to if she does it. But no one badmouths her in front of me, no matter how upset they are, and that's final!'

For all the hard-won energy he had summoned to make this speech, it lost the full attention of his audience. Catherine, Theo, Charles and Rosamund all looked at Romola, united for one moment in a numbing wash of fear. 'Did you say,' Catherine asked quietly, 'that Missy was insane?'

Romola glanced sharply in the direction of her stepfather. 'I think Mr Phocas may have been responding in the correct manner to this crisis,' she said as if the big words might flummox Kavanagh. 'No diagnosis has been made, however, and mine is not adequate. I do think, though, that a speedy recovery of your daughter would be prudent.'

'You do know her, don't you?' Theo said to Romola, his accent thick with distress.

She inclined her head sagely. 'What is the Greek word for playing with a fire like Missy? Hubris? I believe so. Imagine you waking up the sex in Missy!' she said shaking her head.

'I meant what I said, Romola,' Kavanagh said crossly. His voice was suddenly tired and cranky round the edges.

Romola looked at him with magisterial calm. 'Pop, this is serious,' she said, 'and no time for oratory.'

He frowned, his curls bobbing up and down. His earlier dignity was on the wane. He looked a bit like a toy dog fixed to the back seat of a car, which wags its head inanely to the motion of the wheels. 'I tell you, Missy wouldn't harm a fly,' he said, 'and certainly not her own child. Why, Missy is wonderful with children!'

Romola bowed her head and sighed. A vertical frown creased her forehead.

'Why, she's wonderful with Paolo! You never give her credit.'

'Always where it's due, Pop. You know that.'

He looked disgruntled in some way. He fluffed his shoulders and sat back in the armchair, obviously defeated in this round by Romola.

No one knew what to say. They had known each other for decades, Charles, Rosamund, Theo and Catherine. It was as if in the middle of a stupid wrangle, someone had broken an Attic vase and the shards of a thing both venerable and of great value lay strewn about the floor beneath their feet. Catherine sat quietly crying. Theo reached out a hand in her direction, but seeing how vain the gesture was against her tight containment, he let it fall upon his lap. Suddenly he looked old, older than Kavanagh in spirit, as if his many battles had caught up with him and he barely had the strength to move. Out of ingrained habit, Charles and Rosamund exchanged a glance. She looked quickly away. The power of the trust that remained between them unsettled her.

Romola shifted in her chair. Everyone looked in her direction as if for guidance. 'I think it is time for us to hit the Villa Argenti, isn't it, Pop?'

His eyes had taken on that vacancy that Rosamund had first observed in them. He looked into the middle distance as if he had been carried away to this less complicated mental landscape by a puff of wind. 'Missy will phone,' he said, 'You'll see.'

No one contradicted him.

He smiled, nodding at some vague illumination which seemed to jolt him once more into consciousness. 'Missy has a baby now,' he said. He beamed around the room as if only yesterday he had fathered it himself. 'Why, can't you see how this will settle her? Oh, my! It's just wonderful news that Missy has a child!'

Romola's large, dark eyes opened widely as if on a heavy perspective of new sorrow. 'Oh, Pop!' she exclaimed softly. 'No . . . please, no.'

XVI

MISSY HAD declared that they would dress for dinner, and on a whim she had gone out to see if she could get her hair done, leaving Xenia alone in the room to watch the sunset blaze over the Golden Horn. There were flocks of birds rising from the water, wheeling over it; they made the little boats that plied their way towards Üsküdar look laden with silks and spices rather than haggard commuters. The slant of light from the brow of a westerly hill inflamed the Mosque of Suleiman the Magnificent and pierced the waters below, refracting light so that they flashed, now opal, now gold. Xenia's heart was in a panic. The birds moved winged and upwards, first to the left, then to the right. Once, at her Greek school, she had studied Latin and had been made to translate an essay on divination by Cicero. It came to her now, but she could not remember how the birds were to go if the omens were favourable. She knew she should not want to consult a pagan oracle, not put her trust in anything so arbitrary, whimsical and pitiless as nature, but she was desperate. She had half-heartedly searched for a Gideon bible in the drawers of her night table, one that she could cut for guidance. She had read an impressive newspaper story once of the total conversion of a potential suicide by means of an hotel bible which he had opened at random, but Xenia was not sure this was Orthodox . . . almost certainly not. In a way, she was thankful to be removed from the temptation to compound wrongs, for this would only make matters worse. Her friend Sarah was a devotee of horoscopes, but Xenia felt sure that the circumstances of her being a Virgo must lose its application not only in her own plight, but in Constantinople itself. The awfulness of its mystery seemed too profound for stars.

Should she ring home while Missy's back was turned . . . or shouldn't she? In Agia Sophia, she had asked for the guidance of the Holy Wisdom of God, but although she was ultimately sanguine about the outcome of these prayers, they had seemed to cause more trouble in the short run, for she could not understand what had made Missy so angry in the basilica. Had it been she or the Russians or a combination of the two which had put her mother in such a bad frame of mind? For some reason, the Russians set her off. Here Missy was, getting her hair done on the speculation that they would meet the Prince and his cousin in the restaurant she had suggested to them and there, on the other hand, she seemed capriciously unsettled whenever she spoke with the Prince. Perhaps her mother had been in love with the Prince in Paris. She was certainly going to great lengths to make herself attractive for the evening. Xenia tried to think of this as a good thing. It made Missy seem a little romantic, maybe like Georges Sand or Anna Karenina or even Mimi in *La Bohème* – a woman who had loved with crashing chords and lived her life to the full.

On the other hand, Xenia had a deeper sense that it was she who had stepped on an obscure crack and caused pain or displeasure to Missy, who had left the room a few moments ago with a lift to her chin and a look at the telephone that seemed to defy Xenia to touch it. Was she simply imagining this? Maybe she had dreamed some of the other things she had found upsetting during the day. It seemed very hard to tell what Missy would do or say next. At any minute she might come back through the door claiming that she had changed her mind about the hairdresser, or that he had moved, or that he could not take her at such short notice. Leaving Xenia on her own might be a test.

Xenia wondered if she dared to pack her things and go. She could always leave the new clothes behind. But she now realized that although she had a credit card which her 'parents' had given her with solemn warnings against its frivolous use, she actually had nothing in her purse but drachmas, and she did not think this would get her very far on the road to the airport. What was more, she might be expected to pay the hotel bill and not be able to do this. Missy might come in and catch her floundering at the desk. Xenia did not know how one managed any of these things. Every detail of ordinary life had been managed for her since she could remember.

She had the vague impression that one could go to the bank and purchase currency. On her trips between England and Greece, appropriate cash had been placed in her hand. She had the subtle feeling that Mummy – Catherine, as it were – had always been a bit jealous of Rosamund, but Rosamund had always done things for herself and had often shown a timid Xenia how the ordinary world simply worked. Xenia flushed when she remembered the inference she had drawn from Missy's words about Rosamund. Maybe Catherine was jealous for a more pressing reason.

She refused to give time to this thought. Possibly the bank would help tomorrow. But then, how would she get to the bank without Missy knowing? Maybe she should make a clean breast of it and tell her mother that she had decided to go home. The prospect of this filled Xenia with dread. How could she put it? It looked easy, Missy had told her it would be easy, but it now seemed almost impossible. She supposed she could express gratitude. Gratitude was always a good line into anything. Maybe she could suggest that they could meet at a later time when Xenia was older and living on her own.

Xenia wondered if she might even ask Missy to see her off on the aeroplane. Perhaps instead of going back to Chios, it would be more tactful if she were to fly to London. Suddenly, a reassuring vision of her Uncle Charles came to Xenia. In her mind's eye, she saw him in his publisher's suit coming home from work, putting his briefcase in the hall, pouring himself a whisky in the drawing-room. He would ask her vague questions about her studies in which he took no real interest, but his general good will, his general good manners communicated something more.

Xenia looked from the window to the telephone. A pain as sharp as anything she had felt came through her at the thought of Mummy waiting by it at the other end. Such a feeling had never crossed her heart before, and so it had taken some time to identify it as guilt. It was like the shame of not being asked to dance, but it was a lot worse. Once when she was young she had taken another girl's pencil case. She had kept it for a night and returned it the next day, for the desired thing had become an object of dread, almost hot to the touch. The pain felt like that. She thought of Mummy in her clean workroom with quilts and boxes of buttons and her stuffs, her threads and yarns, her lovely loom and how she had let Xenia play with things there in a comfortable cool silence, which was warm at the same time. Unlike the pencil case, she could not return herself to Chios as the same person she had been two days ago. She would be a different person now and always, a person of Missy whose weft went through the warp of her father to make the inextricable pattern of herself.

No, that was morbid thinking. It was sure to be all right. This was an episode, not a career. The cosmic bowl of the sky might sooner change to green than would the universe of her slow-jogging days, days of quiet formality, of nice furniture always in the same place, of forgive and forget, of settled quarrels and of trust given and returned. In any case, it really was a crucial argument here that she had the right to know the truth . . . at her age.

Xenia thought if Mummy answered the telephone, she would not be able to bear it. But suppose her father answered. Her chest tightened at the thought of this. Slightly below the threshold of her conscious mind, but audible to it, a fixed thought dripped, plain and repetitive. It agonized her without pain like water torture. Her father would never be the same to her. Every time her imagination sought him in the places it had found him before, he was absent from them. He had entered a new category of being. Like a verb that has become a noun, he had changed from an active principle into a thing. Maybe if she heard the sound of his voice, it would mend this leak in her thought. What could he say to do this? 'Xenia, I am so sorry. I had meant to tell you this myself'? Would this help?

She remembered a wedding in Chios when she had been quite small: not a grand one, but a local event. Her father was quite firm about honouring this kind of occasion. There had been a huge reception with Greek dancing. The bride and the bridegroom had danced with their handkerchiefs, weaving the ancient, complex steps with consummate grace. Friends and relatives had come up and pinned money to them. Her father had given them a very large amount. Xenia and the other children had raced about in a jubilant Bacchanal of Pepsi until she was quite exhausted and her father had picked her up, her legs still whirling around like cycle wheels. He had laughed so kindly at her burst of tears, for she had cried at being stopped from exploding with excitement, and had said, 'Come along, Xenia, come along, *chryso mou*, it is time to go home now. It is time to go to bed.' Maybe he would say that now . . . or the equivalent. If he spoke to her in that tone, all of this would go away. Missy would achieve her true proportions and Xenia would fall asleep on his chest of lovely smells. Didn't he love her? She remembered he had told her that he had stopped working so hard after she had come to them as a baby because she had taught him that, far more important than vast wealth, was herself. But with the ruby of herself prised from his crown, what would he now do?

Missy had been out for a while now. The door of the hotel room was in shadows, and any minute it might crack open, letting in Missy, a deeper shadow still. Xenia shivered and tried to suppress that thought. She walked towards the telephone. How was she going to put it that she had run away with Missy, that is if she got through? Her father must know by now why she had gone, but what about Mummy? If he had lied to her for so many years, then he would continue to lie. She could hardly tell her mother that she had run off with her mother. She could hardly say that this was an extended shopping trip. Xenia looked at the old-fashioned black telephone on the night table. It seemed to emit a negative force field, forbidding her to touch it. All at once, it struck her that she could ring Uncle Charles and Rosamund in London. Having had a pang of nostalgia for her uncle's decency, she thought of him again. He was Mummy's brother after all and could tread softly with her over this. And hadn't Missy told her that Rosamund now knew the truth? Maybe they could give her some advice, tell her how the land lay in Chios and what was the most politic thing for Xenia to do. She rummaged in her pouchy bag for her address book, but as her hand touched the thing, a shock of memory travelled through her fingers. Only a few days ago, she had heard Lady Simon, her 'grandmother', talking on the terrace at home. Her Uncle Charles was no better than her father. He had a mistress too. Did he have a secret child? Xenia was still half numb with shock in regard to her 'parents', but when it came to thinking of the Simons' analogous situation, a curious emotion came with it. She was not used to feelings like this one, neither in kind nor in degree of intensity. A bitter contempt rose from the gorge of her heart, dragging up with it a chaos of disgust and shame. She sat on the bed, her hands trembling on her bag. What had Missy said to her earlier that day?

She had said that all men were the same.

Xenia sat very still and in an indecent flash of revulsion she saw her uncle in her mind's eye, naked and eager at an amorphous blonde. She squeezed her eyes shut and willed the vision away.

All men are the same.

It had struck Xenia as odd when that afternoon Missy had chosen to take her to visit the medieval cisterns that ran under Agia Sophia instead of the Blue Mosque, which had been on their schedule. But after their meeting with the Russians in the basilica, Missy's mood had become so odd that Xenia had been relieved to do anything at all with a normal purpose to it. Xenia had rather wanted to see the mosaics in the South Gallery, as they were very famous, but when they got there Missy had shunted them through as if the whole exercise had become painful and tedious and Xenia herself a tremendous bore. Xenia had tried to look into the eyes of Christ in the great Deeis on the wall, but she had not been able to face Him. Missy, smouldering now with some obscure dark fire, had given the image an almost insolent stare, as if she had a bone to pick with the icon and all it represented. This had offended Xenia's religious sensibility, but it had been all too vague to challenge. Missy had simply twitched aside, sighing and even tapping her foot until her daughter trotted after her to get a cursory glimpse of the Emperors and Empresses vivid still in chips of stone. Xenia had tried to look at them. After all, they were part of her own history. Instead she had had to fumble inwardly for something to say to appease Missy's inexplicable anger. What had she done to give offence? She had only remarked to the Prince that Agia Sophia was marvellous, and this was such a commonplace that it hardly bore thinking about. Perhaps her mother had caught the impulse she had felt to throw herself into the old gentleman's arms and beg his help. But she hadn't *said* anything! Xenia did not know whether to ask Missy what the matter was and why she fumed or whether to placate her. She decided that the latter course of action was best, and so she thought she would make an appreciative observation on the mosaic of Constantine Monamachus, who had founded the monastery of Nea Moni in Chios. But, by the time she had shifted from sore foot to sore foot and cleared her throat to speak, her mother had sighed heavily and rolled her eyes. 'Look, I'm on out of here!' she had said. Before Xenia knew it, Missy had been halfway down the gallery. There had been nothing for it but to run and catch up with her. Xenia had wrung her hands and racked her brains. 'I'm sorry if I did anything to upset you,' she had said, getting her breath.

Missy had frowned. 'Upset? What makes you think I'm upset? I just need some air.'

It was as if vast Agia Sophia were claustrophobic. Mummy had read Xenia *Through the Looking-Glass* when she had been a child. She felt like a child now, and quite a small one. Pursuing Missy as she strode through the galleries and down the stairs was like a race with the Red Queen. On the pavement outside the basilica, Missy's eyes had darted hither and yon as if the right decision about what to do next would be imperilled by too much thought on the matter. 'I know what we'll do,' she said at last. 'We'll go underground. What d'you say, chicken?'

Xenia could not think what she meant. Also, she had never been called so many nicknames in her life. Even in Greek, there did not seem such a variety of endearments, such a broad system of analogies with sweetmeats and animals. Without waiting for an answer, Missy had taken her by the hand, and before she knew it, they had crossed the wide boulevard and had dived into a small stone building next to some Turkish baths. Missy was silent and tense. She bought two tickets from a kiosk and together she and Xenia quickly descended into a dark and curious underworld.

Xenia peered through the gloom. From the top of a short flight of wooden steps, she could see beneath her a large watery space lit by spotlights. The heavy piers that rose from the cistern supported sturdy arches which cast striking shadows, and under a criss-cross of walkways that had been constructed to transverse the cavern, green, murky water lapped, mildly slapping against the ancient stone. They were alone. Missy sighed and her shoulders released, as if from a bad tightness.

All at once, and obviously on cue at their entrance into the cavern, the scratching noise of a sound system wheezed into life; an orchestra struck up, and the powerful, canned voice of a contralto started to sing. Xenia recognized the piece at once. It was the lament of Orpheus for Eurydice by Gluck, and she loved the aria. The suddenness of the music gave her quite a start. 'They have concerts down here sometimes,' Missy said by way of explanation. 'I came here with my Turkish boyfriend once, you know, the one who sang in the opera. Does still, for all I know. They play tapes so that you can get an idea of the acoustics. Amazing, isn't it?'

' *"Che' faro . . ." I have lost my Eurydice, here on earth, I'm left alone . . .'* Xenia wondered if she were losing her mind, for the music was apt and unreal at the same time. She was listening to an Italian aria written by a German in a Turkish city once Roman, once Greek, with an American mother she had only just met. Or was this Tartarus? Why *Orfeo*? Why now? If they played operatic recordings, why couldn't they have chosen *Rigoletto* or *Tosca*? The pure voice echoed round the heavy piers, the water supply of the Byzantines, their plumbing. *'Where shall I turn? How can I live? Where shall I turn now she is gone?'*

'The cisterns were built by Justinian, I seem to remember,' Missy said. 'Neat, isn't it?' She had cheered up. Perhaps she was agoraphobic. Maybe the size and space of Agia Sophia threatened her. Maybe she felt better underground.

'It's splendid,' Xenia said, swallowing. Condensation dripped from the heavy arches. *'Eurydice, Eurydice! My lost one, I call thee . . .'* It was almost unbearable. For some reason, Xenia could not get it out of her head that Mummy, that Catherine, was singing this directly, was singing it to her. *'Oh, hear me!'*

Missy struck out from the stairs and started to stroll along the walkways that connected over the dark water. She walked with a light, flowing step as if to the music.

'All in vain, I cry again. All in vain, my faithful heart cries out in pain . . .'

'There's a huge stone head down here,' Missy called out. Her voice echoed in the cavern. She looked at ease in the shadowed space. Her clothes followed the grace of her movements into liquid folds. She might have been walking on the water itself, a spirit, a nereid. *'I have lost . . .'*

Xenia felt compelled to follow her. It was as if the import of the song impelled her against its meaning. She took off her shoes and held them in her hand. Suddenly, there was liberty down here with Missy. *'Eurydice!'* the voice repeated in an agonized throb. From what depths had Missy emerged? This was not the myth of Orpheus, but of Persephone. On a sunny day in her ordinary overground life in Chios, Missy had risen from nowhere and offered her pomegranate seeds, and now here she was, bonded to the woman and unable to leave her. Xenia felt heady, bewitched by the drama of all this, the music, the classical reference points. She ran like a little animal along the walk in her stockinged feet. Apples for Eve, pomegranates for Persephone . . . you eat something, you partake of it, and it changes you. To get back to Alice and the caterpillar's mushroom, it was more or less the same – but that was Wonderland, wasn't it? 'Which way? Which way?' You grew with the bite from one side, and you diminished with the bite from the other.

As Xenia reached Missy, the aria reached an end and another scene from another opera began. This time it was *Parsifal.* A golden, German tenor voice sang, but she did not know the words to this one and was relieved. She also felt foolish for having given way to such maudlin flights of fancy over the Gluck.

'Why, you look all barefoot and careless!' Missy said over the strained nobility of Wagner. 'New shoes pinch, eh?'

'I'm sorry, I . . .' Xenia looked down, avoiding the green eyes that always seemed like surveillance cameras in a shop rather than the eyes of a mother.

'Well, that's just your middle name, isn't it, honey? Xenia "Sorry" Phocas. Just how sorry do you have to be all of your life? For what? Now, as for me, if new shoes pinch, I take 'em off, throw 'em in the drink.' For one awful moment, Xenia thought she was about to snatch the shoes from her and hurl them into the water.

'They're very nice, Missy,' she said, not knowing whether her mother was pleased or offended.

She seemed to be neither. The spotlit waters were green underneath their feet. Missy seemed to demand two things from her at once, that she throw off her inhibitions, and that she tighten them up. It seemed so easy to cross her at some times, and yet at others, Xenia had the sense that really she should learn belly-dancing . . . or at least have plans to study it.

'You liked that song they were playing, didn't you?' Missy said, changing the subject. They strolled along together. 'You get music from me!' She said this with a snap of emphasis as if she had slapped a table.

Xenia did not dispute it, but her father had always told her it was a gift from God. 'Do you play an instrument?' she asked.

'Me? No! My Daddy did. He could play or sing anything you liked. Only thing was, you didn't like.' She shuddered slightly, then shook it off. She danced along the track to the grandiose tones of *Parsifal*. Suddenly, she kicked her own shoes off. She pointed her toes this way and that, like a ballerina. 'Now, with me, it wasn't the "opry", it was "dance, dance, dance" . . . "Gotta dance!" I was burning to get to New York and join the chorus line, any chorus line. In fact,' she said, executing a pirouette so graceful that Xenia felt lumpen beside her, 'dancing was my downfall in a way. I ran away from home then fell on evil times. My art was not enough to support me.' She said this with an odd note of triumph in her voice.

They had reached a crossing in the catwalk. Missy stood beside a heavy pier. To the urgent, questing aria of the perfect Christian knight, she started a slow whirl, which made her skirt flare in a perfect circle. Her arms outstretched, her hands arched like an Indian dancer, she lolled her head from side to side, then stopped. 'Whoo!' she cried, shrugging with self-mockery. 'I got into the Sufis one time. There's a dervish museum here in this city, but somehow the phase passed and I never got to see it.' She paused. 'Yes, I've had to be a working girl. Your Daddy saw to that.'

Having been caught up in Missy's exultant whirling, Xenia was all the more caught off balance by this bitter incursion. Again, her mother's face clouded. Perhaps it was the dank atmosphere, the half-light, the dripping arches, the sheer instability of walking across the water on planks above the cistern floor, but the eyes of Missy seemed to bore into her to a point that gave her pain with their coldness. There was a flash of something like hostility, but it was more obscure than an emotion; it was more like an impulse. Xenia felt very uncomfortable. 'I'm sorry,' she murmured, for she realized that it must have been she herself who had caused her mother's sufferings.

Missy turned her head slowly away and looked stonily into the green, lit water. 'It is Theo Phocas who will be sorry,' she said, almost as if she did not know that she had.

Xenia wondered why it was she sensed danger. She had been

frightened of Missy from the outset, but she had taken this as the price of risking the unknown. She had also been afraid that the real mother she had always longed to know would find her wanting in some crucial respect. Now, however, the sense of a larger peril reached her. As they stood together over the water, she felt an instinctual thrill of animal terror. Was it the expression on Missy's face? It was more the peculiar agility of that face to change from one mood to the next without transition. Xenia denied it. She shook it off. It was only the suggestive power of the place, the underworld music, the dreamlike quality of Constantinople itself with its barbed and ancient enmities. Nevertheless, Xenia stood quite still. The track of *Parsifal* had come to an end, and a Mozart aria began: *Laudate Dominum*. 'I am singing this for my audition,' Xenia said very quietly.

Missy looked around cagily, inspecting Xenia's eyes. In a moment of Eastern knowledge, a native expertise, Xenia let her glance be veiled by an impenetrable discretion, just as if she had neither seen nor heard the slightest thing untoward. To her relief, she heard the voices and footsteps of new visitors to the cistern, and they were airily chatting away in French. Although she could not make out what they were saying, it was clear by their gasps of surprise that the drama of the scene enthralled and charmed them. Xenia peered round the massive pillar of stone that stood behind Missy. 'What is that?' she asked, pointing to an illuminated spot in the distance.

Missy gave a little jolt just as if someone had let a door slam on her thoughts. She looked at the French couple, who had managed to make even anoraks look chic, and she adjusted a hesitant smile. 'Why, of course, there it is, your actual Hecate!' she exclaimed to Xenia, suddenly expansive. 'That was what I wanted to show you.' With a light hand on Xenia's shoulder-blade, she steered her forward. 'At least, I always used to tell my clients it was Hecate – more fun that way.' It was almost as if Missy had a recording in her which switched on, Southern, light, joke-cracking, whenever she had an audience. They stopped before a slender Byzantine column, which rose from a vast stone head turned upside down. The murky water lapped at its hair. The face was androgynous, with a bias towards the feminine, but its blank eyes and impassive mouth gave nothing away. Moss had grown on it. On another side of this odd, columnar construction, a similar head lay sideways in the water. It was almost sensuous.

Xenia found the head repulsive, but it attracted her as well. 'Gosh!' she said, to be polite.

'I used to extemporize a bit when I brought them here,' Missy giggled, her mood quite changed again. 'I had to take the dreariest Yankees round. Most of them had never read anything heavier than the *Wall Street Journal* – not since school, anyway – so I would just weave a tale. It is a fact that old Byzantium was sacred to Hecate, and that is as obvious as could be because she is the goddess of the crossroads. I suppose you could say Istanbul *is* the crossroads. So, even though I guess the old Emperors had this lady turned upside down just because she was something pagan and because they wanted a building brick for the cistern, I used to spook my Tartan Trouser Brigade with the Queen of Witches. What d'you reckon? Was I right? Is she or isn't she?'

Xenia glanced at Missy. She was becoming intelligible again as she had been in tombs of the Sultans. The girl shivered. 'I can feel it!'

'I like witches,' Missy said. 'I've always liked them. Up and away on a broomstick! Dancing naked in the moonlight! A lot more fun than sitting at home hooking rugs, I can tell you.'

Xenia looked nervously at her mother.

Missy laughed. 'Don't worry. I don't do spells.' She paused. 'Not on women anyway. But men? They are nothing! Men are all alike. You watch 'em, honey! They want one thing. Put out if you want to, but always keep the whip hand so you can make 'em pay . . . no matter how long it takes.'

The gently moving water flashed reflections from the spotlight on to the pallid, upturned head. Xenia watched it in a kind of trance. Dimly, the nature of her danger became apparent as if the stone head were oracular, a Pythoness, obscure but ominous. Missy had not lured her away from Chios in order to be her mother, but so that her father should suffer. And it was just a question of time before any of them found out just how much Missy wanted this to be. Xenia suppressed a shiver. If this were true, she had to get away.

XVII

'You do realize my sister rigged that whole scene just in order to flush Theo out?' Charles said. 'I can't get over it!' He shifted down to take the hairpin bend on the mountain pass that led to the barren north of Chios and to Nea Moni. A heavy gravel truck hurtled past them on the other side, but Rosamund, usually a nervous passenger, sat oblivious to a near miss. Her slight form had always had a pleasing fragility to Charles, but now she looked like a child, forced into reluctant obedience. Her close-cropped head was rigid on her slender neck. She chewed her lip, and her hands lay slack on her lap as if resisting fate was pointless. They had borrowed the Toyota in order to get out of the house. They were travelling to Nea Moni because it was there. 'You do believe that I made a great point of getting her to tell you I was coming,' he added.

'I believe you,' she said, but she was barely audible. He could not read her mood at all.

The sky had a gentian depth over the hills; it was stony terrain, planetary rather than earthly. The alien landscape stood in absolute contrast to that of the fruitful south. It was a split island. Having reached a peak of aridity where the annealing sun had baked the peaks into a shadowless ochre, the car started to descend into a scrubland where the twisted shapes of stunted trees and bushes stood dead and blackened by a recent forest fire.

'Would you have stayed on if you had known I was coming?' he asked.

'I don't know,' she said. She hesitated. 'I am pleased to see you, Charles.'

'And I you.' He hoped he meant that.

'Saying these things isn't easy,' she said. 'It's a bit like having tea and toast after being violently sick.'

He laughed.

'Goodness,' she said wryly. 'I made a joke. When was the last time I made a joke, Charles?'

'I would say not properly since that bloody woman turned up at our house that Christmas Eve!' He spoke through his teeth and shifted down unnecessarily. 'Missy!'

'It would be an evasion . . . to think that, to blame her,' Rosamund said primly.

'Oh God! Can't you ever evade anything?' he cried. 'In any case, it's true. I've been thinking about it. I've been talking about it to Romola. You made a good stab at it but I don't think you ever really recovered from Mary's birth. And who just happened to be on the scene? Missy! She was disturbing.'

'She was freedom, Charles!' Rosamund said, looking across at him with wide eyes. 'She could do anything she liked and get away with it. You see, I'm so conventional. I hate myself for it, but I'm too much of a coward to be anything else.'

It seemed a bit of a tautology to think of this as genuine honesty from Rosamund, but it made Charles hopeful. As if a bird had landed on his finger and might take flight at some clumsy show of pleasure, he was also cautious. '*Is* Missy freedom?' he asked instead.

'I don't know. All of this has made me think a lot more about it.' They followed the thread of road round the solemn, arid mountains, the massive, protohistoric drums of land. She seemed about to say something else, but evidently changed her mind. After a while, she cleared her throat. 'You do believe that I never suspected that Missy was Xenia's mother until she told me so herself? Even though I told Catherine that I might have concealed it, I don't think I could have endured such knowledge. It must be seen that because I loved Xenia I knew, but I didn't.'

'You were in love with Theo,' he said. 'Platonically, I am sure.' He had not meant to say this. It simply arose to him as the plain truth. 'I'm sorry,' he added. 'I was never there, was I? I really am sorry. I haven't a leg to stand on.'

She was crying softly into her hands. 'Caro isn't,' she said.

He looked at her swiftly. Her thin chest heaved out sighs. They had to tackle it, he supposed. 'Isn't what?'

'Platonic . . . I'm not defending myself, Charles.'

She was, but there was something wistful about it.

'No, it's not,' he said quietly.

She abandoned herself to weeping. He had expected her to be angry, for resentment was endemic to her nature, but she simply cried brokenly. 'You're going to marry her, aren't you?'

The road rose before him and he concentrated furiously on taking the curved incline well. He swung upwards into the next bend and on to the straight track lined with pine woods. 'I don't know,' he said. 'I've given it a lot of thought.'

'Well, she'll expect you to!' Her voice had its old truculence.

'*I* expect me to!' he said with a sudden clarification of things. 'And that seems the wrong reason. I expect me to want to marry a beautiful young woman, but I'm not so sure that I do. It shook me when you ran away, Rozzy, even though I thought you meant to shake me.'

They had reached the height from which it was possible to see the famous Monastery nestling in a deep valley. There was a lay-by on the road overlooking the view. Charles drew into it and stopped the car. His wife, bound up in the seat-belt, was pressed against the door looking at him with open eyes. She looked doe-like and surprised.

'Do you want to make a clean break?' he asked. 'Even if you do, I am not sure that I will marry Caro. She's . . . she's . . .' He did not know how to define it. 'She doesn't understand that life could issue conflicting orders.' He shrugged. It was the best he could do.

Rosamund fiddled with her soggy Kleenex and wiped her nose. It was an ugly gesture, but it touched him with its ungainliness. She was no fairy princess. She waved her hands helplessly in the air, a victim of every kind of conflict and confusion. 'At this stage, how clean could a break be?' she asked plaintively. 'And yet, when I think of trying . . . I *have* tried! And Charles, you really did try. I grant you that. I do.'

The hot car felt like a pressure chamber. 'Let's look at the ancient monument, Roz,' he said. 'Come on.' He opened the door and was surprised to see that she undid her seat-belt with alacrity. She pulled the handle and got out. Rosamund was habitually a great one for demanding more of such a conversation, for picking sores.

They stood for a moment together and took in the view. The Monastery, built with delicacy and splendour, sat prettily as ever in its hollow, its graceful octagonal dome emphasized by a copse of velvety cypresses that surrounded the church. It looked as if it had never been desecrated by Turks or devastated by earthquakes. Instead, it seemed to have transcended all of these disasters as if it actually preached a continuum of peace. The mosaics, which had survived a catastrophic history, were of the finest in Byzantium. It had always been a favourite sight with the Simons, plus or minus whichever children happened to be with them at the time. The family paid a call on Nea Moni whenever they came to the island. Charles remembered with a pang that the ancient nuns had made a fuss over the children and had doled out aromatic sweeties made with rose-water, much to everyone's delight. He shook his head. He had rocked their foundations.

Rosamund had always liked the miraculous icon of the Virgin, which was enshrined in the church and was the cause of the Monastery being built in the eleventh century. The icon had been found by monks in a bush, spirited there, so the legend went, an image not made by human hands at all. Deep down, Charles knew that the Protestant in Rosamund still thought this was idolatry, and perhaps it gave her the thrill of forbidden fruit. It was festooned with thank-offerings, medallions and necklaces, gold and silver plaques engraved with pictures of a particular malady cured. There was a healing balance to the place, the whole scene, as if things could be made right by finding a centre and living in harmonious symmetry around it. They gazed down at the Byzantine gem.

It struck Charles forcibly now that Missy was a kind of iconoclast, but before he was able to utter this new insight, Rosamund spoke.

'You are right about Theo,' she said. 'I confess it.'

Charles glanced at her. She had spoken with great effort, and it hurt him to see her exposing herself in this way. She was a rigorous soul and he often wished that she wasn't. But she looked up at him without the curious guile that usually accompanied her effusions of guilt.

'Theo obeys life's conflicting orders only too well,' she continued ruefully, 'and simultaneously. He lives on two completely different levels, and in a sense I do too, Charles. Maybe that was the attraction in the first place, although I was not aware of it.' She paused and sighed. 'I got sucked into it after Xenia came on the scene, but I wouldn't have if I hadn't found him a temptation in the first place. You say you wished I made evasions, but you really don't mean that because I have made so many, and Theo has been the greatest of these, though it was strictly limited to my caring a good deal for him, I can assure you.' She said this last with her old starchiness, and Charles smiled to himself.

But Rosamund shook her head vigorously. 'I'm not being self-righteous, Charles, I'm trying to tell you something accurately! You and the children were just too difficult for me. It was all too much for my slender resources. I kept letting you all down. I was never good enough, no matter how hard I tried. Theo was so impossible, so exotic that I got the illusion of true involvement without the messy bits. What was more, I deluded myself into thinking it was all far more high-minded than it was.'

She was magnificent, a *Nike*, victorious in her contrition. He winced to think that he had watched her sink into this entanglement with a gratitude born of idleness about her. Theo and Xenia had given her an occupation, harmless on the whole to him, but not, it seemed, to her. Rosamund had been cheated by the family. That was the unstated claim, and he had not had the emotional funds to make her solvent. He wondered now if he could have dug deeper, borrowed on some resource, to have met her needs just a little more adequately.

'And now, of course, you are on the way out of our marriage . . . or not, as the case may be; Mary is on her way to being a stunted neurotic; the other children have lives of their own to lead; I find that Theo has cruelly used me; and Xenia, who turns out to be my first cousin once removed, might be in Iran for all we know!' She sighed, but she did not cry. 'And it is all my self-pity that has done it.'

She had gone far in a short time. Charles put his hand upon her shoulder. 'Rozzy!' He gave her a little shake. 'Eh? Roz? Come on. There's more than one at fault, but let's let it all sink in.' Hesitantly, she reached out an arm and put it round his waist, then withdrew it. Without a word, they turned and slowly got back into the car.

'Shall we go forward or back?' he asked, turning the ignition key.

'Heavens, Charles! That's not like you.'

He puzzled for a bit. 'Oh! I didn't mean the marriage! I meant do we see the mosaics or do we go back to Kampos?' They laughed edgily, but together.

'I don't know. What do you think? It's like Sophocles back there, and I get the distinct feeling that you and I are supposed to be the chorus.'

'Spot on!' he said. Long ago, even with her Gothic sufferings, Rosamund had had a sense of humour. He had forgotten that she could be quite funny.

'Back there on the road you said your sister had rigged your visit here to expose Theo. How did she manage that? Now that our own difficulties have been aired, it seems a little easier to talk about it.'

It was hard to think that she did not know all that had happened. The continued story that long marriages maintain had been disrupted and had lost its thread. 'Romola came hunting for Missy at our house, and together we got it into our heads that she had run away with you. I was terrified!'

'You really can't think I colluded with Missy in any way!'

'Calm down. Of course I don't.'

'Not in a million years did I think Missy would show herself here!'

'Roz, I know! Romola simply happened to be there when Catherine rang and by the time we discovered that Xenia was actually gone, Tom Kavanagh had come streaking back from Ireland. We had to go out and get Diet Pepsi for him. Can you believe it? Romola and I drank Scotch.'

Rosamund laughed. 'But I thought Kavanagh was the great cavalier, charging over here to help.'

'Well, that's how he likes to see himself, but it was really all Catherine's doing. She invited us to stay, then it was she, not he, who arranged the Villa Argenti for the Kavanagh contingent. But the whole thing turned into his show. I can't tell you how awkward I felt during the flight here. What I see now is that Catherine must have guessed who Missy really was, but at the time, we were all in the dark.'

'Oh she did! She did. I cannot tell you how terrible it was when I got here myself from Athens. I would have given almost anything to tell her the truth, but I gave my word . . . a thing I never should have done.'

They looked at each other, neither of them really responsible for what had happened, and both of them aghast for that reason. 'So she really did gamble on it! She assembled an audience like Hercule Poirot . . . each member of the house party with a little piece of evidence, a little guilt.'

'A nice analogy,' Rosamund said. 'The engine is running, Charles,' she added. 'There. I'm already nagging you again.'

He shook his head. 'I'm not sure that is such a terrible thing to do any more in the face of all this,' he said drily. He backed the car on to the road. 'Mosaics? I think so. Perhaps a good idea when one is piecing things together. For the life of me, though, I have never been able to see how anyone ever had the patience to fit all of those minute tiles together.'

'Whatever you can say about Catherine, she is holding up rather well, I think. Do you know how Theo really kept me to my oath? He told me she would crack up if she knew the truth,' Rosamund said.

They descended around the curved road into the piney hollow where the Monastery lay. Charles flushed. 'That is an excuse men make when they want to have a thing both ways,' he found himself muttering angrily. It touched him greatly to feel the pressure of her hand on his shoulder.

'You wanted an angel. I wanted an angel. Look what we both got!' she said.

He stopped the car at the shaded walls of the enclosure. A door in the forbidding gate was being opened by an ancient factotum, but Charles and Rosamund did not get out at once. They sat for a moment in silence.

'What is your sister going to do?' she asked him quietly. 'Whatever happens to Xenia, what will Catherine do?'

'It doesn't bear thinking about,' he said.

Catherine adjusted her half-moon spectacles and rethreaded her needle. When she had entered the study, Theo and Tsamakis had fallen silent, but now, at least, no one could prevent her from keeping watch.

She sat between the men on a straight-backed chair while they sullenly fiddled with their machines. They did not want her in the room, but she was there to stay until Xenia should be found.

She made a firm knot in the end of her thread. She frowned as she took pains in stitching a navy lozenge neatly to a gentian square. The house was finally quiet and she was at peace. She had banished the Kavanaghs to the Villa Argenti, and she had dispatched Charles and Rosamund to Nea Moni. Theo had become incidental to her vigil, for a wholly new and exhilarating perception had come to her in the wake of the crisis:

It was she who was Xenia's mother.

Catherine absorbed herself in the contemplation of this wisdom and its implications. She took tiny stitch after tiny stitch, and the process of knowing became orderly, attached. At first tentative, she groped along the path until a pure conviction opened for her like a road with no natural horizon.

Xenia was her child.

The lozenge was part of a distinctive chevron pattern that ran around the border of the quilt. In front of her, there was a table inlaid with a chessboard on which no one ever played. Her material was laid out there. She took a pale strip of cloth for contrast. Her design was intricate, more subtle than its bold shape suggested to the casual eye. It had been worth eighteen years of watching and waiting for what she knew now.

It was not just Xenia's identity that was at stake now: it was her own. Her unworthiness was of no importance now. She had finally stood out for Xenia, fought and won.

From the very outset, the pain of knowing that she loved Xenia more than any other human being had made the child too precious to acknowledge as her own. Every day since she had come to live with them, Catherine had spoken to herself as sharply as a flagellant on a rock that any self-indulgence in regard to Xenia would be a gluttony she could not afford. All this precarious time, she had worn herself out with the effort of not being Xenia's mother openly so that she could become so secretly. From the moment she had seen the scurfy little baby in the incubator, she had feasted on love and fasted on the demonstration of it for fear of what Theo might do if he found out. He was not a malicious man, and perhaps she had always taken his egoism for granted. Her dread of him had had more to do with the consequences of his obsession with the child whom he had dandled manically, insisting on her undivided attention, her perfect love. There were to be no rivals.

Catherine had never forgotten the agonizing enlargement of her own heart when she had first been allowed to hold Xenia and the wild panic she had suppressed when he had told her the cock-and-bull story of the baby's Albanian mother. The speediness of the adoption process had not been lost on her, with its attendant convoluted, circumstantial lies. What had he done to get Xenia? The question had always had the genius of a ghost which could walk through the highest walls of her defences. There had been a bad time when she had battered Theo with passionate questions about Xenia's provenance but this was lost under a merciful blanket of amnesia. It had been a trancelike time when she had wandered in and out of the nursery night after night when Theo wasn't looking, checking to see if Xenia was still there. Nobody at all knew this. She had stood clasping her hands, not daring to touch the fragile baby in case her clumsy love might damage her.

Later, when she had seen the official papers, and later still when he had managed to get the child British nationality, the grip of fear on Catherine had relaxed somewhat, but for her own sanity, she had always known that she must maintain its clawed manacle, vigilance being the necessary component of peace. As the years had gone by, Xenia had become almost like a mirage to Catherine, a sustaining delusion of perfection in a parched marriage. If she grasped at Xenia, she might melt into a shimmering fantasy.

Catherine could not date the time when her bones had told her that Missy or her analogue would turn up, nor had she ever really admitted to herself that it might actually happen, but she had kept constant watch on Theo and he had given the game away without naming the stakes. She knew the mother was alive. Was it a specific look of anxiety on his face? Was it his remoteness from her? Was it his paranoia about kidnappers? Together she and her husband mapped out their perfect days for Xenia in the beautiful enclosure where they kept her, a prison Catherine herself had built and where it seemed unnatural to keep a child. Often Catherine wondered if it were she who was paranoid. A Greek plutocrat with an adored only child might well fear enemies. Sometimes she would convince herself that the Albanian legend was true, and that she was false to him in her doubt. These blithe moments did not last for long, however, and most of the time she could sense by his guilt – that was it – that her fears were more than justified. Her private terror was that he had stolen the child in some way, and it was for this reason that she was relieved rather than wounded when she began to see that he had fathered Xenia himself. It was a truth she half denied, the unmistakable resemblance between them, body and soul. But if there had been treason against herself, that was nothing next to the bliss of reassurance that it would almost certainly ensure that Xenia would never be taken away from her . . . unless, of course, she made the mistake of loving too much and of being a real mother.

In the north of Chios there were still peasant women who made lace and Catherine was always planning to learn the technique. She had watched them, fateful in black, webbing the weighted bobbins round the pins, winding the skeins on until the central pattern emerged. It was as if Missy were the essential thread; it was as if nothing had ever really hung together without her. Not knowing about her had made their three lives unnaturally close-woven. It had always been certain, and would have been certain under the most honourable terms of a straightforward adoption, that some woman somewhere had given birth to Xenia who was to be the shape of their fortunes . . . a mother who could be regarded almost impersonally . . . like one of the Fates. But as if she had had a genetic disorder and known that the first falter of her hand must come, Catherine had lived with the shadow of an ominous suspicion and she had shifted this burden from one part of her psyche to another, adjusting to its weight so that after a while she did not even notice how heavy it had become. Theo's terror of kidnaps, his moods, his sexual coldness to her, his near idolatry of Xenia, his fascination with Rosamund, all hung together now as one whole crushing load. But at least she understood it.

Suppose she had always understood it. Suppose he had been plain with her, honest from the start. Would she have surrendered so quickly to her enclosed passivity? She honestly did not know. If you were blind from the beginning, how could you judge according to the light? If she had known that another woman had any just claim to Xenia, would she have had the strength to give her up? The violence of her feelings shocked her. She would have fought such a woman tooth and nail with mayhem in her heart, but she would have done so under the law.

Suddenly it occurred to her that Theo had thought that she would not want Xenia if he told her the truth. She could see him thinking that. He judged people rather by his own standards. He had never forgiven her for being barren and simply assumed that she had not forgiven herself. He was no better than Tom Kavanagh with his mares and stallions, his studs, and all the paraphernalia that went with artificial insemination. Theo had not put her down, but he had put her out to pasture. He would have his own will, he would have his own flesh. The worst of it was that he could have had both without lying. Or could he? If one thought about it, and she now did think about it, the lie had given him power over absolutely everyone.

Catherine picked up the sewing scissors and cut the thread, then chose a lemon yellow hexagon from the made-up shapes upon the table.

She was not afraid of Missy Kavanagh and she wondered why. Theo was terrified of her.

She placed the yellow hexagon upon the gentian square and started to tack it in. For some odd reason, she remembered that her own mother had disapproved of this hot combination of colours. She had always disapproved of Xenia too, but that was almost certainly because she sensed that Catherine loved the child. In unguarded moments, she often thought of her mother as 'Lady Simon', an implacable negative in her life, denying the reality of anything she cared for. Had this been another reason for giving up the struggle? Allowing Theo his way in nearly everything about the child? Maybe she could have fought more for Xenia. The only point she had gained in wresting Xenia from his absolute control was to send her away to school. Her school. He liked the security arrangements and now she knew why. Never mind.

Catherine thought of Lady Simon now. She would enjoy this latest news with such rich malice! That her baby was gone with a mad American mother, Theo's mistress, and Rosamund's first cousin to boot, would give her more intense pleasure even than the break-up of Charles's marriage . . . or it would slake the disappointment at a reconciliation. All of a sudden, it seemed finally irrelevant to Catherine what her mother thought, and cowardly, too, to blame her for her cold and limited heart. Catherine knew that all these years Lady Simon had judged her for turning a blind eye. How blind her eyes had been, yet seeing, was a calculation beyond the capacity of Lady Simon to do simple sums. Her mother could not do the algebra of this. It needed love to see what had happened.

'Xenia, come back to me! Please!' she thought.

Theo and Tsamakis were smoking and looking at her. She had challenged her husband in public and she had let Missy Kavanagh into the house. So, he had a mistress, the policeman's eyes seemed to shrug and say. At least he'd brought his bastard up in style. He had even tried to protect his wife and had humbled himself so far as to ask her forgiveness, the great tycoon, the man. Every fibre of Tsamakis seemed to object to her presence in the study. She was bringing open shame on her family when everything had been so neatly closed. Pandora had deserved the nasty creatures from the box.

Catherine continued to sit there and to sew. She smiled to herself slightly when she thought of Theo's 'apology' when everyone had gone and they had been alone together. It had taken the form of a vow. In thanksgiving for Xenia's safe return, he would build a chapel on the grounds of the estate. If she had lost Xenia to Missy, however, he would pardon her, she could rest assured. After all, he supposed, he had given her insufficient information, and Missy had deceived her with the family connection to Rosamund. He was sorry about Missy. Of course he was, but Catherine was his wife and he had never forgotten that. There had followed an odd, ironic fugue developing these themes, when with a voice dry as gravel, Theo had poured out reflexively the story of the love affair. If the structure of his passion for Missy was gone, the content of it remained. He was abject with hatred for her. It was stunning. He had spoken of her blindly as if she had become part of his very self, a part which goaded him to demonstrate that he was still obsessed with her. What he needed Catherine for had become clear. If Xenia had been in contact with Missy, they must find a way to eradicate her from his child's memory. How were they to do this? Perhaps they would travel. Did Catherine think a hypnotist would do any good?

Catherine herself did not wish to be hypnotized into anything.

All of a sudden it came to her like the matching of different hexagons into one flowering whole why it was that she had let Missy Kavanagh in, why she was not frightened of her, and why she had not prevented Xenia from going with her to Çeşme.

Missy Kavanagh had given birth to Xenia, but she was not her mother. The mother of Xenia she had been anticipating all of these years was not that woman with her brittle, sugary affectations. The mother she had feared and somehow sought in long watches of many nights had been herself. She had been denied this gift of motherhood for so long that she could hardly believe that she had attained to it. She had possessed it, but like an heirloom kept in a bank, she had not worn it, used it; she had not even seen it. If Missy Kavanagh had been Xenia's mother Catherine would have recognized her.

She felt extraordinarily free and mobile. She had been like one of the figures on that old chestnut of the Grecian urn that Keats had sung. She had been fixed and stilled into non-being; non-mother and non-child had been captured and enslaved into non-growth and non-movement by the fictive motion of Theo's fluid brush, the artful construction of his awful lies. And now, whatever the consequences of the truth she had so effectively won that day, it had embodied her and given her mind and limbs the power to move. Whatever was to happen, no matter how terrible, it would be real.

If Missy wanted a fight, she would get one. If Theo thought he would browbeat her into staying with him after this, he was mistaken. Even if Xenia were to die at least now she would be able to mourn her. All her life, people had treated her as a decorative object because she had let them make it easy for her not to feel. She put her sewing down. She felt now. Curiously, she thought of her child Xenia in terms of light. And it blinded her like a conversion.

'What do you make of Tom Kavanagh?' Charles asked Rosamund. They had strolled up from the gate of the enclosure and had entered the Monastery church. A black-clad deacon was drowsing into his beard at the door. Rosamund stuffed drachmas into a box and bought two candles from a rack.

'We never knew Kavanaghs,' she said with the haughtiness she reserved for Southern matters. Considering Missy, he thought the snobbery carried less conviction than it had in the past. They drifted into the outer narthex where a large and faded Doom painting filled the north wall. It was incongruously surrounded by potted spider plants, but the space, light and airy, seemed to take some of the gloom out of the prospect of the End of Time. 'I don't know what to make of him,' she added. 'He seems too pitiful a creature to judge.'

'I'm not so sure of that,' Charles said. They stopped in a perfunctory way in front of the fresco. He peered at the Virgin, who with outstretched palms sat in Paradise, flanked by two seraphim. 'Not that I would want to judge him,' he added hastily, eyeing a mighty angel weighing the deeds of souls. 'I'm not in a position to do that. But he is not as gaga as he looks.'

'He's not gaga at all except about Missy!' Rosamund said. 'He wants to get round Theo and hush this whole thing up. That is why he is here. Don't you think?' She looked contritely at the two candles in her hand. 'I don't know that. It's only a guess. Anyway, I don't think I trust him.'

'Snap!' said Charles. They glanced at each other shyly, then back at the faded painting. 'You are right, though, he is genuinely besotted with Missy.'

'Quite.'

She looked at him sideways, meekly interrogative.

'I can't imagine why,' he said firmly and she smiled.

'The one I can't quite make out,' she said after a little pause, 'is Romola. What is she *doing* in that situation?'

They moved in unison towards the interior of the church. The second narthex, more splendid than the first, glowed with gold mosaics. It was like moving to the heart of Aladdin's cave.

'Oh, I'm Romola's intense fan,' he said.

'I like her too,' Rosamund said. 'But do you know why she seemed so horror-stricken when she learned that Missy had a child?'

They stood beneath an arch encrusted with saints and apostles, formal medallions with eyes that seemed to follow every movement with benign intent.

'You gathered that Kavanagh is obscenely rich? Well, he is, but he is not exactly what he seems to be. Apparently, he became a kind of sixties guru on a vast oil well fortune that comes from somewhere in the "Wild West", or the "Tame West" . . . I don't know. He doesn't seem to have much to do with this place here, does he?'

The Simons looked up at the canopy of celestial artifice above them, at the burning jewels of the angels' eyes, their wings, their haloes.

'I don't know. He seems to accept Missy as only God could!'

'Well, be that as it may, he seems to have complicated Romola's life quite unnecessarily. His marriage to her mother dates from his charismatic phase, though he quickly got bored with it – and her. I'll skip the convoluted family history, but the nub of the problem seems to be that Romola's half-sister, his daughter, Paolo's mother . . . follow me?' She giggled. He went on, pleased, '. . . ran off with an Italian playboy, who is not spending Kavanagh's money in the way the old man would like. They lead a jet-set life, and Kavanagh thinks the child is neglected because he has a nanny. So there have been mad will-games, with threats to disinherit if the child does not spend most of the year with Kavanagh himself. I think the daughter has been cut out of the will altogether in favour of

Paolo, or she would be if Romola had not prevented it. She is one of the few honourable people in this whole business.'

As a rule, Rosamund tended to strike poses of awe and rapture at the Byzantine mosaics at Nea Moni, and it had always made Charles uncomfortable to watch her watching herself respond. They stood beside a magnificent wall of gold with Christ washing the feet of the Apostles. The humanity and rhythmic liveliness, the purity and sweetness of the piece were lost on Rosamund now. 'Go on! What about Missy?' she asked, avid for detail. He wondered sadly when he would tell her about her parents' house, how Romola had mentioned the suspicions of the whole community about the fire.

Nevertheless, he suddenly warmed to his story, touched lightly but surely by his wife's eagerness to hear it. 'Well, you can imagine what happened when Missy came on to the scene! Things were bad enough, apparently, without her. Romola thinks that if Missy can provide proof of issue, even by a former arrangement, Kavanagh would be complete putty in her hands. I don't know if you quite got the drift of the old boy's addled idealism, but during the journey in the private jet I got enough sermons to last me a lifetime. You see, if he got the idea that Missy had been wronged, he would see her right – *especially* if the child happened to be illegitimate.'

'No! You don't think Missy . . .'

'Romola does. Romola thinks she is itching to get her hands on the whole revoltingly vast fortune. You see, Kavanagh may look like a horsy old boy who knows his withers and fetlocks, but he has taken to the sport of kings only relatively recently. He bought this huge place . . . what is it called . . . ?'

'Eagles! So that's why I never heard of him!'

'Yes, Eagles, and he thought to get the whole kit, lock, stock and barrel, supplying it with Missy as his chatelaine. You know, sort of a job lot. That is where she has her chief hold. She belongs to an old family. Your family. Kentucky is his newest enthusiasm.'

He noticed that Rosamund had turned her face from him. With her Joan of Arc hair and the candles clasped in her hand, she looked like an etiolated version of the burnished figures on the wall. 'Charles,' she said in a low voice, interrupting his flow.

'Yes?'

'If it's all right with you, I think I would rather that you did not leave me.' She looked up at him. 'I'm not very good at . . .' she shrugged helplessly. 'I miss you,' she muttered.

He was too moved to say anything. In fact, he did not know what to say. He patted her shoulder, feeling just as helpless as she did. She stood peering at him, simple against the background of the heavenly citizens. 'I miss you too,' he said.

She smiled, somehow at peace with herself.

'Aren't you going to light your candles?' he asked. He took her hand, shaking it stupidly. 'I think Xenia needs all the help she can get. Don't you? You ought to light both of them to your miraculous Lady.'

They walked a little awkwardly into the main body of the church. 'Charles, I have become insufferable,' she said. 'I know I have.'

'No, you haven't. You really haven't, Rosamund,' he said. 'Apart from anything else, you've had to suffer me.' And they stood together under the octagonal dome where golden Archangels in flowing robes punctuated bright scenes of the Redemption.

XVIII

SERGE WAS making his way to the bar in the Büyük Londra hotel. Enough was enough. He needed a drink. One drink did not necessarily lead to another. As he entered the lounge, he saw Xenia Phocas sitting alone in a red velvet armchair. She wore an attractive yellow frock, quite new, but everything about her seemed to contradict the bright colour, and for a moment he wondered if she were in physical pain. She was sitting next to an open window. Through it, a warm, fetid breeze blew a jaded lace curtain in mild billows, but the girl's hair remained unruffled, as if it had been fixed in place like that of a doll. She leaned her head against the back of the spindly armchair, her features framed by the heavy maroon draperies. Serge was relieved that she did not see him. Helena had been enough for one day.

He sighed and resigned himself. His weakness had defeated him. It was his old pal and he almost welcomed it. He drummed his fingers on the bar. It was not attended, except, in a manner of speaking, by St Thérèse of Lisieux, who was dressed in the habit of a Carmelite nun and carried a Cross decked with roses. Her smile, from the large sepia engraving, seemed tinged with patience, and her mild eyes pricked Serge's conscience. Two dusty ornamental ferns sprouted from the picture frame. It annoyed him that everything in Constantinople had to be outsized and to do with religion. A chap could not even buy a well-earned brandy except under the watchful eye of a Catholic saint. He cleared his throat discreetly, but still no one came to the bar. The bottles behind the counter were not dusty, but they gave the impression of being little used. He turned to see if he could locate a waiter, and looked straight into the eyes of Xenia.

At once, Serge knew that he would have to postpone his orgy. The young girl gave a timid smile as humble as the saint's. She was dressed to go out. She clutched a small handbag in her lap. Her feet were crossed at the ankles. All she lacked was a pair of white cotton gloves. Although she did not summon him over to her, it would have been simple rudeness to have denied the plea in her eyes. His heart sank at the thought of

Missy's proximity. He made a deal with himself. If Missy turned up, he would have an excuse to buy her a brandy and to have one for himself.

'May I join you?' he asked.

'Please, I wish you would,' said Xenia. 'I dressed, but my mother wanted a rest when she came back from the hairdresser. It seemed better to come down here than to disturb her.' She looked shifty, as if she were lying in some way.

'My cousin is also resting,' Serge said. 'She finds the city quite debilitating.'

'Did you see Topakı Palace?' Her speech was cut out in the pattern of ladies' seminaries and finishing schools.

'Yes, we saw that . . . and the Grand Bazaar, where we were mobbed.' He and Helena had taken refuge from the pressing crowd of hawkers in a shabby café hidden in a corner of the tourist trap. They had taken tea in tulip-shaped glasses under a daguerreotype of a stiffly posed nineteenth-century Sultan. Slow fans had circulated air around the ceiling. Helena had taken it hard that Edgar Jolly was writing the book on Arthur.

'My mother says that we are going to see those things tomorrow, but I don't like jewels.' Xenia hunted his face. 'Actually, I was going to ask you something,' she continued after an uncertain pause. 'I heard you say that you knew someone by my name. I was wondering if you knew my father Theodore Phocas.' She made a brave effort to toss this remark off, but her hands twisted around the clutch bag.

'Why yes!' he boomed. He always felt obliged to be hearty in the face of female pain. 'The shipowner? I do know him. I met him at my club.'

'The Travellers?' She seemed very pleased. 'We are in England a part of the year. We have a flat. Also, my father was brought up in England.' She looked down and blushed. 'He and my mother do not get along, so I would prefer it if you did not mention him when you see her.' She looked up and her eyes darted to the lounge doorway. Serge followed her glance, but there was no one there. The vast piece of furniture, difficult to typify as a sideboard, filled an entire wall with its swelling walnut immensity. More dried ferns were stuck in a brass samovar, which was large enough to have relieved the thirst of a battalion at Sebastopol. A couple of ironed-looking American tourists were arguing politely but firmly with the man at the reception desk, who, with equally good manners, was contradicting them. They were of an age and class to be travelling on the advice of the *New York Times*, which might have urged them to a spirit of adventure they were discovering they lacked. But no Missy came through the archway.

'I don't really know my mother, you see,' Xenia said.

Serge thought that he was supposed to hear but overlook this remark. A liveried waiter, balancing a tray of coffee cups on his upstretched fingers, strode through the lounge. Serge summoned him, and when he had deposited his order with a self-conscious-looking party of Turkish businessmen, he waltzed over. Serge politely indicated Xenia. 'Oh, thank you . . . an orange squash, I think.' Serge miserably agreed that he would have the same, even though his tongue was hanging out for a brandy. Helena had wept in the tea shop in the Grand Bazaar. In the fifty years they had known each other, he had never seen her do this.

'I won't mention him,' he said to Xenia. He felt so sorry for the child, a victim of divorce. Whatever their problems, he and Fiona had managed to stagger on. He thought about Fiona and decided that he would telephone her as a reward to himself for choosing the orange squash. If he told her that Helena had cried in public she would think his journey justified, for she was very tender-hearted. 'Very nice chap, your father . . . thoroughly nice fellow.' He could barely remember Phocas. 'I'm sure he thinks the world of you!'

He had not been able to think of anything else to say, but it had not been quite the right thing. Her face puckered miserably. The orange arrived and there was the relief of the waiter's intervention and the cool drink, which tasted good, when all was said and done. Xenia thanked Serge. 'Do you know how to change money?' she asked him. 'I have some drachmas. I want to make a trip to the airport, you see, and I don't know how much it costs. I don't want to ask my mother because it is a surprise.' Serge noticed that she had to hold the tall glass of orange in both hands to steady it. She would not look into his eyes.

'Where do you live, Xenia?' He found himself asking her this as if she had been five or six.

'Chios!' She seemed so relieved that he had wanted to know. 'But I shall soon be with my aunt in London and then back at school. I go to St Winifred's.'

Serge wondered if he were imagining things. Was this a note in a bottle from the shipwreck of the girl's present situation? It must be instead, he thought, as Helena had supposed. A reunion with a long-absent parent was not going as either of them had hoped, and the girl was mentioning her father's family in order to give herself a sense of balance. 'What form are you in?' he asked her, expecting her to revive with further talk of school.

'Upper sixth,' she said, indeed reviving. 'I mean, I shall be if I go back.'

'Why shouldn't you go back?' He was alert now.

'My mother wants me to go with her to America.' She looked at him directly. 'I am an adult now, you see.'

Oh, dear! he thought. Oh, dear! She looked as if she should be wearing white socks and black patent leather shoes on those little, crossed feet. The breasts on her slender ribcage needed no support. He suddenly saw it. She wanted to run away from Missy. He had been about to offer her Turkish lire gratis, but now he began to wonder if this was wise. It might be an explosive tug-of-love situation. If the girl got to the airport, she might go anywhere to escape insufferable wrangling. She seemed so naïve that she might do something foolhardy. 'St Winifred's is a grand school,' he said, hoping this was sufficiently noncommittal. In fact, it was the ultimate in convent schools for double-dyed Catholics in the 'Brideshead' mould. No wonder the girl had a pre-pubescent air! Serge was for virginity in moderation.

'It's all become rather complicated,' Xenia said. 'You see, my father . . .' She stopped, looked up and froze. 'My mother is coming!' she said. Hastily, she added, 'Prince Mirkovsky, would you? Do you think that you could . . . ?'

'What?' he asked, but Xenia's face had changed. She smiled brightly as Missy bore down.

'Well, hello! We can't go on meeting like this!' Missy said coyly. She had arrived in a cloud of musky scent, heavy with spice and Eastern promise. She was dressed in a light Chanel suit, or something of the kind, which was the pitch of respectability. 'How is my second-in-command getting on with the handsome Prince?'

Serge felt like a dog being dragged into a full bath, but the girl was dying inwardly with embarrassment, and so he said, 'Not so much handsome, but privileged to be in your daughter's company.' He wondered if this was flowery enough.

Missy's hair had been done in a *fin-de-siècle* chignon, which made her look a bit like a character from Edith Wharton. Her nails were newly varnished, and she wore a decorative watch on a thin ribbon round her neck. She picked it delicately from her silken *poitrine* and clicked it deftly open. 'We are popping down the road to Réjans,' she said. 'You'd adore it, Serge, why don't you join us? I think the waiters swam the Black Sea, or something like that, in order to get away from Stalin. Maybe even Lenin, they are that antique!'

He was about to open his mouth to plead an indisposition for Helena worthy of the plague, when Xenia dived in. 'Oh, please! It was what I was about to ask you.'

Missy gave Xenia a very queer look. Serge really was out of his depth. 'My cousin Helena has found the day very strenuous,' he said, and the girl's face fell. 'Well, why don't you both go and eat, and perhaps we will join you later.' He cursed himself. 'Or I will if she feels too unwell.'

Missy's face had a dark sort of triumph on it.

'I will go and wake her, for she will not sleep tonight if I don't, and then I will see how she is.'

'You do that,' she said sharply, then smiled. Xenia looked fearfully from one of them to the other.

Serge was very ill at ease, but he turned to go towards the lift. When he had pressed the button, he suddenly felt Missy at his side. 'Just a word, Serge,' she said, 'before we have our lovely evening. The past is the past in front of the daughter, is that understood? I thought you failed to understand it earlier today when we were in Agia Sophia, because it sort of snuck into the conversation. It's not to be brought up again. Is that clear? Do you follow me? I mean it.' Her eyes and nostrils flared. Every word was soft and intense, each one like a direct blow. 'And you keep your hands to yourself,' she added with shocking coarseness. 'She's not on offer!'

He was too stunned to reply.

'See you later!' she trilled loudly as she turned back towards the lounge to collect Xenia, whose eyes followed him, pleading, as she and her mother made their way out of the hotel.

The Russian restaurant was tucked away in a little thread of passages near the main thoroughfare where cosy trams plied up and down with sleepy, Edwardian reliability. Xenia was watchful, all the more for her mother's sudden good mood. She seemed keen to be out on the town.

When Missy had returned from the hairdressers with her luxuriant chignon she had been in high good spirits. She had been thinking under the drier, she told Xenia, and had decided what to do. Xenia must accompany her back to the United States where she, Missy, would arrange for her to live and study. She had dazzled around the room, rummaging through her wardrobe, agonizing over what to wear. When Xenia had demurred a bit about making such large plans on such short notice, Missy's dreadful coldness had returned. Her good humour had only been restored when, by dint of frenzied effort, Xenia had thanked her effusively for the compliment the invitation implied. She had found herself supplying an enthusiasm she lacked like a prisoner doing callisthenics in a freezing yard under the eyes of a volatile guard. All the same, it was a compliment, and Xenia felt a wretched, sneaking gratification that her singular mother had weighed her in the balance and found her not wanting after all. With one part of herself, Xenia was blindly fixed to Missy's every aspect, almost as if with moving lips and trembling fingers she were trying to recognize and memorize the smallest of her characteristics. The greater part of herself, however, was in an agony to escape. As she followed her mother into the restaurant, the desperation of reckoning overtook her. Something new had bothered her mother in the hotel lobby, something to do with the Prince. That unnerving vertical frown had furrowed Missy's forehead like a long dart, and she had followed the Prince to the lift with the soft, purposeful gait of a hunting animal. Did she suspect that Xenia had been trying to confide in him?

She seemed all right now as they stood at the entrance to Réjans. Missy was all gaiety and elegance, the ghost of old times in Stamboul. She was as ravishing and delicate as a Gibson girl. In fact, the restaurant itself could not have changed much since the turn of the century. The dining-room was as long and as stately as a baronial hall, an impression extended by a music gallery that overlooked the neat, stark tables with their snowy cloths. The whole atmosphere was brown; every inch of paintwork was covered in the slumberous colour of wintry mud. A brace of elderly waiters patrolled the neatly marshalled aisles of diners. They had a proprietorial air and wore boiled shirt-fronts under tuxedo jackets, shiny with age. A few spryer servitors nipped in and out with trays of borscht and blini, bottles of lemon or pepper vodka. In one way, it looked as if time had died and congealed there. In another, it seemed that a lost world had been preserved with an immense frugality of breath and spirit. The Moscow and Petersburg of another age had been spiritually translated to this one, dim spot.

An ancient *maître d'hôtel* creaked towards them, a timeless paradigm of all such figures in his penguin suit, with a spotless linen cloth hung over his arm. He flicked his eyes over them, his face impervious to Missy's gloss and the *grande dame* flourish with which she demanded a table.

Xenia gave him a nervous, apologetic smile. For all her growing anxiety, the seigniorial attitude, which seemed second nature to Missy, embarrassed her deeply. Her 'parents' decried such arrogant behaviour, particularly to people who could not answer back. Missy arranged herself with a regal air and straight away ordered a bottle of lemon vodka. Either she missed the veiled contempt in the waiter's eyes or she did not care. With a little stab of pain, Xenia realized that Missy must be used to it.

'Amazing place, isn't it?' Missy lit a cigarette and waved out the match. The smoke caught at her hooded green eyes and she blinked.

Xenia submerged herself in the menu, which was written in French.

'Cat got your tongue?'

'It's lovely,' Xenia murmured.

'The grandson of a pasha used to take me here. He had one of those old wooden mansions out in Bursa. His family was too refined for words, which was why, I guess, he liked me. He lived in his *yali* with six repressed female relatives who did not know whether they were in purdah or not. So he drank, and mostly here where nobody knew him. I never got the hang of Islam, but I'm not sure he had it either. It sort of puzzled him that he wasn't a European and he resented it because he was.'

The vodka arrived brought by a Turkish underling of the *maître d'*. It was hard to see how the large chunks of lemon had got through the narrow neck of the bottle; they floated, grandly swollen, in the pernicious liquid. Missy snapped her fingers, indicating that she wanted a second glass to be brought for Xenia. The waiter scuttled off and back again, giving Missy a cursory look of awe. With her cigarette clenched between her lips, she poured a good measure for them both from the chilled bottle, then drank. 'Phew!' she said. 'That's better!'

Xenia sipped at the stunning brew in a gingerly way. It produced a fiery hole in her empty stomach, but it did its trick of calming and bracing her.

'You'll have to be teetotal when you come to live with me,' Missy said. 'Tom takes a dim view of drinking. Not that I mind. He's an old sweetie. You'll love him.'

Xenia wanted to say that in no circumstances would she go to live in America. The vodka stung her tongue, but it silenced her confused objections. 'Does he know about me?' she asked instead.

'Not yet. I wasn't sure I would be able to get at you. But when he finds out, he'll be thrilled to bits. If ever there was a Utopian, libertarian guy, it's Tom. He wants the whole world to sing in harmony like the Coke ad. It's always open house for Tom. 'Course, it's his house and that gets mixed up in things.' She took a meditative drag on her cigarette, then abruptly looked down at the menu.

Not for the first time, Xenia caught a sadness in her mother. Behind the glare of self-publicity there was something almost wistful about Missy. A tendril of hair that escaped her lacquered tresses oddly emphasized her age, and in the harsh, dim overhead light, Xenia saw a small map of wrinkles hardened around eyes that often had the cold, blank look of terminal disappointment. Xenia sipped more vodka; it was starting to have its way. 'What were you like at my age?' she asked on impulse.

Missy looked up from the menu, quickly defensive. 'Funny question,' she said. She poured herself more vodka, but not for Xenia.

'I didn't mean to embarrass you,' Xenia blurted out. She had meant to say that she only wanted to get to know Missy better.

'Embarrass?' Missy said coldly.

'I didn't mean . . . I meant . . .'

'What was Serge Mirkovsky saying to you earlier?'

She'd stepped on another land-mine. She swigged the remaining vodka in her glass. 'We were talking about my going to America,' she said. In a flattering imitation of Missy's own desperado air, she extended her glass for another shot.

'What should embarrass me about being eighteen?' The chain from Missy's watch fob dangled from her pretty finger. The watch seemed to swing of its own accord like a dowsing instrument.

'Nothing!' Xenia's voice squeaked with fright. 'I know nothing about you at all. I suppose I said that because I am always so embarrassed myself. It is a word that occurs to me all the time.'

Missy narrowed her eyes. 'That's for sure,' she said, looking Xenia up and down with a curious contempt.

The hostility in her tone caught and winded Xenia; it hurt her terribly. She blushed and looked down at her hands, which were trembling in front of her on the table.

'Aw, go on, have another drink!' Missy said with a bully's largesse. 'But that's the last one, mind.'

She poured. Xenia swallowed. Her face felt irradiated with booze. She had eaten nothing but a kebab all day.

'In answer to your question, at eighteen I was right on out of it.'

' "Out of it"?'

Missy shrugged. 'I already told you I ran away to New York. I didn't get on too well with my Daddy. Until I met yours, I was determined a man like that wasn't going to happen to me twice.' She shot Xenia an ugly look. 'Have some blini. Blini are nice. I'm sure we can get them to rustle up some caviare.'

All at once, Xenia knew that she could not stop herself from committing the unforgivable sin. 'I love my father,' she said.

Missy slowly raised her eyes from her glass and Xenia was immobilized, powerless against the sudden force of her mother's alienation. 'Well, I guess you've made your choice,' she said. Her barely audible voice was soft with menace. 'Pity about that. And here I thought we were going to have some fun. A few laughs.'

Xenia's full heart was knocking. 'But this morning you said I should hear you out.' Her voice rose to a plea. 'I don't understand what is going on. I'm only young, you know!'

Either the elderly *maître d'hôtel* had witnessed Xenia's distress or he genuinely wanted their order. He arrived at the table bearing a tablet and poised his pencil over it with the sphinx-like grandeur of a prophet. '*Konchilace?*' he asked Missy, stonily indicating the vodka. 'Finish?'

'*Nyet!* By no means, *nyet*,' Missy said with sudden joviality. 'We are expecting friends. But I suppose we must order because they are very late. The Prince Mirkovsky is coming, you know. We will have the blini, and then we will see.'

Xenia begged the waiter with her eyes not to rock the boat. He slightly inclined his head to her and departed like a watchful angel.

'Right. So you want to know why Mr Theo Phocas is not my pin-up, do you?' Missy's voice was soft as gauze. 'You're in for a big surprise. What do you know about surrogate mothers?'

Xenia shook her head, wretched but nerved by the proximity of the waiter and the thought of the expected Prince.

'My, you do lead a sheltered life! You do know how babies get there, don't you, sweetie?'

A revulsion, quite unlike anything she had ever felt before, spread into Xenia's whole spirit at this last taunt. 'I may be innocent, even backward,' she found herself saying, 'but I do know how babies are born . . . and how they are conceived. Yes.'

'I see, quite the "Young Miss", aren't you? Well, I suppose it's no wonder you give yourself airs, what with your Daddy and all. To be blunt – and I never mince words – a surrogate mother hires out her womb to a childless couple. She gets together with the husband of said couple with a turkey baster or straight from the tap, who cares? At the end of the production line nine months later, Mom hands over the cute little package and Dad hands over a cheque fat enough to cover the costs of labour. The only thing is, Mom usually knows the score from Day One. Now, yours truly was under the impression that Dad – in this case, Mr Theo Phocas – was going to do the decent thing and make an honest woman of her. To tell you the truth, when I found you were on the way, sweet potato, I had kind of different plans for you, but he got wind of it and radically changed my mind. I got the royal treatment. He stuffed me on health food like a Strasbourg goose . . . and on big, wholesome lies. You nearly broke me in half getting born, chicken, but no sooner than it had happened, it was clear the rubbish away – and that meant me! That whey-faced ninny he married was barren and there was nothing he could do about that. So from the very beginning he had me singled out as his own personal greenhouse. And once the cute little tomato popped into the world, he dropped the bomb on it. Pardon me if I extend the metaphor, but that's the kind of gal I am!'

Xenia was aghast. The waiter brought blini into the absolute silence that followed.

'Well?' said Missy when he had left.

'I don't know what to say.' Did Missy mean she had wanted to abort her? A sense of having been unfairly rooted in her mother's womb made her shudder as if she had a faint memory of having been precarious and unwelcome in that place.

Missy started to sing tunelessly:

> 'She was poor but she was honest
> Victim of a rich man's whim.
> First he loved her, then he left her
> Now she has a child by him.

'That's what you're thinking, isn't it? That I'm improvising on an old story.' Missy was suddenly less malign. Maybe she had been hungry, for she tackled her pancakes with an appetite. 'But that's not the way it was. I was poor all right, and if I have to admit it, indifferently honest, but not by my own lights . . . and he is rich enough, God knows. The twist in this case is that I was not left holding the baby. When you were born, you were put in an incubator, or so they told me, but by the time I was well enough to walk, I discovered that the incubator had gone – vanished, with you in it. Next thing I knew, a policeman was standing at the end of my bed with an air ticket in one hand and a charge sheet in the other. Oh, and I forgot, a large cash sum in dollars. It was settle for a trip home or a trip to jail. They had "found" a juicy little bag of Turkish smack in my apartment, and I am not asking you to guess how it got there. I was supposed to have addicted you to heroin in the womb. In a way, I am surprised his vanity did not extend to showing you the trumped-up doctors' affidavits he got – or bought – to prove me an unfit mother, because his "evidence" was a real triumph. Whether I went home or went to prison, it boiled down to the same thing. He condemned me to a life without my baby.'

Xenia looked across the table at Missy, who was stuffing blini and soured cream into her mouth as if they had just been discussing the Turkish climate. It seemed revolting that she could eat at all, much less with enjoyment. 'I am not a baby now,' she said.

'No, you're an heiress,' Missy said. 'Lah-di-dah!' She gave Xenia a peculiar look as if all the envy she had ever felt was gathered up in her remark and borne into the air like a disease. 'If you had been an heir, he would have married me.'

Xenia's heart was pounding, but she could not move, for everything seemed to hang together like the weight of chains. So, she had been bought and paid for like a doll from Harrods or a slave. The woman across from her was no mother, but a culture in which she had been grown. Xenia's limbs no longer seemed to belong to her: they seemed the property, somehow, of Missy.

'Don't you worry,' said Missy. 'You won't lose a penny by coming with me. Uncle Tom will see us both right.'

Xenia was too appalled to speak. The thought of her inheritance had never crossed her mind. Did Missy think she was making calculations as she sat dumbfounded with the news that she was not a spontaneously created being? With her giddy, bursting head? With the potion of vodka shooting distortions before her eyes?

'Serge! You made it!' Missy rose from her chair to welcome him. 'Helena! We'd just got round to missing you.'

Xenia had the sensation of falling backwards into the two Russians who had come up behind her, but she found her balance as she stood. She reeled slightly towards the white expanse of the old Prince's shirt. He smelt vaguely of eau-de-Cologne. His cousin looked small and gnarled. For some reason, her bright, shoe-button eyes compelled Xenia to steady herself. 'I think . . . I need the Ladies' Room,' she said.

Together, Serge and Helena watched Xenia as she made her way unsteadily across the restaurant towards a flight of stairs that led to the lavatories. Together, they looked at Missy.

'Sit! Sit!' Missy cried. She beckoned the waiter with a commanding finger. 'Name your poison! This is mine,' she said, winking at the vodka bottle as if it had a personality and, Disneyesque, would rise to do a *trepak* on the table.

'Is Xenia all right?' Serge asked. The vodka bottle winked at him too, but he averted his eyes from the power of its suggestion and looked instead after the slender girl in yellow who clutched the banisters for balance as she mounted the stair.

'I could use some vodka,' Helena said, grimly sitting, 'but my cousin does not drink. Not ever. Do you, Serge?'

He began to feel sure that he would not drink with Missy. '*Mineralnie voda*,' he said to the *maître d'hôtel*, whose elderly face broke out in cautious rapture at the Russian words. They exchanged a glance that suddenly seemed to implicate Missy, perhaps in a recent act of impropriety. She seemed sober enough to Serge. In fact, he could not remember that he had ever seen her drunk. The waiter brought the bottle of mineral water with four glasses, which he set upon the table with a pointed look at Xenia's empty place where a plate of untouched blini congealed. Surely, Missy would not let her own child get drunk in public.

'Well,' Missy chirruped, 'have you had a wonderful day?' She flourished a menu. 'Order! Order! Have anything you like. It's my treat.'

Serge watched Helena sipping vodka. With her black suit hanging off the little bird bones, she looked like a starved winged creature of some unidentifiable genus. He could not think why she had insisted on accepting Missy's invitation, but she took in the scene as if she were ravenous for the pickings of what had transpired before their arrival in the restaurant. 'At your suggestion,' she said, 'we visited the seraglio . . . and, of course, the diamonds, emeralds, sapphires and rubies. All quite magnificent, you were right.' Serge wondered if Missy knew she were being patronized, delighted in, as if she were an exotic chocolate, but she did not seem to notice. 'Then, alas, we spent the rest of the afternoon calling to mind old times,' Helena continued. 'Very wearing, I assure you.'

'Well, have some borscht,' said Missy. 'It's a good restorative. As you can see, the young "Miss" has turned up her nose at the blini, and to be quite honest, mine were not very good.'

Serge dawdled nervously with the menu. He could not think what

Helena was up to, and the restaurant evoked the moth-eaten grandeur of his childhood. His mother might have found solace in Réjans, and it made him remember her permanent sense of exile. If he had not been touched by Xenia's plight, her curious desperation, he would never have consented to spend another minute in Missy's company, especially in a place that brought back to him such a sense of failure and despair. All he could think of now was the vodka: that he could have it if he wanted it, just by reaching out an arm. Helena caught his eye as his hand edged towards the bottle, and one baleful glance served to check him. It carried freight from a past in which one drink after another had produced a crushing train of events. He wondered if she were taunting him by drinking with Missy, for she could take or leave alcohol. He supposed she was punishing him for remaining friends with Paul and Marina and for being the bearer of bad tidings about the book. Since their childhood, she had taken reprisals whenever she had been thwarted or disappointed. Why had he bothered to come to Istanbul to tell her, especially when she seemed to want to spend all of their time with Missy?

'Borscht it is, then. Serge?' his cousin said.

'Sure.' He suddenly felt very depressed.

Helena leaned towards Missy with a smile which might generally be considered delightful, but Serge had seen it before and it struck him as ominous. 'Is your daughter unwell?' she asked. 'She looked a bit green around the gills when we came in.'

'Oh, she's fine!' Missy snapped. 'To tell you the truth, she's driving me a bit bananas.'

Serge's wave of temptation towards the vodka passed in the fascination of this moment. Together, he and Helena regarded Missy's outburst with faint alarm. There was a peculiar, explosive force to the words made all the more arresting for her glassy elegance, her lacquered nails and hair. 'Teenage girls!' he said carefully. 'I've had two of them.'

'They're the pits,' Missy said in a cold little voice.

'Lovely girl,' Helena murmured soothingly. 'Charming manners.'

Missy summoned the vigilant old waiter and ordered borscht. 'A bit of an actress,' she said to Helena, a little flash of insolence in her eyes. There was insouciance too, as if the whole business about the girl could go to blazes. Serge forgave Helena at once when he realized that she had been drawing Missy out. That, too, was like her. She liked to manipulate people.

'They do tend to be emotional at that age,' he said, smiling pleasantly.

The *maître d'hôtel* had been hovering around the edges of this conversation. All at once, he leaned towards Serge in a courtly manner bordering on pomposity and spoke rapidly in Russian. 'I beg your pardon, sir, but if the young lady who left the table is under discussion, I feel it my duty to alert you to a situation which might cause Your Excellency some embarrassment.'

So, Missy had advertised the arrival of a 'Prince'. She chafed visibly under the old man's interruption, but there was nothing she could do in the light of Serge's welcoming reply to him.

Helena sighed comically and sipped at the lethal brew. 'Old Russians, old times!' she said to Missy. 'I do not speak the language myself because I was brought up in England, but I am sure that a translation will be forthcoming.'

Serge knew that she perfectly well understood the waiter. 'Please continue,' he told the man.

'The young lady,' he said with ill-concealed outrage, 'is being very sick upstairs in the lavatory. This woman got her drunk deliberately and upset her very badly by something she said. I fear that there will be a scene and I do not wish you to be implicated, sir. I also worry about the girl.'

Somehow, the honour of this unusual, and perhaps undue, confidence warmed Serge. He wondered how long it had been since someone had thought him trustworthy on first sight. With a small puff of his chest, he replied, 'I thank you for warning me. I am here this evening because I anticipated that the young lady might need my protection. Shall I say that we have been discussing the old days in Petersburg? Odessa?'

'We have been discussing your estimable family, sir,' said the waiter, who withdrew with a beatific self-importance that Serge could not begrudge him.

Xenia had been very sick indeed, for she had thrust her fingers down her throat to get rid of it all and had retched into the lavatory pan until she was sure her stomach was completely empty. She was tempted to do it again, but decided to save it up for another time when it would work the wonders it was working now. She felt curiously rested and more in control of everything than she had done since first she had met Missy. She washed a tail of slime from her face and dried it with a paper towel. The reflection of her dark eyes in the mirror gave her a slight shock and she looked away. She had done this once before experimentally at school, but she had felt bad because of Mummy, who worried about eating disorders. Also, one of Sarah's home friends had died of bulimia. In fact, this and anorexia stalked the dorms like a pale horse, fragile girls rattling their bones at the world of grown women, adequate, voluptuous and attaining. She had decided that she would not do this again even though it had made her feel so much better and not so piggy after Rosamund, who always indulged her so. But the person who had made that resolve seemed like quite another Xenia, a child. She was not sure that she even remembered everything that Missy had told her, but an adjustment had been made during the vomiting so that she took no personal responsibility in any of it . . . whatever it was. She rinsed out her mouth and the water tasted sweet and pure, but she did not drink any of it; she spat it out instead. She wished she could stay in the Ladies' Room all night. In another way, she was surprised that Missy had not come to get her. Missy might not get her now, but she would get her some time, that was for sure.

Xenia had begun to realize that there were things that came back and back at you even when you thought you were in front of them. Everyone acted as if life were lived on a path from A to B, but all along it travelled in a circle. It was like one of those revolving doors with Missy grinning at you through glass. Unlike Xenia, Missy had the ability to jump in and then jump out like an expert girl in a skipping game where the ropes twined and twisted. The point went home to Xenia that it really did not matter if she ran away or stayed, although she knew one thing: she would never follow Missy anywhere willingly. What did it matter if she went back to Chios or travelled to London or stayed in Istanbul, for why not call it that instead of 'Constantinople' which it wasn't any more? Whatever she did, she would not escape. Missy with her diamond rings and platinum cards could find her anywhere in the world at any time. If Xenia attained the heights of Oxford, Missy would be there, fudging her way past porters, folding herself into the back of public lectures. And if she hit the depths, then Missy would be there too. She had been knit together in Missy's womb and had been intricately made, not by God as the Psalm said, but by the wilful, sordid, grand design of her father. No matter what she did or where she went, if she were rich, if she were poor, this circumstance would be upon her. In the flesh, worse still, in the spirit, Missy could pop up at any time. Xenia could see her – grinning, winking her green glad eye. 'Well, hi there, sugarplum, it's me, Missy. What is it? Cat got your tongue?' Xenia might see her whirling, expert figure anywhere. In sleep, dozing over books, in the garden, in the house, in the face of

Rosamund, in the map of Turkey. Like a gremlin, Missy could manage to be outside an aeroplane window, across the world, in Tibet. At the hour of her death, Missy would be waiting for her.

Xenia could not go further and she could not go home. It was no longer a question of what she must do now, it was a question of how she could stop doing anything. She decided the quickest way to attain this was to go downstairs. She combed her hair. She felt like wood. This was the best way to feel . . . to become nothing.

'My, you have spent a time powdering your nose!' said her mother when Xenia returned to the table.

'It's powdered now,' said Xenia. The Prince rose as she approached and she acknowledged his courtesy with a nod even though it seemed a pointless gesture. She noticed as she sat that the plate of blini had been taken away. It gave her an obscure confidence to see that it had been removed. There was a darkening glint in Missy's eyes at the smart retort, as if there would be punishment later for rudeness.

All of a sudden, Xenia was on her feet. She felt that she towered over Missy like a great, lumpen giant, stupid and fat. 'Please excuse me,' she said. 'I will return to the hotel. I think I must have eaten something that disagreed with me.'

'Allow me . . .' said the Prince, rising once more to his feet. It seemed terribly sweet that he wanted to accompany such a loathsome being as herself – a real act of charity.

'No!' Missy said sharply and an ugly silence followed.

Xenia reached up and put a hand on his shoulder. 'No, please,' she said, 'it will only make things worse. But thank you anyway.'

And before she knew that she had done it, she had run from them all and was safe on the streets of Istanbul, alone, in the dark, directionless. She took in great gulps of air.

XIX

SERGE FOUND that he could not sleep. He had tried to get the day's events out of his mind by reading a fat, paranoid thriller he had brought to Istanbul, but the hero's race against time to save the doomed world failed to distract him. He concealed his low literary tastes from Helena, whose only prudery was a disdain for popular fiction, and so he had also brought *The Possessed*, which he had been reading publicly . . . in Russian. It sat accusing him from his night table. He picked it up only to let it drop after a few paragraphs. His mind returned again and again to Xenia and her flight from the restaurant. He knew it was no business of his, but a sense of the girl adhered painfully to him like a burr next to the skin. He should have followed her, whatever she had said. The eyes of the Russian *maître d'hôtel* had thinly veiled his disappointment in Serge. And now Serge was disappointed with himself.

But what could he have done? If he had run out after her, there was no telling what antagonism he might have set up between Missy and her daughter. The hotel was only a few hundred yards from the restaurant, and who knew what the quarrel was about anyway? Still, the unpleasantness of tone in Missy and the real sense of emergency in Xenia had made Serge wonder, when he and Helena had returned to their rooms, whether he shouldn't ring Theo Phocas in Chios and report his observations.

Helena had been appalled at this idea. What could he be thinking of? Especially if there were internecine wars between Phocas and his ex-wife, the consequences could be terrible. How could he think of interfering in a family matter when there was no evidence that Xenia was in any real danger? She was hardly the victim of some large plot involving terrorists or ransom notes. Missy had not chained her up or starved her, tortured or abused her. What was more, it had been established that Xenia was, in law, a grown woman. In any case, Helena had pointed out, Missy would hardly have been at pains to thrust Xenia upon them if there had been skulduggery afoot. It was not as if she had anything to hide. The sheer brass of the woman had proclaimed a very high-profile presence in Istanbul. Hadn't it been she who had forced a renewal of their acquaintance on Serge? He had to admit that it was true. And he could hardly ring up a virtual stranger in the middle of the night to say that he had an uncomfortable feeling about the chap's daughter and ex-wife. He was probably, as Helena had suggested, an absentee parent anyway. In fact, it would be very awkward to disturb a close friend with this kind of baseless intuition, much less an unknown shipping magnate, who might, for all he knew, be sipping Dom Perignon in Borneo, bored to tears with the very thought of daughters.

Nevertheless, the more Serge tried to shove Xenia from his mind, the more the idea forced itself upon him that she had fallen among thieves. As busily as he had tried to construct the story of the Good Samaritan around the events at Réjans, however, Helena had deconstructed it. Suppose, she had argued, Missy had been a Professor of Greek or a biochemist? Wouldn't Serge have read another meaning into the scene? He might even have admired Missy's self-control in ignoring the tantrum of a spoiled eighteen-year-old. Was he impugning Missy's motives because she was sexy? Because she had staked out a claim on her sexuality did this make her a bad woman? If she wanted to treat sex as a commodity, why shouldn't she? People traded in drugs, arms and ivory every day, and at least Missy's body belonged to her. He certainly should not infer from her former profession that she was abusing the girl. For all he knew, it could be the other way. Xenia might be tormenting Missy with her past.

Serge had let Helena have her say. He was too pacific a man to defend his theory against an onslaught as able as this one, and what was more he was too tired. He wanted to say that he would have reacted in the same way if he had seen a father and son in the same situation, but he did not hope to be believed. Helena was angry at the way Arthur Holt's biography had eluded her and for many personal reasons that Serge really did understand. He had kissed her angry head good-night, and tenderly. For a moment, she had held his hand to her cheek, not saying anything, and that had healed the obscure, unspoken breach between them. Wounded love was something he could recognize.

Serge turned out the light and thrashed the sheets into order with his feet. He tried to ease his bad shoulder by bunching the thin pillow into his neck. Why did he think of Xenia in terms of danger? Was it her innocence? Did he still think in terms of purity in women? Did it really need special pleading? Missy was not corrupting Xenia, was she? In fact, she would hardly have savaged him earlier that evening in the hotel lounge if she had been some sleazy madam – nor, of course, would she be proposing that Xenia should come and live with her and her husband in the house she had boasted about.

After Xenia had fled the restaurant, Missy had spent the rest of the unhappy evening piling on the respectability of her new social position in life as if she were stacking gold ingots on the table at Réjans, hard currency in a transaction no one but she seemed to understand. To Serge, it had seemed that this had been the real purpose of the ugly little dinner party, as if she were measuring herself, a success at last, against some obscure provincial standard that neither of them knew anything about. Helena had thought it pathetic, this bragging, as if Missy were trying to redeem her sad past from a ghostly pawnbroker. But Serge began to wonder if all along the past had been a means to the particular end of the 'gracious' house she spoke of, its slave quarters that had been turned into flats for the high-tech stable hands with veterinary degrees, the indoor pool, the dogs, the parties on the lawn, on the verandah. It was almost as if the Empress Theodora, whose first career in the Hippodrome was as acrobat and harlot to the Legions, had gloried before them in her signal accomplishment, robed, crowned, embellished and glittering with power.

Serge sat up, thirsty, and drank bottled spring water from the glass by his bed. His shrink, he decided, might say that he had transferred the potential danger in the bottle of iced lemon vodka on to Missy. Whenever he demonized drink, it produced this psychological effect. It was safer to remember that he was allergic to the stuff and that it was not always harmful to others. In suppressing his desire to get plastered, he was projecting on those for whom drink was relatively safe. With a groan, Serge wondered what Dostoevsky would have made of this theory; nevertheless, it worked and he was determined to persevere.

He felt better now he had caught himself out and been clever. His friend Paul was taking a further qualification in psychiatry in Oxford and had recommended the sharp Dr Small. He sighed. Now he acknowledged that he had wanted a drink and had decided not to have one whatever the consequences, he was free to think more dispassionately about Missy and Xenia.

He tried. Again, the girl sailed up to the table in her crumpled yellow dress, her face as blanched as Banquo's ghost, her eyes as terrible. Again, he saw the insulting exchange of looks between Missy and herself. Again, there was the taunt about powdering noses. Again, Xenia rose and fled into the night. But over and over, each time the scene replayed itself in his mind, the factor he could not easily dismiss was a frightening triumph in Missy. For just a moment, she had looked completely slaked, like a boa stuffed with goat. A sleepy look had come into her eyes, and Serge was sure that she had sighed with pleasure. Serge chided himself for weighting the evidence against Missy, whom he disliked. All the same, it suddenly crossed his mind that there was one scenario he and Helena had not explored. He sat up in the dark and drew up his knees. Missy could be mad.

Well, there it was in a nutshell! The splurge spending, the preternaturally vivid behaviour, the footloose past, the moral aphasia, the odd callousness to Xenia's pain, the swings of mood he had observed in Agia Sophia . . . all these added up. Taken with Xenia's evident fear of her mother, a fear that seemed more than rationally explicable, it worked itself into an assured theory. The grandiose ideas, the way she had flourished her platinum card to pay for their dinner, had not been mere vulgar display. It was more as if she inhabited the shadowless world of distorted perspective, the imaginings both shallow and arcane, of psychosis.

Serge was a bit ashamed of himself for this amateur sleuthing. Perhaps he should turn the light back on and read his lurid thriller where such fictions were convention and where implausibilities had a respectable niche. Yet, could she be insane? And if insane, could she be dangerously so? Serge was in deep waters here. Maybe in the morning he could ring Paul in Oxford and ask for his advice. Maybe he could get Xenia alone and question her more closely. Serge began to relax. He had hit upon the obvious solution. He would take Xenia gently aside and see if there was a practical way to help her. He slid down between the tossed sheets, and in a few moments, he was asleep.

He awoke early. The dawn call to prayer staggered and undulated from mosque to mosque throughout the city and it had Serge staring at the ceiling again. Islam was not visible to him, but audible, and this made him profoundly uneasy for some reason. It was as if the disembodied voices challenged his inner map of the universe. It seemed such a single, naked religion next to his own, which always called imagery to mind. Serge was a great one for philosophizing, but he decided to avoid the conflict between Christ and Mohammed for the moment, and got out of bed. He was hungry, and even though he had not slept well, he was restless too. He shaved and a nice old Russian gentleman smiled back at him from the mirror. He looked at his image quizzically, as if to see if it had anything to add to his theorizing of the night before. Had his diagnosis of Missy been 3 a.m. thinking? He would go downstairs and get breakfast. Maybe he would catch the interesting pair, an early bird with worms.

Without bothering to wake Helena, he descended in the lift, and as the doors opened on to the lobby he could hear the voice of Missy at Reception. She was asking the clerk to get her a taxi to the airport, and she seemed impatient that it should come right away.

Serge peered around the corner. Missy was dressed for flight rather like a star from an old Hollywood movie – Barbara Stanwyck or Jane Russell – in a slim suit with a flounced jacket. She did not wear a hat, but she carried gloves and a stack of neat Vuitton luggage stood at her feet. She was startled to see Serge. Her hands flew up in surprise, but she fell to adjusting a large earring snapped to her left lobe. 'Why, Serge! Goodness, you gave me a shock. I was just this minute thinking of you.' She was too arch for words. 'As a matter of fact, I was about to ask this gentleman here for a bit of hotel stationery so that I could scrawl a note to say goodbye.'

'Where is Xenia?' Serge asked. It was the first thing that occurred to him to say, and he made no effort to check it.

'That is just the point I was going to find so hard to write down,' said Missy. 'That young lady and I have had just about enough of each other, if you really want to know. The truth is, her Daddy's just spoiled her rotten. "Whew!" is all I've got to say. I have enough on my plate without that kind of behaviour, and so I was saved just in the nick of time. Thanks for being there for me.' Missy gave a little sigh. The clothes and the oddly childlike voice made her seem more like June Allyson now than any other star. She was almost virginal, disappointed, a mother whose apple pie had been spurned.

'What have you been saved from?' Serge asked. He and the hotel clerk both looked at Missy, who was adjusting the cotton gauntlets on her hands.

'Why, from bringing up the rest of her. I had hoped . . .' and here she let her eyes drift in a genuine expression of puzzlement and sadness. 'Never mind!' she continued, snapping out of it. 'On to pastures new for me.'

'Has Xenia gone?' Serge asked, dazzled from his theory of the night before by Missy's assurance.

'Pouf!' Missy exclaimed, raising her gloved hand balletically.

'You mean to say you do not know where she is?'

Missy shrugged. 'She walked out on me.'

'Last night?' Behind Missy's back, the hotel clerk shot a glance at Serge.

'I'm sure you appreciate, Serge, that some things are just too painful to discuss,' Missy said with a downward sweep of lashes to the vanity case she held by a strap in her hand. 'She's Daddy's girl. Just like him, I reckon.' Missy put her head to one side and gave Serge an enigmatic smile. A gruff Turk with a grizzled moustache lumbered in at the hotel entrance. On seeing Missy, his eyes lit up at the sheer luxury of her. 'Taxi?' she asked, and he nodded.

In a flurry, the manly fellow heaved Missy's impedimenta over his shoulders and into his hands. 'Now, I'd just love to stay and chat, Serge, lamb, but I really must flash or I'll miss my flight.' She made a scrunching little kissy face and bussed him on both cheeks. 'Now, you and Helena just promise to come and see me at Eagles, won't you? I'm absolutely counting on it, and I know that Tom would be delighted.'

'Are you trying to say that Xenia is wandering around Istanbul alone?' Serge exclaimed in a subdued roar.

'No law against it!' She winked. 'Now is there?' She was wearing stiletto heels. In her pencil skirt, she teetered out of the door like a Chinese empress on her way home from a particularly atoning human sacrifice. 'Byee, now!' she said and blew a kiss with an exaggerated pout. 'It's been heaven.' And with that, she vanished.

Serge and the hotel clerk stood stunned by the thunderbolt farewell for quite some moments. He, a Turkish student making ends meet, and Serge were bound together in that sudden, common humanity which transcends national categories. 'The girl!' the young man said. His English was not perfect but it worked. 'I am night clerk. I go off now. The girl did not come back last night at all.'

'What!'

'Look! See?' The young man pointed at the corner. Under a potted palm there stood a small rucksack, a large handbag, and a paper sack with a heap of clothes packed in it like something parcelled up for Oxfam. 'The mother put these here for the girl to come and get them. This is not a good city for a young lady at night.' He was inexpressibly distraught and waved his hands to demonstrate this.

'Oh, no!' Serge cried, 'I might have . . . I could have . . .' He had so nearly followed Xenia out of the restaurant. 'The police,' he said. 'We must get them. And an ambassador, I don't know which. Her father . . .' Already he and the clerk were on their knees scrounging through Xenia's pouchy, studenty bag. 'British!' he cried, holding up the passport, thankful at first that no awkwardness between Greeks and Turks would result from this. It then struck him that Xenia must be wandering around Istanbul without documents, and presumably without money, for she had told him she had only drachmas. She could be anywhere. He sank to his knees. A letter in the duffle bag had on it an address in Chios. 'Please!' he said to the clerk, 'Please will you get the number of Mr Theologos Phocas at this address.'

The young man moved swiftly behind the reception desk and started speaking rapidly in Turkish down the telephone. Serge creaked rheumatically to his feet. 'The police will be here very soon,' the young man said. 'The consulate now or Mr Phocas?'

'Mr Phocas,' Serge said quietly. How could he have failed in this responsibility? What could he say to the poor man? He watched as the Turkish student obtained the number from the international directory; he watched as he dialled. Serge took the telephone and put the receiver to his ear.

'*Herete!*' a harsh voice answered on the first ring.

'Mr Phocas?'

There was a pause and an unnatural click. 'Yes?'

'This is Serge Mirkovsky calling you from Constantinople. I am afraid I have somewhat disturbing news about your daughter.'

XX

Lady Simon sat in the drawing-room and eyed the tree with some misgiving. It really was most inconsiderate of Charles and Rosamund to expect her to change her plans this year, but she supposed she had to acquiesce. She always spent Christmas Day with them in London, but now it seemed she had to stay in Gloucestershire with Theresa. This would mean having to dole out punch and sausage rolls at the ghastly party Theresa gave each Boxing Day for the four corners of the farming community, and she dreaded it. What was more, she was convinced she had been diverted from Holland Park for some dark purpose. Ever since September there had seemed to be a conspiracy of silence. Her every attempt to glean information had been systematically blocked, and she was seized with irritation every time she thought about it.

Where was Rosamund with tea? Lady Simon longed for a cup and felt really that one should have been put straight into her hand the moment she arrived. After all, she had taken the expensive expedient of a taxi from Paddington when in fact she should have been met. This was especially so since she had brought quite a large carrier bag full of gifts for the entire family in advance of Christmas. Why were they not assembled to see her on this St Lucy's Day? It did seem a bit much. She knew, of course, that Charles had to work, but Catherine and Xenia might have made the effort to come the short distance from Bayswater for tea. It was true that Xenia was supposed to have been unwell, but Lady Simon was not sure she believed in that kind of thing . . . breakdowns and so on. Catherine was terribly altered, but no one would tell her why. She had purchased one of those answering machines. Charles had one naturally enough because of his work, but Lady Simon could see no reason why a lady, presumably at home all day, should need one. Catherine rarely returned her mother's messages, and during the three months she had been back in England, she had been to visit Lady Simon only once. And where was Theo? No one would say.

She looked balefully at the decked-out conifer in the corner. The tree was up too early and it was too gaudily dressed with a new star on top made of tinsel. Lady Simon preferred an angel and wondered what had happened to the one she had given them all years ago. She expected Rosamund had let the dog get at it. This new, gimcrack gaiety, she supposed, was a result of Rosamund's paying guest and her little boy (was it her little boy?), who was precocious and tiresome. Lady Simon thought children should be as ordinary as possible and not demand a botany lesson every day as Paolo seemed to – or whatever it was he seemed so keen on, she could not remember. Quite honestly, she had taken the woman for a servant at first, but had been thoroughly slapped down by Charles and Rosamund. Far from divorcing, those two had become as thick as thieves lately, which only went to show Charles's strength of character in overcoming temptation. Lady Simon was a little ashamed that she had wanted the marriage to end, and had mentioned it to Father Henry in Confession. Actually, she really was glad they were back together again. Rosamund seemed a good deal happier, more settled, since last summer. Maybe she had learned her lesson.

As if she had conjured them up by thinking about it, the front door opened and Lady Simon heard the voices of the PG and the child in the hall. They seemed to be untangling coats and woollies, for it was a very unpleasant day. Perhaps seeing the lights on in the drawing-room, the child, still chirruping on about something that had happened at school, burst in. On seeing Lady Simon, he stopped in his tracks. He was wearing a school uniform she could not quite place, even though it looked smart. She supposed this meant he was here to stay in Holland Park.

Oh, where was Rosamund? Surely, it did not take such a long time to make a simple pot of tea and toast a few muffins! As if at her bidding, she heard the clank of cups being brought upstairs from the kitchen, and into the room came Rosamund. Lady Simon was somewhat mollified to see that her daughter-in-law had made a chocolate cake, for she had a sweet tooth. She was a little less pleased when Rosamund greeted Paolo with a warmth and enthusiasm she had not offered Lady Simon. 'Did you have a lovely day at school?' she asked the child, swooping him up in a light kiss. Lady Simon noticed that Rosamund's hair was done in a more attractive way. She probably realized now that if one had a man one needed to keep him. 'Have you said "hello" to Mary's Grandmama, Paolo? You remember, Lady Simon.'

The child shyly disengaged himself from Rosamund and extended a hand. His fluffy hair stood out from having been out in the damp. His doe eyes rested on Lady Simon in a kind of wonder.

'Here, Paolo, I'm giving you the job of toasting the muffins. Now, don't burn yourself or them, will you?' The child seemed very pleased by Rosamund's request. He clambered up on to the padded fender, skewered a split muffin on a toasting fork, and sat with his legs dangling while he completed the task he had been given.

'Will Mary be here today?' Lady Simon asked, thinking of her granddaughter.

Rosamund, on her knees, poured tea and cut the cake. 'I'm afraid not,' she said. 'She has gone to visit Xenia. Catherine is with her every day, as you know, but the rest of us take turns.'

Lady Simon had been told this before, but she kept on forgetting it. Perhaps it was because no one would tell her what precisely was the matter with Xenia or why she had fallen ill. She had been in and out of a private clinic for some time now, but she had not even had the grace to thank Lady Simon for a box of candied fruits she had sent from Fortnum's. Some eating disorder seemed to be connected with 'the breakdown', and Lady Simon was sure that Xenia had scoffed the lot and pretended she hadn't by hiding the fact that she had received the gift. She had always been a sly child. 'Mary is a saint,' Lady Simon said, sighing.

Rosamund vigorously buttered muffins and handed them to her mother-in-law. So, it still annoyed her to hear Mary praised. Well, she must hear it. She had been pushed out of the nest in favour of that cuckoo Xenia, and now she was generously offering her day to her rival. Was this not evidence of sanctity?

'Mary is a dear, good girl,' Rosamund said. Of course, it was impossible to deny it.

'She's teaching me about African butterflies!' Paolo crowed. 'They are *huge*!'

Lady Simon looked up and saw Romola Cardew standing in the doorway. She wore a smart long skirt and a jumper made of subtle wools knit into a complicated pattern. It looked like Catherine's handiwork, but obviously the woman had bought it.

'Oh, Rommy!' Rosamund cried with ill-concealed relief. 'Do come in and have some tea. You must be frozen.'

Miss Cardew raised an eyebrow but entered. She greeted Lady Simon with due ceremony, then sat with the languor of familiarity in the buttoned leather armchair. 'Mary isn't simply good. She is divine,' Romola said enigmatically. She took the cup gratefully from Rosamund and sipped the hot, delicate brew.

The two women exchanged a look of great warmth. 'Ah, yes, so she is,' Rosamund said, smiling at her friend. Lady Simon felt excluded.

'Are you in England for Christmas, Miss Cardew?' she asked.

Romola inclined her head gracefully. 'I hope I shall be here for good. I have found a perfect house in Chelsea . . . with a studio. I am having an exhibition soon. I will send you an invitation.'

'We will miss you when you move,' Rosamund said.

'Oh, we'll be passing biscuits over the back fence before you know it, sugar,' Romola said, wrinkling her nose as if she were guying someone.

'Don't!' Rosamund cried in mock horror. Together, they laughed, but the little boy, who had jumped down from the fender, stood in sombre judgement on them both. 'Missy,' he said.

'It's all right to laugh at her sometimes, Paolo. She can't touch us now . . . nor Mommy.'

'She touched Xenia,' he said. 'Can I have some cake?'

'We are waiting to cut the cake until Charles comes home,' Rosamund said firmly.

But Lady Simon had caught the drift, the whiff, the stuff of information from her daughter-in-law's reaction to the child's remark. 'Who is Missy?' she asked.

'Charles is coming home early from work to see you,' Rosamund said in what Lady Simon thought a rather patronizing tone.

'Paolo, you have homework to do. Now! I'll call you when there's cake,' said Romola Cardew. He did not move and she raised an admonishing finger. 'Your satchel is in the hall.'

The child looked almost too intelligently at them all, but he did as he was told.

Lady Simon suddenly had it. 'I remember Missy!' she said, and she did. 'She is your cousin, Rosamund. She was here one Christmas long ago.'

'Missy was married to Romola's stepfather, Isabelle,' Rosamund said, 'so that makes us all relatives, after a fashion.' She looked demurely at the teapot. The corners of Romola's mouth twitched.

'My stepfather died of a heart attack this fall. He had a horse farm in Kentucky. The Queen of England visited it once.'

So this was what Rosamund had had to conceal all along – that she had black relatives! Poor thing! It was always so unfair on the children. A thought of Missy came back to her. She remembered her sidling up to the fire in silks . . . like a jockey. 'Missy was an adventuress,' she found herself saying without really meaning to. 'Oh, dear!' she added.

But both women laughed out loud. 'That sure is one way of putting it!' Romola cried. 'But she didn't get a red cent that wasn't tied up in trust. She is a pampered slave to its conditions, and I can tell you, she's hopping mad. Tom turned out to be no fool after all.'

Rosamund shook her head. 'We're not laughing at you, Isabelle,' she said to her mother-in-law, who was still bridling. 'And in fact, the whole story is far from funny.'

'Your child mentioned Xenia, who *is* my granddaughter after all.' Both Romola and Rosamund looked down at their hands at this, and Lady Simon could not think why.

'Paolo is not my child, but Tom Kavanagh's grandson . . . and his chief heir along with me and my sister, who is his mother. I am the child's aunt.'

'How did Missy "touch" Xenia?'

'By telling her a pack of lies!' Romola said with extraordinary vehemence.

'Not all lies, I'm afraid,' said Rosamund, looking at the fire.

'No one tells me anything at all,' Lady Simon said plaintively. Although not exactly insolent, Romola Cardew looked at her in a speculative way.

All was forgotten, however, when the door burst open with Charles, who was pink with the cold and hung with parcels. He boomed with Dickensian and seasonal joviality. 'Mummy!' he cried, kissing the air by her two cheeks.

'Lovely, darling . . .' He did look lovely, more relaxed than she had seen him for a long time.

He and Rosamund embraced. 'Oh, yum,' he said looking at the chocolate cake. 'Is there still tea?' He was unwinding his scarf, shedding his coat and parcels right there in the drawing-room, as if the proper order of things was not to be able to wait to see them all. 'The traffic was murder!' he said to his wife as if by way of an apology. 'Otherwise, I would have been here sooner.'

Lady Simon thought that an apology for lateness should be directed at herself, who had come up to London specially, but she supposed that Rosamund made his life difficult now if he did not adhere to times. She probably suspected him. And, after all, one had to realize that now she had him back, she might at last be appreciating the treasure she had so very nearly lost.

'Any news?' Rosamund asked. She poured tea, cut the cake, handed things round. Romola, too, looked at him in an interrogative way as if they were expecting something interesting. Lady Simon was all ears.

'Well, he was very relieved that we had intended all along to consult Helena over the book, and, of course, he guaranteed her full cooperation. But actually, he was far more interested in hearing about Xenia.' Lady Simon could not construe the meaning of the look Charles darted at her. Was she to blame in some way for something? 'He is one of the nicest men I have met.'

'I must say, I liked him.'

'He is anxious to visit the hospital, but does not want to upset – '

'Who!' Lady Simon could bear the frustration no longer.

'Oh, sorry, Mummy.' Charles leaned forward with his teacup. 'I had lunch today with Prince Serge Mirkovsky.'

'I knew his mother!' said Lady Simon, not to be outdone. The chocolate cake and proof of intimacy with the Russian aristocracy restored her mood somewhat. 'Sonya . . . we were on a committee together . . . the Red Cross. You know.'

'Well, we can have him to dinner with Cat, if she's not too exhausted. She has wanted to thank him all along, and we can take it from there. Dr Gresham might think it a little too soon after the event.'

They had paid absolutely no attention! The expense of the taxi, Rosamund's new intimacies, the large, mysterious shifts in her children's lives . . . all these things had taken their toll on Lady Simon. Charles had not even asked about her journey to London, nor enquired about her health. And now, to top it all off, he was exchanging significant looks with Rosamund about having Catherine to dinner with Sonya Mirkovsky's son! She hadn't a clue to what was going on. Were they scandalously trying to make a match for Catherine with this Russian prince? It was too intolerable! They even seemed to take their paying guest more seriously than they did herself! Who did they think she was, after all? Even Theresa cruelly withheld information from her. She decided to come out with it after all. 'Where is Theo?' she asked. 'I demand to know.'

There was a very awkward silence. With a muted affront at this outburst quite worthy of Lady Simon herself, Rosamund raised delicate eyebrows. 'Poor Paolo wanted his cake. I quite forgot,' she said. She cut a wedge of it and slid it on a plate. In one lithe movement, she was out of the room.

'As it happens, Mother, Theo has just taken off for the United States. He's got himself tangled up in suing someone, and no one is going to get rich on this one but the lawyers.' Charles shook his head with far more sadness than this could have warranted.

Perhaps there *was* to be a divorce. 'Is he suing Catherine?'

'Hardly,' her son said, giving a thin smile. 'Actually, Mummy, it's all a bit complicated at the moment. Let's not spoil our lovely evening by getting bogged down in it. The outcome will emerge when it does, and not by talking about it.' He slapped his knees twice heartily. 'Right! Well! I have to wrap our prezzies, haven't I? And I may say that Rozzy is making us the most elaborate meal tonight. I am the custodian of the secret ingredients which I have gathered from the wilds of Soho, and I must take them to her.' He got up and flourished his parcels in the air. Taking a little pity on her, he kissed her indignant cheek. 'Mummy, you will find everything out in due course, with the rest of us . . . but now is really not the time. Cheer up, old girl! There are truffles in here,' he said, wagging a small, smart carrier bag. 'I shall be back in a minute, then we can have a lovely drink and a chat.'

Lady Simon watched the retreating back of her son, his arms laden. She supposed he really was in charge. After all, he had been brought up to take command . . . and she did feel a bit silly for having lost her temper.

'What is it that you want to know?'

She had forgotten that Romola Cardew was still sitting in the leather armchair, and it startled her. She had seemed to speak out of the shadows of stillness and repose, like an unexpected oracle.

'I simply do not know what is going on,' she said, hoping for an ally, however strange.

There was a pause. 'What is going on, Lady Simon, is that Xenia nearly died a few weeks ago. There is hope that she's turned the corner now, but she's still a bag of bones. She is in a wheelchair. She is on a drip.'

'What!'

'They protect you,' Romola said. 'They think they are protecting themselves by not telling you, but really everyone is afraid of exposing you to any unpleasantness.'

Lady Simon stared at her in amazement.

Romola shifted forward in her seat. 'This last September, Xenia was discovered in Istanbul by the Turkish police trying to throw herself off the Galata Bridge into the Golden Horn. It took some time for us to get her back because they put her in custody and she refused to speak. In the end, Serge Mirkovsky found her. He saved Xenia's life, in a manner of speaking, but now she is back in London, she has, until fairly recently, been doing her best to finish the job. This is really serious, Lady Simon. Xenia has been very, very ill . . . is.'

'But, she . . .' Lady Simon did not know how to begin a protest at this unwelcome news. 'Can she really be dying?'

'Not if your daughter Catherine has anything to do with it! That woman is heroic. Don't you see? Can't you tell? If you want a family saint, you have *her*! And that is why you have been kept in the dark. Catherine simply cannot cope with anything else, like questions about her marriage, for example. Every ounce of her will goes into Xenia.'

'She's not even Xenia's real mother!'

'Now, that makes me mad,' said Romola, but casually, 'because this is as real as it gets! Please do not make me regret speaking to you. If there is one thing that poor little abused skeleton clings to, it is that very reality. Her father, of course, is acting like a raving lunatic . . . in my humble opinion.'

'I never, never approved!' Lady Simon hardly knew where to lay blame.

'Actually, you and he have something in common. You have not visited Xenia at all, and his presence at the bedside has been fairly catastrophic. Everyone is more than a little relieved that he has gone off, even if it is only to try and lynch Missy . . . for it is she who has played the major role in Xenia's decline. Charles and Rosamund are more charitable than I am about it. They put his irrational behaviour down to grief. I say, however, that his own pride was his child, not Xenia at all. If I could get my hands around his neck, I would kill him.'

'And me?' Suddenly, it mattered to Lady Simon what Romola Cardew thought.

Romola shook her head slowly from side to side. 'You? You haven't had the chance if no one tells you these things.' Although her eyes were exacting, she had a gentle smile. 'Now, you are "A High-Toned Old Christian Woman", as the poet says, and believe me, you can make a real difference.'

'How?' The thought of Xenia in a wheelchair began to sink in.

'Well, first of all, don't tell a soul you know any of this that I have told you. Secondly, go to see Catherine and Xenia tomorrow. Thirdly, act horrified. Fourthly, don't ask any questions or irritate anybody or get on anybody's nerves for just one hour. And fifthly, just give love.'

'We're not demonstrative.' Lady Simon put her head to one side and considered the fire in the grate.

'Why should you be? Of course you're not! You don't have to be false to yourself. That would be worse than anything.'

'She's not dying!' Lady Simon said, quivering suddenly with the awfulness of it. 'She can't be, poor lamb!'

'If you knew the half of it . . .'

'Poor Catherine!'

'That's the stuff!'

'Imagine them not telling me . . .'

Romola smiled to herself and sank back into the armchair. 'Now, you won't get me into hot water with Charles and Rosamund, will you? If you do, I'll never tell you another secret, and believe me, I have lots of them. But not a word if I can't trust you, all right?'

Lady Simon wondered if she had ever met such a perplexing, confounding individual in her life as Romola Cardew. It was not often that she felt able to be utterly frank with people. 'I never liked the child,' she said, 'and I expect that is what they hold against me, particularly if she is dangerously ill. You see, I always thought she was Theo's . . .'

'Shhh!' Romola's index finger went to her lips and she raised her eyebrows. 'Oh, the tea things!' she cried as Charles came back into the room. 'I have been having such fun with your mother that I completely forgot. I meant to bring them down.'

Lady Simon was very touched by this remark.

Charles was bearing gifts – a heap of incredibly badly wrapped Christmas presents. He put them under the tree. 'Never mind, I'll clear them,' he said, loading cups and saucers on the tray. 'Time yet for a drink?' he asked. 'We had such a late tea.'

'Darling,' said Lady Simon, 'I think I would like rather a large gin.'